DEATHLESS
DIVIDE

JUSTINA IRELAND

Deathless Divide

BALZER + BRAY

An Imprint of HarperCollins*Publishers*

Balzer + Bray is an imprint of HarperCollins Publishers.

Deathless Divide

Copyright © 2020 by Justina Ireland

All rights reserved. Printed in the United States of America.

No part of this book may be used or reproduced in any manner whatsoever without written permission except in the case of brief quotations embodied in critical articles and reviews. For information address HarperCollins Children's Books, a division of HarperCollins Publishers, 195 Broadway, New York, NY 10007.

www.epicreads.com

Library of Congress Control Number: 2019944665

ISBN 978-0-06-257063-5

19 20 21 22 23 PC/LSCH 10 9 8 7 6 5 4 3 2 1

❖

First Edition

For every reader who found something worthwhile
in Jane and Katherine's story.
★ *Thank you* ★

In Which I Arrive at Miss Preston's

The first thing you should know about me, the truest most important thing, is that I ain't never really had friends. Not back at Rose Hill Plantation, where the kids regarded me as some kind of outsider, the daughter of the plantation mistress and uppity besides; and definitely not at Miss Preston's School of Combat for Negro Girls. Sure, Big Sue had some affection for me, and the other girls tolerated me well enough, but there was never a point I had a person that I could confide the deepest yearnings of my soul to in the manner of close acquaintances.

It was my own fool fault.

After the Negro and Native Reeducation Act enforcement officers took me from Rose Hill, the only home I'd ever known, they loaded me on a train and sent me east. It wasn't because there weren't any combat schools in Kentucky—there were—it was because there was a greater demand for trained Negro girls in the Eastern cities than there was anywhere else. I didn't know it at the time, but the whole Attendant business had become big money for folks, churning out girls they could sell to the highest bidder, those fees taken by the schools as reimbursement for the training they provided us. And if the rates they charged us colored girls for our government-mandated training was higher than what families paid for tuition at the fancy Eastern colleges, well, who were we to complain? Life as an Attendant had to be better than whatever hole we'd come from.

So the boys were sent to local schools, to one day be hired out for patrols and die defending a wall somewhere, guarding some town that had no right existing in the first place. But girls like me were put on a train and delivered to fine cities like Philadelphia, New York, and Baltimore.

The trip is a blur, mostly because I cried my way through it. Adventure is only swell so long as a body is enjoying the trip. After that, it becomes an ordeal. Mine took me through Ohio and Pennsylvania, and finally to Baltimore, which stank of human misery, fish, and death. It's a stench you get used to, although it would never smell like home.

We were unloaded from the train, hungry and tired, while the fine ladies of the combat schools haggled over us like animals at market. There was pushing, and maybe some hitting, and the next thing I knew I was on a pony—a smaller, over-land version of an armored train—bound for Miss Preston's.

I didn't cry once I was gathered with the other girls on our way to the school. There were four of us: doe-eyed Jessamin, who would run off our second year, never to be heard from again; Bessie, who died one spring when she accidentally stepped on a shambler buried in a bramble patch; Nelly, a girl who was fond of reminding everyone how she could read, not that it kept her from dying a week into her stint as an Attendant; and me. We sat in the pony, each trapped in our own private hells as we silently considered our futures.

The pony pulled into Miss Preston's, and for the first time since I'd left home I felt a stirring of possibility. See, Miss Preston's looked like home to me. Oversized oaks, white split rail fence, deadlier exterior fences, a wide lawn. The school had been built in the manner of a plantation house, and while such a design caused the other girls to suck their teeth and shake their heads, it made me feel something that few places have made me feel: safe.

I do realize that there is a fine bit of irony in the architec-ture of oppression granting me a measure of peace, but keep in mind I was not always the woman awoken to the dynamics of power I became during my tenure at Miss Preston's.

As we tumbled out of the pony and into the front yard of Miss Preston's, the headmistress and school's namesake descended the front steps to greet us. She was a large woman, and an excess of ruffles accentuated her size. She gave me the impression of a very fancy cake, all layers and joy, and the memory now makes me cringe. Had she been calculating our value to her own plans for ascension, like a villain in a Shakespearean tragedy, even as she greeted us with warmth and affection? I'd like to think not, but I know people too well to believe any differently. Folks are, at their heart, selfish, and anything they tell you is more often than not designed to meet their own goals.

I know, because I ain't any different.

"Welcome, girls, to Miss Preston's School of Combat for Negro Girls," she proclaimed. "Here you will leave behind your old lives and find yourselves transformed into women of the world. It will be you who attend to and protect the finest and most elite women in this country. You will lead lives of bravery and service, and your future is now full of limitless potential."

Silence was our only response. Because every single one of us would have done anything in that moment just to get back home.

"The upper-class girls behind me will escort you to your rooms. You'll each start with form-one lessons. As you get settled in, the girls will explain to you the household rules. Welcome once again to Miss Preston's, and I hope you take advantage of the miraculous opportunities afforded to you here at the school."

With that, we were whisked away to our rooms.

The thing that stuck with me from Miss Preston's little speech was the idea that we were embarking on a new life. But the problem about starting a new life is you bring your old self with you. Even though I was told that this was a great opportunity and I had a responsibility to grasp it and work toward greatness, I was still the same Jane McKeene that couldn't help but run off at every opportunity to get into trouble. Back at Rose Hill, rules had been breakable as eggshells, and just as easily disposed of. My impetuousness had, more often than not, been rewarded with indulgence, not punishment, and I suppose part of me had expected somewhat of the same at Miss Preston's. But that wasn't to be, and I learned right quick where I stood with the instructors at the school.

Two days after I arrived, I got my first lashing.

That initial night at Miss Preston's, I had lain in the dark and listened to the crying and sleep sounds of twenty or so other girls. I would have been the oldest girl in my class, if it hadn't been for a pretty blond-haired girl named Katherine Deveraux. I couldn't say why I hated Katherine so much on first sight. Maybe it was her bossiness. Maybe it was the way all the other girls gravitated to her, as though her friendship and approval could change their lives. Or maybe it was because she smiled all the time, always smoothing things over when a mistake was made—but there to witness the mistake, every time, without fail.

And so when I committed the crime of taking an extra piece of corn bread at dinner without permission and Miss Anderson dragged me into the yard before the whole school for my first-ever whipping, Katherine was right up front, hands folded in her skirts, looking like an angel sent down to witness my punishment.

I'll spare you the details of the ordeal. There were ten lashes, and it was more pain than I'd ever endured in my life. After it was done, Miss Anderson made some grand pronouncement, as despots are prone to do, and I knelt there in the dirt without a single regret, because that corn bread was delicious.

But when Miss Anderson left, it was Katherine who came over to me, who helped me to my feet.

"Jane," she said, her voice high and clear, loud enough for all the girls to hear, "it will be okay. There is no need to cry. This is a trial of your own making, one many of us will surely endure, sooner or later. We are, so often, our own worst enemies." She smiled that smile of hers. "But the rest of us, we are here for you."

See, this is the kind of nonsense Katherine would spout, like she just couldn't help herself. A barb wrapped in cotton, some sort of admonishment tucked into platitudes.

And I was not one to stand for it.

I looked at Katherine, my tears drying cold on my cheeks. "A trial of my own making."

She blinked, as if surprised at how her own words sounded coming out of someone else's mouth. "Well, yes. We all wanted an extra piece of corn bread, but only you were fool enough to go into the kitchens and snatch one."

"There was plenty of corn bread. Why shouldn't we all have an extra piece?" I crossed my arms even though it made my back scream in pain. A few of the other girls murmured in agreement, and I could feel the questions sprouting beneath them, taking root in that moment. Why did we have to be sent halfway across the country to care for some fancy white ladies that wouldn't even let us have an extra piece of corn bread? Where was the justice in that?

But Katherine didn't understand the change in landscape, and she muddled along on her high horse just as best as she could. "Because there are *rules*. You cannot just go around breaking them. And if you do, there must be consequences. Otherwise everyone would just do as they like."

"That don't sound half bad to me," a girl said, and there were more murmurs of agreement.

Katherine huffed a little in frustration. "You all are missing the point. I was trying to tell Jane we understand how she feels, that we are here for her after her punishment."

Maybe it was the way Katherine said *punishment*, like it was something I deserved. Or maybe it was the way she kept saying that she understood how I felt, even though I was sure that fair skin had never borne the brunt of the lash. Either way, something in me gave way, and my black temper rose up, blotting out all reason.

I drew my hand back and slapped Katherine with all the force I could muster in that broken moment.

It was a good slap. The sound carried throughout the yard, silencing conversations and eliciting a few gasps. Katherine's eyes widened, impossibly large, and tears filled them, though none fell. A thin tendril of horror uncurled in my middle, and in the back of my mind Aunt Aggie chided me for being too quick to resort to violence to express my feelings, but mostly it felt good to take all the ugliness of the past week and direct it at one person, to give it to them, a gift of pain.

"Maybe," I said, my voice low, and a few girls took a step back lest the slap become a real dustup, "maybe *now* you understand a little bit of how I feel."

Katherine blinked, and her tears finally fell. I was ready for her to hit me back, and I'd have a chance to work out the rest of my homesickness and heartache in a bit of fisticuffs. But instead, she turned on her heel and fled, back toward the main building of Miss Preston's.

And that is the story of how Katherine and I became sworn enemies.

Sometimes, when sharp-edged personalities like ours rub against each other, it generates nothing but sparks and heat. But after a while, well, they can wear each other down until the pieces fit together. If it hadn't been for what happened at Summerland, Katherine and I facing the worst ordeal of our lives and each of us only surviving for the companionship of the other, I suspect we would still be adversaries. We're too different to be anything else.

Which begs the question: What comes next?

PART ONE

In the Garden of Good and Evil

In a wide sea of wax; no levelled malice
Infects one comma in the course I hold,
But darts, an eagle flight, bold, and forth on,
Leaving no tract behind.
—*Shakespeare,* Timon of Athens

— J A N E —

Chapter I
In Which Our Sequel Begins

It's a curious thing, to watch a town fall to the dead.

Usually, you only discover a place that's been overrun after the fact: hollowed-out buildings full of shamblers, broken windows marked with the blood of fleeing occupants, scattered ephemera, cups and combs and bottles, the small things that people drop in the midst of headlong flight. It's an eerie sight, the aftermath of a shambler attack, but it's an echo of the horrors, not the actual carnage.

DEATHLESS DIVIDE

Seeing it in action? Well, that's something I'd hoped never to bear witness to.

And yet I'm actually enjoying watching an ocean of undead overwhelm Summerland.

The dead are too far off for me to smell them, but the sound of their moans carries on the hot summer air to where I stand. The buildings of town are matchboxes; the dead are ants swarming all around. I ain't never seen so many shamblers in one place, and I can't help but wonder if this is what it looked like when the dead first rose in the midst of the Battle of Gettysburg, back in 1863.

"Jane."

I turn. Katherine stands nearby, her arms crossed. Even in the midst of running for our lives, she is beautiful. Her golden skin is flushed, and a few tawny curls have escaped her updo to blow in the wind, her eyes as blue as the hot summer sky. The bonnet she wears should look homely, a fashion relic, but on her it's lovely, if a bit blood-spattered. You might not know Katherine was a Negro from looking at her—she's that light—but there is a dusky hue to her skin that belies the truth.

"Do you think Gideon made it out?" I ask. Gideon Carr, a boy about whom I have entirely too many opinions, was nowhere to be found as we escaped. And even though the boy ain't my problem . . . with his muddy hazel eyes, pale skin, and tousled curls, I kind of want him to be. Which is hard to contend with, since nothing of consequence can come from any such feelings.

"Gideon is resourceful," Katherine says, an answer that ain't an answer, "like Ida, your acquaintance from the Summerland patrol. I am certain she was able to see to matters and cleared out before the dead could complicate escape. But we have dawdled long enough. The wagon with the others is going to be out of sight soon, and we should get moving. The restless dead are not going to stay within the town forever."

Katherine is a bit of a nag, and usually all of her bossiness puts me into a provocative mood. But today I am feeling quite fine, since we have survived a near slaughter, rid the world of some particularly unsavory characters, and found our freedom all in the same fell swoop.

We stopped here because I wanted to take one last look at Summerland, the hellhole where I nearly lost myself. The town had been a Survivalist utopia founded by an unholy minister and lorded over by his sheriff son—a town where Negroes had been put in their place, which was in brutal service to the well-to-do white folks that had come to make it their home. It had been hell, but I'd survived. All that effort, however, had been driven by a single thought: that I had a place to go when all was said and done. Rose Hill Plantation, my childhood home.

Now, from the letter I grip in my hand, the last one my mother had tried to send to me, I know that to be false. I've got nothing now but a dream of a faraway place—California—and the hope of finding my beloved Momma and, more importantly, Aunt Aggie. I ain't seen either of them since Rose Hill Plantation, and my letter-writing campaign was thwarted by Miss Anderson, one of the most vile people ever born and an instructor at Katherine's and my alma mater, Miss Preston's School of Combat for Negro Girls.

But that was all then, and this is now. Momma's last note says California is where she was headed, but that don't mean much in these end times. The question that matters more: Is she even alive? And what about Aunt Aggie, the woman that mostly raised me up? What do I do if she's gone to the great beyond?

It's too much to consider in one go. Before I can answer any of those questions, I have to keep surviving today.

"Yeah, okay, let's go," I say.

"Would you mind relacing my corset before we set out?" Katherine asks, pointing to her back. "Not too tight. Just enough to give me a little bit of security."

I manage not to roll my eyes, but just barely. "I don't know what it is about you and corsets," I mutter, but oblige her request anyway. On the way out of town I'd cut the lacings to the contraption so that Katherine would have a bit more range of motion with her swords. We were fleeing from the restless dead, after all. But now that the danger has passed it's apparently time to return to a modicum of respectability.

I lace and knot where necessary but leave the whole thing

looser than I'd learned in my sartorial training back at Miss Preston's.

"I suppose that will have to do," she sniffs, and by that time the wagon with the rest of our party is far enough down the road that all we can see is the dust cloud it kicks up behind it.

It ain't hard to follow. It makes such a creaking racket that if there are any shamblers around they'll show themselves quickly enough. But unless it's a horde, I ain't worried. Jackson Keats, my sometime beau, walks beside the wagon that carries his sister, Lily, and the rest of our ragtag group. The Duchess, the former madam of Summerland's house of ill fame and a white woman of fine moral character, sits in the back with tiny Thomas Spencer, while her girls Nessie and Sallie sit up front and drive the wagon. We are a merry band of survivors, and no one seems all that upset about leaving Summerland behind us. One day, our time there will be just another terrible memory.

"How long until we get to Nicodemus?" I ask, running up to the front, where Jackson leads the way as we walk the dusty track. We're the only ones on the road, which makes me think anyone else who had fled Summerland must've taken a different route. There'd been a crossroads a little ways back, and Jackson had conferred with Sallie in a low voice before we'd continued on, taking a turn that hadn't borne the same deep wheel marks that the other road did. At the time, I'd thought Jackson knew an alternate route, one that would leave us less open to attack, since Jackson was more familiar with the land in these parts than I am. But still, I'm a mite bit worried. Not because I don't trust Jackson, but because I don't like being beholden to a plan that ain't my own.

And maybe the for-real truth is that I do have misgivings about placing my faith in Jackson. After all, once upon a time he was my beau before he decided to put me aside, and the only reason I ended up in Summerland was because we went looking for Lily and uncovered the mayor of Baltimore's plan to build some kind of peculiar utopia out in the middle of Kansas. Now here we are, in between a whole lot of nothing and a ravenous shambler horde, with nothing but our wits and a handful of weapons. No plan, no rations, just hope.

It makes me nervous, how alone we are in the big, wide-open prairie. I don't like feeling so exposed, like the entirety of my sins are being laid bare before that watery blue sky.

"Yeah, you and I need to talk about Nicodemus," Jackson says, gaze steely, hand resting lightly on the revolver hanging by his side. "Not now, but once we stop for the night." His jaw is set, and whatever warmth I might have seen in him back in Summerland has faded. Red Jack is back, ruthless and cutthroat, the boy who used to make my heart pound.

Today his attitude just annoys me.

I stop walking and pull him with me onto the side of the road, out of the path of the wagon. "What are you talking about? What's going on in Nicodemus?"

Jackson crosses his arms. "I just said we'll talk when we stop for the night. The town is a two-day ride, and we're exposed out here. My words were about keeping us all safe, not an invitation to fight about it."

"Fighting is how we get to safe, and it seems like maybe you got a plan that the rest of us should get clued in on."

Behind Jackson, Katherine has left the wagon's side, brows pulled together in a frown. "What's going on?" she asks.

"Jackson says there's something he needs to tell everyone about Nicodemus, but he wants to wait until we stop for the night. I think we need to have it out now before we get too far down the track."

Katherine sighs. "What's the problem with Nicodemus?"

"Nothing," Jackson says. He takes a deep breath and then lets it out. "Your classmates from Miss Preston's are in Nicodemus. There was just a conversation I wanted to have with Jane. Later. When there ain't an audience." He gestures with his head toward the wagon.

"Is something the matter?" the Duchess calls. The wagon has now passed us by and is slowly making its way down the road. I imagine the Duchess ain't too fond of all the folks with weapons falling too far behind.

I tug Jackson by the arm and we start walking, keeping to the side of the road to avoid the worst of the dust. "Look, this ain't the time for half stepping the truth of the matter, no matter how bleak. At some point that horde back behind us is going to be on our tail. If there's something we should know about Nicodemus, out with it."

Jackson sighs and rubs the back of his neck, lowering his

voice. "All right, fine. The town, well . . . it's a bit crowded. There was hardly enough room for the people who were there back when I left. And with the rest of the folks fleeing the horde heading there, I think it would be a better plan to not go there at all but to rather head to the eastern part of the state, make a run for Fort Riley and the Kaw River." He presses his lips together.

I look at Katherine, and her expression of confusion mirrors my own feelings. There's more to his decision than that, and we both know it. "What ain't you telling us?" I ask, but Jackson just shakes his head.

"Drop it, Jane, and trust me for once, will you?" He takes off his hat and swipes away the sweat with the back of his hand before resettling it into place. His bowler is flecked with ominous-looking dark spots just like my wide-brimmed hat, and I wonder if he stole his from a dead man like I did. "There ain't nothing worth seeing in Nicodemus. It's just as cursed as Summerland, the same old evils prettied up with whitewash." He takes a deep breath, lets it out, and starts walking. "It's a Negro settlement, founded by Freedmen and runaways from the Five Civilized Tribes. But that doesn't mean it doesn't have issues. You can't trust those Egalitarians any more than you trust the Survivalists."

I have no doubt what Jackson is saying is true—the Egalitarians were against using colored folks to bulk up patrols and defend towns, but they were still hardheaded in their own way. The best-case scenario would be to avoid a town altogether and just strike out for California. But that's a fool's errand with no rations, and Jackson knows that just as well as I do.

"Runaways?" Katherine says, bringing me back to the matter at hand.

"Some of them Indians kept slaves the same as everyone else," Jackson says, his words clipped. "Ain't a single body in this entire cursed country that didn't have a hand in trying to own the African."

I shake my head, because neither the words nor the tone beneath them sound like the Jackson I know. But I got bigger problems than a bit of proselytizing. "I don't think the Duchess or Sallie will care about going to a Negro town," I say, deftly changing the subject. I'm pretty sure Sallie and Nessie are sweet on each other, and the Duchess was one of the few allies I had in Summerland. Gideon and Ida are both in the wind, and while I hope they made it out of Summerland safely I can't worry about that just yet. I still haven't saved my own miserable hide.

Jackson shrugs. "Maybe not, but we really should head east. If we skip Nicodemus altogether, we'll have a better chance of getting to the Mississippi, and from there we can go anywhere, quickly and safely."

"But there are Miss Preston's girls in Nicodemus," I say. "Sue might still be there. And Ida and the Summerland

Negro patrols were planning to make their way there. If Nicodemus is crowded or compromised, we have to find them and let them know. They'll want to come along with us. And there's safety in numbers, especially when they know how to put down the dead."

Katherine crosses her arms, and a look I recognize all too well comes over her face. Jackson is about to get an earful. "Jane is right. Our friends are in Nicodemus, Jackson. There is no way we could abandon them like that. It's unconscionable."

Jackson presses his lips together. "Since when do you have friends?" he asks me.

"What, you think there ain't anyone I care about more than you in this world?" I shoot back. "Don't forget why we're in Kansas in the first place."

"Fine," he says, hightailing it toward the wagon.

Katherine and I exchange a glance.

"What got into him?" she asks.

I shrug, and jog to catch up to where Jackson is stopping the wagon.

Love does not delight in evil but rejoices with the truth. It always pro-
tects, always trusts, always hopes, always perseveres. Love never fails.
—1 Corinthians 13:4–8

— K A T H E R I N E —

Chapter 2
Notes on a Broken Heart

Once the wagon is stopped, Jackson, or Red Jack as Jane sometimes refers to him, addresses the group. It is easy to see he
is uncomfortable. There is a reason he avoided the discussion
of Nicodemus, and even though it is not immediately clear, I
believe it has something to do with Jane. His gaze skips over
her as he surveys our group, like whatever the boy is about to
say is something that she will not want to hear. It is curious,
and, like Jane, I want to know just what is going on.

But his nerves are catching, and I press in at my sides, trying to find some security in the relaced corset. The familiar panic is still there, just as it always is, right below the surface. I take a deep breath and recite Scripture in my mind to distract myself from the feeling.

Jackson shifts his weight a couple of times, and we all watch him warily, except for the little Spencer boy, who is fast asleep in the Madam's lap. Red Jack takes off his hat, and I know for a fact I have never seen him look this unsure of himself. Granted, we have not been long acquainted, but even while we were on that miserable train ride west, a consequence of an overzealous investigation into affairs that did not concern us, he still looked like he was out on a lark. This is a different Jackson, and he chews on his words, as though weighing them carefully will somehow make them more palatable. "We ain't headed to Nicodemus."

Jane and I exchange a glance. She shrugs. I twist my hands in my skirt, as though the material can absorb the anxiousness I am feeling. My only comfort right now is the knowledge that Jane has no more of a clue as to what is happening than I do.

The Madam—I refuse to refer to her as the Duchess; it is a ridiculous nickname—pushes her red hair out of her face and adjusts her grip on the little Spencer boy. "Then just where is it that we're headed? Jane said Nicodemus was our best bet." Her face still bears the bruising of Sheriff Snyder's wrath, and a fiery rage swells within my breast, pushing back the panicky feeling. I would never tell Jane this because her penchant for violence does not need any encouragement, but I am glad she killed him. That man deserved to die.

I hold close to my anger, because it is a much more welcome feeling than the fear that some terrible thing waits just around the bend.

Jane crosses her arms, Sheriff Snyder's hat, now her hat, pulled low over her eyes. "It is our best bet, but Jackson thinks we should head east to Fort Riley."

One of the other soiled doves, a white girl named Sallie with long, dark brown hair and a defensive jut to her jaw, crosses her arms. "That makes sense to me. Fort Riley is on the way to the Mississippi, and we could go anywhere from there. We should find the Big Muddy and try to head up north before winter gets on. One of my weekly callers heard tell of an enclave up around Saint Paul. Hardly any dead up that way, and they say Fort Snelling is big and strong enough that those who can get there won't have to worry about anything."

Nessie, a colored girl a bit darker than Jane with mournful eyes, frowns. "What's wrong with Nicodemus?"

"Nothing, if you're a fan of those temperance biddies," Sallie says, her expression going stormy. "They're all about *respectability* in Nicodemus. They like to say they survive by being a better class of people. It's not as if I think Negroes ain't good people or nothing, but those folks in Nicodemus make a big deal about it. No drink, no whoring, no swearing. It's like a town made of a church."

I look to Jackson. "Is that true? Is that why you want to go east?" I cannot keep the edge out of my voice. I get the sense there is something he still is not telling us, and I despise secrets.

Nothing good ever comes of withholding the truth.

"Sallie is right, Nicodemus is a bit . . . restrictive." It is not an answer, and it is a vexing response to say the least. "And it's not nearly as safe as Fort Riley. I'm not putting Lily in danger again, if I can help it."

"Hey! I can defend myself," she says, cheeks going ruddy. "I've been taking care of me and Thomas for months. Don't treat me like a baby."

Like me, Lily is light enough to pass. It was looking for her that got Jane, Jackson, and me carted off to Summerland in the first place. She is a plucky girl, and seeing her gives me some idea of just how Jackson and Jane fit together. Jane says the two of them are no longer an item, but I see the way her expression softens when she glances in his direction. And I saw that kiss he gave her outside Summerland. Jane might deny it, but she has a soft heart, and one too easily given, in my opinion. Her love affairs were a constant source of conversation at Miss Preston's School of Combat for Negro Girls, although to hear Jane tell it she was as discreet as they come.

"It seems to me making a beeline for Fort Riley only makes sense if you think there's somewhere to lay on for supplies along the way," Jane says, crossing her arms. "If it's further than we can walk in a day or two we're setting ourselves up for trouble, especially in this miserable heat. Just how far you think the lot of us is going to get without food or clean water?"

"There are some abandoned farmsteads we can scavenge along the way," Jackson says, giving Jane a hard look.

"You got a map of these farmsteads? Because that doesn't sound like any kind of plan to me," she shoots back. "Hoping that we can find supplies."

"I have to agree with Jane," the Madam says. "Lily here might be able to fend for herself, but little Thomas most definitely can't. And to be truthful, me and the girls aren't exactly used to fighting the dead or hunting for our food."

"And I'm not even sure I want to go to Minnesota," Nessie says with an apologetic look to Sallie. "Forts mean soldiers, and I don't have good memories about any of that business."

Sallie's expression is stricken, and Nessie takes her hand. But the rest of our party is looking more vexatious by the moment, and I clap my hands three times to get everyone's attention.

"All of this arguing is not going to get us anywhere," I finally say. Panic thrums in a low key through my veins, like a plucked guitar string. That horde might not be upon us just

DEATHLESS DIVIDE

yet, but if we keep at this they will. "Perhaps there is some logic to Jackson's idea, but as Jane points out, it is still not a plan. How far to Fort Riley?"

A muscle in Jackson's cheek twitches. "Three days, maybe a little more, depending."

"And Nicodemus is what, another day's walk?" Jane asks, needling. At Jackson's slow nod, she snorts. "We've got no provisions, no water, and a bunch of tired, hungry people. I don't think there's a real choice, here."

"Jane is right," I say. "We should head north to Nicodemus, and once we have gotten our bearings and procured some supplies, we can discuss how we might head east to Fort Riley. Besides, with that horde behind us, we should send word out to all the nearest towns and encampments so that they can prepare."

"That makes sense," the Madam says.

Jackson opens his mouth to reply. "But—"

"Perhaps we should vote on it?" I interrupt him.

The Madam and Nessie both look uncertain, and Jane's eyebrow has a cock to it that I dislike. She is plotting, and whatever has gotten the gears of her mind turning cannot be good. But a vote is the best way to put to rest hurt feelings, and there is no sense in setting off with someone out of sorts. This is not a pleasure trip. We are literally running for our lives.

"I know how I'm voting," Sallie says. "I ain't fond of

Nicodemus, especially seeing as how they ain't exactly going to be rolling out the welcome wagon for working girls like me and Nessie. But I'm even less fond of shamblers, and it's only a matter of time until that horde starts to follow the rest of the food. We need a chance to prepare, no matter where we decide to go."

Jackson does not appear convinced, but the rest of the group murmurs concurrence, and it seems like the majority has spoken. But that is when I notice that Jane is barely paying the discussion any attention. Instead, she watches Jackson like a hawk.

"I'm not voting on anything until I know why Jackson is so damn eager to run to Fort Riley," Jane says, as direct as ever, her eyes narrowed.

Here we go. I swear, Jane lives to fight. It is her daily bread.

Jackson looks at Jane, but his expression is not angry. It is sad, almost regretful. "Fine, Jane, you win. The truth is that I heard there were survivors from Baltimore in Fort Riley, come west on the same train that brought Miss Preston's girls out this way, and I'm hoping my wife is there."

My breath catches. Jackson's words fall into the oppressive heat of the afternoon like birds from the sky, sudden and unexpected.

Jane takes half a step back, as though she has been struck. "Your wife?"

He shrugs. "I got hitched back in May. I was going to tell you eventually . . . but, yes, Jane. I'm married." His tone is gentle, but even so, the soiled doves all bear similar expressions of sadness and anger. It is impossible to ignore that this is a blow to our poor Jane.

"You went and got married? Without even *discussing* it with me?" Lily yelps. The girl is too young to parse the subtext of Jackson's declaration.

All of my attention is for Jane. I remember how she looked when she thought Jackson was dead, the anguish that had crossed her face before she twisted her expression back into her usual scowl. The naked despair on her face now puts that past sorrow to shame.

Jane tries to recover, and Jackson watches her expectantly. I am not quite sure why. Does he want her to cry? I know they were close, close enough that I am sure Jane has compromised the boy a few times. But there is something here I just do not understand.

"Well, congratulations!" I say, forcing all the brightness I can muster into my voice. "Lovely that you, sir, have been able to find a wife amid the tragedy and death of these end times. You are quite the enterprising fellow."

Jane makes a choked sound that is somewhere between laughter and a sob, and I keep talking, hoping no one else has heard her. I have found that when all else fails, a sunny disposition can save the moment.

I continue. "While Fort Riley does sound like a potential goal for us eventually, how delightful to be able to reconnect with other Baltimoreans, it seems that the only reasonable plan of action is that we seek out the nearest settlement, no matter whose wife may or may not be in residence there." Once again, the group murmurs its assent. I look to Jackson and Jane, and they both give curt nods.

I give everyone my best smile and clap my hands once like Miss Duncan, my old instructor at Miss Preston's. No one could redirect a mishap like Miss Duncan, and her poise was unimpeachable.

"Excellent, then let us stop wasting daylight." I gesture for Sallie to take up the reins again. "Jackson, can you man lead scout? Jane and I will take the rear."

He stalks off toward the front of the wagon and sets out with long strides. Jane and I fall behind and slightly to the left of the wagon, doing our best to stay out of the considerable cloud of dust the wheels kick up. After a short while it becomes clear that it is a wasted effort, and, using my boot knife, I slice off a strip of my petticoat to tie around my nose and mouth. I slice a piece for Jane as well, and she takes it without a word.

"Are you okay?" I ask in a low voice. I daresay Jane and I are not exactly confidantes, even after our trials together in Summerland. Our friendship is newborn, and I am wary of placing a strain upon it that it will not bear. I remember too well our first meeting and how quick Jane is to take offense at the least little comment. But it is plain to see that she is hurt. She cares about that boy in a way I only understand in an academic context. I know love, of course, but not the push-pull of whatever Jane shares with Jackson. I have come to believe that it just is not in my being to feel such a powerful longing for a person, not physically nor romantically. I am sure that there are lots of reasons why, and folks most likely would try to blame my upbringing, which I would say is wholly incorrect. I am the way God has made me, and I shall not question the wisdom of my Creator. But whatever the reason, the true fact is that I have never had to deal with the complications of romantic entanglements, because they are just not something I desire nor will seek out.

But no matter how she may feel about me, I care about Jane deeply. And even if I do not understand the pain she feels right now, it does not mean I cannot support her through it.

That is what friends do.

Jane does not answer, and I bump my shoulder into hers, give my boot knife a few quick flips. "We could kill him if you would like."

That gets Jane's attention, and she looks at me with wide-eyed surprise. For a brief moment I think I am going to have to explain the joke, but then she bursts out in a hearty laugh.

"Kate, you are too much."

"Perhaps you are right. But we should at least cover him

in honey and leave him out for the ants. I am still rather sore at him for getting us shipped out west. Kansas, of all places! And now he has hurt your feelings? That definitely warrants some kind of retaliation."

Jane sighs and shakes her head. "It's fine. I'm fine, Kate. But thank you. I'm going to fall back a little more, this dirt is all up in my eyes." She swipes at her face, and I know the tears are not because of the dust at all.

She drops back a little ways behind me, turning and watching our rear as we walk. I draw up alongside the wagon a bit more, and smile brightly at Lily and the Madam. Thomas is still sleeping, poor thing. Does he even realize his plight?

"How is Jane doing?" the Madam asks.

"Oh, she is just . . . tired. She was up all night killing the dead, and I daresay today has been even more eventful." The briefest memory of the sheriff's office in the aftermath of our shootout flashes in my vision: dead men, blood everywhere, Pastor Snyder yelling expletives at us as we armed ourselves and departed. My smile turns brittle, and I have to blink hard to keep back the anxious sensation that plagues me like a restless beast. "It will be better for all of us when we find a place to rest."

The Madam nods, and if she notices my momentary lapse in composure she does not say. As an Attendant, it is my job to always remain in control of my emotions, no matter how strong they may be.

I turn my attention back to the tall grass on either side of the road, taking as deep a breath as the corset will allow, and try to will myself calm. The old panic gnaws away at the edges of my mind, a constant catalog of worries that now includes all the terrible things Jane must be feeling and a fair bit of guilt over the dead men back in Summerland. My pulse thrums, and if I were to stop walking I fear that everything would overwhelm me. I wish my corset were tighter. Even though Jane hates the thing, calling it certain suicide in a shambler fight, the control the garment provides helps me to keep the panic inside. Jane would surely laugh at the thought, a bit of satin and bone holding back all the awful that prowls through this world, preying on the wary and unwary in equal measure. But when I am dressed and looking my best, I feel like I actually have power over something.

And even the smallest feeling of security is a comfort in a brutal, unforgiving world.

I pray you, do not fall in love with me,
For I am falser than vows made in wine . . .
—*Shakespeare,* As You Like It

— J A N E —

Chapter 3
In Which I Have an Uncomfortable Chat

I can feel Katherine's eyes on me all through the afternoon. I
scrub my face with my sleeves, smearing around dirt and snot
and tears, and try to untangle my feelings while we walk.
Katherine thinks I'm crying because Jackson broke my heart,
but really my tears were brought on by rage. How dare that
boy kiss me outside Summerland, a kiss that felt like a promise, when he was already hitched to another? How dare he get
me all tangled up in the cutthroat politics of Survivalists and

a quest for his missing sister when all along he was bedding down next to someone else?

How dare he?

But I say none of this, and I keep myself in control by uttering not a sound as we walk, the slice of petticoat Katherine gave me tied around my nose and mouth. If I let loose the tenuous hold I have on my feelings, there will be blood. And it won't be mine.

We walk all through the day, not wanting to give the dead a chance to catch us resting. The sun beats down on my neck, and our lack of water soon takes its toll. My mouth tastes like the wrong side of a boot, and I cough and fight to work up enough saliva to spit. I'm only moderately successful, and the aftertaste of my effort is even worse than the dust coating my teeth.

At this rate, I ain't even sure we'll make it to Nicodemus.

Still we press on, never stopping, though we take frequent breaks whenever we see anything that looks like it could be a creek. But this late in the summer everything is dry, and the cottony hotness that coats my mouth grows thicker by the minute.

Instead of thinking about my thirst I think about Jackson. His shirt clings to the strong muscles of his back—he's stripped off his waistcoat to combat the heat, and I ain't one to skip the view. I remember all the times I saw that fine red-brown skin of his. Jackson and I ran together for nigh on a year, and even after our falling-out he still came around, roping me into schemes that promised adventure and money but never panned out quite the way we thought they would. But in all that time together, not once did he ever mention the idea of marriage, even in the abstract. Not that I would have agreed to any proposal from him, mind you. I got goals of my own, and I ain't never seen a woman get hitched and keep on with her business. Hell, I ain't sure I ever want to set up housekeeping, let alone do it with a man. And having babies? Lord save us all.

No, Jackson never even mentioned it, the possibility of children and "till death do us part" and a life less chaotic. And yet, in all that time we were still up to our adventures he never saw fit to tell me he'd gone and jumped the broom. Where was this wife of his while Katherine and I were help-ing Jackson poke around the Spencers' homestead? Where was she when we crashed the mayor's fancy dinner? Why wasn't she the one that got uprooted and sent west to a set-tlement that was little more than a reinstated version of the old South? Which makes me wonder what kind of girl he married. If she's all the things I ain't.

I ain't sure why I'm fixating on Jackson and his marital status when there's a horde less than a day's march behind us, but I am. A bleak mood taps at my brain, and I let it in without a second thought. The killing from earlier in the day is still with me, and with this newest revelation I just want to lie down in the long grass alongside the road and let the dead find me. It has to be better than this miserable existence.

Just as the sun is beginning to head home for the night, we come upon a cabin, and Jackson calls for a halt.

"This is likely the best we can hope for as far as shelter goes," he says. "I figure we're about halfway to Nicodemus, and if we rest we can make good time tomorrow."

No one objects, and once Katherine and I have cleared the cabin to make sure there ain't any shamblers lurking about, everyone gets to making the best of a bad situation. At the very least, there's a pump, and after a good bit of work water comes up, first silty, then cool and clear.

"Well, at least something is going right," Lily says, saying what we're all thinking.

We cup our hands and drink our fill, scrubbing our faces as we do so. The water makes me feel a little more human even though there's an ache in my middle that no amount of water can relieve. A loud growl comes from Katherine's belly, and she flushes.

"I beg your pardon, but it has been a long moment since I last ate," she says, as though we ain't all powerful hungry. Only Katherine would apologize for a breach of etiquette in the midst of fleeing for her life.

Jackson and Lily head out into the prairie to see if they can scare up a rabbit for dinner. The Duchess sets to stoking a fire in a long-disused hearth inside the cabin, tiny Thomas at her side, while Sallie and Nessie unhook the horse from the wagon and set him to grazing in a fenced area that looks to be built for just such a thing, complete with a wooden trough they fill using a bucket found in the cabin. That leaves Katherine and me to keep watch in the gloaming, and we perch on a couple of empty wooden crates we find on what would've served as the porch.

"Jane, I think the wounds on your back have opened again," Katherine says after a few moments. Her voice is low and her words are careful, but I already know she's right. There was never any doubt that I'd carry a reminder of Sheriff Snyder's lashes, but at this rate I'll be lucky not to get an infection. My dress tugs and pulls at the welts on my back, and even though I've been mostly ignoring the pain, the hotness lets me know I've let it go too far.

"Well, at least I'm alive," I say with a sigh, trying to push aside my fear and worry.

"Let me see to them, Jane. We can at least clean them up." Her tone is gentle, and it makes me want to laugh. If anyone had told me six months ago I'd be mixing it up like this with Katherine Deveraux I would've punched them in the mouth and called them a fool. Guess the only fool here is me. I nod, and Katherine disappears and returns with a bucket. She slices off another piece of her garments and gently dabs at my back.

"If you're not careful, you ain't going to have but four petticoats left," I say.

"Jane McKeene, you know full well I am wearing only

two petticoats. It is far too hot for more than that." She winks at me, and I can't help but smile.

We sit in companionable silence for a few moments before Katherine clears her throat. "Are you sure you do not want to talk about Jackson? Because I cannot help but—"

"Why the hell would I want to talk about him?" I ask, deciding anger is an easier emotion to cling to at the moment than despair.

Besides, Katherine ain't going to be able to answer the only question I have at this moment: Why? Why ain't I good enough? For him, or for anyone? Because everyone sets me aside, sooner or later. My momma, who tried to drown me when I was little even though I loved her more than the moon and stars. Aunt Aggie, who urged me to go with the school officers when they came calling for kids for the combat schools. And now Jackson. Everyone I've ever loved has pushed me away, in one way or another, and I ain't keen on rehashing a lifetime of angst with the one person who might give a fig about me now.

Best she find out how unlovable I am in her own good time.

Katherine mercifully doesn't press me; she throws the bloody rag back in the bucket and gestures at me to button my dress up. "The sheriff, then? You have had quite the emotional shock today, and killing a living person is no small thing. There is a toll it takes on the mind and the soul, and I worry that after all we have been through . . ." She trails off, her words as delicate as her touch.

But kindness ain't what I need right now. I stand, my body smarting, my belly aching, and sigh. "I'm fine, Kate. Besides, we got bigger problems. What are we going to do once we get to Nicodemus? Jackson told us before that the rest of Miss Preston's girls ended up there after escaping Baltimore, but you and I both know that no town is safe for long."

Katherine shakes her head. "I do not think we should make any decisions until we can take the measure of the town for ourselves. It is clear that Jackson and Sallie have their reasons for not wanting to go there, but survival is the thing that matters now, and I think the only people we can trust are one another. You urged me to have patience back in Summerland, and I think that is the proper course of action here as well. After all, a cautious and cool head is the hallmark of a Miss Preston's girl."

A rustling comes from the edge of the grass, and both Katherine and I jump to our feet, she readying her Mollies—short swords with a blade the length of my forearm—and me pulling my revolver, leaving my sickles in their holders. It wouldn't be the first time either of us have seen the dead crawling along looking for a meal, legs too broken or ruined to walk properly.

But it's a rabbit that bursts out, zigzagging toward us. I don't hesitate. My first shot misses, but the second hits, the small body flopping dramatically as it dies.

"Jane!" Katherine gives me a look of wide-eyed horror.

"What?" I ask. I gesture at the prone form with the barrel

of the gun, which still smokes. "That's dinner."

She shakes her head again. "The way you go off pulling that thing out at a moment's notice, I swear . . ." She trails off and walks over to grab the rabbit, holding it up by the ears. There's another rustling sound, but this time it's Jackson and Lily, their silhouettes clear with the bright of the setting sun lighting them from behind. They come walking out of the tall grass at the far edge of the property, Lily clutching her shotgun with a grin.

"We got two of them," she announces.

"You mean *I* got two of them," Jackson says, his voice warm with affection. "You need to work on your trigger pull."

"Jane also got one, and if you had arrived a few seconds earlier she probably would have plugged you full of holes as well." Katherine sniffs.

"Pffft. I know the difference between a girl and a rabbit," I say.

Katherine looks meaningfully at me and then Jackson, and gives the group of us her best smile, before she gestures to Lily. "Come along, let us get these dressed so the Madam can cook them."

"She likes to be called the Duchess," I say.

Katherine huffs. "That is not a name," she tosses over her shoulder as she and Lily round the corner of the house, heading to the pump. It ain't until they're gone that I realize I'm all alone with Jackson.

Dammit.

He must be feeling the same thing I am, because he takes off his hat and draws a breath. "Don't start."

"Start what?" I ask, even though I want to pummel him until the story of how he got hitched falls out.

"Playing inquisitor. You got that look, Jane, and I'm tired. Our course is apparently set for Nicodemus, despite my recommendation, and there's still a long way to go before we get there."

"So that's how it's going to be?" I ask.

"Seems like. You're the one who wanted me to make a pretty speech while we were running for our lives. You're always thinking of yourself and never the people around you."

I want to hit him so badly that I can taste it. "That's pretty rich coming from a liar."

"You know what, Jane? I ain't got time for this backbiting anymore."

"Fine, then . . . congratulations on your nuptials." There's no legitimate goodwill in my tone, I'm far too angry for that. I think of a million things I could say, how I could provoke him into having the argument I want to have, but then I realize it doesn't matter. None of this does. I've already lost him, and I'm a fool for never even noticing the game was finished. "I really mean it, Jackson. I hope you find your wife."

He gives me a sidelong glance, like he doesn't quite believe I'm sincere. "You expecting me to believe you?"

"Yes. You don't want to fight, and that's fine. You're right, there's no point to it."

He crosses his arms and gives me an assessing look. "Why the sudden change?"

"Like you said, it's a long way to Nicodemus, and fighting that whole long way is only going to waste energy we don't have. We can be civil."

"Can we, though?" he asks, his voice low.

I make my way over to sit back down on one of the crates, and Jackson takes the other. "How come you waited so long to tell me?"

Jackson shrugs. His posture is stiff, but if there's anything Jackson enjoys doing it's relating a story. "When was I supposed to tell you? When we were hiding out in that shambler hole on the Spencers' farm? While we were chained up in a train bound for Kansas? In the middle of shooting some drovers trying to steal a wagon, or while I ran for my life ahead of an approaching horde?"

"Right before you kissed me outside of Summerland would've been a good time," I say, propping my feet up on the railing that runs the length of the front porch.

"Ah! There it is. I knew you were going to be difficult," he says, and it's a spark to the tinder of my hurt feelings.

"I ain't being difficult, Jackson, I just think it would be nice if the boy who got me upended from Baltimore and sent to the middle of Kansas told me about getting hitched to some trollop."

"My wife ain't a trollop, Jane, and you ain't being fair."

"I ain't got to be fair about anything, Jackson. I can be as bitter and petty as I want to be." I can almost hear Katherine lecturing me that you catch more flies with honey. Why bother catching flies in the first place when you can just smash them with a minimum of hassle? I jump to my feet, pacing back and forth across the boards of the porch, my anger too much to be contained now that I've loosened its leash.

"If that's the way you want to play it, Jane. Then let's go; let's have it out."

I stop. "You want me to fight you?"

He laughs, the sound a rusty blade, and leans back, crossing his legs at the ankles. "I ain't about to fight you, I know better than that. You want to talk about this, so let's talk. You want to know why I married some other girl and not you, because we wouldn't be having this conversation in the first place if you weren't feeling some kind of way about the whole matter."

I freeze, because he's seen through me in a way that makes me feel naked and cold, despite the lingering heat of the day. And right now I hate him for that.

"Okay," I say, lowering my voice and choosing my words wisely. "I want to know why."

"You mean, you want to know why her and not you. Be specific." The mirth is gone from Jackson's face, his expression stony, and I know I've made a mistake. I've overstepped the boundaries we silently set for ourselves, our flirtation and rebuke, the easy push-pull that's characterized our friendship ever since he put me to the side. I've made the mistake of demanding something from him, something I never did even in the time we ran together, and now he gives me the same calculating stare I've seen him use on a dozen marks.

It ain't a feeling I like.

"Yes," I finally say. "You wanted a wife. I've been around longer than any other girl you know." Shame fissures through me at being so weak, so needy. But I have to know.

Jackson climbs to his feet, paces, and takes a deep breath, scrubbing his hand across his face. "Would you have even said yes if I had asked?"

"You didn't ask," I say. Because that's where my brain gets stuck. He didn't ask because he didn't want me. Even if I maybe wanted him.

Jackson leans forward again and stands. The sunlight is fading fast now, and pretty soon there won't be much light to see by. But I ain't worrying about that, I'm thinking about weddings and families, and the joy of being wanted. I got a whole lot of experience with folks wanting to see less of me, and knowing that maybe Jackson was one of those folks makes the whole situation even more painful.

Jackson points off into the yard, and I follow his finger with my eyes. "That's why I didn't ask you." It takes me a moment to figure out what he's pointing at, since the daylight is fading and the world is going to shades of gray, but I finally get it. He's pointing to the puddle of blood left by the rabbit I shot. "I married because Lily needs a mother. She needs someone who can look after her. And that ain't you, Jane. You ain't the nurturing type. You're a survivor, and I had to do what was best for Lily."

"How are those two things any different?" I ask. "This world is about surviving."

"Maybe, but you're the Angel of the Crossroads, the girl who ran out of a safe place like Miss Preston's in the middle of the night to put down the dead." His words remind me of the first time we met, he and a troupe of other folks, their pony nearly overrun. I'd saved their lives, but the next morning I'd ended up getting the strap because I'd overslept and missed morning drills.

"You're mad because I help people?" I ask, unable to temper my surprise.

He shakes his head, his frustration etched in the taut lines of his shoulders and his fisted hands. "You can't help but get involved in things, even when you know better. How can I depend on a woman who finds it appropriate to run off into the fire instead of away from it? It's who you are, Jane, and I've always loved that about you. But while that may be admirable in a Miss Preston's girl, it ain't in a wife. I want someone I know is going to be there, day after day, not off running on some adventure."

"Why is that okay for you and not me? Why is it okay for a man to be out running around and not a woman?"

Jackson shakes his head. "I ain't saying it's fair, but that's the kind of woman I want. Someone to keep my sister out of danger, and maybe give me some little ones of my own. But you'd never have wanted to be strapped down, chasing after babies. You know that, even if you don't want to admit it to yourself."

He shakes his head, and I can't help but feel that in all our time together I didn't know him like I thought I did, not really.

He doesn't want a wife. He wants a doormat.

My anger melts away like sugar in the rain, and my shoulders slump. How do I argue with him? Jackson is right. There are a few things I'm good at, but none of them are domestic chores. I'm good at putting down the dead.

I'm good at killing.

And what little girl needs that in her life?

Jackson's expression starts to go soft, but then he grabs hold of himself, putting his hat back on and resettling the bowler at a jaunty angle. "We done here?" he asks, voice hard.

"Yeah, we're done," I say, throat clogged with emotion.

Jackson nods once and stalks off, long strides taking him around the edge of the house, following the same path Katherine and Lily took only moments earlier.

⁂

My body is too heavy to carry, my heart is a stone in my chest, but I don't cry. Instead, I collapse on one of the crates, draw my knees up so that I can hug them, watch the horizon, and try to imagine myself pledging my troth to someone, anyone. To love someone else, to follow them even if it means giving up the fight.

I can't.

Jackson is right. I'm a survivor, and in this world, that means doing what needs to be done. I think of all the choices I've made to get here—the shamblers I've put down, the lives I've saved, and the ones I've taken, all of it coming together in the long, dusty road that stretches behind and before us, a path I will keep walking until the end of my days. That feels more realistic to me than any kind of fairy-tale ending.

I realize, as the last of the sun sinks below the plains in a brilliant show of pink and orange, that I will forever be alone.

Because that's how a killer survives.

And ye shall know the truth, and the truth shall make you free.
—John 8:32

— KATHERINE —

Chapter 4
Notes on a Restless Night

After an unexpectedly tasty dinner of roasted rabbit alongside roasted potatoes—Nessie had found some in a long-
abandoned garden—we settle on who will sleep and who will
take watch. Jane, her face an inscrutable mask, volunteers for
the first shift, despite my objections. This is the second night
in a row that she will be running on limited sleep. There are
more than enough adults in our group for Jane to sleep the
entire night. But no amount of reasoned discussion will get

her to budge, and I know better than to keep arguing with her once she has that look on her face, jaw set and gaze distant, an unmistakable sign that her mind is made up. So, like everyone else, I make myself as comfortable as I can in the small house and drift off into an exhausted sleep.

I am startled awake what seems like only a few moments later by Jackson, shaking my shoulder. "Your watch," he mumbles, stumbling off to find his own rest. I grab my weaponry before making my way out of the small house: my Mollies as well as several throwing knives and a rifle. I attend to my bodily needs before washing my face at the pump. There is enough moon to see by, as it is waxing, thank goodness, but not enough to cut through the darkness beyond the edges of the property, so I have to listen very carefully for the dead, trusting my ears to sense what my eyes cannot.

Which is how I hear Jane's approach before I see her.

Her soft footfalls are as familiar as my own thanks to lives lived parallel to each other, our identical training. It is strange to know a person so well without really knowing them, and I turn toward her as she stands in the moonlight, painted in silver and shadow, her face hidden by the brim of the hat she still wears. Sheriff Snyder's hat. It is a gruesome reminder of all that we have been through, and yet Jane refuses to part with it. I fail to believe she could not have found something else to keep the sun out of her eyes, and besides, there is no sunshine at night. But I do not bother querying her on the matter. She has had quite the day, and I know how Jane can take offense at even the most benign of comments.

I stick to an easier topic. "You should be sleeping."

"I tried. The Duchess had second watch, and once she'd relieved me I laid down in the wagon out back, figuring that tiny little house was already full up." She goes to the pump and drinks deeply, as though whatever restless sleep she took left her parched.

"Sleeping out of doors? Is that wise?"

"If the dead are gonna come for me, my penny will let me know, wake me up before anything happens," she says, fingering the necklace tucked into her shirt.

I have long known about Jane's penny. The story goes that her aunt gave it to her before she went east to Miss Preston's, and that it is some sort of hoodoo. And I believe it. I spent nearly a year in the swamps with the Laveaus, the most famous voodoo queens in all of Louisiana, and what I learned in the bayou was that there are things that those with experience in such areas can do that defy explanation, and it is better to just keep an open mind.

But that does not ease my worry over Jane. She is going to push herself too hard, because that is her nature, but out here in the wild mistakes can be deadly. I need her fresh and ready to fight. Despite urging Jane to caution earlier, I have no doubt that once we get to Nicodemus we will find an untenable state of affairs. Perhaps it is cynical, but after

Summerland I no longer believe in happy endings for Miss Preston's girls.

At least, not without a fight.

"Jane, you need to give sleep another try. It is going to be a long walk to town."

"I know that, Kate, but it's too damn hot. And don't give me that 'language, Jane' nonsense. The sun's gone down and it's still sweltering. Only hell can be this unrepentantly hot."

I grin and swallow my laughter. "I fail to see the difference between this and Baltimore."

Jane snorts. "And that was too damn hot in the summer as well. Plus the stink from the wharf? I miss Rose Hill. I never remember it being this blasted hot."

I stare into the dark, letting myself think of home, my for-real home, for the first moment in a very long time. The memory is delicate, and I crack it open like an egg, swift and precise. "Louisiana is just like this. Once summer gets on, with the mosquitoes and the fever, I swear, you start to think you will never be comfortable again."

"Louisiana? I thought you were from Virginia." Jane moves out of the yard and comes closer. She leans against the porch railing, and I know I have piqued her interest with even that small bit of my history. At Miss Preston's, I had been happy to let the girls think I was from somewhere else, mostly because it made it easier to pretend to be someone other than who I truly was. What girl wants to try to explain that she comes from a long line of women who made their living on their backs? Especially knowing the scorn folks like to direct at fallen women? I know Jane would give me a tongue-lashing if she were to know I felt such shame, but it is not easy to just throw aside something you have lived with your whole life, and I will never forget the way some people would look at my mother when they realized she was not an independent free Negro of means. I never wanted anyone to look at me that way.

Maybe it is wrong to care what people think. But I do. Deeply. I suppose that is the remnants of my mother's instruction. She was sure to teach me very early of the need to be able to slip on a second self like it was a corset—an identity that men would find pleasing and would protect the fragile truth of oneself. I did it at Miss Preston's in the hope that being the perfect student would somehow win me an early appointment, a way to earn some money so that I could one day do something with my life. Even though I have eschewed many of my mother's teachings, that was one trick I never completely unlearned.

Jane is too taken with the possibility of a secret to notice my maelstrom of emotions. I sigh and stand, head out into the yard to take a walk around the house, checking on the horse and patrolling the grounds to make sure the dead do not sneak up on us. "Louisiana is where I'm from. Nawlins," I say, letting my voice fall back into the distantly familiar lilt of my hometown.

She raises an eyebrow. "Well, ain't you just full of surprises."

"A girl needs to have a few secrets."

"Indeed."

She follows me like an out-of-sorts shadow, dogging my heels with her black mood. I ignore her and see to making sure our temporary homestead is safe. The dead are not the only concern out here on the prairie. While we have not seen any Indians in our time here I know they must be out there, living their lives unfettered since the Army headed back east to confront the dead so many years ago. I have no idea whose ancestral lands we might currently occupy, but the tribes in this part of the world have no love for Easterners, and rightly so. Some people I had met in Summerland, a family of white homesteaders, had related tales of the Comanche they had run into in the southwest, near the Texas border. "Between the dead and the Indians, heading west is near impossible," they had said. "One wants to eat you, the other just wants you gone, however that might be accomplished." I had no quarrel with anyone, but that did not mean I could ignore the potential dangers of the world.

It would be anyone's guess who or what might come wandering through the area where we had set up for the evening. So even though I want Jane to get some rest, I appreciate her company here in the stillness of the night. Four blades are always better than two.

Once I am satisfied that things are as safe as they can be,

we make our way back to the front of the house and the crates there. I have no sooner sunk onto one, adjusting the corset to keep it from digging into my hips, when Jane says, "Tell me about New Orleans. Or *Nawlins*."

She is making fun of me, but I am too tired to even pretend to be cross about it. And if tales of my hometown can distract her from whatever it is going on between her and Jackson, I am happy to oblige. "What do you want to know? It is like most of the Lost States: miserable in the summer, slightly less so in the winter, and the dead chomping after you all the time."

"How does such a place exist? Felt like Baltimore was only survivable because come winter the dead lay down and you could spend all of the spring harvesting them. Without such a culling . . ." Jane trails off, and I know she is mentally trying to calculate how large the hordes must grow in the Deep South.

"Nawlins' canals trap many of them," I say, my voice low. "After the dead rose, the people of the bayou were pretty well protected. The dead cannot swim, and the natural water currents would drag them out to sea by the thousands. A few folks got the idea that that same mechanism might be used to fortify the city, so they got to building canals. The ones used by the shipping industry had always been an important part of the city, so dredging new ones was not as hard as it might sound. And the city has stood ever since."

"Wait, are you saying that the entirety of the city is made

up of waterways? You don't have any walls? Or bobbed wire?" Jane's voice echoes the awe and surprise of most people when they first see the city.

"Nawlins is at sea level, pert near below sea level in a few places now," I say. "There are the sea walls, too. They used them to keep out the storm surge during hurricanes in the old days, but now they also keep out the dead. Between the brackish water, which speeds along the decay of any dead that get caught in it, and the city patrols, it is enough to keep the city safe. Movement inside and outside the municipalities is tightly monitored, and there are ferrymen who will secure your passage into each area. Yellow fever is a bigger danger than the dead, the way folks tell it. I grew up in the French Quarter, and Maman used to say that nothing was prettier than the Mississippi sweeping away the dead in the morning."

Jane snorts—so loud that I almost do not hear the terrified whinnying of the horse.

We jump to our feet. "Shamblers," she says.

"Get everyone up," I say, unsheathing my swords. For once, Jane does not speak, just heads inside the cabin while I make my way silently around the side of the building, hoping that I am not too late for the poor animal.

The eastern edge of the land is sliding to pink as the sun begins to rise, but there is enough moonlight to see a group of lumbering, grasping figures trying to climb the corral to get to the horse. Those are not rustlers—their strange, jerking movements mark them as only one kind of creature.

The dead.

I count seven dead before they turn their attention to me, deciding I am likely the easier target. They are fast, recently turned, and I have barely swung my sword to decapitate one before another is upon me.

My Mollies are not about flash and dash, like Jane's sickles. There are no spins or kicks or any kind of full-body theatrics. The Mollies are about discipline. Keeping two swords moving at all times, marking the interlocking patterns and defending while also ending the dead—decapitation being the preferred method for such a task—it is all a difficult endeavor, one that requires an inner tranquility. That is why I love the weapon. There is nothing that brings me greater joy than killing the dead, and the only time my brain quiets, where my fears and worries seem far away, is when I wield the swords like an avenging angel.

Moonlight catches on my dancing blades as I step forward, swinging them through necks, removing heads and working the perimeter. The Mollies are not the kind of weapon you would want to use in a crowd; they shine in one-on-one combat, a quick and efficient weapon to put down a single target, and I have to keep moving so as not to be overrun. But by the time Jane comes back with Jackson, I have felled the lot of them.

And I did it all while wearing a corset. Stick that in your eye, Jane McKeene.

"You okay?" she asks.

I nod. "There were seven of them, fresh turned. I cannot tell whether these were folks from Summerland, but there are surely more on the way. As soon as the sun is up, we should move."

"I'll take another look around the perimeter and make sure there ain't any others," Jackson says. He moves off, gun drawn.

I wipe my swords off on the long dress of one of the dead. It is hard not to think of her as a woman—some homesteader, or maybe a fine Eastern lady—who found herself out on the prairie hoping for a new life beyond the terror of the woods. One of the women I met at Summerland had spoken about Kansas as being the new Promised Land. "Any place where you can see the dead coming is a blessing. All of this flat, nearly barren earth is a godsend." Of course, seeing the dead coming does not mean that a body is safe, but I was not about to dash her dreams.

And now, this dead woman, so recently grasping and hungry, is nothing more than a dress to clean my sword. I sometimes wonder if people would hope less if they knew it was inevitable that it would end in tragedy.

I shake the thought and turn my attention to Jane, taking the opportunity to let her notice that I harvested seven all by myself and while wearing a corset, but she is just scowling at the bodies like they have somehow personally wronged her. "What has got you so vexed?" I finally say.

"Do you think we're killers, Kate?"

The query catches me off guard. Not because it is a line of thought I have not considered before now, but because I am not used to Jane wanting to discuss moral quandaries. After all, she rebuffed my efforts to discuss her killing of Sheriff Snyder but moments ago. She has always seemed to me to be a person of uncompromising beliefs, even if she and I disagree on the nature of those thoughts.

More important, Jane's question tracks too closely to my own train of thought, and I am uncomfortable with the coincidence. "What do you mean? You think I am morally compromised?" My heart begins to pound, and the old anxiety returns, the fear of judgment, of failing, of not being enough. I never expected to feel that with Jane. I have never expected her to find me . . . inadequate.

"No, that ain't it; I just been wondering if putting down the dead, doing what we have to do to survive, well . . . if it makes us bad. And not going-to-hell kind of bad, because I ain't sure I believe in all that folderol, but bad like old, dead Sheriff Snyder. Are we murderers?"

Jane talks so fast that I am having trouble following her, and I take a deep breath before I answer. I do not want my words to be inadequate, because I know she needs to talk about what happened with the pastor and the sheriff back in Summerland. After all, it has been less than a day since Sheriff Snyder pointed a pistol to my temple and promised to end my life. But this is a conversation of another sort, although I truly believe the two matters to be linked. I do not understand Jane's mind well enough to be sure I will not provoke her into some sort of irrational nonsense in response.

And so I give her the only response I can in the moment. The truth.

"I think . . . that we become whatever we need to be to survive," I say. "Back in Nawlins, my mother was a placée— um, a kept woman." I cannot quite see Jane's expression, and it feels like too much effort to look up as I unearth this bit of my soul, so I just keep cleaning my blades as I talk. "But she was shrewd, and when she realized she could make more money operating a brothel, she did just that."

I take a deep breath, willing the tightness in my chest to loosen just a bit. Talking about Maman always does this, and it seems silly that after being away from her for nearly five years I should still have such a reaction. I force my voice to remain light. "Maman said that a person becomes whatever they need to be to survive. And that is what I think we are, Jane. Not killers. Survivors. The only goal of this world is to stay in it as long as possible. And no one gets to judge how a body does that, especially when the alternative is being eaten."

I stand and give Jane my best smile, the one that is friendly and open and accepting. The dawn is beginning to paint the world in shades of gray, and there is an expression on her face that looks near enough to relief that some of the tension drains out of me. It is as though my feeble attempt at eloquence has helped her set to rights something that was troubling her, and the way her shoulders relax—as though for one second she can just *be*—gladdens my heart.

"Thank you," she says. "I needed to hear that."

A shout comes from the back side of the house, as well as a shot and then another. It is nothing good, but even worse is the heavy silence that takes its place.

Jane and I exchange a look and then sprint toward the sound, running over the uneven ground as fast as the watery morning light will allow.

. . . Nothing in his life
Became him like the leaving it. He died
As one that had been studied in his death,
To throw away the dearest thing he owed
As 'twere a careless trifle.
—*Shakespeare,* Macbeth

— J A N E —

Chapter 5
In Which My Heart Breaks

Jackson meets Kate and me as we round the corner of the cabin. I heard only a couple of shots, and I don't see any shamblers behind Jackson, though the light still ain't great. But I'm tired and out of sorts, and I don't even rightly know my own mind. I can only hope I'll be useful in a fight, if it comes to that.

"We got to move," he gasps. "Now."

The fallen ladies run out of the front of the cabin, wide-eyed with fright. "Sorry," the Duchess huffs. "We were trying to get ourselves together." She holds Thomas, who sucks on a leftover rabbit bone, and my stomach gurgles angrily in response. With the dead descending upon us we don't have time to look for anything to break our fast. But going hungry looks to be the least of our problems.

I turn to Sallie. "Can you get the horse and wagon ready to move?"

She nods. "Nessie, you come help. It'll go faster with the two of us."

They run off, and I turn back to the Duchess. "See if there are canned goods of any sort and fill whatever buckets or jars we can find before we move. We're still a day from Nicodemus, and at this rate it'll be a long way on an empty belly."

The Duchess nods and heads back inside, nearly running over a bleary-eyed Lily coming out, a rifle clutched in her small hands.

"Shamblers?" she asks. She rubs her eyes and yawns. "How many? Where?"

"The dead," Jackson says, voice calm, "are everywhere. Always. Don't ever forget that." There's a tone to his voice that I don't recognize, and his eyes are strange, intense. I wonder if he had gotten hold a bottle of spirits to make the night go easier.

But it's Lily who sees it first. I follow her gaze to Jackson's left arm.

To the dark trail on the light brown skin of his wrist, dripping onto the ground next to him.

"What happened to you?" she asks. Her voice is slow and careful, carrying with it a lifetime of fear, loss, and worry. The worry we all feel, looking at him now. My heart pounds in my head, rattling my brain as I hold my breath, wanting for it to be something other than the inevitable.

Wanting for him to lie to me.

"You'll have to go without me," he says, voice flat. "It's okay, it's okay. . . ." He's unsteady on his feet, his movements erratic, and I instinctively push Lily behind me, into Katherine's arms.

"No," Lily begins, trying to fight against Katherine's embrace, swinging her rifle wildly. I holster my sickles and catch the firearm on its next pass, jerking it out of Lily's hands so that Katherine can wrap her arms around the girl, keep her away from Jackson.

"Let her go," he says, voice thick.

"Jackson—" I start, but he shakes his head.

"Let us say good-bye. You and I both know I ain't got long, and the last thing I want is the two of you fighting about this moment after I'm gone." He moves his gaze to Lily. "You can't do anything, Lily-bird. So settle."

Lily walks toward Jackson, her steps slow and deliberate; Jackson falls to his knees, and Lily nearly bowls him over. She's crying and he's clutching her tightly, murmuring soft things that are for her alone. I feel a pang of jealousy. Jackson was never so soft with me, and now he never will be. If I hadn't already lost him, I'm losing him now.

What a spiteful girl I am. Even in his last moments I'm thinking about myself.

Lily steps backward when Jackson releases her, walking over to Katherine, who opens her arms once more. Lily throws herself into her chest and begins to sob, turning to hide her face in Katherine's bosom. Katherine looks down at the girl in her arms, her expression goes from shock to misery, and she wraps her arms around Lily, murmuring soft words.

"They came up out of the grass. I ain't even see them," he says. "They were just kind of crouched down. Almost like they were waiting for me." He looks over my shoulder to Lily and lowers his voice. "Get her out of here. I don't want her to see."

"You're—" The words catch in my throat; I have to force them out. "You're not going to change for a little while yet."

"I ain't talking about changing. I'm talking about you finishing this."

I open my mouth to object, and Jackson grabs my wrist, his hand sticky with his lifeblood.

"Please," he says, voice husky with all the things that have passed between us, years of fighting and kissing and all those messy emotions in between.

I understand why he's asking me and not Katherine. Especially right now as she comforts Lily. It's everything he said to me earlier. And I hate him for it. I should yell at him, I should fight him, because it ain't fair. It just ain't. Not more than a handful of hours have passed since he broke my heart, and now to do this, to have to deal his mortal blow. That ain't something I should have to do.

But this world ain't ever just. And I can't tell him no.

I never could.

"Kate, you and Lily go wait with the wagon," I say. "Jackson and I are going to take a stroll." My voice is even and an unnatural calm descends over me. Tears threaten, and I take a deep breath and push it down. All of it. My shame over murdering the sheriff, my heartbreak over Jackson's revelation, my fear over the fate of my mother and Aunt Aggie, and this: my rage at this no-good world taking every damn thing I care about. I will feel nothing, and once all those emotions are locked away tight I can do anything.

I can survive.

"Let me come with you!" Lily screams, fighting to get free of Katherine. She ain't too little to know what comes next. She's grown up in this world of misery and loss just like the rest of us. She knows that Jackson ain't coming back, and that there ain't no way to survive a shambler bite.

But Jackson shakes his head. "No, Lily-bird. This ain't for you to see." He walks over and embraces her for a short moment before kissing her on the forehead. He kneels and whispers something in her ear, and she's crying too hard for me to hear what he tells her.

I want to cry, too. I want to sob bitter tears of grief and disappointment and rage. But I don't, because I ain't got time.

There are more dead headed right for us, and if we don't get moving, Jackson won't be the only one we lose today.

Lily sobs brokenly, and I hand Katherine the rifle as she pulls the younger girl away, toward the wagon and our escape. Jackson and I don't move, just watch them leave.

"You got the chills yet?" I ask. Everyone knows how the change works. First, the numbness, then the chills, making a body shake so hard that anyone nearby would think they're having a fit. And then, right before it happens, a yellowing of the eyes and drooling, like they got the scent of frying pork chops stuck in their nostrils. I've seen it happen, heard people scream and snap through the change as it overtook them.

But it's never been someone close to my heart. Jackson is the first. He's been a handful of firsts for me; this one is by far the worst.

"No chills, but I can't feel the bite anymore. We need to move," he says, setting off back the way he came. His long legs eat up the distance, tracking through the knee-high grass, and I damn near trip over the shambler remains lying in the weeds.

"At least you gave them what for," I say, pulling out my sickles. It's cold comfort, but I ain't sure what else to say.

I walk behind Jackson, watching the way his shirt plays across his back, thinking to yesterday when I did the same thing. How dreadful the memory is, how unfair. It's a doorway to all sorts of better memories and worse ones besides. I have to fight to lock them down. It's too seductive to wish for simpler times, to get lost in the softness of nostalgia.

"They were fast, too fast, which means there's most likely more of them out there." Jackson stops. We're far enough away from the homestead that all that's visible is the rough outline of the house. He starts to shake, and tears leak from the corners of his eyes. "Do it now, Jane. Don't make me go through the change."

I shake my head. "I can't. Not until I know it's real." I won't risk killing him if by some bit of luck I don't have to, and his shoulders slump with the realization of it. For some reason, I think of Gideon's vaccine—his confidence that he'd found a way to render a shambler bite harmless. But here I am, watching my best boy turn, helpless to do anything but witness his end.

Hope is deadly, and some part of me wants to believe that all those lies about Negroes being immune to the bite are true. But my eyes tell me otherwise.

Jackson is turning, and there's nothing I can do about it.

The sky is brightening by degrees, the sun painting colors into the rough landscape. Now I can see the fear naked on Jackson's face, the realization that there's no way out of this.

"You know it's real. I wouldn't lie about something like this," he says.

Tears break free, and I laugh and wipe them away. "You can't blame me, though. You never were any good with the truth." I need him to joke with me, to be as dismissive as he was when we ran together. Even last night, as he tore out my heart and stomped it to smithereens, he still wore that cursed half smile of his, as though it was just another bit of meaningless conversation. Earnestness ain't something I can tolerate right now.

I am barely holding myself together.

But Jackson ignores the unspoken plea in my voice. And who am I to dictate the tone of his last moments?

He falls to his knees, wrapping his arms around himself. He shakes, and behind him the sun is rising in a bloody sort of way. It makes me wish I was some kind of artist, that I could render the beauty of Jackson and the sky in oil paints, shades of red and love. I want to stop time, to freeze this moment forever.

"It's funny, I ain't got a lot of regrets, Janey-Jane," he says, the old nickname cutting through me like a dull, rusty blade, lodging right in the softest spot of me. "I've always lived my life knowing just what kind of man I was. But I'm sorry things didn't work between us. I'm sorry I wasn't the man you needed."

"It ain't supposed to end like this," I say, and look away.

"Jane." He waits for me to look back, and that's when he stills for a moment. In the growing sunlight he is a vision. The red in his curls glints like fire, and his eyes are as green as spring leaves. He's a creature out of myth and lore, a satyr dancing and luring innocent maidens into his wood. Jackson ain't looking at me so much as looking through me, like he sees a world much better than the one we live in. A slight smile parts his full lips. He is everything I have ever wanted. "You know that ain't true. It was always gonna end like this."

I take a shaky breath, but halfway it lodges on a sob. This time, I let the tears fall.

"No one gets out of here alive," he continues, and for half a heartbeat my penny goes icy before warming back up. "Like my daddy used to say: it begins bloody, and it ends the same way."

It ain't the kind of thing I'm expecting, and I have to fight to swallow around the lump in my throat. It's all so damn unfair. "Damn you, Jackson. Damn you for this."

"I know, Jane. I know." A shudder passes through him, and he stills. He closes his eyes. "I love you, Jane. I know what I said before, but I'm asking you now: keep Lily safe for me."

"How am I supposed to do that in this godforsaken world—" I start to ask, but there ain't going to be no answer forthcoming.

Jackson's shoulders slump and he falls forward. The sun is up now, and the world has gone bright.

And I can see lurching, stumbling forms in the distance.

I know I need to get our band of survivors back on the road to Nicodemus, but I can't leave. If there's one thing Jackson could always be counted on for, it's getting himself out of one situation after another. Part of me is hoping this will be one more story he'll be telling out the side of his mouth with half a smile, the danger long past.

But then the form on the ground lets out a growl, a shambler's moan, and I know Jackson is gone.

So I raise my sickles, and do what I must. Swiftly.

And as Jackson's head separates from his body, I fall to my knees, sobs wracking my body.

I will never let myself love someone again.

I'm still sobbing as I drag myself to my feet. I want to run out to the middle of the prairie and just lie down, see if I can pull myself together, or if my parts just disintegrate and float away on the wind. But time ain't a luxury I have.

I also can't leave behind the valuables on the body. If anything, Jackson wouldn't want me to. I clean off my sickles before I grab his hat and tip it upside down like a basket. Into it goes his pistol and the big knife in his belt. His pockets yield a gold watch on a chain and not much more. I'm just about to leave when I decide to pull off his boots and find a letter inside the left one. It's written in a messy hand, and I only have to glance at the first few lines to realize that it must be from his wife.

Curious—Jackson didn't know how to read. Did he begin his marriage by lying to the girl? It makes me ache for him and hate him at the same time.

I tuck the letter in with everything else and make my way back to the homestead as quickly as possible.

Everyone is in the yard when I arrive, the wagon laden and set to go, and the short run has given me time to compose myself. I'm numb, the loss too fresh to hurt properly just yet, and there's still our own necks to consider.

"There's a whole mess of dead about a mile away. Maybe two. We have to move." I force myself deep, deep down into the place in my mind where everything is quiet and cold and my heart ain't breaking. Luckily it ain't as hard as a body would think.

How does one go on when they've lost their heart? By being heartless.

I hand the pistol to Nessie, and she eyes it hesitantly. "I don't know how to use this," she says.

"You want the knife instead? We're about to move fast and hard to Nicodemus. Everyone needs a weapon, and no more than two people plus Thomas on the wagon at a time. We cannot let that line of dead catch up to us, or we're all shamblers." My voice is hard, but I don't have any softness for Nessie, nor anyone else. And not a lick of pity, besides. "If any of you fall behind, I will leave you."

"Jane—" Katherine begins, but I shake my head at her.

"We don't have time for kindness, Kate," I say, and she says nothing, just nods.

Nessie takes the pistol. "Keep it pointed at the ground until you're ready to use it," I tell her.

My words are blades aimed at everyone around me. I'm taking my fear out on them, and it ain't fair, but I can't quite help it. I refuse to lose anyone else today.

"I'm sorry about your friend," Nessie says, her voice soft.

The words create a fresh lump in my throat, and I say nothing, just tuck the knife in my belt before I move on over to Lily. She watches me with a sullen expression, tears leaking down her light brown cheeks.

"Here. This is yours," I say, handing her the hat and the pocket watch. I keep the letter—of course I do. I ain't proud of it, but I want to see what love looked like to Jackson, to see what he'd say to this girl that he never said to me. Even with him gone, I'm still jealous and petty, but it's the only connection to him that I have.

Even if he ain't anything that was even remotely mine.

"I hate you," Lily says, her eyes locked on one of my sickles.

I glance down and realize that, in my haste and anguish, I missed cleaning a spot, Jackson's blood drying near the hilt.

"I know," I say.

And with that, we run for Nicodemus.

Be ye angry, and sin not: let not the sun go down upon your wrath.
—Ephesians 4:26

— KATHERINE —

Chapter 6
Notes on a Horde

Jane sets a grueling pace away from the homestead, her usual scowl back in place, barely bothering to check the underbrush that lines the road away from the house for shamblers. At first I think to engage her, to caution against recklessness. With the loss of Jackson fresh on everyone's mind it is too easy to panic, to run like frightened livestock. But once we have crested a slight rise and I look back toward where we spent the evening, I understand Jane's urgency. A mass of dead lurches toward us, a mile or so behind. It is impossible to tell how fast they are moving, but even if they are strolling all we need is for the wind to shift, for them to catch the scent of us. At top speed, they will close that distance quickly.

And out here in the open, with nothing for defense apart from the few weapons between us? Well, our odds are not good.

Sallie, at the reins of the lightened wagon, and with Thomas seated behind her, sets out with the horse at a trot. Jane and I can keep that pace beside them—our stamina comes from years of training at Miss Preston's. But Lily, Nessie, and the Madam do not have that experience.

We have only gone a mile or so before everyone is winded and their steps falter.

"Jane, they need to get into the wagon," I say, voice low.

"The horse will wear out," she says. "If that happens, we're all done for. They're just going to have to keep up."

"What do you know about horses, Jane McKeene? How many have you raised and cared for?"

She says nothing, only presses her lips together, a muscle working in her jaw.

Just as I thought. I am trying to be gentle with Jane because of what she has been through; over the past few days, she has experienced a lifetime of pain and danger. But my patience is nearing its end. "We must put distance between ourselves and that horde," I say. "The farther away we are, the less we risk them detecting our scent. What we need now is speed."

This time, she ignores me, and that is when my temper flares.

"Sallie, please stop the wagon," I call.

"What do you think you're doing?" Jane demands, but the wagon is already stopping.

"Lily, Nessie, Madam, please climb into the wagon." I look to Jane, but she has fallen silent. "Sallie, keep the horse to a quick walk, make sure not to strain him."

"Oh, he's a big boy. It'll take a lot to do that," Sallie says, smiling as an exhausted Nessie climbs up next to her. "But, Jane, let me know if you think we need to change the speed."

Jane is not the only one who is scared, and Sallie's words make me realize that these people will do whatever Jane tells them to. They see her as a fighter, someone who knows what it takes to endure in these end times. No matter the command, they will follow rather than argue.

I doubt Jane realizes that.

Once everyone is settled, Sallie flicks the reins again. I strip off my swords as I run, putting them in the back of the wagon. "Jane, put your weapons up."

She looks at me, eyes wide. "What?"

"Disarm yourself and walk with me."

"There's an army of dead on our heels and who knows how many around us, and you want me to put up my sickles?"

"Yes. Disarm or be disarmed." The challenge in my voice is clear.

Jane's scowl deepens, and she drops her sickles and pistol in the wagon.

"Sallie, have the horse trot for a little while," I say.

She raises a hand in acknowledgment, and the wagon picks up the pace, pulling away from Jane and me.

I put my hands on my waist and wiggle. The corset is not very flexible, but it allows enough movement for what I have planned.

"Kate, I don't know what's got into you, but—"

She does not get to finish the sentence, because I slap her full on the cheek. Not as hard as I could, but enough to get her attention.

"What the—"

I hit her again, this time the other cheek. Her brown skin is ruddy, and I take up a defensive stance.

"This ain't the time for such nonsense," she yells.

"This *is* the time. You are frustrated and out of sorts, and your grief is a fresh brand that has not begun to heal. I know what you have been through, and the Lord knows you are entitled to deal with your emotions as you see fit. I personally would find solace in the Scripture, but there is no Bible about. You need to work through what is going on in your heart and, well, I figure this is as good a way as any." I put up my fists.

Jane shakes her head. "What are you blabbering on about?"

"It is going to take time to deal with the events of the past few days, but time is something we do not have right now— and in the meantime, you cannot take it out on them." I point at the cloud of dust that marks the wagon's passage.

"So you think you and I should just have at it in the middle of the road until the dead catch up?" she asks. She is breathing hard, and her expression has gone stony, a sure sign that my words found their mark.

"I am going to do what I can to get you to focus, Jane. I am going to be your target because I can handle your ire in a way they cannot. Sometimes a little physical release, directed and controlled, can quiet the heart just a bit." I do not tell her about the way my heart breaks for her loss, nor the constant, creeping waves of panic that lap at my consciousness. Heartfelt confessions have never moved Jane the way that actions do, and if I want to help her, if I want to show her that I am her friend, I have to do that in a way that she understands.

And if there is anything Jane understands, it is combat.

"I am sorry . . . I am sorry that this world demands more of you than you should have to give. But that is not a reason to expect more of these untrained women and children than they have to give. We have the ability to protect them, and so we have the responsibility to do so, as long as we are able. Putting their survival solely on their own shoulders? Making them run alongside the wagon like livestock while they slowly succumb to exhaustion? That is not who we are, Jane. We can survive without being cruel to one another. I refuse to believe that we have to be like those we hate in order to carry on."

Something in her face shifts, some piece of whatever she is working through falling into place. I am jubilant that I am getting through to her.

And so I am not watching for the fist that comes flying toward me.

The punch is a good one, aimed right for the space below my corset. I backstep too late, and she catches the corset's edge. My breath whooshes out of me, and the force of the blow sends me stumbling back a few steps.

"You want a fight?" she says as I gasp for air. Her face is a blank mask. All of her emotions have retreated, leaving nothing but an expression of polite interest. She has locked herself down tight, focusing on nothing but the moment. "Well, then, let's go."

I take a deep breath and straighten. The corset absorbed some of the blow, but not enough. Jane is not pulling her punches.

So then, neither will I.

It was customary to spar at Miss Preston's. The instructors ignored no aspect of our education and knowing how to defeat a living person as well as the dead was part and parcel of our instruction in protecting well-to-do women. While the dead may let their hunger overwhelm them, the same may be said of live men and their passions. A Miss Preston's girl was tasked with protecting her charge against all ravenous monsters, not just the undead sort.

Grappling in the middle of a dusty road, with a cadre of dead on one side and a wagon of terrified women on the other, however, is definitely not something a Miss Preston's girl should do. But if I cannot help Jane through this, these emotions she would rather bottle up than contend with, then she will misstep when it matters most. I cannot let that happen. I owe her my life for saving me back in Summerland.

And I have few enough friends as it is. I need to hang on to the ones I possess.

I sidestep Jane's next punch, and the follow-up that comes behind it. Her swing is wild, uncontrolled, and I easily land a blow of my own to her midsection. She doubles over, and I place my hands on my hips. "Honestly, Jane, you are fighting angrily, and your form is amateur. Remember your lessons for once, will you?"

I barely have time to dodge the kick that comes for my head, and as I dance out of the range of Jane's foot my own anger surges, hot and fierce.

"You looking awfully red in the face there, Kate," Jane drawls.

She is right. A slap or a punch is just sparring; a kick has the ability to immobilize me, if she were to land it, maybe long enough for the horde to overtake us.

"Jane, that was a very bad decision."

I step in close, faster than she is expecting. Not everything I know about combat was learned at Miss Preston's. After running away from home, I spent several months living in Bayou la Southe. That had not been my plan, but life cares not for the plans of Negro girls, passing light or otherwise. I learned a lot running with the Laveaus, a group of disgraced voodoo women who dedicated themselves to stopping the slavers that ran their cargo up and down the Mississippi River. And one of the things I learned was how to fight dirty while wearing a corset.

I wait for Jane's next swing, catching her arm and pulling her forward. Her momentum means she falls into me, her torso open and unprotected, so it is easy to bring my knee up into her midsection.

The breath goes out of her, and I take the opportunity to spin around behind her, locking my arm around her throat.

"You are out of sorts. You need to rest, to let yourself grieve and come to terms with what happened in Summerland. Losing Jackson is just compounding your distress."

She flails, making a terrible gurgling sound that I ignore. In my mind I recite Psalm 23, it is much more pleasing than listening to Jane choke. Before she loses consciousness, I release her. "Look at yourself," I say, my voice made of razors. "You are sloppy, your moves are reckless. I know feelings are never something you want to talk about, but you cannot handle this all by yourself. You just. Can. Not."

Jane coughs and heaves. Tears fall from the corners of her eyes, and murder is writ large on her face. I really cannot blame her. I did best her but good.

For a moment I am worried Jane will swing at me again, but then her shoulders slump and a long, low wail comes from her.

"It ain't fair," she says, her voice almost too quiet to hear.

"No, it ain't," I agree, my tongue tripping over the improper English and my heart aching for her once more. "And I am so, so sorry."

Jane sobs brokenly, her body shuddering. I pull her into my side, supporting a good deal of her weight, and let her cry, the kind of release she would not allow herself. We begin to walk.

The day is still, and our luck holds. We are able to keep pace with the wagon a hundred yards ahead of us, and the horde behind keeps its distance.

And for now, this is enough.

This is the excellent foppery of the world that when we are sick in fortune—often the surfeits of our own behavior—we make guilty of our disasters the sun, the moon, and stars, as if we were villains on necessity, fools by heavenly compulsion, knaves, thieves, and treachers by spherical predominance, drunkards, liars, and adulterers by an enforced obedience of planetary influence. . . . An admirable evasion of whoremaster man, to lay his goatish disposition on the charge of a star.
—Shakespeare, King Lear

— J A N E —

Chapter 7
In Which Our Luck Runs Out. Again.

A dozen or so miles from the homestead, and a couple of headachy hours after I've managed to stop crying, the dead catch up to us.

I walk sullenly beside Katherine after our middle-of-the-road fisticuffs. I'm still sore about her using that neck hold on me, and my throat aches every time I swallow. But I'm also impressed that she could be so ruthless. I ain't ever seen that side of her before, and I wonder what other kinds of tricks she has up her sleeve.

I'm also planning on making her show me.

But the truth is, since having it out with her, I have felt a bit better. The loss of Jackson is still an aching wound, and I know it will be for some time. But focusing on keeping our group of survivors alive gives me something else to think on. I have to get us to Nicodemus. Only then will I let myself fall to pieces over Jackson—and ponder the difference between a survivor and a killer in this cruel world.

I'm thinking about Jackson's letter from his sweetheart when under my shirt my penny goes icy. At the same moment, Sallie stops the wagon.

"Jane! Katherine! We got a problem!" she yells.

Katherine and I don't hesitate. We run around to the front of the wagon. We'd been expecting the dead to come up from behind us, the horde that's been trailing us from Summerland, but it turns out they weren't what we needed to worry about. A dozen or so shamblers have congregated in the road, like flies on manure, swarming a wagon that looks very much like ours.

"Looks like some fellow travelers ain't make it," Nessie murmurs. She holds the pistol I gave her, Jackson's gun, in a white-knuckle grip. Shame for lashing out at her earlier washes over me, heating my face. I reach up and take it from her, tucking it into my belt loop.

"Don't want you accidentally shooting me in the back as we clear this mess," I say, my voice full of the apology I can't bring myself to say. Katherine was right. She and I are the ones trained to put down the dead. Not everyone is cut from that cloth, and expecting Nessie to be something she ain't is unfair.

This part is best left to the killers amongst us.

Katherine and I walk toward the shamblers, slowly and cautiously. The dead are so busy feeding that they haven't even turned to look at us. They're down on hands and knees on the left side of the wagon, using teeth and hands to gorge themselves on the entrails of an unrecognizable man. They dined on his face and neck first, and the road beside the overturned wagon is scarlet with his blood. The attack must have been sudden, violent, and recent.

A few moments earlier, and it could have been us.

"Got any ideas?" I ask Katherine.

"Normally I would say we shoot them, but I am afraid that gunshots might spook the horse at this distance," she says.

"Not to mention bring the other horde running."

"Yes, the horde." Katherine looks briefly behind us before turning her attention back to the dusty, blood-soaked road before us. "Well, I reckon we go in hard and fast. You want to lead off?" She eyes me warily; this is no doubt a peace offering for the thrashing a few hours earlier.

I unsheathe my sickles, turning them in my hands until my wrists are warmed up. "You're going to have to show me that fancy hold you got me in," I say, and her answering smile has more than just a smidge of relief.

I take a deep breath and sprint right at the dead. My skirts are high enough that they don't tangle my legs too easily, but

I have the momentary thought that trousers would be even better. I really miss the ones I used to wear when I ran the roads back around Baltimore. Maybe I'll find myself some when we get to Nicodemus.

And then I'm swinging my sickle to take off the head of the nearest shambler, a man that wears the garb of a homesteader, work boots and rough homespun garments, all covered in splotches of red and black, his blood and that of his victim. A gurgling scream, a slice, and I'm moving on to the next one.

Whatever advantage I may have had in running up on the dead is now lost. They abandon their meal and come after me, growls rumbling deep in their throats. I take out four more, leaving another five, before Katherine draws even with me, her swords dancing complicated patterns that catch the sunlight as they sever heads.

I move wide left to give her room to work, taking out a couple of dead that decide I'm the easier target, and we've just cleared the last shambler when a shout comes from behind me.

"Hurry up! The horde is on the move!" Lily screams, the terror naked in her voice. She points to the rising cloud of dust on the horizon behind us, the air heavy like a deadly storm.

"Dammit!" I yell. The felled wagon is smack-dab in the middle of the road. Our wagon might be able to make it over the bodies, but there's no way we can make it around the wagon without risking the wheels falling into the rut on either side of the road or snapping an axel. And the fallen horse attached to the damaged wagons is in no condition to move. Poor creature. Now I understand why we always used iron ponies, the horseless carriages driven by steam, back east. The dead don't devour steel.

"Quickly, we need to unhook the horse and push this contraption out of the way," I say.

Katherine glances over her shoulder, her blue eyes going comically wide. "There is no time," she says. She hurdles the dead and runs to the front, hacking at the leather straps with her sword. I lean against the back of the wagon and get ready to push.

"Jane!" comes the shout from behind me.

"We're clearing the road!" I yell. I don't look back, don't turn to see how much ground the horde has covered in just the last half minute. The stink of putrefaction fills my nose, a smell stronger than the ten shamblers we just downed could manufacture.

We are out of time.

I shove against the back of the wagon with all my might, grunting from the effort. The thing moves a little, but not enough. I turn around, putting my back against the wagon, and now I can see why folks are hollering at me.

The dead are less than a quarter of a mile away.

I push again, but it's impossible with the bodies of the dead blocking the wheels. And there's no time to move them all before the oncoming mass of shamblers reach us.

"Help me lift it!"

Katherine is next to me, and I immediately place my palms flat under the bed of the wagon and heave. Flipping it over won't clear the road completely, but it's enough space that Sallie should be able to squeeze our wagon by.

We grunt and strain, splinters digging into my palms from the rough wood. But the thing finally begins to rise, tilting over and landing with a crash that is swallowed by the terrified screams coming from our wagon.

"Go, go, go!" I shout.

Sallie doesn't need the prompting. She stops the wagon just long enough for Katherine and me to clamber aboard, and then we're flying down the track, the dead now at a full sprint behind us.

Most times, the dead ain't fast, especially those that have been wandering about since the Years of Discord, those dark times just after the dead first rose in 1863. Some of the shamblers from that time are still dragging themselves around—one can often tell by the remains of their Union or Confederate uniforms. But these are fresh, and they continue to gain on the wagon even as Sallie urges the horse into a gallop.

These dead can't all be from Summerland. There's too many of them. Could there be other towns lost to the horde recently? It's a grim thought, and I wonder—not for the first time—if we're running toward salvation or ruin. Jackson had wanted us to forget about Nicodemus all together and make straight for Fort Riley. And maybe he was right. Is Nicodemus going to be able to withstand a horde like this?

And what if Nicodemus has already fallen to the same fate as Summerland?

"Jane," Katherine yells, pointing at the dead. "They are gaining on us!"

"The horse cain't maintain this pace," Sallie yells back at us. "The wagon is too heavy!"

"We have to slow down the horde," I say. I pull out my sidearm and take aim at one of the nearest dead. My first shot misses, but I cock the hammer again and pull the trigger, and this time I manage to clip its knee. It goes down, tripping a few of its neighbors and causing a moment of localized catastrophe.

My third shot misses widely again, and Katherine lets out a huff beside me.

"Save your bullets," she says, pulling out her rifle. "This wagon is bouncing all over the place, and we both know you are a middling shot, even in ideal circumstances."

I swear, that girl would criticize God himself if he were to come down and grant her a few miracles. Still, she's right. I put my gun away. "Here, I'll play tripod," I say as she begins to take aim down the length of the rifle.

She takes up position in the wagon, sinking down onto her left knee, and she plants her right foot on the floor, propping her right arm on her upper thigh. I sit in front of her, legs crossed, and plug my ears with my fingers as she rests her left hand, which cradles the rifle's forearm, on top of my right shoulder.

"Call the count?" she says, yelling to be heard over the noise of the wheels as we hurtle along the road.

I nod. "Old white woman with a blue dress," I say, picking out a target. "Fire at will!"

The wagon bounces along, and there's a momentary pause as Katherine takes a shallow breath and releases it before she pulls the trigger. The shambler's head explodes in a spray of blackened blood, its body falling sideways and collapsing the column so that at least a dozen of the others fall with it.

"Next," Katherine calls.

"Um . . ." My mouth goes dry as I spot one of the dead toward the edge of the pack. It's an old white man, his shirt-front covered in dried blood, and a stab of recognition zigzags through me.

It's Pastor Snyder, the miserable preacher from Summerland.

I'd left him bleeding out from a gunshot wound in the sheriff's office. The bullet hadn't been mine—an errant shot from his dying son had been the cause—but I'd left him to the approaching horde all the same. Either the shamblers found him before death did, or he returned on his own with no one around to drive a nail into his forehead after he expired. And seeing him run toward the wagon ignites a fire in my chest, a determination that ain't been there the past few hours.

I did not survive the miseries of Summerland to die on some dusty road in the middle of Kansas.

"Jane?" Katherine yells, and I realize she's still waiting for me to call the shot.

"Indian woman wearing homespun," I say, picking out a more centrally positioned target.

Katherine fires again, and again the shambler falls. Her rifle is a repeater, so she has four more shots before she has to reload. I thank whatever misbegotten funds supplied the armory of Summerland. The place was terrible in every single way, but at least their weapons were top-notch. The dead have already fallen a ways behind us thanks to the commotion that Katherine has caused.

We continue, me calling out the shots and her taking them until the horde falls back far enough that they're out of range of the rifle. We can still see them, maybe a mile away.

Katherine didn't miss a single shot.

"Best at Miss Preston's," she says, a mischievous grin on her face as she reloads and stows the rifle.

I roll my eyes as I turn around and sit against the back of the wagon. "If you say so."

Sallie glances over her shoulder at the horde. "I'm glad you girls gave us some breathing room, but we got another problem."

"What else is new," mutters the Duchess. She holds Thomas and Lily toward the front of the wagon, and while the children both look scared, they've got their wits about them for the moment.

"The horse is wiped," Sallie says. "He's gonna run himself to death if we're not careful."

And, as if on cue, the horse goes down.

I grab for the side of the wagon as we skid to a sudden stop, everyone sliding around. Nessie takes a tumble, and I vault out of the wagon after her.

"You okay?" I ask as I help her to her feet.

She nods, but her face crumples immediately. "We're going to die, ain't we?"

I shake my head. "No. No we ain't. Not today."

The horse lies on his side. He's not dead, but he's dog-tired. I know how he feels. There have been a dozen times I've thought about just lying down, giving up. But that ain't my nature.

Which is why I'm going to do what I'm about to do.

I pull the knife from my boot and cut the horse loose. He looks at me with wild eyes, panting, his sides heaving, and I feel terrible. I push the sorrow aside and swallow thickly.

"You've been a good horse," I say to him. To Sallie I ask, "Is there a way to get him on his feet?"

Her eyes widen as she realizes what I mean. "We can try," she says, coming to stand next to me.

She grabs his reins and tries pulling him to his feet. At first he refuses to budge, so I walk behind him and push his rump like I can will him to rise. The horse tries to roll over, back onto his feet. It's no use.

He's finished.

"Let's try once more," Sallie says.

She pulls on the reins, and I get my shoulder behind the horse. This time he gets up, unsteady. His sides heave and there's a wet, soapy-looking coating all over him. But I'm hoping he can serve one last purpose.

One of the first tenets of instruction at Miss Preston's is that an Attendant must be willing to do whatever is necessary to protect her charge. Anything, no matter how distasteful.

Katherine draws up beside me. "Jane," she says. She knows what I'm about. It seems that today is all about doing the most regrettable things.

Once the horse has gained his footing, I take the reins from Sallie and turn the horse toward the plains. I draw my pistol and fire a shot right next to him. Just as before, it's enough to spook him. And this time, no one is holding the reins to keep his burst of speed under control.

The horse takes off across the prairie, perpendicular to where we stand. How light and free he must feel without the weight of the wagon behind him. But as he runs, so, too, does the following horde, shifting to sprint after the movement of a potential meal.

"Come on," I say after it's clear that the horde is on the horse and not us any longer. I don't wait to watch the horse fall again. I can't.

I won't mourn the horse. I've already got enough grieving to do.

I take Thomas and help the Duchess out of the wagon. "Let's not waste any more daylight."

The Lord is my shepherd, I lack nothing. He makes me lie down in green pastures, he leads me beside quiet waters, he refreshes my soul.
—Psalm 23: 1–3

— K A T H E R I N E —

Chapter 8
Notes on a Struggle

It is with a dark mood that we set out after losing the horse. Jane carries Thomas, and after only a little while Lily begins to fall behind, so I carry her as well. We had to abandon all but a few of the provisions we were able to scrounge up at the homestead, and after only a short ways I realize that having to leave behind the jugs of water we pumped is a huge blow. The landscape is desolate, nothing but grass and a few scrub trees, and the sun unforgiving. We will be lucky to make it to Nicodemus.

As we walk I try to push my panic to the side and focus

on each small thing I am doing. Walking down the road. Balancing Lily on my back and the rifle in my hand. Taking small shallow breaths to allow for the corset, which is still much looser than I like. I watch Jane walk, her head held high, and her resilience gives me strength.

As long as Jane can keep going, I can as well.

We have only gone a mile or so when we come upon another scene of carnage: a man who has been shot between the eyes. His boots are missing, as are any weapons he might have been carrying.

"Bandits?" I ask.

Jane nods. "I've never known shamblers to steal a man's boots." She hands Thomas off to the Madam and checks the man's eyes. "No yellow." She looks the body up and down, waving her wrist limply. "I don't see any bite, either."

"Then it was a murder," the Madam says, pulling at the low neckline of her dress in worry.

Jane nods. "Looks like. It's possible he asked someone to end him before he turned, but . . . it's probably too much to hope this was a mercy killing. Let's pray we hit Nicodemus before nightfall."

Everyone nods and continues to walk, with renewed energy. The dead are one thing, but highwaymen are another. Though Jane and I are trained in combat, a coordinated band of ambushers will likely be more than we can handle. And our party will provide a tempting target to any ne'er-do-wells that might spy us.

We walk for what seems like hours. I put Lily back down when I start to falter myself, handing her the rifle to carry. We left hers back in the wagon, since it was best to travel as light as possible and she admitted she was not much of a shot anyhow. But even without the added weight, my feet ache. I still wear the garb of a modest lady, not the functional attire of an Attendant. My boots are meant for sitting in a parlor, not walking miles on a dirt road. I am considering asking for a halt—if I am exhausted I know the soiled doves must be as well—when we round a curve in the road. I blink.

There, in the distance, is a town.

"Jane?"

"I see it," she says.

We continue to walk, and if our pace picks up a bit there is nothing but hope fueling it. The collection of structures grows in detail and shape, and we are nearly to the town proper when we come to a sign that bids us welcome to Nicodemus.

"We made it," I say, and relief loosens the tension that has been riding my shoulders.

"For now," Jane says, pointing behind us. In the fading daylight on the horizon, a cloud of dust that could only be the oncoming horde is visible. We may have confused them temporarily with the horse, but it was only a matter of time before they were back on our trail. "Let's hope the fine people of Nicodemus will let us inside of their walls before the dead get here."

We keep walking, past a handful of out buildings, and

take in an impressive sight. We are at a triple-wire fence, the barbed wire sturdy and shiny, the integrity well maintained. There is another barrier of angular stakes, and then farther along the track another fence of barbed wire and then finally a taller barrier wall made of bricks. Actual bricks! It is a fine wall, and it puts the heaped dirt barrier of Summerland to shame.

Did Sheriff Snyder know there was a town this well fortified so near? If so, no wonder the man's control over Summerland was so fierce. If we had known such a place was so close, we might have just taken our chances and ran.

There are a handful of girls standing guard at the first gate. For a moment I wonder to myself why they appear so familiar. Squeals jar me out of my haze of confusion.

"Jane! And Miss Priss! Now ain't that something!" Sue comes forward, her height and girth completely unchanged since the last time we saw her. She is a head taller than any of the rest of us, and with her massive size she could clear a path like no other Attendant we have known. Sue's skin is dark, her hair shorn since last we saw her, and the dress she wears is one of the ugliest calicos I have ever set eyes on, only coming to just below her knees. But she grins widely, bright-eyed and happy. She carries a scythe that looks to be well used, and the girls who follow behind her watch with an expression of adoration. Sue was one of the most formidable girls at Miss Preston's. To say I am glad to see her would be an understatement.

I am less thrilled that my derisive nickname seems to have found me in the middle of the prairie.

"Big Sue! Ruthie! Jenny!" Jane calls out each girl's name as she embraces her. She knows more of the girls than I do, and after a moment I realize these are not all Miss Preston's girls—some of them must be girls Jane knows from her time on the patrols at Summerland. "Are Ida and Lucas here?" she asks.

Sue nods. "Yup, they got here this morning, talking about a horde on the way to eat us all. Their group was followed by a whole bunch of skittish white folks. That's why we're out here."

"Surely they do not mean to have the few of you take on the horde, on your own!" I cannot quite keep the horror out of my voice.

Sue laughs, the sound low and deep. The other girls titter as well, and my face heats with embarrassment.

"Nope," Sue says. "These Nicodemus folks, they got a machine some fella invented that kills the dead when they get close enough. We just offered to come out and keep watch because we got nothing else to do. This town is getting awfully crowded."

It is more than I have ever heard Sue say in the entire time I have known her, at least two years. Something has definitely changed.

She turns back to Jane. "Speaking of, did that pretty boy find you and get you that letter of yours?"

Jane folds in on herself a bit, and nods.

"There was a tragedy," I say, stepping in to say the words for her. "It has been a long trip."

Sue straightens, her mood dampening. "Aw, sorry to hear that. Annie, why don't you take these fine folks to the sheriff's office so that Miss Duncan can get them settled?"

"Miss Duncan? Oh, well, that is a relief," I say, ignoring the smug looks of the girls. They think I am happy to see her because I am the teacher's pet, but the truth is Miss Duncan is a seasoned veteran of the War Against the Dead and a knowledgeable woman when it comes to survival. Hopefully, she will have some sort of strategy for this approaching horde. Machines might slow them down for a time, but everyone knows it is only bladework that stops the dead.

A small girl with perfectly straight braids—most assuredly done by Sue; she was the best braider at Miss Preston's—walks up and beckons for us to follow. The Madam and the tiny Spencer boy, now asleep, lead the way. I let the other soiled doves and Lily go ahead of me, and then I pull Jane back so that I might have a word with her privately.

"Are you okay, Jane?" I ask.

She shrugs. "Fine enough, I suppose."

"Once we get inside, let's see to finding us both a place to get some rest—"

"Murderer!"

I look toward the town's proper front gate, where a crowd has gathered, blocking the way. A group of red-faced white men come barreling toward us, and I recognize quite a few of the drovers from Summerland as well as men from the more privileged families. Without thinking I ready my rifle. They slide to a stop when they see the end of my barrel.

"What is the meaning of this?" I demand, and the men seem confused. A few take off their hats respectfully; most of them know me as a delicate lady of the East, thanks to Jane's shenanigans of passing me off as white. The rest of the men look to be trying to judge just how good a shot I am and whether they can make a run at us.

They might not know it, but that is a gamble they would regret making.

There is too much yelling to understand what is happening, until we hear a voice over the din. "Back up, back up," he says, and a familiar face pushes through the fray. I relax my hold on the rifle just a bit but do not stow the weapon.

Daniel Redfern, a Lenape Indian man who once worked for the terrible Mayor Carr back in Baltimore but later helped Jackson escape certain death, stops a few feet in front of us, his back to the crowd. I am not sure whether to shoot the man for helping us be shanghaied to Summerland or to ask him for his help.

"Mr. Redfern." I nod. "I must say, you are looking hale and hearty."

"Miss Deveraux, it is a pleasure to see you looking similarly well, despite the obvious hardship you've been through." It is nice of him to say such, even if it is a lie. I feel like a dress four seasons out of fashion, raggedy and pathetic. I know my appearance must look a fright as well.

Mr. Redfern turns to Jane. "Miss McKeene," he says, his voice taking on something of a tone as he says Jane's name. "I'm going to need you to come with me."

Jane finally recovers enough to grin. "The last time I saw you, you were abandoning us to our fate at the hands of the men of Summerland. You look taller, Mr. Redfern."

"Sheriff Redfern," he corrects.

"What?" Jane's smile melts away and then reappears once she notices the silver star upon his chest. "Well, how about that. You used to break the law, and now you enforce it. This town really is something else. You got a Negro deputy, too?" It is meant as a lighthearted inquiry, but there is an edge to Jane's voice.

He sighs, already exasperated by her presence. It is a feeling I know well.

"Jane McKeene, I'm going to have to ask you to come with me."

She puts her hands on her hips. "Well, I wasn't planning on staying out here. In case you ain't noticed, this here prairie is infested with shamblers."

"You don't understand my meaning." He grabs her arm, and only then does the crowd of people between us at the gate to Nicodemus part. "You are under arrest for murder."

My fate cries out,
And makes each petty artery in this body
As hardy as the Nemean lion's nerve.
—*Shakespeare,* Hamlet

— J A N E —

Chapter 9
In Which I Learn the Fate of Baltimore

My entrance into the town of Nicodemus is a grand one. I am allowed to walk without chains, but I suspect that is because Mr. Redfern doesn't have any rather than faith in my honor. The white drovers from Summerland howl for my neck as I pass by them, my head held high. I fight the urge to give them a little smile and a jaunty wave, figuring I should try to contain my baser instincts for once. After all, it's only a single line of armed girls keeping them from stretching out my neck then and there.

I recognize the girls from Miss Preston's School of Combat and those from the Summerland patrols holding back the men, but there are other colored girls I don't recognize, their features stranger than any Negro I've ever seen before. There are also a few Indian girls, though I do not know from what tribe.

"Those girls are from Landishire Academy," Miss Duncan offers helpfully, appearing to my right. Her color is high, and there's a strange tone in her voice. Contrition? "Many mixed-race Negro girls found their way here from there. It's a school for the offspring of Indians and Negroes. Miss Preston wasn't fond of them, said the mixing of the Negro with any race but whites made the girls intractable."

"Well, seeing as how Miss Preston did like to sell her girls into bondage, I can see where that might get to be an issue," I mutter, more to myself than to Miss Duncan.

My former instructor's lips thin. "Yes, I'm afraid I didn't know the extent of Miss Preston's treachery until the night you and Katherine disappeared. It's not something I'm proud of. I should have been more astute."

I shrug inelegantly, ignoring what I suppose she considers to be an apology. After the time I spent in Summerland, I'm not exactly feeling charitable. After all, my back still ain't completely healed from the whipping Sheriff Snyder gave me.

Sheriff Redfern walks behind us, gun drawn in case I get any ideas about running, but it's Miss Duncan who seems to be doing the escorting. She wears a tin star on the lapel of her riding jacket—apparently, she is a deputy. What kind of town is this Nicodemus if an Indian man and a white woman can be the law?

We clear the innermost fence, which is easily ten feet tall and made of sharpened logs driven into the ground. As I glance at it, Miss Duncan, ever the teacher, says, "The town was once a fort, before the Army abandoned it during the War Against the Dead. There are several tribes that claim this land—the Kansa and the Kiowa; the Pawnee to the north. The town was originally fortified to protect against them, but now these same walls protect the people of Nicodemus from the dead."

A couple of girls stand on the wall, one with a rifle, the other with a spyglass. They wave at me as I pass, and I wave back.

"You are something of a legend amongst the girls here," Miss Duncan murmurs, too low for Redfern to hear.

"How's that?" I ask.

"The Angel of the Crossroads," Miss Duncan says, her lips pulled down in disapproval. "There is not a one of them that has not heard the tale, thanks to Sue."

I don't smile, but hearing that makes me a wee bit glad. It's good to know I got some allies.

Back in Baltimore County—before I found out that Mayor Carr was sending folks west to Summerland, and before I had the misfortune of getting shipped out there myself against my will—I would patrol the roads at night and lend assistance to travelers. I thought my exploits were mostly my own concern, but Sheriff Redfern had enlightened me to the tales surrounding my heroics. "The Angel of the Crossroads." It was a ridiculous name for a homesick girl who cut down the dead in order to work off her loneliness and anger.

Thinking about it makes me think about Jackson. The memory of our last argument is like a letter opener through the ribs, small and deadly. I take a shuddering breath and blink hard and fast.

I will not let a single one of these bastards see me cry.

Once we clear the gate I get a better view of the town proper. It's a smaller parcel than Summerland, with houses and buildings tucked tightly together in military precision. The structures are made of clapboard, the wood silver with weathering. The roads are also smooth and dusty, and there's no horse manure dotting the lane like there had been in Summerland. The boardwalk extends the full length of the town, and the house of worship is set off from the main drag. It's smaller than Summerland's, without the impressive spire. There's no saloon, but I'm surprised to see there is a library— it's a small whitewashed building tucked next to the church, and is just as well maintained.

Well, this is a whole different animal from Summerland.

We make our way up to one of the first buildings we encounter, which must be the sheriff's office. There's no markings on the window and no signage outside the door, but half the room is taken up with a cell made of iron bars, so that's really the only thing it could be. A large Negro man waits on the walkway, and my heart jumps as I recognize the pale man standing beside him.

Gideon Carr.

It seems traitorous that my pulse should pick up at seeing the boy, especially with Jackson just passing, but my emotions are unsteady at best and I cannot help but be glad at the sight of him. He looks better than he should, clean and composed, and when his eyes light on me he gives me a smile that pulls one from my own lips.

"Jane McKeene, well met," he says as Redfern guides me onto the boardwalk.

"Better met if I wasn't in custody," I shoot back, and he laughs.

"True."

"Ladies and gentlemen, please, folks, can I get your attention?" The colored man standing on the boardwalk yells to be heard over the din of the crowd, and people grudgingly turn to him, tearing their angry glares away from me for the moment. I ain't exactly terrified, but I will say that having this many people call for my neck ain't giving me a whole lot of peace of mind.

I'm beginning to think there might have been some wisdom in that Fort Riley idea.

"Thank you, folks, thank you. Although I know a few of

you, I have not had the chance to become acquainted with the bulk of you. I am Hamish Washington, mayor of this fine town. Welcome to Nicodemus!"

I laugh as the crowd falls silent, and I swallow the sound at Redfern's dark look. The looks of confuzzlement on the white folks' faces as they look from Gideon Carr to Mayor Washington and then around the very lovely town of Nicodemus are like a vaudevillian act. They cannot fathom a colored mayor, which is no surprise when so many of them thought Summerland was the best idea since bobbed wire. Any place that sends colored folks out to die to protect white folks is fundamentally flawed, and so is any muttonhead that would support such a system.

"While you can see that our small town here is growing more and more crowded by the minute, Nicodemus is a town founded on Christian values of hard work and charity. So you are all welcome to remain as long as you are willing to work." Mayor Washington ignores the surprise and disgust that twist the pale faces before him. "We are also a town of laws, and we believe in fairness above all."

"That girl is responsible for the fall of Summerland!" a white woman with a hideous tan bonnet yells.

"She murdered the sheriff in cold blood, and there was no one left to protect us!" another man yells.

I stare at him, openmouthed. These fools somehow believe that Sheriff Snyder and his henchmen were keeping the town safe. No wonder they're so angry with me. They think I was the cause of their undoing. And why not? A mouthy Negro girl without any kind of sense? I am the world's most perfect scapegoat.

The crowd begins to holler, and Mayor Washington holds up his hands once more. "I daresay that the horde outside our gates is responsible for that, friends. No single man could have kept your town safe." Mayor Washington chuckles, but his humor only riles up the crowd even more. I look to Gideon with wide eyes and a slight tilt of my head, silently imploring him to step in. It's clear that the folks from Summerland won't respect a colored man, and maybe Gideon can use that family name of his for good.

But he just gives me a wink and says nothing.

"Either way, fine citizens of Summerland," Mayor Washington says, redirecting the conversation once more, "we believe in upholding laws. We take your accusations against Miss McKeene here very seriously, and if she is responsible for killing your sheriff she will be punished accordingly. Gideon Carr and I will begin interviewing eyewitnesses forthwith, so that we can put this matter to rest, one way or the other."

I cannot help but stare at the mayor as he attempts to placate the citizens of Summerland. Trying to talk sense to this group of enraged white folks is the silliest thing I've witnessed in a spell. It's like watching someone try to reason with the dead: dangerous and an absolute waste of time.

People begin shouting once more, but I am hustled into the sheriff's office by Redfern and Miss Duncan, my piece in this tableau apparently complete.

Inside the office, the shouting is muted. My eyes take a moment to adjust to the darkness, but at least it's a mite bit cooler than it is outside. While I'm taking stock of the office, desk, cell, and not much else, Redfern opens up the barred door and gestures for me to head inside.

"Strip off your weapons first." A muscle in his jaw flexes as he looks at me, and I'm struck once again with a kind of sadness at knowing he doesn't care for me. I don't often give a lick that people don't like me, but every now and again I do. Something about Redfern—perhaps his ability to adapt so easily—makes me want to be able to call him a friend, even though I know that ain't happening.

I've dawdled too long, and he takes a step toward me. I raise an eyebrow at him. "You think I'm a murderer, too?"

Redfern frowns. "What? No, I just need you in the cell until the council can organize a trial for you."

I snort. "You do understand that there's no way I'm going to get any kind of a fair trial?"

"Nicodemus is a town founded on Egalitarian principles by former slaves and a few Quaker settlers. I daresay you'll get treated just like everyone else." He says it with the certainty of a man who has spent the better part of his life believing in a system.

I laugh, harsh and bitter. What was it Ida had told me

back in Summerland? Something about white folks twisting the law to suit themselves. I have no doubt that there ain't any justice to be found on all the continent for the Negro, and not even the promise of a town full of colored people is going to change that doubt. I watched the fine, educated, affluent Negroes in Baltimore turn a blind eye to the lives squandered in the name of keeping white folks safe. In my first few minutes in Nicodemus I've already seen Mayor Washington dancing for the Summerland folks. I ain't got a lot of faith in the colored men of Nicodemus, either.

They're gonna hang me, as sure as the sun will rise tomorrow, and while they do they'll find some way to twist it so that I should thank them for the pleasure of having my neck stretched.

But Redfern is hardheaded; I don't give him a philosophical debate, just point out the obvious. "Half of those folks out there calling for my neck are the same who stood by as hundreds of Negroes were forced into slavery and killed in Summerland. They're trying to blame me for their town falling to the dead. You really think they care about justice?"

"Jane," Miss Duncan says, her voice kind, "we aren't going to let you be lynched, but we have to do this the right way."

I scowl at her. Funny how the right way for white folks always ends up with someone else taking the blame. Or dying. But I don't say that, because I'm tired and more than a little maudlin.

For a second I wonder whether I could overpower the two

of them. Redfern, maybe. But Miss Duncan is a whole other matter, and, with a sigh, I turn over my weapons. My sickles, boot knives, and sidearm make a tidy pile on Redfern's desk, and he gathers it up and places it in a drawer while Miss Duncan locks the cell door behind me. And once more, I despair, my freedom taken so easily. It seems I am a caged bird; no matter how far I fly, I inevitably find myself beating my wings against bars.

The cell contains nothing more than a moth-eaten cot and a filthy bucket. "The cot is clean," Miss Duncan says at my askance look, "and I'll fetch some water for you."

"And this?" I ask, nudging the bucket with my foot.

Miss Duncan says nothing, just presses her lips together. If she thinks I'm going to perform my bodily functions with Redfern for an audience, she has another think coming.

It doesn't matter, I tell myself. I'm not long for this cell. There's only two ways this ends: with a noose around my neck, or with me hightailing it across the plains.

And hemp ain't my color.

Miss Duncan leaves while Sheriff Redfern settles into the chair behind the desk. I can't help but remember the greeting Katherine and I got from Sheriff Snyder when we arrived to Summerland, and for a moment the dead man swims in my vision. But then I blink and it's just the bland expression of Sheriff Redfern.

"Miss McKeene."

"Sheriff Redfern."

"Mind telling me what happened between you and Sheriff Snyder at the end there?" he says.

I shake my head. "I'm sorry, Sheriff, but I'm invoking my Fifth Amendment, as is my right as an American citizen."

"What makes you think there's an America anymore?" he says.

I am, for the second time in a day, left speechless. It's an unnerving pattern.

Miss Duncan returns with a bowl of stew, a crusty roll, and a full canteen. She hands it all to me through the bars, and my stomach rumbles. I settle on the cot then drink from the canteen, washing the road dust from my mouth before I turn my attention to the food.

I clear my throat dramatically, since Redfern is still waiting for me to start spilling my guts, a confession that ain't never going to happen. He might be the law in this town, but a tin star doesn't change anything about the man wearing it. And what I remember of Redfern is that he was only too happy to play by the rules of a broken world as long as they protected him. "Perhaps, Sheriff, you should tell me what has transpired since you left me in the none-too-gentle hands of Sheriff Snyder."

Redfern gives me an inscrutable gaze while I enjoy the stew, which probably ain't that great but tastes like manna to me, half-starved as I am. We sit like that long enough for

Miss Duncan to let loose with an impatient sigh, and it's her irritation that finally provokes Sheriff Redfern to speech.

"After I saved your friend Jackson and sent him off onto the prairie, I hitched the train back to Baltimore. Mayor Carr had asked me to ensure the delivery of the lot of you as well as some provisions and the first load of his property to Summerland, and then to return. The mayor was planning on leaving Baltimore within the month and wanted me to escort him as well. After the episode with the shambler you put down at his dinner party, it was only a matter of time before his ruse collapsed, and someone discovered that Baltimore County wasn't as safe from the dead as the Survivalists were claiming. And the mayor had no interest in being around for that revelation."

I think of Jackson, the pain sudden and swift, and I have to blink rapidly to stave off the tears. Not yet. I can't break just yet. I have to get through this, whatever this is, and then I can mourn his loss.

Just a little bit more.

Nothing of Sheriff Redfern's story surprises me. Mayor Carr had been a clever bastard, but now he was most likely dead just like all the rest of them. Well, not dead. Undead. I want to imagine Mayor Carr as a large, roaming shambler, but that just brings back the images of Jackson's last moments, so I force myself into a scowl and stare at my stew instead. I do feel better knowing that Mayor Carr will no longer be able to ruin the lives of Negroes by offering them up as shambler chow, but it's a cold comfort indeed when weighed against my own personal tragedies.

Sheriff Redfern reaches into his desk and produces a bottle of whiskey and two glasses. He pours one for himself and another for Miss Duncan, and she takes it up without question, even as it's the middle of the day. I'm supposing those stories we heard about Nicodemus and its temperance laws ain't accurate after all. No one offers me any, and I'm a mite bit put out, truth be told. Ain't I been through a trial?

After taking a small sip of his drink Redfern returns to his tale, expression pinched as though relating his story is one of Hercules's labors. "I had just returned to the city when he asked me to take one more trip south before we were to head west. He wanted me to go down to a compound in the Lost States in order to unload some bitten Negroes he had for a tidy sum. So I saw to loading up the train and set off.

"That's when the city fell."

I shovel stew into my mouth and nod along to Sheriff Redfern's story. Back in Summerland, my friend Ida told me how criminals and "bitten" Negroes have no rights under the Thirteenth Amendment and could be sold into a version of servitude that persisted down in the South. The reasoning went that, once bitten, a body is no longer "human," and thus had no rights; combined with the accepted wisdom that Negroes have some sort of natural resistance to the bite of a shambler, it created a situation where Negroes could legally remain in a state of "bitten-but-unchanged" in perpetuity, and thus be sold like any property. It made no matter that there was no evidence a colored person was any more likely to survive the bite of the dead than a white one, it was a convenient lie that no one much bothered to debunk, especially when it meant that a person could lie about colored folks getting bitten and make a quick buck on the open market down in the Lost States. Most white folks are eager to believe the worst about us, anything to make us seem less like people.

Plus, there were more than a few folks who were looking for some way to reinstitute slavery, that peculiar institution. Claiming Negroes had been bitten and survived was just the answer they'd been searching for.

Redfern's words are also a good reminder that no matter his title now, he used to work for Mayor Carr. Sheriff Redfern might not be spouting the "divine supremacy of the white race" nonsense that Pastor Snyder lived by, but I still can't trust him.

Redfern continues his tale. "We were only perhaps a half mile outside of Baltimore when the engineer stopped the train. The tracks were swarming with dead, and we couldn't ram them without the risk of derailing. There were too many for me and the small train crew to fight on our own. We were about to be overrun—until Amelia and her girls came to our aid."

Sheriff Redfern gives Miss Duncan a soft look, and she blushes prettily, sipping at her whiskey before speaking. "The horde came upon the school quite unexpectedly. It was everything we could do to get out with what weapons we could salvage. The place was utter chaos. We lost most of the instructors, including poor Miss Preston." Miss Duncan shakes her head at the memory.

I don't blink at this. Getting eaten by shamblers is the least that woman deserved. "What about Miss Anderson?" I ask. She and Miss Preston were both responsible for sending Katherine and me west to Summerland. I'd like to be able to close the book on them both.

Miss Duncan sighed. "Miss Anderson took her leave of the school a couple of days before the attack. No one is sure where she is now."

I grip the canteen so hard it bends a little as Sheriff Redfern picks up the story. "The Miss Preston's girls had fled toward the train tracks, knowing that their best route out of the city was to stay off the main road and follow the tracks until they were well clear of the city walls. When they saw us stalled with the dead they cleared them out, and the engineer and I figured it might be good to have some assistance as we left out of Baltimore County."

Miss Duncan nods. "We found the Landishire girls a little way down the track, as well as some other folks. And then we all rode to the next interchange, switched tracks, and headed west. And we were not a moment too soon—from the train, we could see another horde the likes of which I'd never envisioned in my worst nightmares, making its way, glacier-like, toward Baltimore. I daresay I have no idea what is happening in the Lost States, but the East is done for. I cannot see how the cities are going to survive, when the shamblers we saw are combined with the masses they will add to their ranks in Baltimore itself. No wall can stand against a hundred thousand dead. A normal city would have trouble fighting back a horde a fraction of that size, even with the advanced defenses we have here in Nicodemus."

"Funny you should mention that," I say. "Because Nicodemus has got a horde of its own heading right for it."

Sheriff Redfern and Miss Duncan exchange a look. "The horde that overran Summerland?" she says. "We had a feeling that horde might be headed this way, but at the speed they travel, we should have weeks to prepare. If they even make it here at all before they change course or disperse."

"Well, I've got some bad news for you, because it was nipping at our heels all the way here. Like dogs tracking a rabbit."

"A horde that has adapted to move so quickly and deliberately? Can it truly be the same one?"

"That's what I'm telling you."

Miss Duncan purses her lips, and Sheriff Redfern scowls. "There is a difference between coincidence and causation," he says, his tone dismissive. "Gideon Carr said as much himself."

"You spoke with Gideon on this?" I ask, and they nod. "Before Summerland fell he had a theory that shamblers have some way of communicating with one another over long distances, some kind of survival instinct. A sort of adaptive behavior, something that helps them to find food as it becomes more scarce—as we collect ourselves behind walls that no small cadre of shamblers could hope to breach on its own. It's what makes them horde up like they did outside Baltimore's walls, or at Summerland. As we get better at defending ourselves, they're getting smarter, more capable. Adapting to the exact tactics we've used to outrun them, keep them out, and beat them back. And if you ask me, that's probably why you got a horde on its way to Nicodemus."

Redfern laughs. "That's some kind of supposing."

"You go out and say howdy to that horde, and then you come and tell me there ain't something strange about this new crop of dead," I shoot back, leaning forward against the bars. They think the idea is foolish, but they told me themselves how the hordes of Baltimore baffled and terrified them. And they didn't see the way the dead waited for us the first time the walls of Summerland were breached. Poor Jackson even said that it seemed like the dead that got him were lying in wait, almost like a living man might do. The dead aren't as mindless as everyone wants to pretend. Not anymore.

There's a knock at the door, and Gideon pokes his head in. "Sheriff, Miss Duncan. I hope you don't mind the intrusion, but I am here on the behalf of several concerned people."

My heart pounds in a glad rhythm, and this time I don't even bother chiding myself over the reaction. I am happy to see Gideon, there's no use shaming myself for it. Jackson is gone, but he'd put me aside long before he turned. Before he'd pledged his troth to another. Not that I have any less tragic expectations for the feelings I have for Gideon, if I'm being honest with myself. But for now I am going to hold the glad feeling in my heart, however fleeting it might be.

Redfern bristles. "I ain't the one accusing Miss McKeene of murder, and Miss Duncan is here to make sure nothing improper happens. What do folks have to be concerned about?"

"These are dark times, Sheriff. I daresay we have enough to occupy us with just regular living," Gideon walks into the room, his spine straight. He seems even taller than usual, and his characteristic limp is completely gone as he strides confidently to stand next to the cell. His eyes meet mine through the bars and a slight smile curves his lips. "Miss McKeene, I take it you are well?"

"There's a horde bearing down on our current location and I'm behind bars with a murder accusation hanging over my head, but all things considered I suppose so."

Gideon laughs, the sound rich. Under my shirt my penny takes on a slight chill, but it's gone almost before I can ponder what it might mean. My lucky penny ain't a normal penny, it's hoodoo, and usually warns me of peril. Was the chill of the penny because of Gideon, or the steely-eyed gaze Sheriff

Redfern is giving me? Or something else entirely?

"Sheriff Redfern, you know as well as I do that Jane will never get a fair trial as long as those ruffians from Summerland have their say. Mayor Washington has asked me to speak with Jane, since we are acquainted, and get her side of the story."

"Is that so?" Redfern says, giving me a narrow-eyed look.

"It is. The council is debating whether to even prosecute, knowing what they do about the denizens of Summerland, so I daresay this is of the utmost importance. If you don't mind, I'd like to take a few minutes to speak with her, alone." There's a tone to Gideon's voice that very clearly says he doesn't much care whether Sheriff Redfern minds.

I look from one man to the other. Redfern worked for Mayor Carr, Gideon's father, so the two must be acquainted. Whatever the history between them, it's clear there's no love lost there.

Sheriff Redfern shakes his head and stands. "We'll give you some time to speak with your . . . acquaintance." Redfern says the word in a way that makes clear he thinks we are more than that, and Miss Duncan's lips purse with displeasure. My face heats, and I sit up a little straighter. I might be known to steal a kiss or nine, here and there, but I will not have my honor called into question by anyone's uneducated assumptions.

Even if there's a good chance the man was reading my traitorous mind.

"Thank you, Sheriff." Gideon's tone is bland and polite, and if he noticed the emphasis in Sheriff Redfern's words, he gives no indication of it.

Sheriff Redfern and Miss Duncan leave the office, the door scraping closed behind them. As soon as they're gone I bound off the cot and grab the bars.

"What in the seven hells is going on?"

He grins. "It's good to see you, too, Jane."

I cross my arms, because he is far too relaxed for someone who just fled the dead. And I never trust a person that ain't at least a little bit anxious in these perilous times, especially considering that horde heading for us. It ain't escaped my notice that Gideon is here in Nicodemus looking comfortable and settled. Just how does one set themselves up to be a mayor's right-hand man in only a day?

"How'd you get out of Summerland, Gideon?" I drop the question like it's a shambler, quickly and without any kind of shame.

His satisfied expression falters, just a little. "The same way you did, I imagine."

"The day the town fell, I saw you in your lab not an hour before we were overrun. You didn't seem to be in any hurry to leave."

My momma once told me I have a particularly annoying habit of not letting go of a topic until I've gotten a satisfactory answer. *Jane, I swear, you are as relentless as the dead when you set your mind to something*, she'd said in exasperation. And she's right. When something doesn't smell right I'm not one to let it be. Because what you don't know might kill you. Whatever it is that Gideon is hiding, I want it out before it comes calling at the worst possible moment.

An expression somewhere between shame and embarrassment crosses his pale face. For the first time I notice that he has a faint smattering of freckles across his nose, and I have to work to quickly squash the warm, twinkly feeling the discovery evokes.

The boy is a distraction, I swear to God.

"The truth is . . . I left right after I spoke with you and Katherine." He pulls a handkerchief from his pocket and then takes his glasses off and cleans them as he talks. "I knew that the town was going to fall—not as soon as it did, but soon enough. The evidence was overwhelming. So I decided to take my chances running. I was busy loading some of my lab equipment onto a wagon when I saw your friend Ida and the rest of the Negro patrols running for the town's border. I broke open the lock on the armory door for them, and then we all fled. Does it help if I told you I had no doubt that you would survive?"

"Not especially," I say, my tone dry. I can't really blame him for hightailing it out of there. Truth be told, I would have done the same thing if I hadn't had Katherine in my ear talking about helping folks and the like. I grab my canteen off the ground and drain it. I still feel impossible thirsty. "Either way, it's finished now, Summerland is just another dream turned to dust. So what's this grand plan you have to save my neck? At least, I'm assuming that's why you're here?"

"Oh, yes." He leans forward in the chair, and an odd expression comes over his face. It's somewhere akin to the way my momma would look when she'd read a particularly inspiring passage of poetry or verse, a little bit crazed and a lot bit excited. "I want you to help me convince the people of Nicodemus to let me inoculate them."

"I'm sorry, what did you just say?"

"My vaccine. I've injected it into various subjects, including yourself—to great success, by the way—and I do believe it's ready for wider testing. I want the people of Nicodemus, and now Summerland, to let me inoculate them as well."

I laugh, the sound ugly and harsh. "If I remember correctly, I ain't exactly had much choice when you gave me the poke."

He flushes at the possible double meaning and clears his throat. "Yes, I know, and I apologize for that. But I only made sure you got it because you were headed for the patrols—the most dangerous job, the people most likely to be bitten. It was important for everyone working the patrols to have any possible protection I could give them."

I shake my head. "Gideon, you're a damn smart man, I know you're just trying to help people, and I don't want to rain on your parade. But you ain't Edward Jenner, and whatever it is you're sticking in people ain't the smallpox vaccine. I ain't ever seen it work. What I *have* seen is a whole bunch of people get dead."

He purses his lips. "It's worked on you."

"I ain't been bit! That's the problem here. As soon as someone gets bit, that's when you can start figuring out whether your inoculation works or not, and I don't know people who are lining up to let shamblers bite them. Not to mention that most folks get devoured by the dead, so most times it ain't just the problem of a little nibble."

Gideon continues on, ignoring my outburst. "Nicodemus is the shining light on the hill. They're open to the promise of science in a way that Baltimore and Summerland never were, and if I can show the townsfolk that it's not walls and blades but vaccines that are the future, then we can change the world."

"Gideon, my problem ain't with vaccines—it's with *your* vaccine. It's based on the same faulty science as the one that got me all caught up in this mess back in Baltimore, ain't it?"

"Professor Ghering's formula was promising, but it had fundamental flaws. Ones that I've since addressed."

"Fine—even so, how is it that you think we're going to convince everyone that the vaccine works? You want I should march out to that horde, bid it good day, get bit, and then come skipping back like the prodigal lamb?"

Gideon takes off his hat and runs his hand through his hair. "I think you're mixing your metaphors, Jane. And look, I understand your reluctance. Here's the issue: most people here aren't worried the inoculation won't work; they're afraid that getting injected is going to turn them. If you could tell folks that you got the vaccine and didn't turn, that would convince a fair number of people to submit."

"No, Gideon. And not just no, but hell no," I say. "And now that you mention it, how is it you came to be such a fixture in Nicodemus in the first place?"

"I've been splitting my time between here and Summerland in secret for the past year," he says, not quite meeting my gaze. "I'm in charge of the town's defenses, and they've been giving me the resources I need to do what I never could in Summerland. We've taken to manufacturing our own gunpowder efficiently, and we've increased the strength of the fences as well as added an electric fence that's powered by a series of windmills and a nearby creek."

I study him for a long minute before crossing my arms. "I don't understand. If you knew this place existed, only a couple days' journey, why didn't you help folks get out of Summerland and come here, where they wouldn't have to risk their lives with shoddy defenses and forced patrols?"

He grimaces slightly. "I tried, but . . . I failed. I've been living here in town for the past year or so, pretending my trips away from Summerland were for research on the movements of the dead out here on the prairie. I only made my way back to town often enough to make sure Sheriff Snyder and the preacher didn't get suspicious, take my lab from me, or report anything back to my father, whose grace was the only thing keeping me safe out here. Even so, I was ready to run, to make a clean departure, but that's when you and

Katherine arrived and, well, I knew I couldn't leave. Not yet."

"Well, I suppose that's something," I say. The mention of Katherine's name revives a bit of the old jealousy. I imagine Gideon watching Katherine's arrival with interest, thinking what a lovely bride she'd be. And then I squash the feelings, because she's one of the few people I trust. I'm quickly running out of allies, so there's no room for pettiness right now.

Gideon clears his throat nervously and starts talking faster. "The council will most likely be meeting tonight to discuss what to do with you. Let me tell them that you've volunteered to help me with my vaccine—to allow it to be tested on you. I won't send you out to be bitten; I'm sure there are other ways to test the efficacy other than direct contact with the dead."

"Gideon . . ."

He's a brilliant scientist, it's true. Maybe he could find some way to concoct the miracle shambler cure that could finally curtail the plague. But then I think of Othello, the poor Negro that made no mistake but to believe in the fantasy of Professor Ghering's anti-shambler vaccine. He was fine until he got bit, and after that, well, he turned shambler just like everyone else. Gideon would have just thought of him as another negative test. And I ain't signing on to be part of anything like that, cure or no.

"You can't go around lying to people to get them to participate in your experiments," I say. "It just ain't right. You're playing with folks' lives here."

Gideon shifts in his chair uncomfortably. "I understand

that, but this vaccine is worth it. It could save the world. It will save the country, at least! Imagine, a land where the dead have no interest in the living, where no man or woman turns shambler ever again, where the undead are just another nuisance to be exterminated. We can make that a reality, and you could be a part of it."

I laugh, some of my desperation leaking through. His expression falls. "We have to put all the old ideas aside, Gideon. Fortified towns, newfangled defensive technology . . . none of it ever makes a difference. While you're busy experimenting and failing and experimenting again, more and more people get turned, and that just means more dead around to hunt folks down. Nowhere can be safe forever. And I'm sorry, but your vaccine ain't the answer. I watched people turn on the patrols back in Summerland. And that's all the evidence I need."

His expression goes slack. "Jane, I'm sorry you feel that way."

His words are like a slap, his tone dismissive and haughty. All the things I've been telling him, facts and truths, he just dismisses as the opinions of a woman. The boy is a muttonhead. A very cute one, but a straight muttonhead nonetheless. He's willing to ignore what is right in front of him, and why? Hubris? Or something else?

Just pondering it puts me in a bleak mood, because I get the feeling that nothing I can tell him is going to sink in.

He's going to do just as he pleases.

I shake my head. This is the last thing I need right now. I need to change the subject, because it's clear as day that we ain't going to come to any sort of harmony on this inoculation business. "And when exactly were you planning on evacuating Nicodemus, in between all these science projects and murder trials?"

He frowns. "What are you talking about?"

"You might have hightailed it out of Summerland before the proper horde arrived, but Kate and I watched that wave of dead overwhelm it. And while that horde snapped at our heels, we stumbled upon another pod on our way here. The whole mess of them might have slowed down a bit, but by nightfall, this town will be overrun."

Gideon shakes his head. "Oh, there's no concern there. I have something that will keep the town safe, you'll see." He gives me a secretive smile, and I decide right there that whatever Gideon's got up his sleeve, I probably ain't going to like it.

"The dead won't get through our fences. They are far more advanced than Summerland's."

"You think a bit of wire and science is going to keep out thousands of hungry shamblers?" I ask.

He flushes and stands. "Look, I didn't come here to fight, Jane. I'm trying to help."

"I get that, Gideon, but so far you've ignored the fact that every plan that you or anyone else felt was the one to finally stop a shambler horde has failed completely. Do you even know what it's like to fight the dead?" I'm yelling, and all I can think of is Jackson on his knees, begging me to end him sooner than later. "First your nonsense about your vaccine, now keeping out a horde with a fence and whatever else you've tinkered together? The world ain't your lab, Gideon! You can't go back and redo the experiment when you don't get the results you hoped for."

His expression goes stony, and I know I've misstepped at some point, but I can't seem to stop the flow of emotions.

"Jane, you have no idea what I have experienced."

"I don't, but this? This is madness!" I pull at the ends of my braids in frustration and start pacing.

Gideon stands and retrieves his hat. "I just wish you could have some faith in me."

I collapse onto the cot and rest my head in my hands. "Faith is for people that got hope, Gideon, and I'm afraid that's been in short supply for a long minute."

The silence stretches on into something ugly, and he sighs. "I'm going to go. You seem to be out of sorts, and it's understandable. You've had quite a trek across the prairie, and I think maybe you just aren't seeing things clearly right now."

I press my lips together, because I see things more clearly than he knows. Nicodemus ain't any different than Summerland, or Baltimore for that matter. Same old nonsense, just prettier packaging. And none of that is going to matter anyway if we don't do something about that horde. The thing about shamblers is they don't care what a body believes in, as long as they can sink their teeth into it.

"Thanks for stopping by," I mutter, because I know Gideon is trying to help. His brain has only been taught to think about problems one way. He doesn't understand that sometimes it takes a bold solution to solve a problem, one folks ain't expecting.

Like a well-placed bullet.

Gideon is almost to the door when he turns back, walking all the way up to the bars. "Consider my proposal, Jane."

There's no way on God's green earth I'm letting him poke and prod at me again like some kind of specimen. And I sure as hell ain't letting the good people of Nicodemus and Summerland decide my fate.

As Gideon leaves the sheriff's office I make a decision.

First chance I get, I'm running.

Behold, how good and how pleasant it is for brethren to dwell together in unity!
—Psalms 133:1

— KATHERINE —

Chapter 10
Notes on a Plot to Save Jane McKeene

I pace the boardwalk in the front of the Nicodemus sheriff's office, trying to listen in on Gideon and Jane's conversation without appearing to eavesdrop. A day-old biscuit and a thin stew, which was the food the kind women of Nicodemus had passed around to the refugees, sits uneasily in my belly. I want a proper bath and a change of clothes, but I refuse to have either until I know that Jane's welfare is assured, at least for the time being.

The entirety of Miss Preston's, as well as a good number

of girls from the other combat schools, are gathered outside the sheriff's office as well. Our presence has proven enough to keep the Summerland folks at a distance, for now. Most everyone has dispersed to whatever other tasks they might have. A small knot of people still watch the sheriff's office, but they are not a threat as long as there are Miss Preston's girls about. It is strange to see people I once shared meals with—a fair number of the fine folks of Summerland seem to have escaped the horde as well as the drovers and roughnecks—scream their rage out over their inability to kill a girl. It is monstrous, and yet another reminder that the dead are not the only threat in this world.

The combat-school girls are wound tight due to the approaching horde, which is now close enough that I get a whiff of decay on the hot breeze every now and again. Nearby, Sue leans against a wall, sharpening an overlarge knife with a whetstone and a bit of oil. She is out of sorts. She keeps advocating a strategy of flight, but no one seems to be listening to her.

"That horde will be here by nightfall, and after Baltimore I ain't of a mind to fight my way out," she said, and jutted her chin at the town's main gates, once again securely closed. "That ain't going to keep a determined horde out, not forever."

She is right, but before we can do anything we need to get Jane out of jail. This accusation of murder, on the heels of Jane having to administer last rites to Jackson? Well, I am not sure what her emotional state might be, and I worry that her brashness will only find her swinging from a rope, justice or no. Jane is the proverbial bull in the china shop, and while she is highly effective against the dead she is terrible at navigating the intricacies of human interaction.

Which is why I feel as though I should force my way into the sheriff's office and do the talking for her. Gideon might draw water with the leadership here in Nicodemus and be clever besides, but he has not spent the past three years watching Jane flit from one near disaster to another.

Truth be told, I am also not sure I trust the man.

"Jane in there?"

The voice pulls me from the runaway train of my thoughts. I turn to find the girl Jane was friendly with—Ida—standing behind me with a few of the other Negroes that I recognize from Summerland's patrols. Next to her, looking as nervous as a cat in a kennel, is a Negro girl with brown skin and straight hair pulled back into a single braid. She is not redbone like Jackson, but there is something vaguely different about her. It is something about her eyes, and as I am studying her she smiles.

"Cherokee," she says.

I blink. "I beg your pardon?"

"You're thinking that I ain't just a Negro, and you're right. I got Cherokee in me, too. My people came on the long walk with the Five Civilized Tribes. Not of their own accord, mind you, but come west we did."

I realize I have been staring, and a powerful flush comes over me. "I apologize. My journey here has been long and fraught, and I may have lost some of my manners along the way. I am Katherine Deveraux."

"Callie," the girl says, grinning, and I am reminded of Jackson saying that the town had been settled by runaway Negroes, some of them formerly enslaved by the Five Civilized Tribes, along with a group of Quakers. I do not think the girl is a Quaker, so I peg her as the former. Her front tooth is chipped, and it gives her an impish air.

"It is a pleasure to meet you," I say. I gesture behind me to where Sue has paused in her knife sharpening to watch my conversation with this new group of women. She pushes off the boardwalk to stand next to me. "This is Sue."

"Uh-huh," Ida says, looking Sue up and down but ignoring me altogether. I get the idea that she does not care for me, and the usual litany of reasons runs through my mind. My pale skin? The way I carry myself? The way a few of the fellows in the gaggle behind her have taken off their caps and are now giving me that thrice-cursed look men always give me? I do not know, and I do not especially care. I know how to work with a woman who does not like me, and I refuse to let a bit of pettiness stop me from saving Jane's ungrateful hide.

"I suppose you are here about Jane?" I say, crossing my arms.

"Yup," Ida says, resting her hands on the sword she carries. "There ain't no way we're about to let those folks from Summerland lynch her."

"So you're here to break her out?" Sue says, twisting her lips to the side. "Because that's what I'm about."

I draw myself up. "No one is rushing in and breaking anyone out without any kind of plan. What do you aim to do after you secure her freedom? Will you run? With no supplies, and a horde bearing down on us?"

A few of the folks behind Ida shift and mutter something under their breath, but Ida is unmoved.

"Better to die out there, fighting for our lives, than to die in here scrabbling for food and getting told what to do by white folks." Ida holds her hands out to gesture to the town.

I frown. "I thought this was a Negro settlement?"

Ida shakes her head. "Maybe now, but how long do you think that's going to last? Them Summerland folks are already running around, trying to push everyone this way and that. How long until they got the colored folks running patrols while all the white folk stay safe inside the wire?"

I drop my arms, all the fight going out of me. Ida is right. I could see the looks of disbelief on those pale faces when the mayor introduced himself. The peril outside might have some people behaving themselves for now, but it will not last.

However, I cannot let the panic of a few folks take hold, either. That is the problem with fear—it is like wildfire, traveling fast and hot, leaving only ashes behind.

"It seems to me that it is in our best interest to make sure that does not happen, that we can keep the people of Summerland in check," I say, gesturing a little ways down the street where people gather. "There are definitely more of us than there are of them."

"That's what my daddy figures," the girl—Callie—says. She flushes and ducks her head. "He's the mayor, and he and the council figure that with a good number of well-trained folks they can keep order and ensure that nothing bad happens. He says that at their heart, people want to do the right thing, and as long as the right thing is an option, nothing can go wrong."

"That seems to be overly optimistic," Ida says, glancing down the road toward everyone lining up for the evening meal. "Especially given the number of angry white people stomping around town."

Ida is right. Mayor Washington sounds a bit naive. How is a man with so little sense going to keep order in the maelstrom churning beneath him?

My heart begins to pound, and I take a deep breath and let it out. I can feel the edge of one of my panicky moods trying to settle over me. When I was younger, Maman used to call them my "worrying fits." I would find myself frozen with indecision for fear that any choice I made would be the wrong one, earning the wrath of Maman or one of the other ladies of the house. Later, when Maman found a protector, I would lie awake at night worrying that we would be put out on the street like Amelie Dupree, whose companion had dumped her and her children unceremoniously after he decided he could no longer afford her small house in Tremé. Life out here is fraught, but even life within city walls is dangerous. It is just that the danger takes different forms. And for some blasted reason my mind was convinced that if I did not worry through all the possible pitfalls, they would befall me sooner rather than later. Folks might think my pretty face made my passage through this world easy, but that was far from the truth.

I take another deep breath and realize that Ida and Callie are giving me a peculiar look. I muster a wan smile and fan my cheeks. "This heat is getting to me, I apologize. What was it you just said?"

"I said that I don't think those Summerland people are going to take direction from a Negro mayor," Callie says.

Ida nods. "Agreed. Especially not as terrified as they are right now. And when white people are scared it's the Negro that bears the brunt," Ida says with a twist of her lips. "This place is a powder keg. We need to make haste before it explodes, because we all know what's going to happen when it does."

"It'll be Summerland all over again," says one of the colored girls behind Ida.

"And I ain't about to let that happen," says one of the Negro men next to the girl. "I'll fight folks before I let them turn me into a mule again."

A chorus of murmurs follows his proclamation.

"I see your point," I say, and Ida raises an eyebrow. There is no use telling her I was considering the exact same line of thought, everything is philosophical until we deal with the matter at hand. "But if we are going to get out of this town, we need a plan. And that means we need Jane."

Ida grins. "Now you're thinking. No one plots like that girl."

I sigh. "You are more correct than you know."

The door opens, and Gideon walks out. The expression on his face is that of a man who has just gotten an earful from Jane McKeene. I hurry over to him, Ida on my heels.

"Well?" I ask.

"Jane was quite adamant that she did not trust the council and wouldn't even consider my proposal," Gideon says with a deep sigh.

"What proposal?" Ida asks.

Gideon turns to Ida with a polite smile, though it is clear he is not fond of being interrupted. "When Jane arrived in Summerland, I gave her the same inoculation as I gave you and the rest of your associates who came from the Lost States. I need help convincing the town council that the formula is safe and a good first step in going beyond guns and walls for defense."

"But who says your vaccine works?" Ida asks, looking Gideon directly in the eye. The midday heat could cause his resulting flush, but I daresay it is not.

"I do, and as I am the scientist here, I think that should be enough."

"Well, obviously it ain't if you need Jane's help to convince folks to let you poke them," Sue says, her voice low and steady. Gideon's Adam's apple bobs as he swallows, and his discomfort is almost palpable.

He turns to me. "Either way, Miss Deveraux—Katherine— please stop by my house when you are finished here. I saw the rest of your traveling companions a little while ago and have already sent them on ahead. Accommodations in town are quite cozy at the moment, and I would be glad to welcome you into my home." With one last sharp glance at Ida and Sue, Gideon walks off, irritation in every line of his body.

As he walks away, I catch Callie's eyes following him, her expression somewhere between sad and hopeful. It is clear to me that this is not the first time she has met the tinkerer. Interesting.

"What in the Lord's name is he thinking?" Ida exclaims once he is outside of earshot, bringing my attention back to the matter at hand. "Trying to use Jane to convince folks to become part of his research?"

"Yes, I daresay he has greatly underestimated Jane's dedication to justice, even if she is a bit liberal with her misuse of facts every now and again," I say.

Sue laughs. "That's a very pretty way to say Jane's a liar. But true enough, she'd never lie to folks if she thought they might get hurt by it. Any of us could have told him she wasn't going to go for that silly proposal. Remember what happened back at that lecture in Baltimore?"

"Sheriff," Ida says with a cough, and I turn.

Sheriff Redfern approaches, a stony look on his face. Jane told me once that Daniel Redfern is too pretty by half for a man, and while I can understand her attraction I just do not feel it. To be fair, I think Jane is attracted to just about any human who gives her a passing glance. Though Jane's tendency to jump without looking is so often a source of vexation for me, I cannot help but be charmed at times by the way in which she so gleefully gives in to her appetites.

"Sheriff Redfern," I say with a smile. "How are you this fine evening?"

The sheriff stops with a tip of his hat in my direction. "I am well, Miss Deveraux. And you all?" He gives Ida the kind of look that tells me the two of them have tangled in the past. Ida sets her jaw and glares daggers right back.

"Everything is brilliant," I say with a laugh. "Ida here was just helping me understand how things work in Nicodemus."

Sheriff Redfern shifts his weight, resting his forearms on his twin revolvers. Those guns are new—the last time I saw him was in Summerland, and the only weapon he had carried was a long Bowie knife tucked into a sheath by his side. The knife is still there, toward the middle of his belt.

"Well, Callie there might have enlightened you to the fact that gathering in large groups in the street is frowned upon in Nicodemus," Redfern says, gesturing to the rest of the patrol. "Y'all need to start moving on along. It's time for chow." He gives me a polite smile, one that I suppose is meant to be reassuring. Men have been giving me that smile my entire life. I do not return it.

"My apologies, Sheriff, but I distinctly remember walking past a lynch mob when I entered town but a few hours ago. Was that unruly group also given the order to disperse?"

Redfern's smile fades. "Just get a move on and mind your business. You'll have an easier go of it if you do, Miss Dever-aux." He tips his hat at me and opens the door to his office.

"I need to see Jane," I say.

"I'm afraid that isn't possible." And without another word he shuts the door in my face.

Ida snorts. "I could've told you that was going to happen. Now, if we're done wasting time with pointless debate, maybe we can get going on the plan we've been working on."

We walk back toward where the rest of the patrol is, and with a whistle from Ida folks begin to disperse. I wonder how she came to be the leader of such a motley crew in such a small time. What transpired in their flight from Summer-land? I get the feeling it was not quite as uneventful a journey as ours.

Ida gestures for me to follow her, Callie, and a powerfully built boy with midnight-dark skin who introduces himself as Lucas. Sue dogs my heels; Lucas keeps glancing back, and it is a moment before I realize he is actually looking through me and right at Sue. I elbow her, and she gives me a hard look.

"What?"

"You have an admirer," I say in a low voice.

Sue looks up, startled, and meets Lucas's gaze before he gives her a small smile. She quickly looks down, and I grin.

"Stop laughing," she says.

"Who is laughing?" I ask. Sue is the only one of us at Miss Preston's that ever talked about getting married and having children. I think the rest of us figured that death would be the only embrace we would ever know. But not Sue. She was set on having little ones. The more terribleness I see in this world, the more I hope that just one Miss Preston's girl might get a happily ever after. Maybe it could be Sue.

We weave in between the houses of Nicodemus until we stop by a spot near a heavily secured gate toward the rear of the settlement.

"So, this plan of yours?" I ask, feeling nervous and exposed.

"Get Jane and make a run for it," Ida says. "I'm still figuring out the first part, but Callie has the second worked out."

Callie nods. "This gate might look secure, but it's actually used in the fall to bring in the harvest. It's light enough for a single person to open, if the block is removed."

"Once we get out of town, we head east, to the Kaw River," Ida says. "From there, we can keep going east on the water until we get to the Mississippi. And from there, we can get anywhere." Her eyes are bright just considering the possibilities.

"Even California?" I ask, remembering Jane's letter from her momma.

"You can get anywhere you want, eventually, and traveling by water should mean we can avoid any run-ins with shamblers," Ida says. "But it's going to be a long walk to the Kaw, and we ain't got nothing in the way of provisions. Even if we could find a way to steal from Nicodemus's stock, it's like to be nearly depleted by now, with all the new people from Summerland here."

I nod. "That is my single greatest worry. Any ideas?"

"There's a town not far from here, Arleysville," Callie says. "It fell to shamblers about a year ago. It's three days' walk, but there's supplies there—enough to get a hundred people to the river, easy."

"But the town fell to the dead?" I say.

"We aim to clean it out, take what we need, and keep moving. We reckon that the horde that hit Summerland had the Arleysville dead in with them, since they like to group up and all," Ida says.

"This all sounds like something we can do," Sue says, testing out the gate. It creaks as she leans against it, giving truth to Callie's declaration.

"It certainly seems like a good idea," I say. And since I do not have any of my own I do not feel a need to elaborate any further.

"But we still don't know how we're getting Jane out of

there," Sue says, with a nod back toward the Nicodemus jail. "If we don't, she's dead."

"Any way you slice it, we need Jane," Ida says. "I fought with her in Summerland. No one knows shamblers like her."

"Right," I say, biting my tongue. I want Jane with us as much as the next woman, but I was first in our class at Miss Preston's, and I am no slouch when it comes to shambler killing. Same with Sue. But there is no reason to provoke disagreement when I finally have allies, so I go back to the most crucial matter at hand. "Any notions as to how we might win Jane her freedom?"

Lucas clears his throat, and we all turn to him. "I think I might have an idea."

— J A N E —

Chapter II
In Which I Cool My Heels

Being trapped in Nicodemus's jail cell has me pensive. I've got nothing to do but think, and there's too much I'd rather not be thinking about as the sun marks time against the far wall: Jackson, Gideon's enraging proposal, getting my neck stretched, Rose Hill being no more, my momma and Aunt Aggie somewhere out there struggling to survive. Neither Momma nor Aunt Aggie are trained in the fine art of shambler disposal, and although Momma is fair enough of face to find a male protector, that thought just takes me down another path of worry and concern. It's my experience that most men in the world are ne'er-do-wells, only too happy to compromise a lady the first chance they get, and Momma is too delicate to deal with the rough sort that tend to thrive in this dangerous world.

Great, now I'm thinking about the exact thing I didn't want to be.

I roll over on the straw-filled mattress with a sigh. Sheriff Redfern sits in his office chair, feet up on the desk, snoring loud enough to summon the dead. If I wanted to skedaddle, now would be the time, but I'm no good at picking locks. Not like Jackson.

And just like that I'm crying.

I start off low and easy, but soon enough I'm biting my arm to keep my sorrow quiet enough that I don't wake Redfern. I squeeze my eyes shut. I wish I believed in all that nonsense the clergy are always spouting off about heaven and eternal rest, but all I can think about is Jackson on his knees, begging me to end him before he turns.

"You all right?"

I glance up and Redfern is standing next to the bars, his face twisted up with something like worry. The sight is a right fine surprise, and I shake my head, tears falling hot onto my hands.

"I'm not going to let them hang you, Jane," he says, perhaps mistaking my sobs for fear instead of grief. "Sheriff Snyder got nothing more than what he deserved, and the townsfolk here know that. You will walk out of that cell a free woman. I promise." His tone is mild, but his words say more about him than he can know.

"I don't know if that's a promise you'll be able to keep, Sheriff, but I appreciate the sentiment all the same."

He nods and sighs. "Here, I'll get you some more water."

I hand him my empty canteen, and he leaves the office. While he's gone I make use of the bucket; it might be a foul enterprise but I'm going to take my privacy where I can get it. I've just finished and am adjusting my skirts when there's a commotion from outside.

"Jane McKeene!"

I place the bucket back in the corner and stride over to the small, barred window. I'm too short to see out properly, but on my tiptoes I catch a glimpse of Big Sue and someone else, a girl I don't recognize.

"Big Sue, what're you about?"

"Aw, it's just Sue now. And this is Callie."

A brown face appears in the window for a second before it disappears. "Hello!" the girl calls, and her face reappears as she jumps up to the window again. I get the impression of a slightly upturned nose, freckles, and a messy braid.

"Hey," I respond, and to Sue I say, "So, what's the plan?"

"What you need a plan for, Jane? Miss Priss said that

IN THE GARDEN OF GOOD AND EVIL

white boy was going to get you out." I can tell from Sue's tone what her opinion is on that.

Despite my predicament I smile. "That white boy wanted me to play science experiment."

"What you got against science? You were always going on and on about different discoveries you'd read about in those newspaper articles of yours."

"Yup, but that was real science, not some fairy story made up by some boy with less sense than facial hair."

Sue laughs, the sound low. "And Jane McKeene said, 'Thanks, but no thanks, I'd rather hang.'"

"Hey, I got my honor."

"Since when?" Sue jokes, and I laugh. It feels good after the day I've had.

"Well, either way I'm still here."

Sue harrumphs. "For now."

"Sue, gimme a boost," Callie says. "It's irksome trying to conversate with a person you cain't see." Her face appears in the window and she grins, a chip in one of her front teeth. "Did you really kill Sheriff Snyder?" the girl asks. I'd thought she was younger, but she actually looks like she might be older than me. Despite her carefree demeanor there's a cold-ness to her eyes that puts me on my guard.

"I reckon I ought to plead the Fifth on that one since that's why I'm in here," I say. "Speaking of which, I need to get out of this place before these white folks decide they need a little

149

show with dinner." I stick my tongue out and mime being hung.

"Oh, my daddy won't let them do that, don't you worry," she says.

"'Daddy'?"

"Mayor Washington. That's my paterfamilias."

I blink. "You speak Latin?"

"You don't?" she shoots back, and I smile. There's something incredibly appealing about the girl, and not just because she reminds me of the stories of pixies my momma used to read me.

"Girl, you are heavy," Sue grumbles from out of view.

"I am not, stop being mean. Anyway, Jane, I figure you've got a couple of days before anyone tries to run a lynch mob on you again. The council has been holding meetings all day, talking to all those survivors and taking statements. But right now they're all too busy at the wall, getting ready to watch the rail gun take out the dead," Callie says, her voice positively chirpy next to Sue's lower timbre. "That's why we're here."

"Rail gun? What's that?"

Just then comes a sound, like a cannon shot but without the echo. And it doesn't stop. It's like a barking dog, but louder, dominating the still afternoon. I'd think it was thunder, but the sound is too close and the sky is as clear as can be.

"Did that answer your question?" Callie says. "Gideon

built it. It uses magnetic fields to fire bullets, instead of gunpowder. It's powered by electricity!"

"Ugh, you're heavy," Sue grunts. "And your boot is on my spine. Hurry up."

"Sorry!" Callie says without really meaning it.

"Electricity," I say, remembering Gideon's experimental lab back at Summerland, his horrific shambler wheel. "How is it generated?"

"Windmills! That tinkerer sure is smart."

I remember now that Gideon had mentioned something about windmills. It's better than keeping a bunch of shamblers inside the town walls to run his machines, anyway.

"So, you knew Gideon in Summerland?" she says. Her tone is light, but there's an edge to it, a curiosity, and something in her face that makes me think that there's more to her question than she's letting on. I don't know who this girl is or what she's about, but I'm not about to give her any more information until I find out.

"I did."

"Did he help you escape the horde there?" she asks.

"No. Let me talk to Big Sue," I say. None of this is going to help me escape.

"It's just Sue," she says as Callie disappears and she comes back into view. "Don't call me that no more."

I open my mouth to tease her, but if she's saying not to do something, there's no fun in pushing her. Not the way there is with Katherine. "Okay, okay. So, back to the matter at hand. Getting me out of here."

Just then, the gun falls silent.

"You see how that thing makes a racket, right?" Sue asks.

"Yep."

"They're going to fire it regular-like until that massive horde is gone," Sue says.

"Every hour on the hour!" Callie says, jumping up behind Sue's shoulder. If this wasn't a life-and-death situation it'd be funny, the way Callie keeps bouncing back into view every now and again like an overeager puppy. "They can't fire it for more than a minute or two at a time because it overheats."

"They think they can take out that horde out there with these inventions," Sue says. "But you and I know better, Jane McKeene. At some point, the bullets and the electricity and whatever else are going to run out, but the shamblers are just gonna keep on coming."

I snort. "I already told them that."

"They ain't about to listen," she says. "We saw the eastern horde when we were fleeing Baltimore. They can try fighting the dead all they want, but them shamblers never get tired. Never."

It's the most I've heard Sue talk in almost forever. But it ain't ever about what Sue is saying, it's about what she ain't saying. She knows that there's nothing to be done about a horde but to run from it, and that's real life talking, not academic inquiry. I don't care if Gideon's got some of his fantastical inventions working here—if I was ever of a mind to put my faith in walls and guns, that time is past.

I stretch a little taller and eye what of Sue I can see. "You feeling sharp? Because you know there ain't no one like you that can clear a path, and we're going to need your bladework to get out of this place."

Sue snorts dismissively. "Sharp enough, I suppose. Just be ready later tomorrow night, close to dawn. We're going to do what needs to be done."

"You know where to find me," I say. It's meant to be a joke, but nobody laughs.

Sue and Callie take their leave, Callie giving me one last inscrutable look over her shoulder, and I turn just as Miss Duncan walks in, carrying my canteen and a plate of food. My stomach rumbles; I'd been so preoccupied I'd almost forgotten how hungry I am. I have to keep myself fed; there's no telling when the next opportunity for food will arise.

I lean against the bars of the cell, arms hanging out. Miss Duncan pauses. "Planning something, Jane?"

I grin at her, then retreat until my back is against the wall. "Eating. Is that for me?"

"Yes, compliments of Gideon Carr. He wanted to make sure you got an extra portion this evening." An expression I can't name crosses her face. Disgust? Fear? "You do know that he is Mayor Carr's son?"

I shrug. "Yes, ma'am, that's what he said."

"So why exactly has he taken such a shine to you?" Her voice is heavy with suspicion, and I know what she's on about: a freewheeling Negro girl getting cozy with an affluent white man. There's only one way that story ends, and it ain't happily ever after.

Plus, they got names for girls like that. And I'm sure it ain't escaped Miss Duncan's notice that I rode into town in the company of women who make their living on their back.

The extra food is straight bribery, his not-so-subtle way to try and convince me to champion his cause. But I ain't got any use for standing behind rubbish like his vaccine, and no amount of extra helpings is going to change my mind.

But I ain't about to tell Miss Duncan any of that.

"Miss Duncan," I say, giving her my best smile even though my tone is far from polite, "I promise that there is nothing going on except that this town is about to be overrun. And at some point you folks will think the answer yet again is to throw us colored girls at another problem of your own making."

I don't bother to keep the cold rage from my voice. Miss Duncan worked to train girls for years, girls who were packed off as little more than slaves, sent west to die just because they were cheap and expendable and no one would miss them. She's got no room to judge me, and I'll be damned if I let her start now.

"Jane—"

"I'll thank you to hand my supper on through. Seems like some folks could stand to think on their own sins and stop worrying about how I account for mine."

Miss Duncan purses her lips before handing me my canteen through the bars. She unlocks the door and hands through the plate, nearly catching my hand as she quickly slams it shut.

An ominous silence settles over the sheriff's office once again. "You know they ain't going to be able to stop that horde with the gun, no matter how fancy it might be," I say. "The dead are going to take this town, and this county, hell, all of Kansas. Our best bet is to run, and keep running."

She turns away, but not before I hear her soft reply. "I fear that you are right, Jane. That we will all find our end here."

Her despair was almost enough to put me off my food.

Almost.

Have mercy upon me, O LORD, for I am in trouble: mine eye is con-sumed with grief, yea, my soul and my belly.
—Psalms 31:9

— K A T H E R I N E —

Chapter 12
Notes on the Ones Lost

After leaving Lucas, Ida, Sue, and Callie to their planning, I make my way to Gideon's house, which after a bit of inquiry I discover is in the middle of town. I am still desperately in need of a bath, and the Madam had promised to find a change of clothing for all of us when I had headed out to find Jane. Here is to hoping she is as resourceful as my maman.

As I walk up to the house I am quite stunned by its beautiful simplicity. It is a fine structure, with an actual gable and a porch. The entire structure bears the signs of a recent whitewash and it makes me wonder just how the house came to be. This is no barrack. Was this once the home of a post commander, or maybe a chaplain? I do not know much about Army forts, but the building seems incongruous in a place that is mostly utilitarian in nature.

Either way, the house is the finest that I have seen out here in Kansas, and I wonder how it was that Gideon came to be in possession of it. I cannot see the fine people of Nicodemus giving over a house so easily; they must truly revere Gideon and his upgrades to the town's defenses.

I enter the structure to find the Madam and her soiled doves talking in hushed whispers in the sitting room. They stop when I enter, their eyes wide. I pause on the threshold. "Did I interrupt something?"

Sallie is the only one who looks me in the eye. "We were discussing leaving. Sooner rather than later."

I sink into a nearby chair. "No one is going to keep you from leaving," I say.

The Madam straightens. "That wasn't what we were concerned about."

"Well," I say, forcing a smile since the silence has pressed on a bit too long and no one seems to want to elaborate, "what is the matter at hand, then? I assume you have a plan? A destination? A way through or around that horde bearing down on us?"

The Madam looks embarrassed, and Nessie seems uncomfortable.

"We got enough of a plan, but our biggest concern is Lily," Sallie says. "The Duchess thinks we should take her with us, on account of her being so close to Thomas and all, but me and Nessie think the girl should have her own mind to make up as she chooses."

"Since her brother is gone," Nessie says, her voice soft, "she should be able to choose her own path. Stay here with you and Jane, or head north with us."

"You're planning on taking Thomas?" I ask.

"You have a problem with that?" the Madam asks, leaning forward in her chair a bit.

I shake my head. "Of course not. It is clear he has become attached to you in a very short time, and there is no one here in town who would raise an argument. I am just considering that the difficulty of any trek is magnified by the presence of little ones. And none of you is trained in the art of defense."

The Madam leans back and crosses her arms. "Well, that is something we've considered. There's a group of Summerland roughnecks planning on leaving come dawn, and they've invited us to go along with them. We're going to head up north where I've heard tell it's safer."

I purse my lips, because just what exactly is a group of Summerland drovers expecting as payment to escort a group of fallen women? I have to believe those men are not helping them out of the goodness of their hearts, but I am not so crass as to point that out.

"Are you sure this is a good idea?" I ask, changing the subject. The Madam does not seem to trust me completely, and that is fine, but I know Jane would not want me to let these women leave Nicodemus without any sort of plan. As much as Jane pretends toward indifference, she is fiercely loyal, and I know the Madam to be one of the few people Jane cares about in this wasteland.

"No, but it's the one I got," the Madam says.

I am tired and my temper is frayed from too many days of hardship. "There is a horde out there!" I say, unable to keep my terror out of my voice. "And I do not believe a single one of those drovers will be able to protect you all from the dead."

"Maybe not," the Madam says. "But there's something about this town that makes me uneasy, and the sooner we take our leave the better I'll feel."

"Exactly," Sallie says.

I take a deep breath and let it out. There is no use in yelling at a grown woman about her life choices, even if they are poor. "So in light of this revelation, I think I agree with Nessie and Sallie," I say. "We should ask Lily what she wants to do."

"I want to watch Jane hang," Lily says from the doorway.

"What?" I ask, while the soiled doves gasp.

"You don't mean that," the Madam says.

Lily storms into the living room, rage and tears in her eyes, and I wave the rest of the women away. "I will take care of this," I tell them. The women nod and take their leave.

Lily stands before me, arms crossed and expression fierce. She wears clean clothes but there are tearstains on her face. She has been crying. I do not know the girl well, but even I can tell when a child is crying out for help.

So I do the only thing I can think of. I gather her up into a bone-crushing hug.

Lily flails, and I hold her tighter, my lips near her ear. There is no way past this but through, so I start talking.

"We did not get to talk much on the road here, did we? You might not remember me from Miss Preston's, but I remember you. You and the Spencers used to bring us lemonade and cookies while we trained. You would scowl and chase Thomas around while his mother served us, and once you asked me if it was hard, killing the dead." I am not glib like Jane, and I do not have her knack for spinning words into stories that ease the worries of those around her. And I am not clever like Jackson was, I cannot tell Lily the one thing she wants to hear so that she will trust and believe me. But I know how to spot a problem and solve it, and Lily's broken heart is not so strange a thing.

We have all lost someone we have loved. It is practically the only guarantee in this terrible world.

Lily stills as she remembers, just enough that I loosen my grip a bit, but I do not let her go. "You said it was as easy as harvesting wheat in a field," she whispers, voice clogged with emotion.

"Well, that day, I lied to you. Killing the dead is not easy. It is the hardest thing you will ever do. Not physically, though swinging a blade hard enough to sever a neck is no cakewalk. But because it takes a piece of your soul. No matter what you tell yourself, you know those folks were once just like you. They loved and fought and did all the messy parts of living you and I do.

"For us to keep on living, they have to die. There is no way around that. But that does not make it easy. And for the Negro to be the one to carry that burden, to bear the brunt of all the awfulness, well, it is far from just. Life is not fair.

"Lily, I knew your brother, and I know Jane. And it was Jane helping your brother find you that landed us all out here in Kansas in the first place. She knew it was dangerous, to go poking around in whatever awfulness we would find in the Spencers' deserted house. She knew that it would mean bad things, for all of us. And yet she went, because it was you. And because that was what Jackson asked of her."

Lily says nothing, her breaths coming too fast, and my heart breaks for her once again. But I keep talking, because that is all I can do. I know that there are not enough of us in this world taking care of one another, and I cannot let Lily go while she carries hate in her heart for the only person who loved her brother as much as she did.

We can fight together or we can die alone.

"Jane ended your brother because she loved him. And he asked her to do it because he knew that she loved him enough to carry it through. Watching someone turn, keeping them company in those last, final moments in the world . . . that is not easy, either. That is hell. Jane went through hell for your brother, because he asked her to, and she would do it again if she had to."

I release Lily and take a step back. She does not move, and I gently take her hands, squeezing them tightly. Her eyes are closed, tears leaking from beneath the lashes.

"She didn't even cry," she finally says, ripping her hands out of my grip and slamming her fists against her thighs. "She just came back, handed me his belongings, and started barking out orders. If she hurt so bad, why didn't she cry?"

"Because she knew in that moment that saving the rest of us was more important," I say. "Losing Jackson broke Jane, but the thing about Jane is she is never going to let anyone see the cracks. She is going to do her healing in private. Because she knows she has a job to do, which is making sure the rest of us are as safe as we can be.

"But we have a job, too. Letting them lynch Jane, letting her die—that is wrong. Jane fought to save us all in Summerland, and you cannot turn your back on her no matter how angry you are right now. Not just because it is the last thing Jackson would want, but because if there is anyone in this world who understands your broken heart, it is Jane Mc-Keene."

Lily sniffs once, then twice, and then throws herself back into my arms, her small body wracked with sobs. I hold her until the storm subsides, rubbing her back. Once she has calmed, she pulls away, still crying softly.

"I'm still cross with Jane," she says.

I nod. "I would recommend you get used to it. I spend much of my time the same way. But she is a good person, and good people are so hard to find. Now: you have a decision to make. Do you want to travel with the soiled doves and Thomas, or do you want to stay with Jane and me?" Jane is in no position to travel anywhere or make any kind of offer to the girl, but I know that if I were to let Lily run off with the Madam and her girls Jane would string me up herself. I still plan on convincing the Madam to stay until a more opportune time for leaving, maybe with the patrols once we have rescued Jane, but one step at a time.

Lily shrugs in answer to my question about her future. "I don't rightly know."

"Well, no one is going anywhere tonight, so you have some time to consider. But just know that there are few people I have had cause to admire as much as Jane McKeene, and she feels more affection for you than she lets on."

She nods. "I'm going for a walk," she says. I watch her leave through the door I just entered not long ago before taking a deep breath and letting it out.

A bath and a change of clothing is in order. And after that?

I need to see Jane. Because if Lily is in this kind of state, how can Jane be holding up? She needs someone by her side. Despite her bravado I know that Jane is scared. And what she needs right now, as much as an escape plan, is to know that someone is on her side no matter what.

By the pricking of my thumbs,
Something wicked this way comes.
—*Shakespeare*, Macbeth

— J A N E —

Chapter 13
In Which I Get a Visit from the Dead

Through the night, the rail gun keeps up its maddening rhythm—*whoomp whoomp whoomp*—firing for about a minute before going silent. It fires every hour on the hour, and it is the world's worst timepiece. I can't see what it's doing, but I can hear it, and it's enough to make a body go insane.

Of course, so is being trapped in a tiny cell.

By the time the sky begins to brighten outside of my prison and no one has come to liberate me or string me up, I

start to get antsy. Miss Duncan comes by to feed me breakfast—a cold biscuit and some kind of greasy meat—and to
empty the bucket. But other than that I am left to my own
devices. No Katherine, no Sue, no Sheriff Redfern. And no
Gideon, though that last one is a relief.

I take a peek out the window of the cell to see what I might
be missing, but the streets are empty, the day near burning
hot even as the sun is not near its highest point in the sky.
Autumn is near, and beyond that a winter I've heard to be
harsher than what we're used to back east, but you wouldn't
know it from the current temperature. I wonder if the heat is
what's got the streets so empty, with not a soul out and about
seeing to their business. The only sound in all of Nicodemus
is that rail gun and its clockwork firing.

But I am not without entertainment. And when my racing
thoughts get to be too much, and when I've cried whatever
tears I have to give at any given time about Jackson's loss, I
read my letters. The one from my momma, and the one I
took from Jackson.

At first, I feel guilty reading the purloined letter. There's
a whole lot of waffling before I pull it out and open it. This
remorse is a new thing, because in the past I have never let a
bit of thievery put me off my game. But now, every time I do
something questionable, I hear Katherine's voice in the back
of my head—*Jane, what an awful thing to do* and *Jane, you are
better than this* in that way she has—and I get all twisted up.

But at the same time, I can't *not* read the letter. I have to know why Jackson married this girl. I keep thinking about him and this mystery girl, limbs entangled, and it sets off a whole new spell of crying.

And sometime around the dozenth or so firing of the rail gun I realize that my chances of leaving Nicodemus alive are dwindling by the second. See, I've been in the cell a day and a night. And that rail gun has been firing most of that time. How many rounds has that infernal device sent hurtling toward the dead? And how many are still left? It ain't like bullets are easy to come by, even if Gideon got his own work-shop set up here in Nicodemus. The fact that it keeps firing means nothing good. Even if I survive the coming trial, there ain't no way any of us are surviving that horde if we're not gone soon.

So, figuring that my immortal soul is already beyond all redemption, I open the letter and begin to read it.

And immediately wish I hadn't.

Jackson,

You will not read this. You cannot read this. But it isn't right to send someone off into the world without a love note, no matter what you might say. Protest all you want, this is mine.

I know you hate hearing this, but I am entirely devoted to you. Every morning waking up next to you has been the best day of my life, and when our child is born I know it will be even better. You've felt the way he kicks! I have no doubt that he will be just as mischievous as his papa.

Never doubt I am sworn to you because you saved my life in all the best ways, and that's not something I can ever repay.

Be safe, Jackson. Find your sister and bring her home. And if you do find someone to read this to you, know that every word I'm saying here is true, as well as quite a few I've left unsaid so as not to appear wanton.

All my devotion,

Rosamund

I drop the letter and pick it up. I read it and read it again until I have to force myself to put the letter aside.

A baby? Jackson's wife was expecting a child. One that most likely has either been born or devoured by the dead.

My heart pounds, and I reread it again and again. That was why Jackson was so hot to find his sister, beyond the obvious reasons. He really was starting a whole new life, a life he used me to rebuild. I want to be angry at him, want to scream out my frustration, but instead I'm just heartbroken all over again.

Jackson had a chance at a real future, one full of love and family, and all he got was dead.

"Now you're reading my personal correspondence. That's a new low, Janey-Jane."

I nearly fall off the bunk at the voice, and my heart thunders in my chest. Under my shirt my lucky penny has gone to ice, and when I stand and move toward the bars my eyes refuse to believe what they see.

There, with his arms crossed and a hip propped up on the sheriff's desk, is Jackson, smiling his smile, looking no worse for wear.

I rub my eyes, and a terrible gladness comes over me. "Jackson?"

He laughs, a sound I would recognize anywhere. "None other."

I grip the bars so hard that my hands ache. "But you're dead."

"So I am, thanks to you."

The simple sentence wounds me to the quick, and I take a stumbling step back. "You here for revenge?" I ask.

Jackson shakes his head. "I need a favor."

"You always did," I snort.

Jackson laughs again, and I cross my arms. I have read many a weekly serial featuring ghosts, and the one thing I know about them is that they're supposed to visit the living in the dead of night. Leave it to Jackson to be contrary even in death, showing up with sunlight streaming in the windows. "You for real?"

"You tell me, Janey-Jane. Am I here? Or am I just the manifestation of your guilty conscience? I would urge you not to dwell on it. Would it change anything that's about to happen, either way?"

I shake my head. "I suppose not."

He grins again. "Questioning the truth of things doesn't change them. Whether I'm a true haint or just your addled brain trying to make sense of your grief and remorse, that doesn't alter the fact that you've got unfinished business to attend to. Mine, specifically."

"So what's the favor?"

"You have to get Lily out of this rotten town. You know as well as I do that guns and walls ain't never saved nobody. At least, not forever."

"There is a way past every wall, and all guns eventually run out of ammunition," I say. It was a common argument between Jackson and me. He'd never much trusted walls, and he didn't much care for guns. I thought the right kind of walls could keep a body safe, and I feel no shame in saying I quite enjoy firing a weapon, even though I am nowhere near as deadly accurate as Katherine. But now, I have to agree with Jackson, haint or no. There is no way the walls of Nicodemus can keep that horde out forever. Eventually it will grow large enough to push the walls down, and when that happens there won't be enough bullets in all of Kansas to save our necks.

Jackson laughs. "Funny I have to die to get you to see things my way. In either case, promise you'll keep Lily-bird safe."

I sigh. "You see that I'm trapped in here, right? Not a lot I can do behind bars."

Jackson purses his lips and then sucks his teeth like he always used to do when he was annoyed. It cuts right through me, the heartache as fresh and sharp as the moment I lost him. "You'll get out of there, no worries about that. I need you to promise me you'll keep the vow that I can't."

I take a deep breath, wipe away the tears that just keep coming despite my best efforts, and sigh. The stink of the dead filters in the window, carried on the hot breeze, heavy and redolent. Whether it's from the pile of dead that the rail gun is leaving outside the walls or the undead hordes continuing to assault us, I cannot know—but either way, we don't have much time. Maybe that's why I'm getting visitors from beyond the grave. Perhaps the situation is desperate enough that Jackson gave up his eternal rest to ensure that I was vigilant.

And maybe Jackson is just as much of a pain dead as he was alive, bossy and obstinate.

"I already told you I'd take care of Lily," I say. "But if you need to hear it again, I swear, I'll keep her safe."

Shouting comes from outside my tiny window, along with the commotion of running feet. I turn to spy folks hurrying this way and that, panic writ large across their movements.

It's just a heartbeat's distraction, but when I turn back to the desk, Jackson is gone.

I take a deep breath and collapse onto the bunk. My penny slowly warms, and my heart pounds from both fear and excitement. Was that truly Jackson I just saw?

Back at Rose Hill, one of the other aunties, Auntie Eve, used to talk about how a haint led her to freedom in the early days of the dead rising. "He was a fine-looking man, tall, with pale skin and long blond hair. He appeared at the foot of my bed one night, just standing there. Now, mind you, this was when I was just coming into bloom, and my first thought was that the master must've been having guests over, and I'd unfortunately caught one's eye. So when he gestured for me to follow him, I went because I figured it couldn't be as bad as the whip. He led me clear through the woods and across the river, walking until the sun came up."

The story from there would change depending on the mood Eve was in. Sometimes that white man's ghost looked into her eyes and tried to speak but couldn't because his voice didn't work. Other times Eve gave up and sat down, too scared to continue running and even more scared of going back. In those times the man's ghostly touch gave her the strength to keep moving.

Either way, the ending of the story was always the same: Eve's haint had saved her life, since the undead swept through the plantation that same night. Only a handful of souls were spared.

Aunt Aggie, however, had a different theory about Eve and her ghost.

"She didn't see no ghost. The girl's got guilt weighing her down. That's what happens when you go on living while so many folks you knew died." Aunt Aggie said this to another one of the aunties while shelling peas. A little ways off, Eve was telling her ghost story yet again. As Eve got to the part where the ghost led her through the dark woods and west to something like freedom, Aunt Aggie shook her head. "Sometimes, when the world doesn't make sense, it's easier to pretend like there are other forces at work. But there ain't. That's just life."

Now, I'm sitting in my jail cell, wondering if my guilt—over killing Jackson, over the pain I caused Lily, and over the future I stole from Rosamund—is provoking me to visions, or if it was something like what Auntie Eve said she saw. I can't help but think about my penny, warning me whenever danger is near. That's pretty darn unexplainable. I suppose I ain't as skeptical as Aunt Aggie would be.

The door to the sheriff's office opens, letting in light and heat and a large colored man with a full beard fashioned into mutton chops. I scrub my face as the man saunters in with a politician's smile.

Mayor Hamish Washington has come to see me.

Behind him is a gangly youth about my age, looking put out. The boy's skin has a ruddy hue to it, and I suppose he's fine-looking enough, but I can't help but notice his hands, which look entirely too soft to have seen any real work.

Lord have mercy.

"Miss McKeene! Well met," the man booms, his voice filling the room and overflowing it so that I wince. "My name is Hamish Washington, and I am the elected mayor of Nicodemus. We met briefly yesterday before you were incarcerated."

"I remember—you're the one who seems to think indulging

the Summerland folks is a good idea," I say, gesturing weakly at the bars between us. "And not so well met, sir, as you can see that I am in quite the predicament." I still sit on my bunk, and I make no effort to climb to my feet. I might've been brought up as a Miss Preston's girl, but I am quickly leaving tiresome etiquette behind. However, neither of my guests seems to notice my breach of decorum. The man laughs and claps the boy next to him on the shoulder.

"A clever girl, Cyrus! I told you, did I not?"

Cyrus looks like he's as happy about this meeting as I am, and the corners of his mouth pull downward. "Father, we don't have time for pleasantries. There is a horde at the gates. Shall we get on with the business at hand?"

I swallow a laugh as the mayor's smile falters for a moment. So, it seems that the mayor is the glad hand while his son is the voice of reason. Which makes this meeting all the more interesting.

Which one of them wanted to speak with me? And why?

"Yes, of course, my boy, of course. Jane, Mr. Carr—Gideon—has spoken very highly of you. Very highly indeed." The mayor talks like we are old friends, and I lean back on my bunk, because I learned long ago that you should never trust a man who treats you like a longtime friend.

"Mayor, that is good to know, but my immediate concerns are of my pending trial—"

"No doubt, Miss McKeene, most assuredly. But please

keep in mind we expect to have those charges cleared up post haste—once your moral character is accounted for."

"And my secondary concern," I continue as though the man hasn't taken the opportunity to talk over me, "is that horde outside your gates that is about to overwhelm the town."

The man nods, and Cyrus gives his father another nervous look.

"Which is why we are here, Miss McKeene," the mayor says, his insistence on saying my name over and over again fraying my temper. "As I'm sure you've heard, the town's defenses are nigh impenetrable—far beyond those of Summerland. But the former residents of Summerland—white and Negro alike—have impressed upon us the threat that this extraordinarily large horde presents. As such, the council has been debating whether we should require that residents of Nicodemus receive an injection of Gideon Carr's inoculation. These hordes of late present a threat the likes of which we have not seen since the Chaos Years. Mr. Carr, the architect of our marvelous defenses, says he has perfected an inoculation that he has been working on for a number of years. That vaccine will greatly improve our chances for survival, should our walls be breached." The mayor's voice remains polished as ever, but beneath his tone is a note of fear, one I might not have noticed if I hadn't heard such a thing before.

The same tone laced the speech patterns of Sheriff Snyder back in Summerland. The mayor might seem composed, but

I reckon his fear will be his undoing.

"If you think the town will be breached, then why not evacuate now when it could be done in an orderly manner?" I ask.

Mayor Washington covers his unease with a deep chuckle. "No one is saying that Nicodemus will fall, my dear girl. I suspect we've all witnessed the fall of a town in our time, terrifying as that sight is, but it remains the truth that most towns are brought down from the inside, the carnage instigated by a small group of infected persons finding their way in and turning the town. Rotting it from the inside, as it were. Mr. Carr's vaccine would prevent that threat. And we have the walls for the more obvious challenge of the hordes."

"I, on the other hand, believe the risk is simply too great," Cyrus says, interrupting his father with a pointed look. "If Gideon's formula is imperfect, it could result in the very outbreak within the walls of Nicodemus that Father just spoke of preventing. Mr. Carr, to my mind, seems overly confident in his vaccine, without any real evidence of efficacy. The majority of the council shares my concerns."

"Which is why we are here," the mayor concludes with an indulgent smile.

"You want me to tell you that the vaccine works," I say, my face heating. I barely manage to keep my aggravation from my voice. I told Gideon I wasn't going to provide him with any sort of support.

"Oh, indeed, that would be quite helpful, Jane," the mayor says with a nod.

"Have you been bitten?" Cyrus asks.

I shake my head.

"So then you cannot possibly know," Cyrus says with a note of finality in his voice, and I like him a great deal more.

"Now hold on, Cyrus," the mayor interjects, holding up a hand to forestall his son's next words. "You have received the injection, correct, Miss McKeene?"

"Yup," I say, "right along with every other Negro that had the misfortune of spending time in Summerland."

"And yet, you seem quite fit," the mayor says.

I frown. "I ain't died yet, if that's what you mean."

"There, you see?" he says, clapping his son on the back. "The vaccine is safe."

"That is not even remotely what she said," Cyrus says, exasperated.

"You said it yourself, son," the mayor says, turning his back to me, as if I have served my purpose and am no longer part of the conversation. "It's the risk of accidental infection that constitutes the only argument for not administering the vaccine. If it doesn't prevent one turning into the restless dead, well, we are no worse off than when we started. But if it does work, we will have saved the town" He smiles now, his voice filled with relief, and his foolishness is unbearable.

I leap to my feet. "You're damned for a fool if you put your faith in Gideon's serum," I growl. "The last time I listened to a man tout some injection and how it's going to save us from the plague, I ended up having to put down a handful of freshly turned shamblers in the middle of a university lecture hall. All it's going to take is one of those things inside these walls, and we're done for, no matter what your sainted Mr. Carr tells you. You need to start getting people out of this town in a coordinated manner. The time you fritter away waiting for the tides to turn is time you ain't got."

Mayor Washington takes half a step back. "Gideon Carr is a man of science—" he begins, but this time, I don't let him finish.

"Gideon Carr is the son of a man who was a staunch Survivalist and whose actions led to the fall of Baltimore. I'm sure you've heard tales about how that ended. And Gideon himself was only too happy to watch colored folks be sent out to their death day after day in Summerland. I saw his vaccine in action, coursing through the veins of those folks—when those walls were breached, they turned, the same as the rest of us will. It. Doesn't. Work!"

My words are too fast, nearly hysterical, and I want to call them back. How I wish sometimes I could be more like Katherine, sweet and disarming and always winding up with everything I need. But I ain't like her, and it seems like my honesty will be my end.

But I still do not understand how this conversation came

to be in the first place. How can Gideon peddle these lies to unsuspecting folks? How could a good man convince others to rely on unfounded truth? I cannot fathom why Gideon Carr is so adamant about using his vaccine on every person in the surrounding area, but it makes me question my earlier assessment of the man. How can one be an ally and ignore the good counsel of all those around him?

I look over at Cyrus, whose skeptical expression has transformed into one of keen interest. But his father does not appear so moved.

"The council has only demanded to have proof that the injection is safe, that our townsfolk would suffer no ill effects. You, and the rest of the colored folks from Summerland, meet that burden of proof," the mayor says, heading for the door. His step is light and carefree. He's gotten what he came for. "As for your legal troubles, I wouldn't worry too much, Miss McKeene. We have almost concluded our interviews, and thus far have not found a single eyewitness who can confirm you murdered the sheriff. You should be free by supper."

With that, he sweeps out of the office, and I bury my head in my hands, groaning. In the same way the pastor sold folks on religion saving them from the undead masses, Gideon has peddled rubbish science and sold people on a hope that doesn't exist. And like the pastor, he's built a town around it.

I have to save the people of Nicodemus from themselves. But I'm also thinking about my own miserable hide. I don't want to die in this place, whether hanging from a noose or mauled by the dead. Even though the mayor seems to think I'll be freed, I doubt the veracity of the man's assertions. He obviously lives in a delusion of his own making, especially if he's of a mind to go along with Gideon and his garbage vaccine.

The sound of a throat clearing echoes in the office, and I lift my head up. Cyrus remains rooted to his spot, his gangly stature perhaps a little less awkward without the imposing bulk of his father beside him.

"I told him the same things you did," he says. "But he, and everyone else on the council, are simply too afraid to listen. I've spoken at length with Gideon. He's revised the serum dozens of times, even since he administered it to you, and the reality is that he doesn't have conclusive evidence that it works. And there is, as you say, abundant proof it doesn't."

"Your father is sentencing this whole town to death," I mutter. "There ain't any kind of inoculation against fear and false confidence."

Cyrus nods. "I know. I've tried to convince the council that we must leave, to make our way out the back gate before we're completely surrounded. But so far, no one wants to take the chance. And now Gideon's serum will give them every reason to stay." His eyes go distant, seeing some memory I ain't party to. "I think they remember what it was like, walking out of Indian Territory with little more than the clothes on our backs. A lot of us didn't make it, and some said we should've stayed, that we'd have had a better chance with the Five Tribes." Cyrus shrugs. "All I know is that I would rather take my chances running than stay here and wait for death to find me."

I nod. "That makes sense."

"Yes, most of the council thought so. Myself included. It's only been Gideon Carr's assertions of safety that have kept us here."

"He saw Summerland fall, why would he think Nicodemus is any safer?"

"Better walls," Cyrus says with a laugh. Any soft feelings I might be harboring toward Gideon these last few weeks have died on the vine, like young fruit in a late frost. I cannot believe that he would give this town such terrible counsel.

But then I think about the interactions I had with his daddy, and maybe I can believe it.

Cyrus gives me one last long, inscrutable look and says, "Good luck, Jane McKeene."

"Good luck to you as well, Cyrus Washington. Let's hope we both make it out of here alive."

And then he's gone and I'm left with nothing but my dark thoughts.

For wrath killeth the foolish man, and envy slayeth the silly one.
—Job 5:2

— KATHERINE —

Chapter 14
Notes on the Foolishness of Men

There is a knock at the door, and for a moment I consider not answering it. I have been avoiding Gideon and the soiled doves since yesterday, and Lily seems to have been avoiding me in turn. It has not been easy. Everyone's emotions were high when we arrived after our headlong flight, especially after Jane was arrested, and the evening meal had not been much better. The soiled doves gave Gideon baleful glares when he casually brought up the matter of his vaccine at the supper table—their feelings on being on the wrong end of a medical procedure were clear—and Thomas had fussed through the entire meal, no doubt responding to the tense atmosphere. Lily was sullen, but at least she was alert, which is all the more anyone can ask of a girl mourning the death of her last remaining relative.

For my part, I had spent the entire meal struggling to breathe. It had been my hope that at some point the tight feeling in my chest would relax enough for me to do the things that need doing—to secure Jane's freedom, to facilitate a quick exit from this doomed town. But I barely managed to hold myself together through the meal. And when I went to bed, heart pounding like a panicked rabbit over everything and nothing, I had prayed that the morning would offer me a bit of respite.

It has not.

I woke this morning paralyzed by an unnamed fear, and the day's progression has done nothing to ease it. My corset, which I had been wearing looser in response to Jane's incessant nagging, is now back to its usual rib-clenching tightness, in the hope that the physical discomfort can loosen the grip of the nameless terror that clenches my heart.

And yet, it is still not enough!

I close my eyes and take a deep breath as the knock comes yet again. I sit in the room off the kitchen, a pantry into which I threw a sleep pallet and renamed a guest room yestereve, and I slow my breathing. I want to scream and cry and rage, but none of that is going to be any kind of use.

At the fourth knock, it becomes clear that the person on the other side is not going away. So, finally, I open the door.

Callie and Sue stand in the kitchen, their expressions twisted with worry. "We let ourselves in," Callie says with a wan smile.

I struggle to summon a polite smile. "Did you speak with Jane?" I ask.

They nod. "Yesterday, but that ain't why we're here," Callie says.

"There's a town meeting, and we think you should be there," Sue says.

"What is it about?" I ask, smoothing a few wayward tendrils of hair so that I at least look presentable.

"I ain't quite sure," Callie says. "But my brother, Cyrus, he's on the town council, he and my daddy went to see your friend Jane this morning. So I'm thinking it might have something to do with her."

I take a deep breath and stand as straight as I can. I push aside all my anxiousness and give them a bright smile. "Well, then, we should make haste."

The sun is high in the sky as we make our way to the church where everyone is gathering. As we enter, it is easy to see that people have segregated themselves into various factions: the white folks from Summerland congregate on the left side of the church. They number fewer than I thought. The group that seemed to be fifty or so folks when they were calling for Jane's neck turns out to be fewer than twenty men and women. I am uncomfortably surprised to see the Madam and her girls sitting on the edge of the Summerland crowd, Thomas bouncing happily in her lap. I suppose when lines are drawn it is easier to go with what one knows than to forge new paths.

The displaced Summerland folks wear identical scowls directed toward the right side of the church, where the residents of Nicodemus sit, men and women of color dressed in finer clothes than anything the Summerland folks wear. Here and there is an Indian man or woman, and I spot a lone white family in the plain dress of the Quakers, but for the most part the right side of the church is a sea of dark skin. A few of the Nicodemus folks meet the glares of Summerland's displaced with their own haughty glares.

Tossed into this mix are the Summerland patrols, standing with arms crossed in the back of the church. Their weapons are clearly on display for all to see and the murmur that arises makes clear the white folks from Summerland are none too happy to see it.

There is a shifting of bodies as the town council and the mayor walk to the dais at the front of the church. The council is mostly colored, although there are two very elderly white people who make their way to the front as well. Sheriff

Redfern files in behind them, and he tips his hat at me as his eyes meet mine. It is incredible to see so many colored folks in positions of power.

The outrage coming from the white Summerland folks is nearly palpable, and my spirits lift a bit at realizing that for all their bluster and outrage the principles they clung to in Summerland will do nothing for them here.

There are maybe two hundred people crammed into the church, and the heat is unbearable. The stink of unwashed bodies competes with the scent of decay from the horde outside the gates, and I am not quite sure which one is worse. Either way, I am not distracted by my discomfort for long as the mayor pounds on the podium to get everyone's attention.

"Ladies and gentlemen, thank you for coming to this town hall. I am sure you are all wondering what this could be about, and instead of bloviating at you as I usually do"— he pauses to chuckle here, although no one in the audience laughs along with him—"I figure I would let our lead science man, Gideon Carr, speak instead."

"When are you hanging that darkie?" someone yells, and a chorus goes up from the Summerland section of the church. Mayor Washington gives them the kind of smile one would give a child demanding a sweet before supper.

"We are still conducting our investigation into that matter, rest assured. But this town meeting is about a more pressing issue, namely that group of restless dead gathering outside the main gate."

This seems to mollify folks a bit, and Gideon grins winningly as he climbs onto the dais from his position in the front pew of the church.

"Nope," Sue mutters next to me. "I sure don't trust that white man."

"Aw, Gideon ain't so bad," Callie says. She catches me looking at her and ducks her head. I have seen that expression before, more than once.

Callie is besotted with the man.

"Good afternoon," Gideon says, pitching his voice to be heard above the crowd. I turn my attention back to him, and whatever Mayor Washington believes to be pressing enough to summon everyone in the middle of the day.

"As many of you know, I'm Gideon Carr, scientist and inventor. I've advised extensively on the defenses of both Summerland and Nicodemus, though I daresay that the good people here in Nicodemus have given me resources and support to execute plans that far outstrip my efforts in Summerland." A heavy silence greets the statement, and Gideon clears his throat and continues. "For nearly twenty-four hours you have heard my electric rail gun firing, and thus far it's been successful at keeping the undead away from the town's perimeter. We estimate them to currently be about a quarter of a mile away, just beyond the outside edge of the fencing. They since seem to have stopped their forward progression, for reasons we do not quite understand. They have made no move to surround the town and remain to the south." Gideon removes his spectacles and cleans them before resettling them. "By my count—and please keep in mind this is only a rough estimate—there are currently between two and three thousand restless dead outside the gate."

His pronouncement is met with a chorus of gasps. I cannot help but wonder how the man thinks making everyone panic over the very obvious problem of the dead is going to help anyone.

"Ladies and gentlemen, please, please, I am not quite finished." Gideon stands a little straighter and begins to pace across the dais, eating up the space with his long stride. His gait is uneven because of his slight limp, but his voice is powerful and carries above the ruckus. People begin to quiet once more.

"There is a solution that has not yet been explored, and that is what I would like to present to you all today." Gideon looks out over the room and gestures toward the back. "Ida, would you join me up on the dais?"

Ida pushes past us without a word, making her way to the front of the church. I turn toward Sue in surprise and see my shock echoed in her expression. "Do you know what she's doing?" I ask Sue.

She shrugs. "I get the feeling not many are privy to that girl's truest thoughts," Sue says.

Ida stands next to Gideon, looking about as happy as I've ever seen her.

"Ida here was a member of the Summerland patrols. I have been experimenting with an inoculation, a type of medicine that is injected into the bloodstream, and can counteract the effects of the undead bite. Should a person be bitten, the vaccine would keep them from turning. Assuming the wound is not fatal in itself."

The room quiets even further. The only sound is a stray cough.

"Since last fall, I have been vaccinating each and every member of the Summerland patrols, including Ida here. As you can see, she remains healthy. The inoculation is safe. I know the council has some reservations in recommending everyone in town get the vaccine on account of the risk of turning—the vaccine is a distilled serum made from the blood and saliva of an infected person, after all. But as you can see, there is nothing to fear."

The room explodes into chaos once more as people shout their questions at Gideon and Ida. She crosses her arms and stares defiantly at the back of the room, and I want to ask her why she is all of a sudden allied with Gideon Carr. Just yesterday she praised Jane's reluctance to endorse the vaccine, and now she is up on the stage next to Gideon. What changed her mind?

A man surges to his feet yelling loud enough to be heard over the rest of the crowd. "So this injection of yours will cure the undead plague?"

"It won't cure it, no," Gideon says as people settle down enough to listen to his answer. "Once someone is bitten and begins to change they are lost. But my vaccine will prevent the plague from spreading in two ways. First, those who do not survive an undead attack will not rise upon expiration. And second, those who are bit but survive will not change. In short, not only will the vaccine enable you to survive an attack but no new restless dead will be created in the event of a town being overrun."

People are yelling all kinds of questions, but Mayor Washington returns to the front of the room, thanking Gideon and clapping him on the back as he departs the dais.

"Ladies and gentlemen, you have heard our resident man of science and his proposal. The need is self-evident. As such, the council has decided that everyone in town is to be inoculated. Mr. Carr will be visiting each home personally to administer the injection. From there, we will begin assigning people to teams, and we will start launching small-scale attacks against the horde in the hopes of thinning out its numbers. Every man and woman will do their part. And I do mean *everyone*. Make no mistake, our fight is for the very fate of Nicodemus. We either survive or perish together, and I for one would like to keep on breathing this sweet Kansas air."

"The man is a muttonhead," Sue murmurs with a sidelong glance at Callie. If she is offended by the slight to her father, she does not show it. I nod, but as I listen to the muttering around the room, I wonder if Gideon's little presentation has convinced some folks. The promise of a cure is a seductive one.

The mayor and his council take their leave, ignoring the shouts and questions that follow them out the door. Ida walks past us, and I grab her by the arm.

"I thought you did not believe in Gideon Carr's vaccine," I say, my voice low enough that it does not carry.

Ida smirks at me. "No one asked me whether I believe in it. They asked whether I got the shot, and I did. But Gideon promised me that if I did what he asked, he'd ensure that the patrols wouldn't just be us colored folks all over again. That was enough for me."

"Do you really think the mayor or anyone else is going to get those lily-livered white folks to pick up a blade?" Sue asks. "And, besides, I thought you wanted out of this town?"

Ida shrugs. "Still do. But least this way, I have a better chance of surviving until the getting is good. And maybe that horde will be a little smaller when we take our leave." She turns on her heel and strides away. I cross my arms and look at Sue.

"Well, what now?" I wonder aloud.

"Ida is right: nothing's changed," Sue says with a heavy sigh. "Let's go rustle up something to eat, and afterward we'll tell Jane everything that's going on. Hopefully Lucas and his boys are working on that plan to get her free. Because I want out of this place sooner rather than later."

I nod and make to follow. Callie, however, hangs back.

"Callie? Are you coming?"

"Not just yet, I have something I want to do," she says. Her gaze is locked on Gideon Carr, and I stifle a knowing smile.

"Well, good luck," I say, even though I am not sure I honestly mean it.

Nothing good can ever come of a Negro girl chasing after a white boy, but I suppose that is a lesson Callie will have to learn for herself.

Men in rage strike those that wish them best.
—*Shakespeare*, Othello

— J A N E —

Chapter 15
In Which I Spoil for a Fight

I'm lying on my back in the Nicodemus jail, pondering Gideon and what his motives might be (nothing good from where I sit), when Katherine enters the sheriff's office. She is such a welcome sight that I can't help but smile as I climb to my feet.

"Well, look what the cat dragged in," I say.

In truth, she looks fresh as a daisy. She's wearing a day dress in pink calico with just enough ruffles to be ridiculous, if it were on anyone else but her. Her hair is swept up in a complicated style that a typical woman would need a lady's maid to accomplish, but I know Katherine probably did it all by herself. She makes me viciously envious, not because of how pretty she looks but because I've been wearing the same sweat-soaked dress covered in shambler blood for going on a week. All I want is to burn it and dance on its ashes before soaking for a whole day in a tub. But there ain't a lot of bathing in jail. I mean, the facilities consist of a bucket, for the love of God.

Katherine huffs predictably before looking around for a chair. "Do you know how difficult it is to find acceptable clothing in the middle of the prairie?"

I raise an eyebrow and cross my arms. "I was joking with you, Kate. What's got into you?"

Katherine purses her lips before moving over to the bars. "Well, there is a giant horde outside our gates and now the entire town believes that somehow Gideon Carr's vaccine is going to save them," she says. "Well, if not save them then at least keep them safe. We should be fleeing instead of trying to fight."

"They want to fight the horde?" I say, feeling the world fall away a little.

Katherine waves away my words like she's brushing off a mosquito and turns back to me. "Never mind about all that, we have more pressing issues. How are you doing, Jane?"

The warmth and worry in her voice undo a little of my

control, and I have to blink hard to keep from crying. "Oh, you know, well enough. Just seeing ghosts, is all."

Katherine frowns. "Sheriff Snyder's?"

I laugh, the sound harsh and loud. In my grief over Jackson I've mostly forgotten all about the other man I killed. "I wish. Him, I'd know how to deal with. No, Jackson."

She leans forward, eyes wide. "What did he say?"

"You believe me?"

She snorts. "Of course I believe you, Jane. I am not sure that any Christian who believes in the good Lord above could ignore the possibility of souls being trapped here in our world, unable to pass on. Haints are a real thing. I saw them when I was younger, out in the bayou. Ghost lights that will lure you to your death, angry spirits that got unfinished business, and the kind ones who will give you a gentle nudge when you need it. Since you are still here and relatively unscathed, I am assuming Jackson was the third sort."

I shake my head, because the last thing I expected was to discover that straitlaced Katherine Deveraux believes in ghosts. "He told me we have to get out of town and that I have to keep an eye out for Lily."

"That makes sense, and exactly what I would think his spirit would say. But I do not understand why that has you so shaken. You look like you ate week-old oysters."

I blow out a heavy breath. "It's not just that. I . . . Jackson was going to be a father."

Her pale brows shoot up so fast I'm afraid they're going to launch right off her face. "And just how do you know that, Jane? Did his ghost tell you that?"

"No, I nicked a letter off Jackson after he died. A letter that was from his wife back in Baltimore. I gave the rest of his belongings to Lily but that letter I kept because . . . I wanted to know."

"Know what?" Katherine asks. There's something in her face, a kind of worry or sadness or something that I can't rightly place, but I ignore it because I'm too busy wallowing in my own feelings.

"I wanted to know why he got married! I wanted to know why and what she was like." I start to pace, but there's only so much space in the cell, and sooner than I'd like I'm turning back toward Katherine and her unnamable expression. She doesn't say anything for a while. And I wait for her exclamation of surprise, of something, but there's none.

I stop my pacing and spin on my heel toward her. "Did you know that Jackson had an expecting wife?"

Katherine shakes her head. "No. But now that you mention it, it does not surprise me."

"And why's that?"

She laughs. "Jane, that is what most people want, is it not? To find love, settle down, share their life with someone. A family . . . I must admit, the whole idea has never appealed to me, but I do understand why Jackson would chase after such a dream. Regardless: Why would you begrudge Jackson the opportunity? Not everyone wants to spend their life killing the dead."

"And you think I do?"

"I think that you have never once stopped to consider that a life beyond killing might be possible."

"You think I like putting down shamblers, that I enjoy it?"

Katherine sighs. "I think you have accepted it as your path. But that is not the point. Jackson is dead, and still you let his choices in life upset you so?"

"Well, what else am I supposed to do? Jackson was all I had, I ain't got anybody else!"

Hurt is writ large on Katherine's fine features, but it ain't a match for my incandescent anger. Anger at myself, for trusting in Jackson, and in Gideon Carr, and believing that I could one day find happiness despite the misery of this world. I ain't got a single person I can rely on.

"Jane, you are far from alone. You have Sue, and all the other Miss Preston's girls. Ida and the rest of the Summerland patrols are loyal to you to a fault. And, believe it or not, you have me."

"Kate, you know we ain't friends. We were at best uneasy allies, two people pushed together by fortune and necessity. But that time has passed. I don't expect a lick from you, and you shouldn't expect a damn thing from me."

"Jane . . . ," she begins, but she doesn't go on, and I ain't in the mood to wait around for whatever honeyed words she's trying to manufacture.

"Say what you need to say and go. I'm sure you've got other places to be." My gaze is direct, and she lifts her chin a little at the challenge, just like she would when I'd lay into her back at Miss Preston's.

Maybe it's just easier to tread familiar ground instead of forging new paths.

"I came here to tell you about the vaccine and the town meeting, but I can see that you are in one of your moods. So all I will say is this: if you want to feel sorry for yourself, that is fine, but do not sit there and pretend that you are the only one in danger. This entire town will be overrun by the dead inside of a week, and unless we figure a way out—together— we will all of us be dead."

As if to punctuate her point the rail gun takes up its cadence, booming just outside the office. I want to come back at her with some kind of witty rejoinder, but the truth is I ain't got a thing to say. She's right.

But that doesn't mean I'm going to tell her so.

Without another word she sweeps out of the sheriff's office, leaving me alone with nothing but the sound of the rail gun and the churning of my stomach.

Make no friendship with an angry man; and with a furious man thou shalt not go.

—Proverbs 22:24

— KATHERINE —

Chapter 16
Notes on a Friendship

I leave the sheriff's office before I start crying. Damn that Jane McKeene. She is hurt and lashing out, just like she has been since Jackson died, but directing all that anger outward instead of reckoning with it is just going to get her deeper into trouble. Between the approaching horde, her murder accusation, and the plots afoot in Nicodemus, she is going to need to be at her sharpest, and this definitely is not it.

I restrain the urge to stomp my foot in frustration, and instead I adjust my hat with a bit more force than necessary, nearly jabbing my scalp with the hatpin. Once it is resettled I take a deep breath, enjoying the reassuring grip of the corset on my ribs before I set out to find Sue and plan our next steps.

I spot her on the boardwalk a little ways up from the sheriff's office, and she turns toward me at my approach. She is fully armed, and her scythe swings as she walks. She looks like an omen, a dark personification of the grim reaper, beautiful and relentless.

"You should get your weapons," she says, noting my lack of arms. "That gate could come down when we least expect it, and it would be a shame for you to have to run to find blades."

She is right, of course. Things are rapidly spiraling out of control in Nicodemus and a good pair of swords is always the best accessory. "Excellent idea. I will head back to the house to get them now."

"I'll walk with you. I haven't been able to find Lucas or Ida anywhere, so I guess we might as well let them find us."

Lucas was supposed to tell us his plan for breaking Jane out, a plan that was supposed to go into action that very night. But I had the feeling that things had changed, especially in light of Ida working alongside Gideon Carr.

It was difficult to ascertain whose side anyone was on at the moment.

We stroll in silence for short while until Sue asks, "You talk to Jane?"

"Yes. We have to get her out of there. She is . . . unraveling. Emotionally. She is nearly hysterical." I do not mention Jane's claims of being visited by Jackson's ghost. I believe Sue catches my drift without any elaboration.

"That ain't surprising. Jane doesn't do well on her own. Did you tell her about the vaccine? And the mayor's plan to save the town?"

I nod, and take a deep breath and let it out. "She agrees that there is something happening here, something of which we have only seen the beginning. But . . ." I trail off.

"She being tetchy?" Sue asks, her eyes taking in the whole of the street.

"Yes. She pinched a letter that was not meant for her and learned something she did not want to know. Jackson had secretly gotten married, and his wife was with child."

Sue lets out a low whistle. "Now that is some piece of news to stumble upon. For what it's worth, I told her that boy was never any good, but you know how stubborn she is. Like a mule, that one. Sets her mind about a bit of business, and even when it goes sour she's still set on seeing it through."

There is an opportunity to glean some information here, and I blink at Sue, making my face seem as guileless as possible. "Do you know what happened between the two of them? Jackson and Jane? How they met? I never really understood how Jane could take up with such a ne'er-do-well."

That makes Sue laugh and stop walking. She rests the hilt of her scythe on the boardwalk and leans on it. "Don't try to use that honey on me, Miss Priss. I know what you're up to. But it's no secret, that history between Jane and that boy of hers. Once Jane makes up her mind about someone that's all she can see. Nothing short of the fires of Revelation raining down upon her head will change her course. She met him while out and about on one of her nightly adventures, saving people from shamblers. Angel of the Crossroads, they called her."

I nod, because I had heard the stories back at Miss Preston's. Reckless nonsense, I had thought back then, but I had jumped at the opportunity to tag along with her when Jackson asked her for help finding Lily. I understood then why she had done it, sneaking out all those nights. There was no freedom, no place to breathe at Miss Preston's. Our movements were carefully coordinated and controlled, everything geared toward turning us into biddable handmaidens with killer instincts. But running along the dirt highways of Maryland in the dark? There were no rules out there in the wild.

Sue continues her story, and I force my attention back to her tale. "Jane would sneak out and watch out for wayward travelers—rich or poor, Negro or white, it didn't matter—for no other reason than because she could. She met that boy out and about one night, and I'm sure he was up to no good, but she saved his life. He was grateful, and she decided she was in love. Right up until she found him tumbling Mary Beth Jefferson."

"Wait, she found Jackson with another girl and she still was preoccupied with him?"

Sue sighs and nods. "Like I said: muleheaded. I'm sorry about Jackson, may he rest in peace, but darned if he wouldn't keep finding ways to break her heart for the rest of his days. It's probably good for Jane that he's gone, but she won't see it that way. She's so stubborn, she'll keep carrying that flame for him even after he's dead."

I tap my finger against my lips as I think. "Whatever happened to Mary Beth Jefferson? I somewhat remember her from Miss Preston's."

"Oh, Mary Beth ran off. Left the school real quick after Jane caught her out. Our girl has a mean streak a mile wide once you cross her, and I reckon Mary Beth felt she was better off taking her chances out in the world than sticking around Miss Preston's."

I put my hand to my temple and massage the spot as a headache begins to bloom behind my eyes. "This is entirely too much. It is barely noon."

Sue laughs and slings a heavy arm across my shoulders, pulling me into her side. "Welcome to being friends with Jane McKeene, the hardest job in the world."

I bite my lip and blink back sudden tears. "I am not sure Jane and I are even friends, Sue."

"Nonsense. Once Jane decides she's attached to you, there's no way you're prying her off. And you, my dear, are most certainly attached. She might be contrary right now, but give her a few minutes to cool down and it'll be fine. She's quick to anger, but just as quick to regain her wits." Sue releases me and jerks her head toward the far end of the boardwalk. "There's Miss Duncan."

We watch as our former instructor approaches, but she seems to be preoccupied with thoughts of her own. I start to wave at her, but Sue catches my hand and pulls me backward so that we rest fully in the shadows of the boardwalk.

"What?" I ask, voice low.

"Miss Duncan seems like she's about some sort of dark business. Look, she's got that furrow between her brows like she always used to get when Jane started back-talking."

Sure enough, Sue is correct. Miss Duncan is vexed about something, and as she disappears toward the stables toward the rear of town I get an idea.

"We should follow her, see what is going on."

Sue nods. "Good idea. Ruthie ran up to the wall just a short while ago, must be she was running to fetch Miss Duncan."

"If there is mischief afoot then we should definitely see what it is."

Sue pushes me playfully with a grin. "Jane's rubbing off on you. See, it ain't all bad."

I roll my eyes at her, and then on quiet, catlike feet, Sue and I skulk after Miss Duncan to ascertain what she could be about.

For there is nothing either good or bad, but thinking makes it so.
—*Shakespeare*, Hamlet

— J A N E —

Chapter 17
In Which Things Begin to Unravel

After Katherine departs, I feel six kinds of awful. I took every last bit of anger and sadness and threw it right at her for no other reason than because I could. Even if we ain't friends, if everything that we've been through up to now ends up being the only kind of kinship we share, there's still no reason to go back to being how I was at Miss Preston's.

It's a revelation that causes me to lie down on the bunk and stretch out like a starfish. The Jane that I once was, that girl is gone. All the dreams and hopes I had back then are ashes, and that means I need to build something else in their place. I'm still aching to get out west and find my momma, but that ain't happening if I don't survive today.

I've been living so long for the future that I haven't been focusing on the now. And I ain't sure I know how to change that.

The door to the sheriff's office opens and Sheriff Redfern strides in, his expression grim. I climb up off the bunk and watch him warily as he unlocks the cell door and swings it wide.

"What's this about, Redfern?" I ask before I take a step, because he seems to have his own agenda, and I don't have time to puzzle out what it might be.

"You're free to go. It seems that the good folks of Summerland have zero eye witnesses, and the council has decided to drop the charges."

It's good news, of course, having won my freedom without having to put a bullet in anyone, but a heavy disappointment fills my middle. I wish Katherine were here to celebrate my liberation with me, but I went and chased her off like a spoiled child screaming for a bigger piece of cake. I take a step out of the cell and stretch, working through myriad, conflicting emotions. "Well, then, Sheriff, looks like the system actually worked. Color me surprised."

"I promised you that you wouldn't hang," he says, voice

steady. His expression doesn't change, not even an eyebrow twitch. Wordlessly, he goes to his desk and pulls out my weaponry, laying out an entire arsenal on the smooth wood. I strap it back on, piece by piece, watching Redfern the whole time. I feel a good deal better having all my edges back, and my relief at being on the right side of those jail bars makes me bold.

"You really don't like me, do you?" I finally ask as I secure my sickles to my belt.

He sighs and props a hip on his desk. "Jane, it has nothing to do with not liking you. It's knowing that somehow, some-way, this is going to end badly for you. And there's nothing I can do to stop it."

I raise an eyebrow at him. "So we're on a first-name basis, now?"

That raises a glimmer of a smile. "Our paths continue to cross in a way that feels like more than coincidence, and I've learned not to ignore patterns in my life. But I'm telling you this: you need to learn to watch your back."

It ain't the answer I'm expecting, and I rock back on my heels as I ponder his words. "How's that?"

His lips thin. "I know your kind. I've seen what becomes of them."

I cross my arms. "My kind?"

"The brave, the bold, those who would do the right thing rather than save their own skin."

"How're you going to make that sound like a bad thing?"

He shakes his head. "You aren't listening. Like you, I went to a combat school, mostly Indian kids taken by a white family, the Redferns. They gathered us up from whatever place hadn't been overrun by the dead. My first year there, most of my friends ran away, off into the nearby woods, anywhere to get away from that school." He pauses to take a breath, as though the memory is too much to bear.

"You stayed, though?"

He shrugs. "I've always been practical. The school fed us and provided a measure of safety, and I had no idea where my people were or if they'd even survived the dead. This was during the Years of Discord. Whole towns disappeared overnight. I was scared, so I stayed." He shakes his head. "I should have run like my friends, but I didn't."

I nod, because I understand that feeling. Sometimes it can feel like the unknown is worse than the hardships you're enduring. Didn't I stay at Miss Preston's, thinking there was a pot of gold at the end of that rainbow? The beatings, the lies, I endured it all because I thought that my pain and suffering would be repaid. But now, knowing what I know, I should've run back to Rose Hill the first chance I got. If I had, maybe there'd still be a Rose Hill in Haller County, Kentucky.

Daniel Redfern scrubs his hand over his face and continues his tale. "The Redferns were the kind of people who thought they were making the world a better place. That they were doing the right thing. Nothing could stop them, not the kids who ran away or even the kids who died of simple things, like fevers and lung infections. No matter what happened, they carried on, dogged in their faith and their beliefs."

This is getting worse by the minute. "Are you comparing me to the people who took you from your home and tortured you?"

That gets a laugh out of him, the sound rich and deep. "No, Jane, listen. You're so damn impatient you won't even listen to the lesson long enough to properly ignore it."

I take a deep breath and let it out. "Okay, fine."

He nods and continues. "The Redferns had a daughter, their own flesh and blood, and she insisted on coming to combat classes with the rest of us. Betsy always looked out of place—her pale skin unmistakable in the drill line, working just as hard as anyone. She didn't even have to be there, but she was, because she thought everyone should do their part to fight the dead. Because it was the right thing to do.

"The first time the school sent my class out to clear a field, Betsy was with us. There were dozens of shamblers; it turns out, the farmer who'd engaged the Redferns to bring us out there and clear his field had lied about the size of the cadre. In the fight, Betsy got bit. She didn't tell anyone at first, just kept putting down the dead. But soon it was clear that there were too few of us, that we would be overrun, and that's when

Betsy sent us all back to fortify the farm's fences and rearm ourselves while she covered our escape. She knew she was done for, so she kept fighting until she turned."

I stare at Redfern, waiting for more, but that appears to be the end of the story. "I don't get it. She saved your lives."

"But she shouldn't have been there in the first place. She died because, rather than stay in her place, she decided it was up to her to try to make things right, to make them fair. Betsy was convinced that she could fix the world, show by example that it shouldn't just be the Indian and the Negro out killing the dead, that it was a job for everyone."

I sniff, because it seems to me that Redfern should be thanking his lucky stars some well-meaning white girl saved him rather than using her to prove his point about . . . what? I'm not sure what his argument is exactly.

"Betsy was a hero," I say.

"Exactly," Redfern says, nodding. "Heroes die. But survivors live to tell the story. When the dead got to be too much for us to handle, most of those fools wanted to keep fighting, because that's what we'd been taught. I was one of the first to cut and run. I knew what the score was. The things you're taught are only useful if they keep you alive."

I shake my head. "Daniel, I think you must have a very lonely life if the only person you care about saving is yourself."

He shrugs. "Maybe. But I'm still alive, and most of Baltimore isn't."

His words wake a little voice that I've tried to ignore for a very long time. It's the part of me that wonders what my life would be like right now if Jackson hadn't asked me to go find his sister. The truth is, my momma would probably agree with the whole of what Daniel Redfern is saying. She was always quick to offer a helping hand to other folks, but never so much as to put our family at risk.

"It's the American way," she would say, watching from the porch as another family took up residence at Rose Hill. "You help as much as you can—but no more. You don't think those founding fathers wrote all those pretty words about independence just to help the poor, do you? The books are right there in the library, Jane. They did it because they didn't want to pay taxes, to have some king tell them the price of tea. And for that, they went to war, and hundreds of people died. If that ain't capitalism, I don't know what is."

I love my momma, and I surely trust her more than I do any founding fathers I've never met. But I have to believe there's more to life than just surviving.

"So, then, how is it a man who runs at the first sign of a threat to his own well-being ends up sheriff of Nicodemus?" I ask.

Daniel Redfern grimaces. "Sometimes, Jane, you do things because you don't have a choice."

And he saith unto them, Why are ye fearful, O ye of little faith? Then
he arose, and rebuked the winds and the sea; and there was a great
calm.
—Matthew 8:26

— KATHERINE —

Chapter 18
Notes on the Follies of Science

Sue and I follow Miss Duncan as she wends her way through
Nicodemus, leaving the more settled part of town for the animal pens and well-laid-out gardens. The stink of manure is a
harsh greeting but it also makes me glad to know that there
are some resources here inside of town. The plots of land we
pass are well tended, and even though no one is minding the
gardens as we pass, it is clear they will feed us for at least
another couple of days.

"Might I ask just what it is you think Miss Duncan is about?" I say, adjusting my hat so that at least a bit of my face is shaded by the narrow brim. I am not vain, but with this much sun I am going to have a plethora of freckles running rampant on my nose, and that is bothersome.

"I don't know. She's been acting strangely ever since she took up with Sheriff Redfern."

I frown. "Do you mean romantically?"

Sue gives me an incredulous look but does not slow her stride. "How else would I mean? They were all sorts of cozy on the trip out here, and they've spent an awful lot of time off on their own since arriving here. Ruthie even says she saw them kissing once, so if they ain't romantic then they're at least sinning something fierce."

"Well, I think that is lovely," I say.

Sue snorts a half laugh. "I didn't say it wasn't. But Redfern is a councilman, and he used to be Mayor Carr's man as well. I don't trust him, and neither should you."

Sue is right, of course, but I say nothing and just follow along. We have come to the far edge of Nicodemus, and here the houses are smaller and more run-down than on the main road. Most are little more than shacks and look a stiff breeze away from collapsing in on themselves.

"This is where the white folks from Summerland stay," Sue says, glancing at the open doorway of a house. A pale face stares back at us from the gloom. "Frankly, I ain't quite sure how you and Jane survived there."

"It was a trial," I murmur. This part of town makes me uneasy. We quicken our pace.

Sue suddenly halts, and I skid, barely avoiding running into her back. She ducks behind the side of a stable, pulling me along as well. Just up ahead, a line of white folks shout angrily, their words unintelligible as they talk over one another. Miss Duncan strides up to them.

"Folks, what seems to be the problem?" she asks, her voice carrying clearly through the day to where Sue and I crouch in the shadow cast by the stable.

A scrawny white woman in a blue bonnet steps forward. "That scientist never showed to give those injections the mayor promised, so we came to find him. But he said he doesn't have any more!"

"You gave them to the Negroes, now you need to give them to us!" yells a short white man. A chorus of people shout agreement.

Miss Duncan holds her hands up for calm, just as I have seen her do a thousand times. "Folks, settle down. I am sure there will be enough serum for everyone. Let me go in and speak with Mr. Carr and see what seems to be the problem."

She pushes past the crowd of people, and they part like the Red Sea. Miss Duncan raps on the door of the building. A very harried-looking Gideon opens it just enough to let her inside.

"If the colored folks hadn't gotten stuck none of them would want to, either," Sue says, her tone mild.

"Did you get an injection?" I ask.

Sue snickers. "I'll take my chances with the dead."

I nod in agreement. I like my chances with a pair of Mollies a great deal better.

Miss Duncan reappears and gives everyone a calm smile. "Thank you so much for your patience, and I have excellent news. Mr. Carr is distilling a new batch of serum as we speak. He assures me that it will be available after supper, so please feel free to come back then and he will see you."

This settles the crowd somewhat, and people begin to wander off. Sue gestures for me to follow her. "Stay low, we don't want Miss Duncan to know we were spying on her."

"Sue, what are you not telling me?" I ask, once we are out of earshot. We head back toward the center of town to Gideon's house. I still need to grab my Mollies, after all.

She glances at me askance. "What do you mean?"

"Miss Duncan. Why did you not want her to see us?"

Sue huffs out a breath and stops in a patch of shade, wiping her sleeve across the sweat glistening on her dark brow. She leans against the side of the building and gives me a direct look. "I don't trust her. She's been strange ever since Baltimore fell. Furtive, maybe a tad bit guilt-stricken. And not just on account of her getting romantic with Redfern. The way the school fell, well, it was odd. I woke to screams and the dead were already inside the walls. You know how things work, it never should have gone that way."

"You think Miss Duncan fell asleep on her watch?"

Sue nods. "I think she would've left us all to die if she hadn't needed help clearing out the dead. But she knew it was too much for her, so she came back to find us. I think all this time Miss Duncan ain't been any better than the rest of them, just a bit nicer about hating us."

I blink, a sensation like falling coming over me. "Not Miss Duncan, Sue. She would not have done that." I have to believe there is at least one person in the world who gives a fig about me. Miss Duncan has always been kind and fair.

"Why not? Summerland was the plan for all of us all along, you and Jane just got an early introduction. You think Miss Duncan somehow was the only one at Miss Preston's who didn't know?"

I shake my head. "Just considering it is terrible."

"Maybe. But you know firsthand that we weren't nothing but lambs to be sent to the slaughter. Just because they dressed us nice doesn't change anything," Sue says sadly. "Anyway, I'm going to find a spot to hide out until this heat passes. Come find me after supper, we'll take a turn up on the wall and see about that horde."

I nod, and Sue goes about her business, wending her way back through town. My heart is heavy as I enter Gideon's house, the possibility of Miss Duncan's duplicitous nature a weighty matter, and sprawled on the chaise like she owns the place is Jane McKeene.

"Hey there," she says, grinning from ear to ear. "What's a girl got to do to get a bath around here?"

My heart leaps with gladness to see her on the right side of iron bars. I should be happy that she is free, and I am. But I am also sorely vexed that the last time I saw her she treated me abysmally.

Even though I would like nothing more than to share with Jane the things I have learned over the past couple of days, to plot and plan like we did in Summerland, I give her the cut direct and make my way to my pantry to spend some time by myself, mulling over the events of the day.

Nothing emboldens sin so much as mercy.

—Shakespeare, Timon of Athens

— J A N E —

Chapter 19
In Which I Get the Lay of the Land

I stretch languidly as I wake, enjoying my first day of freedom in a very, very long time.

Well, free from jail, anyway. There's still the horde outside the Nicodemus gates, biding their time and waiting to get in.

After Sheriff Redfern set me free I was at a bit of a loss as to where to go. My acquaintances from the Summerland patrols were staying in a barn just outside the middle of town, and Miss Preston's girls and the girls from Landishire Academy weren't far off from there. But the Duchess and her girls were staying with Gideon, and even though I was vexed with the scientist for selling the town the scientific snake oil I figured this last option was the best one. After all, I wasn't quite sure whether the fine white folks from Summerland would try lynching me again. I figured the last place they'd look for me would be in the house of the son of Abraham Carr.

Katherine came in a short while after my arrival, still quite a bit cross with me, but I had yet to see anyone else. The Duchess, Sallie, and Nessie all seemed to have disappeared. Even little Thomas was gone. Lily skulked past at one point, her glare nearly enough to set my clothes aflame, but there was no point in poking that hornet's nest just yet. I'd talk to her eventually, but not when feelings were so raw.

I know when to leave well enough alone, even if it might not always seem like it.

I was most disappointed to realize Gideon was nowhere to be found. Even after our last conversation there was still a small part of me that thought I might be able to talk some sense into him. It didn't even matter if he'd stuck half of the town with his silly serum. If I could just convince him to talk to the mayor about an evacuation plan, we might yet stand a chance. There was a time when the self-important bastard had listened to me, and if I could get him to see the truth in things, well, perhaps we could save a whole bunch of lives.

Because despite all my conflicted feelings about him and his foolhardy belief in his own brillance, I still felt a little soft toward him. It ain't my fault. The heart wants what it wants, and I was still entirely too fascinated by Gideon Carr.

But Gideon was also out and about, so I rooted around in the kitchen until I found a hard crust of bread and a rind of cheese that was mostly fine, ate my makeshift dinner, and then fell asleep while debating whether to bathe.

Now sun streams through the windows, open to let in a bit of air, and the stink of the dead carries on the breeze. It's a grim reminder that my freedom is tenuous at best.

A rap comes at the door, and another. It sounds like an official sort of knock, so the last people I expect to see when I open the door are Sue and that strange girl, Callie.

"Jane!" Sue says, grabbing me in a one-armed hug so that she doesn't have to put down her scythe. "You stink."

"Well, there ain't exactly a lot of chances to bathe in jail. Callie, good to see you again."

The girl gives me a ghost of a smile. She looks like she's been crying.

"You all looking for Gideon?" I ask.

Sue shakes her head. "You and Katherine. Where's Miss Priss got to? We ain't got a lot of time."

"I am right here," Katherine says, sailing into the parlor. She ignores me, and I realize that I got some groveling ahead of me if I want to get back on her good side.

Callie greets her with a nod. "Sue and I will explain what's happening as we walk."

They set a good pace, and Katherine and I follow along

behind. I reach out for her wrist. "Kate, about yesterday—"

"I have no interest in talking to you, Jane."

I take a deep breath and let it out. "I'm trying to apologize, Kate."

"That ain't an apology," Sue calls from up ahead. "Try starting with 'I'm sorry, I was wrong.'"

I twist my lips. "Thanks for the help, Sue."

"Anytime."

I grab Katherine's wrist again, this time holding her until she stops walking. She gives me a scowl, and I give her my best smile. "Kate, I was wrong, and I'm sorry. I ain't got a lot of friends, and I said things yesterday that came from a place of hurt and fear and . . . I don't know, rage. Not anger at you, but at the world. Still, I ain't had any kind of right to point those feelings at you, and I'm sorry."

Katherine blinks once and again, and then she nods. "That will do, Jane. Thank you. But I am still quite hurt, and you are going to live with that for now."

I sigh as she takes back her hand. "Don't stay mad at me too long. We got dead to fight, and you know how aggravation makes you sloppy."

Her lips nearly quirk into a smile, but she manages to subdue it. Still, it tells me things will be fine between us. Eventually.

We run to catch up with Sue and Callie up ahead; by the time we do, they've reached a group of Negroes I quickly recognize as the Summerland patrols. They greet me heartily, and I let myself be welcomed with a wide grin while Katherine stands a little ways back from the group.

"Good to see you free," Ida says after everyone else has acknowledged me.

"Good to see you still in one piece. How's that cavalry sword treating you?" I ask, pointing to the blade by her side.

"Well enough, but it might not matter in a bit," she says, gesturing behind her. She leads us down a path that bends behind the last building before the wall.

And I cannot help but swear at the sight before me.

Someone has destroyed the back wall of Nicodemus, pulling down the rear gate and leaving the town exposed to any dead that might find their way to the rear of the town. The wood bears the markings of an ax, ruling out the dead, and the work looks hastily done. I stare at the wide opening to the rest of the prairie. I got a strong urge to run through and keep going, but I know better than to think that's any kind of option. I've got no supplies and no clue where to even go.

"Who could've done this?" I wonder aloud, not actually expecting an answer.

"No clue," Ida says, spitting as she studies the damage. "But even if we were to try and plug that hole up there ain't no way it would keep the dead out."

"Nicodemus is finished," Callie whispers. She's trembling something fierce. For the rest of us this is just another rest stop on a never-ending road to nowhere. But for her, this dusty town is home.

"It could not have been just one person," Katherine murmurs. "Dismantling such a large gate would take many hands, especially if it were done quickly."

The rail gun fires up, as if to remind us just what is at stake. The dead will find a way into Nicodemus, and it's almost like someone has purposefully invited them in.

It's only our good fortune that has kept the horde from surrounding the town up to now, but it seems like we might be running out of luck, and fast.

"There's a whole lot of boot prints. Did anyone see anything?" I ask.

Everyone shakes their head, and Ida stamps her foot. "Ain't no sense in worrying about who's responsible now. We need a plan."

"Ida's right," Sue says, resting the hilt of her scythe in the dirt and leaning against it, easylike. "There's always been something funny about this town, and I don't like it one bit. I think we get what we can and skedaddle."

"We have to tell Miss Duncan," I say, surveying the damage. There are wagon tracks, and I crouch down to inspect them. "And we have to warn the folks that live here. They need to know their flank is compromised." My pronouncement sits uneasy with folks, and I hold up a hand before any of them can argue. "I know that you want to take off, never look back. And I ain't got no kind of softness for this place, either. But this town was built by Negroes like you and me, and I think we owe it to our folks to at least give them a chance to evacuate with us."

"They won't listen," Ida says, expression hard.

"That doesn't mean we don't try," I say. It pains me to care, to want to save Nicodemus. Daniel Redfern's words come back to me, about heroes and minding one's own damn business. But a world where everyone just looks out for themselves? That ain't the kind of world I want to live in.

"Before we do we might want to puzzle out who could have been behind this destruction," Katherine asks, stepping forward and surveying the damage more closely.

"Maybe it was the Summerland folks?" I offer.

"None of the wagons are missing, though," Callie says. "I checked after I saw what had happened." I nod and return to my examination of the boot prints around the gate. I'm no tracker, but I can recognize a woman's shoe imprint. One woman and one man, it looks like. Curious.

"You should tell your daddy," Sue says, and Callie's face scrunches up in distaste. But she eventually nods and runs off.

While the others begin to talk amongst themselves, I motion to Katherine and Sue, and point to the prints. They both share a look, something I'm not privy to passing between them.

"Do you think—" Katherine begins.

"That it was Sheriff Redfern or Miss Duncan?" Sue says. Her expression is hard. "I don't know."

"What are you two about?" I ask.

"I am going to find Miss Duncan," Katherine says, ignoring me. "If it was not her, she can help us talk to the council.

And if it was . . ." She trails off with a sharp shake of her head and dashes off.

"Just what is going on?" I demand.

Sue waves me off. "Later, right now we need an exit plan."

I huff but say nothing, because she's right.

Sue walks over to Ida, drawing her attention away from her conversation with Lucas and another girl I don't know. Sue gestures at the gaping hole in the perimeter fence. "Do you think you and the rest of the patrols can guard the breach while we send up the alarm to folks?"

Ida nods. "We still got folks back on the other side of town as well. If a few folks will stand guard Lucas and I will go round the rest of the patrols up."

It's about as good a plan as any. "Grab whatever supplies you can find as well," I say as they run off.

Sue nods her agreement. "The quicker we quit this town, the better."

Sue and I wave to the girls guarding the breach and begin jogging toward town. I give Sue a little extra elbow room as she runs with her scythe. Her dark face is pensive. "This place has more plots than a graveyard."

I snort. "I never took you for the conspiracy type, Sue."

She shrugs. "You ain't the only one who's been through a trial these past few months."

I sigh. "True enough. Come on, let's try to save a damn town. Again."

The crown of the wise is their riches: but the foolishness of fools is folly.
—Proverbs 14:24

—KATHERINE—

Chapter 20
Notes on Foolhardy Endeavors

I hurry toward Gideon's house, mindful of both the smell and sound of the dead. Perhaps it is just my imaginings, but the horde sounds closer now that I know the rear of the settlement is vulnerable. The mystery of the destroyed gate picks at me, but not nearly as much as the rising panic over our newly discovered vulnerability. It steals my breath and sends my mind hurtling down path after path of imagined disaster. It is the worst sort of time to fall into one of my worrying fits, but the more I try to push away my questions and fears the greater they grow.

Could it really have been Miss Duncan behind the breach in the wall? What kind of person would so wantonly destroy that gate? And if it was her, what was her goal? At some point the horde will find their way to the opening. Is it possible that we are playing into the hands of some larger plot? I have a plethora of questions and not a single answer, and so I hurry until my breath comes in gasps.

Truthfully, I cannot imagine Miss Duncan destroying the gate, no matter what Sue says about our instructor's strange behavior. But I want more than just the Mollies strapped to my back when I confront her, just in case.

By the time I thunder up the steps to Gideon's house, the whalebone and cotton of my corset is not enough to tamp down the fear blooming in my chest. I enter the house without knocking and find Gideon in the sitting room, his head in his hands.

"Gideon. Is something amiss?" I ask.

He looks up at me with a stricken expression. "I've made a mistake. A grave one. And now, all of you are at risk."

I want to take the time to draw the story out of him, but there isn't time. "Do you know the rear gate is down?"

He nods. "Yes." His answer is short, and the tension that rides his frame leads me to believe that there is much he is not saying.

"Have you notified the council? What is being done about it?"

"As far as I know, nothing. The rest of the council doesn't know about it yet."

I blink, and my chest tightens with panic. "What? Why not?"

Gideon's gaze slides away from me, but the guilt is writ large in his expression. "I destroyed the rear gate, with some help. I . . . I was hoping that my mistake would take care of itself if provided with the proper opportunity."

I collapse into a nearby wing chair, my worry too heavy to keep me upright. "Gideon. I need you to explain to me what is happening. Slowly."

He takes a deep breath and lets it out. "The people from Summerland were willing to be vaccinated, but I was running low on my stores of the vaccine, so I decided to try a faster method of distilling the serum. And I made a miscalculation somehow . . ." He pauses, but it's not a sentence that needs finishing. After a moment, he continues. "It was one, then another, then . . . It was a bloodbath. I managed to escape, to bolt them into my lab. But there was no way those flimsy walls would hold them for long."

Gideon scrubs his hand across his face and I am rooted to my seat by my horror. He either does not notice or does not care, he is so fixated on the telling of his tale.

"What about the patrols from Summerland? And the girls

from Baltimore? Why did you not ask them to help you put the dead down?"

He shakes his head. "I asked Callie to help me, but we panicked . . . I . . . we panicked. The dead instinctually gather, and the rear gate is not all that far from my laboratory. I was hopeful that, given a path to the rest of the horde, they would head in that direction."

I struggle for breath and jump to my feet. "You've killed us," I say, everything slowing to the rhythmic beat of my heart. The panic has honed my rage, and I want to throttle Gideon. "You have killed us all."

He says nothing, and I take that to mean that our conversation is at an end. Any minute the dead will come a-knocking, whether it is the horde outside or the results of Gideon's failed experiment, set loose upon the town, and I have faith in neither man nor science to save what is left of us.

"Lily!" I shout, all manners forgotten, and she comes thundering down the stairs, fully dressed, a rifle clutched in her hand and her brother's knife strapped to her waist.

"Is it the dead?" she asks.

"Ain't it always?" I say, as Jane might. And with that, a new thought springs forth, stealing my breath anew: Jane and Sue have no idea what they are about to run up against. I swallow hard and wave Lily toward me. One thing at a time. "Come on, we have to go."

"I'm sorry," Gideon says. Anguish coarsens his voice, but

all I can think about is the danger he has put us in. The world is terrible enough without the addition of men like Gideon Carr.

I cannot bear to listen to him one more moment. "Is that what matters now? Your absolution?" He does not answer, so I yank a saddlebag off its hook next to the front door and run into the kitchen. I fill the bag with day-old biscuits and whatever other food I can grab. "Somehow, Mr. Carr, I do not think you being sorry negates the very real danger you have put us in."

I cannot even consider the lives he took at this moment. Those angry people, desperate to get their share of the vaccine. I had no love for the Summerland folks, the drovers and well-to-do white folks who let Jane and Ida and the rest of the patrols keep them safe for months, but they did not deserve to die. If I let myself envision their last moments, I will be swept away in a wave of despair and I do not have time for that right now. I can only focus on the one thing: getting provisions and getting the hell out of Nicodemus.

There is a canteen on the counter and I fill it quickly at the kitchen sink, pumping hard and fast. My anxiousness is a familiar friend, and this time it is most definitely warranted. The dead are going to quickly overwhelm the town, especially if they are already inside. Considering their numbers, fighting them would be like trying to dam up a waterfall with matchsticks.

And I, for one, am not fond of foolhardy endeavors.

Once I have grabbed what provisions I can along with the rifle sitting near the kitchen door, I throw the bags over my shoulder and turn to where Gideon still stands in the living room, hands fisted. His head is down, and my fear and anger are so great that I cannot help but volley one last parting shot.

"Mr. Carr, you may be a genius, but you have very little common sense. I hope you live long enough to regret this."

And then I grab Lily's hand and run out the door.

Thou know'st 'tis common; all that lives must die,
Passing through nature to eternity.
—*Shakespeare,* Hamlet

— J A N E —

Chapter 21
In Which I Err

No one in Nicodemus seems much inclined to save their own fool necks.

Sue and I are running from home to home, shouting about the coming horde, but no one answers or even peeks through the curtains to see what the fuss is about. We pause long enough to put our ear to a couple of doors, and it's clear that there are folks there. Just no one that wants to come out.

"Come on, enough of this," Sue says. "We can't save those who ain't interested."

It pains me to leave anyone behind, but Sue is right.

"Well, then I suppose there's nothing for it but to find the rest of our folks and get out of town." For a moment I wonder where the Duchess and her girls are. And little Thomas. Were they at Gideon's house? I hate leaving them behind, but it's only a matter of time before the streets are thick with the dead, and I have no intention of being in Nicodemus when that happens.

I follow Sue down the streets, each one dust and clapboard, and as we round a corner we're met by a horde of undead. They're only a few feet away, but they haven't noticed us quite yet, and we freeze.

"How did the dead get into town already?" I whisper.

"That is a mighty fine question," Sue says, readying her scythe. "It couldn't have been that breach in the wall. But more important, where do they think they're going?"

I slowly draw my sickles, but even the small motion is enough to attract the attention of one of the shamblers. She lumbers toward us at a run, more following, and I pause as I recognize a few of the faces. My heart thunders in my ears, and a keening that ain't the moans of the dead starts up in my brain, like the sound a wounded animal makes when it's just asking you to finish the job and put it out of its misery. It's a grief wail, and it takes me a long moment to realize the sound is actually coming from me.

Because running toward me, hair loose and drool streaming from her mouth, is the Duchess, with Sallie and Nessie not far behind.

Seeing them puts lead in my feet and drains the fight from my body. My hands fall to my side, and I take half a step back, not because I'm scared but because I am already too close to breaking to handle this. What is the point of fighting if everything you care about ends up devoured? For the first time, I can't see a way forward, and so I freeze.

It's a hesitation we can't afford.

"Jane!" Sue yells, bringing her scythe up and across.

There are too many for her, and I am half a step behind, moaning like a broken thing.

"What's the matter? What are you doing?" She falls back enough to give herself some more space to work with and grabs me by the front of my dress, shaking me. "You have to fight!"

The jostling is enough to break through a small bit of my pain. I blink away my tears and spring into action, but it's like I am a being wholly separate from my body. Part of my brain is trying to understand just how the soiled doves could have ended up turned, and part of me is raging against everything, all of it. What kind of miserable world is this when everyone you give a fig about can end up a monster?

I begin to move through the dead, ending their misery even if I know there will be no end to my own.

I tell myself I am doing the Duchess a favor as I separate

her head from her body, her fiery hair catching the sunlight as her head rolls off toward the boardwalk. I tell myself the same again as I put down Sallie, pretend I am sending her off to her eternal reward.

But when I get to Nessie, and as I part her head from her body, I don't see her. Instead, I see Jackson in those final few moments, the new day's sun catching his yellowed eyes, the boy I loved wrought into a monster right before me.

I hate this miserable world, every last thing about it, and I take that grief and pain and rage and direct it where it needs to go. I slash and tear and scream.

But if I am all frantic bladework, Sue is constant and rhythmic, and she begins to sing "My Faith Looks Up to Thee" as she works:

My faith looks up to Thee,
Thou Lamb of Calvary,
*   Savior Divine;*
Now hear me while I pray;
Take all my guilt away;
Oh, let me from this day
*   Be wholly Thine.*

Sue's voice is deep and even, and even though I don't much believe in salvation I find comfort in her singing.

My swings slow, become more deliberate. But as I kill the rest of the turned people of Summerland, working with Sue to put them down, all I see is Jackson, my guilt and regret a tangible thing, so that by the time we've finished I'm covered in shambler blood and tears.

As soon as the last body falls Sue rounds on me. "Jane, what is going on? You nearly left me out to get swarmed! You off your oats since coming west?"

I shake my head. "Sue . . . I'm tired. I'm tired of all this killing and mourning and hoping for safety that doesn't exist."

Sue raises her eyebrows at me. "Are you having another one of those existential crises you told me about?"

I laugh and use a cleanish part of my skirt to scrub at my face. "I can't believe you remember that."

Sue rests the hilt of her scythe on the body of a shambler and tilts her head at me. "Aw hell, Jane, I remember most of what you say, even if I know to only believe about half of it. But that doesn't tell me what's gotten into you."

I gesture weakly at the dead that litter the ground, cluttering up the dirt lane. "Those are my friends, some of them at least. I think that destroyed gate is the least of our worries, now."

Sue looks down at the bodies, her deep brown skin going to a shade closer to gray. "Jane, I ain't smart, but I've been here in town for a good while. There ain't no way a shambler got in here who could have turned this group of people, open gate or none. The rear gate ain't been down long enough."

I shake my head, trying to think of how this could have happened. How could so many people have turned shambler within the city walls? Especially without any kind of undead presence. It ain't a riddle I have an answer to.

A thin cry comes toward us, and we look back down the street, past the dead. My penny is an icy weight against my neck, and next to me Sue takes a sharp breath.

"Sweet Jesus," she says.

The thing about the dead is they can move fast when they're fresh turned, but only as fast as their legs could have carried them in life. And well, little ones don't move that fast. Especially if they ain't all that good on their feet.

Thomas, sweet Thomas, lurches toward us.

The dead ain't got any nurturing instincts, and they'd most likely left him behind once they'd scented a meal nearby. Now that the fighting has passed, it's easy to see the barn door hanging askew a little way down the lane. These dead folks must've been locked up in there, and there's only one way that could have happened.

Someone must have done the locking. And I don't need more than two guesses to figure who it could be.

Sue hasn't moved, and her scythe ain't any good at putting down one tiny little boy, anyway. So I walk forward to the thing that was once Thomas, swallow the scream that wants to well up, and end it.

"Told you this town was no good," comes a voice. "There's

too much scheming about for a body to live in peace."

I whip around at the interruption, but Sue is scowling into the distance, puzzling out something on her own and paying me no mind.

And so I turn my attention back to Jackson.

He stands a little ways down the lane with his arms crossed, dead scattered at his feet. It has occurred to me that I see him because I'm going mad, because there ain't no other explanation, but that doesn't mean he is full of nonsense.

Besides, I could use a little otherworldly guidance right about now.

"Those dead will be inside the town proper in about a quarter of an hour," my personal haint says, digging a cheroot out of a breast pocket and lighting it up. I swear I can almost smell the sweet smoke. "That Gideon fellow might have some interesting tricks for slowing down those dead, but ain't nothing stopping a horde that size. Nicodemus is finished. Don't forget you made a promise. Best keep it or I will harry you the rest of your days."

I squint as one of his vest buttons glints and blinds me for a moment, and the next I see, Jackson has dissipated into sunshine and dust.

"Jane! Sue!"

Katherine and Lily come thundering around the corner running at full tilt. They skid to a halt when they see the carnage around me, and Katherine raises her gloved hand to her mouth in horror. "Oh my God."

"God ain't got nothing to do with this," I say. "This is all the province of man."

"You do not know how right you are," Katherine says.

"What's that mean?"

"It was Gideon," Katherine says, expression somber. "He said there was a miscalculation."

"That's a hell of an error in arithmetic," Sue says, mumbling a quick prayer to herself.

"His serum? It turned them shambler?" Lily's eyes are wide, and a host of emotions flicker across her face before settling on disbelief.

"I knew it. I just *knew* it," I say, voice hard, stamping my foot. "That boy is a damned dangerous fool. And if I get the chance, I swear I'm going to make him pay for what he's done here."

"Later, Jane," Sue says. "Where's everyone? Ida? Callie? Lucas? We need to shake a leg, that horde ain't gonna wait forever."

As if to punctuate her words, a crashing bang comes from behind us. We all turn toward the front of town, when the banging comes again. Sue leads the way as we run toward the sound, and we skid to a stop in the middle of Nicodemus's main street as the front gate, our last, best defense against the dead, comes crashing down.

"Well, hell," Sue swears.

Katherine nods. She is calm, even as the dead begin to lurch into town. "Let us go find everyone."

Sue leads us, and we run down the last couple of empty streets to the livery where everyone has been staying. Lucas sees us first, jumping to his feet. "We ready?"

"More than ready, we got dead in the town. Time to shake a leg," I say.

Lucas nods. "We don't have much in the way of provisions, but we got canteens and a bit of jerky."

Ida walks up, rolling her shoulders as she tries to loosen up for a fight. "Then let's take what we've got and get moving. If we head east, we'll eventually hit the Mississippi. I figure that's as good a goal as any," Ida says.

"Rear gate is our best bet. Front gate is bound to be swamped," Sue says. Katherine and I nod in agreement.

"We got to get everyone out and in an organized way," I say, swinging my sickles and limbering up my wrists.

Katherine draws her Mollies and moves the blades in slow circles.

"Sue, we got enough Miss Preston's girls to do a decent wedge?" I ask.

Sue nods. "Yep," she says, hefting her scythe. "I'll take point."

Katherine takes a deep breath and forces a tremulous smile. "Well, then, let us lead the way."

The wedge is a triangular formation that's meant to punch

through large groups of the dead. It would be impossible to take out the entire horde, but it's a good protective strategy that will keep the kids and folks that don't know how to put down the dead a little safer as we make our way out of town.

"The Summerland patrols will take flank," Ida says, drawing her cavalry sword and lifting her chin. It's a dangerous role, and from their grim expressions, they know what they'll be up against. But there is confidence there as well. They have real weapons now, and their audacity speaks not to foolishness or pride, but to an understanding of their own worth. It's a fine change. I nod at them so they know that I see them, even if it ain't something that I have time to say out loud.

"Let's go, then," I say, feeling heavy with dread at trying to flee yet another horde.

At some point this has to get easier.

We move out quickly. It doesn't take long before we hear the sounds of more dead. Their moans echo through the town. It's a maddening chorus, the breathy rise and fall of it, and it's curious to hear only the dead and no sounds from the living, no screams of terror or shouts for help. It's only half of a two-part harmony of terror, and hearing the dead alone raises goose bumps on my arms and quickens our feet.

The people of Nicodemus still haven't left their houses. I've seen this nonsense before. The fools are hoping to ride out the storm.

We move down the dusty street, careful and alert, Sue

having taken point, her scythe at the ready. I am surrounded on either side by Miss Preston's girls, and behind me, Lily prays in a low voice.

It doesn't take long to find the dead. They clog the wide avenue, pouring in through the main gate like water through a busted damn. The walls to either side of the opening sway under the press of the dead on the other side, and, as we arrive, the horde begins to reach the houses closest to the wall. Now we hear the familiar duet, screams of fear and surprise coming from several of the houses as the dead push their way in, then, too late, the sound of gunshots.

"We need to run," Sue says. "Forget the wedge. If the shamblers are all concentrated on the southern end of town, we can make for the northern gate, but we have to move quickly."

"To the northern gate," Katherine says, adjusting her grip on her swords. I glance over my shoulder and give Lily a reassuring smile, even though she doesn't return it. But that's no bother. The only thing that matters is that she stays safe. I don't aim to break that promise.

Sue leads our group through the town. I follow, Katherine and Lily hot on my heels, Ida and the Summerland patrols guarding our rear. Sue was right; the further we travel from the main gate, the easier the trek becomes.

Ida falls into step next to me, cavalry sword glinting in the sunlight as we run in the opposite direction of the breaking

IN THE GARDEN OF GOOD AND EVIL

horde. "That gate might be open, but we've still got an electric fence and bobbed wire beyond that," she says. "Any ideas on how to get through?"

"If the dead got through the electric fence in the front, then the circuit is broken. As for the bobbed wire, well, I reckon we have a lot of motivation to get through," I say. Ida snorts in amusement.

We're moving quickly, a moderate pace that can accommodate everyone, when a shout goes up.

"They're coming!" yells a voice from the rear of our group.

"Move!" comes another.

"We gotta run faster, Sue!" I scream.

My penny goes icy.

And then we round the corner of a house to where the northern gate is—and run right into a pack of shamblers.

It takes only a heartbeat to see what happened. Our friends guarding the gap lost their nerve and broke ranks, skedaddling out onto the prairie, leaving the breach open. They didn't get far. The horde must have sensed them leaving and, within the barriers of the exterior fences, swung around the city wall, the edges of the pack catching the folks fleeing out ahead of us. Several prone forms lie just beyond the gate, shamblers upon them. The wet sounds of feasting turn my stomach.

But not only did their cowardice spell their doom, it's about to spell ours as well. A dozen or so dead meander in the shadow of the log fence. Lily screams and raises her rifle, getting off a single wild shot.

It's a lucky thing the girl doesn't shoot anyone in the back.

Our formation goes to hell, and we're stuck in the midst of a proper melee, everyone spreading out to give themselves space to work. Katherine's swords flash, but I don't have enough room for my sickle swings. I push Lily behind me, and I get my left sickle up just in time to put down a tall male wearing Union blue. But swinging my right sickle would mean hitting Ida or Katherine, and I can't do that. There's nowhere to run.

And the dead are lunging right for me.

The world slows. The shambler in front of me was once a young white woman, blond hair, milky eyes. I have just enough time to admire her dress—a blue brocade frock that belongs in a ballroom. She throws her entire body at me, and I throw up my forearm to catch her throat.

But I am too slow, and my penny is ice-cold, and I miss her throat.

I miss.

But she does not.

I scream as her teeth sink into my forearm, but I don't hesitate. I push her backward, using her body to block the rest of the oncoming dead and to give Katherine and the rest of the girls behind me space to fight. The girl doesn't let go easily, and it's only my boot in the shambler's midsection that gets her off me, a fair chunk of my forearm going with her.

Blood sprays across the remaining dead, but I'm swinging and swearing, the sounds of the girls from Miss Preston's and the Summerland patrols matching my own.

We fight like our lives depend on it, even though I know, my life's blood falling into that Kansas dust, that mine is over.

Soon there's just the gate, littered with the remains of harvested shamblers.

The world is quiet, everything fading away, blood thrumming in my ears. I can feel the gazes as they land on me, the soft inhalations as people realize what the blood steadily leaking down my arm means.

"Jane," Katherine says, taking a step toward me.

I have no words for her. I have no words for anyone. But I lock eyes with Sue, and she understands.

"Come on!" she says, pointing out the gate to freedom. "Jane will cover the rear, but we need to move, now!"

Ida and Lucas and Lily are frozen, and everyone else hesitates as well, but only for a moment. They know that I'm done for, and ain't no amount of sentimentality is going to change my fate. They all move past me, not looking back, and I'm glad for it.

But Katherine doesn't budge.

"You need to go," I tell her. I hate the way my voice shakes, and how my head feels too light by half. Tears burn hot trails down my cheeks, but I ignore them.

"You are going to bleed out if you do not see to that arm," she says, voice as cool and calm as a lake on a hot summer's day. She rips off one more strip of her dress and uses it to bind my arm tightly. My left hand tingles, my fingers going numb. For some reason, that makes me laugh.

Katherine quirks an eyebrow at me. She is still so composed, so controlled, as always.

"It doesn't hurt," I say.

"Jane—" Her voice cracks, and her eyes well with tears. She clears her throat to speak, but before she does I point toward the prairie with my sickle.

"I'm bit, Kate. Get the rest of Miss Preston's girls on a line and escape while you can." My heartbeat echoes in my head, and I wonder how long I'll have until I start to turn. Ten minutes? Thirty? It doesn't matter. It ain't enough.

"I'm not going," Katherine says. "I'll stay here with you."

"Y'all need to keep moving. I'm going to hold them off as long as I can. Here," I reach under my shirt and pull off my penny, the leather breaking free easily. "Take this."

Katherine shakes her head but holds out her hand, and I drop the luck charm in it. Tears fall down her face now.

More shamblers have met the group just outside the gate, and a little ways away Sue and Ida hack at the dead, trying to clear a way for everyone.

"I'm going to wait with you, give you a proper end, Jane," Katherine says, setting her jaw like she does when she gets it in her head about the right way to do a thing.

"No. You do that and you're going to need last rites right

along with me. Besides, who is going to look after Lily?"

Katherine looks over to where the girl cowers, eyes wide as the dead close in. Lily won't make it on her own, and there's no one I trust more than Katherine to keep her safe. Either way, we're wasting valuable time, and they need to get out of Nicodemus while that's still a possibility.

"Don't be sad, Kate. Jackson told me that life starts off bloody and ends that way, and I've always believed him. I guess I'll get to see him again, even sooner than I expected. Keep Lily safe. Maybe go home, see your momma. Have a good, long life, do all the things you dream of." Emotion makes my words stick in my throat, and I cough to force them out past the lump of everything I want to say to her. "And, Katherine—"

Her eyes widen at me and I pull her in for a quick hug, and these last words I say near her ear so no one else can steal the moment from us.

"Thank you for being my friend."

I let her go. She is speechless; tears now fall unchecked down her cheeks, and it's too much for me to bear. I give her a quick grin, one more memory for her to carry with her, and then I dash off back the way we came.

If I'm going to die, I'm going to do it fighting.

My left hand is completely useless, quickly going to pot as the loss of blood and the shambler's bite work against me. I barely notice when my sickle falls out of my hand. I can't feel anything down my whole left side of my body, not even the chills. It's just a slow-spreading numbness, and I ignore it and turn my attention to the dead.

They seem to be moving slower. They've gathered after eating their way through the houses, and there are too many of them now for them to run much, so they just do their slow stride down the dusty lane. They don't seem to care much about me, but I care a whole lot about them.

Putting down the dead with a single sickle ain't easy, but I keep swinging, taking down as many as I can, jamming them up so they can't go loping after Katherine and the rest of the colored folks fleeing the town. It ain't as much as I want to give. But I can only pray it's enough.

Too soon the shakes are on me, and I drop my remaining sickle. My body is wracked with chills, and it's hard to think about any one thing. I can feel my mind slipping away, turning to something else.

Something hungry.

I have a memory of Jackson, the way he lunged at me, and I imagine shambler-me doing the same thing to Ida, or Sue, or Katherine, stealing away their life, their freedom, everything they've fought so hard to keep.

I have to make sure I can't do that.

The sheriff's office ain't too far from where I am, and I stumble toward it, pushing the dead out of the way. They ain't interested in me at all, and I wonder if I smell like spoiled meat to them. I'm already half shambler, and they know it, even if my heart doesn't.

I manage to let myself into the office and stumble into my old cell. The room is dark and empty. I shut the bars behind me, but anything more than that is beyond my abilities. The shambler bite steals my strength and my sense. I fall to the floor, hot and cold and disconnected, not unlike the time Jackson and I got drunk on rum in the woods behind Miss Preston's, stupid and vulnerable, without the sense the good Lord gave a house cat.

Thinking of Jackson brings the tears, and I begin to cry. I lie on the floor of the cell and sob in mourning of my own life, all the things I'll never get to do, all the places I'll never get to see. Not that there's any place in particular I want to be; but lying on a dirty wooden floor, arm bleeding and slowly dying, ain't it.

I roll onto my back, look at the ceiling. I manage to cross my arms over my chest and I hug myself as tears leak down into my ears.

Alone and heartbroken, I die.

And that is the end of Jane McKeene.

But his flesh upon him shall have pain, and his soul within him shall mourn.

—Job 14:22

— KATHERINE —

Chapter 22
Notes on a Heartbreak

Jane disappears into the mass of restless dead overrunning the town, and I dash my tears and whirl toward the northern gate.

There will be time to mourn later.

Sue and Ida slash through the undead in tandem, the two of them a lethal combination. They move like they have fought together for years, and a sharp stab of grief nearly doubles me over. How am I supposed to navigate this mess without Jane? And how have I come to rely on her so completely in such a short span of time?

The dead press in on all sides, and for a moment I fear we will be buried, until Sue pushes clear of the wall and we are on the other side, out of Nicodemus. After clambering carefully over the dead electric and barbed wire fences, there is nothing but plain before us.

"Let's move!" Ida yells, and everyone takes off, running as hard and fast as they are able. I holster my swords and follow, staying close to Lily, who has started crying quietly, the dead no doubt a reminder of the terrible end at their last visit. Running like this is not sustainable, especially in a too tight corset, but at this moment it is our best bet. We have to put distance between us and the horde, and while it is not very Christian of me, I very selfishly hope that they find enough to occupy them in Nicodemus that we have ample time to escape.

I hope they find Gideon Carr and chew his face off.

We have gone about a half mile across ground uneven with holes and rocks before we find the road. We all come to a disorganized stop, some folks bending over and retching from the exertion, others just panting heavily. My vision swims with black spots, and for a moment I fear I will faint.

But then Sue is behind me, unbuttoning my dress and loosening my stays, all the while muttering at me, "You and this corset are a recipe for disaster."

I take a deep breath, and Sue laces me back up, looser this time.

"Thank you," I gasp.

"Sit. Breathe," Sue says.

I take a few moments, and while my breathing is nowhere near regular, it is better than it was. I have been away from Miss Preston's long enough that I fear I am no longer in top form, and I make a note to spend some time each morning running through my drills. Maybe I can talk Jane into sparring with me—

The thought dies a sudden death, and fresh tears prick my eyes. No, not Jane. Not anymore.

I shake my head, and the tears fall unchecked once more. "Oh, Sue! I should have kept her safe. I should have—"

I let myself fall into my grief, and as I sob Sue wraps me into a hug with her strong arms.

"Jane wouldn't want us to cry," she says, even though her own voice is froggy with emotion. "She'd want us to keep going. She'd tell us some half-true story about Rose Hill Plantation and then berate us for wasting time." She puts her hand on her hip and cocks her head in a familiar way. "Y'all better stop being maudlin and get moving 'fore that pack of shamblers catch up and make you supper."

I laugh and pull back, swiping at my cheeks. "That is an excellent Jane."

Sue shrugs, wiping away her own tears. "I've had some practice."

When I am feeling a mite bit better, we go to find the rest of what I have come to think of as our New Negro Council. Ida and Lucas have been watching us, and Ida starts speaking as soon as we walk up.

"I'm sorry about Jane, but Sue is right. And we need to figure out just what to do about *that*." Ida points to the road.

Heading toward us is something large enough to kick up a whole mess of dust. It is moving too fast to be a horde. A quick look around shows that there is nowhere to hide from the thing bearing down on us, so I square my shoulders and adjust my bonnet. "Please see that everyone gets off the road, and tell them not to say a word. I will handle this."

Ida and Lucas nod, waving everyone back with quick instructions. Sue gives me a bit of side-eye, her face scrunched up in a puzzled expression. "What are you about, Miss Priss?"

"I have spent the past few months pretending to be someone I am not, and I have a feeling those skills might come in handy once again. Oh, and if anyone asks, you are my Attendant."

Sue's eyes go wide, and then she nods. "I don't much like where this is going, but it's a Jane-quality plan."

This time, the mention of her name fills me with pride. I cock an eyebrow at her. "Where do you think I got it from?"

The contraption speeding down the road gets nearer, and louder. Soon, we can see that it's a pony, larger than any I've ever seen before, with a shambler catcher on the front and great billows of black smoke filtering out of the chimney as it speeds along the road. It nearly draws even with us before it comes to a halt, the hiss of steam shattering the relative peace of the landscape.

A man leans out of the driver's compartment, waving happily. His skin is deeply tanned, and I cannot quite tell whether he is a white man or some other pedigree entirely. The cars he hauls behind him are empty, as if he is on his way to make a pickup. But where on earth could he be going?

His smile is genuine as he takes in the motley crew standing on either side of the road. "Hello there, fellow travelers. Might you be able to tell me what territory this is?" His English is slightly accented, but I cannot tell what his original language might be. It sounds as though it could be French, but what could an Acadian be doing this far west?

I give him a polite smile and nod. "This is Kansas, but if you are heading west, I fear you might want to rethink your plans. My household and I have just fled the settlement of Summerland due to it being overrun by an undead horde, and have been imperiled ever since." The insinuation is clear, and he nods at the group standing around, mouths shut and eyes hooded with distrust. As much as I hate pretending to own other human beings, all of us are smart enough to know that danger comes from many directions, and the dead are but one. Slavers still work these uncivilized lands and sometimes the appearance of a certain kind of order is enough to keep people from resorting to their baser instincts.

"Well, miss, you're in luck, because I was just on my way to find y'all."

I pause, and the air grows thick. "I am sorry, sir, but whatever do you mean?"

"I'm from Fort Riley, and a few days ago we received an S-O-S out of Summerland. Would've been here faster, but I ran out of fuel. And, well, buffalo chips are hard to come by now that the dead have taken to harrying the herds."

A sense of relief, strong and profound, washes over me. My legs are nearly weak with it. Finally, for once, something has gone in my favor. "Good sir, I do believe you have saved us."

The man grins, and his low chuckle is anything but reassuring. "You should wait until you see Fort Riley before you say that. Why don't you have your people climb aboard while I navigate a path to turn this thing around?"

I nod and turn to Sue. "Please get everyone on the . . . well, I suppose it is a pony."

She moves off and pretends to start bossing folks around, and the man climbs down from the driver's car and comes to stand next to me.

"Are all these people yours?" he asks, his tone conversational. But there's something in his eyes that makes me wary, and I lift my chin, haughty as I answer.

"They are indeed. I had a plantation in the east. Kentucky. Rose Hill Plantation, it was called. Perhaps you have heard of it?"

He shakes his head. "No, I haven't. What brought you out west?"

"The dead," I say, sighing. "Always the dead. Why, this frontier is such a mean place that we have been left to travel on foot. And I have not had a new dress in ages." I say pouring on my accent, sweet as a mint julep. "I had a mind to find a new homestead out here on the plains, but as you can see the pickings are slim."

The man nods, but it is clear from the shrewd look in his eye he is considering everything I say. "Pardon my forwardness, but I don't see a ring on your finger."

"That is because I am a widow," I say, quickly. "My husband died on the trek west. My girl Sue minds me."

"If you have an Attendant, why carry swords? Seems to me that a lady such as yourself shouldn't have such a need for so base an occupation."

My stomach drops as I realize my mistake, but instead of getting defensive I look down my nose at the man, crossing my arms. "Sir, I beg your pardon for being so forthright, but just how long have you been out here on the frontier?"

The man begins to laugh. "Not long enough, apparently. Only a few weeks. I came north with a group from Nawlins, looking for a new life."

I purse my lips. "Well, it has evidently been long enough that you have forgotten your manners."

The man's face reddens. "Mighty sorry to overstep, miss, the swords just look, um, well used."

"You, sir, are going to find that even a maiden must protect herself out here. Between the dead and the elements, survival is only of the fittest."

The man does not say anything, but there is a sly look in his eyes that I do not care for. "Captain Shaw is just going to *adore* you."

And with that, I am less certain of our rescue.

A good leg will fall; a straight back will stoop;
a black beard will turn white; a curl'd pate will grow bald;
a fair face will wither; a full eye will wax hollow:
but a good heart, Kate, is the sun and the moon;
or, rather, the sun, and not the moon,—for it shines bright,
and never changes, but keeps his course truly.
—Shakespeare, Henry V

— J A N E —

Chapter 23
In Which I Am Saved

A headache is the first thing I know. It pounds through my temples, rhythmic and heavy, like a marching band with nothing but a drumline. I breathe through the pain, trying to open my eyes, half of me just wanting to drift back to sleep, forget the whole damn consciousness thing.

It's the sound of the dead that pulls me from my stupor.

I force my eyes open. Sunshine pours through a nearby open window, bright and harsh. It takes me a moment to realize I'm inside a house, on a settee. It ain't nowhere I recognize at first, and I sit up in a blind panic, immediately regretting the move. My head swims, and I fall back with a groan. My mouth is hot cottony dryness and everything aches.

"I wouldn't try moving around too much just yet. You've got a fever, and you're going to need at least a few days to adjust."

The voice is familiar, but it ain't until I struggle into a sitting position that I realize who sits in the nearby wing chair. Gideon's hands are behind his head, and his long legs are crossed at the ankle. His spectacles sit on a nearby end table and I get the impression that he was dozing in the chair, watching over me, waiting for me to wake. The notion makes me more than a little uncomfortable.

"Is this hell?" I ask, my throat scratchy and the words hoarse.

Gideon laughs, the sound bitter. He's aged since I saw him last. There are dark circles under his eyes, deep lines bracketing his mouth. "No, it's Nicodemus."

I look around a bit more slowly, and this time I recognize the furnishings of Gideon's house, even if my presence in the place doesn't make a damn lick of sense.

"But . . . I got bit." My brain is slow, and I'm trying to piece together what happened. I remember collapsing on the floor of the cell in the sheriff's office, staring up at the ceiling as the bite overtook me. And then I remember—

Nothing.

"I got bit," I say again, and Gideon smiles, the expression indulgent.

"I know, Jane," he says. His tone is teasing and warm. "But you survived. Did I not tell you? My vaccine works."

"Try telling that to the Summerland folks." I might be half dead, but I ain't about to pretend that I don't see Gideon for who he is. And the fact that I'm sitting here with him in a room that is well appointed while the dead meander outside is setting off every alarm bell I have. There is something very wrong with every damned thing about this situation, and I for one ain't about to pretend otherwise.

The mirth drains away from his face. "That was a . . . mistake."

"No, it was a *choice*, Gideon. You took advantage of their fear, all for your damn experiment—" I start to heave, and Gideon springs up, dropping a bucket down next to me. I retch, a disgusting greenish black concoction that doesn't look like any vomit I've ever seen before. In that moment, I think I'd rather be dead.

Bright side: at least my mouth ain't dry anymore.

Once I've finished, Gideon says, "You're going to feel terrible for the next few days as the infection works its way through your body." He carries the bucket into another room and comes back with a cup of water. I have never seen a more delicious offering. I'm Eve and the cup is her cursed apple and I make the mistake of reaching for it with my left hand. Pain explodes up and down the limb, and I discover that the stink of putrefaction ain't just coming in the window from outside. It's coming from under the makeshift bandage around my forearm.

I drop my arm, unbalancing myself and nearly falling off the settee. Gideon catches me, gently setting me upright, and tears spring to my eyes, the combination of his attention and the agony of my arm loosening my hold on my emotions.

"Easy, there. Easy. You're alive, but just barely. You're going to need to rest and regain your strength. Trust me, it's going to be a while before you go overthrowing any more frontier regimes." He says it like all of this is a lark, a poker game and he's just pulled four aces.

"Why are you in such a good mood?" I grumble, reaching for the water with my right hand, my good hand, and downing it so fast that it nearly comes back up.

He just smiles as he takes the cup and goes back to the kitchen to refill it. I lean against the back of the settee and focus on breathing. Turns out that when you're mostly dead, doing any sort of living is harder than getting a shambler to waltz.

I turn my head to the side and look out the windows. The dead meander through the streets, walking in slow patterns that mean nothing to me. But what is of notice is that not a single one seems inclined to come through the window and try to take a nibble out of us.

Gideon returns and hands me the cup of water. I sip it this time and tilt my head toward the window, where dead seem completely unconcerned with us. "What's that about?"

He takes his seat once more and puts his spectacles on. It's like those glasses change him somehow. The mirth drains away and he sits a bit straighter, his brows knitting together as he speaks. "The antibodies the vaccine has helped to create in your blood are now fighting off the infection, and one of the side effects of that process, I've discovered, is that the dead are no longer a threat. Something about it suppresses the feeding instinct. I haven't had the time or opportunity to parse out why yet. Basically, they see you as one of them. Well, us. They see us as one of them. Or, two of them?"

I remember his limp, the brace he sometimes wears. "You got bit."

He nods. "A year ago, back in Baltimore. I was assisting Professor Ghering in the lab—I had been experimenting with my own variations on his serum, and I made a fatal error. I was bitten . . . but instead of dying, I survived. I went through much of the same suffering you went through, and when it was over, I had a terrible scar—and an immunity to the dead."

I laugh low, the sound bitter. "All this time they've been saying that Negroes are immune to the bite of the shambler, and here it was that white folks held the key to surviving the bite." A thought passes through my mind and I look up. "Unless you're really a Negro?"

The question causes Gideon to stiffen. He adjusts his glasses, taking them off again and cleaning them before resettling them on his face. His hair is long enough now that his curls fall into his eyes, and he pushes them back impatiently. "I am not. But it wouldn't matter. Human anatomy is identical across color lines."

"Uh-huh." I'm still thinking about all the colored folks who have had their lives stripped away from them for a lie told to keep certain folks safe. Meanwhile, Gideon and his like are traipsing around the country without a care in the world, turning people left and right in pursuit of science. "Is this why you bolted in Summerland? And why you kept to the back of the fight when we had to take on the dead?"

Gideon nods. "I think it might also be why the dead's behavior changed that night of the skirmish. Something about my presence maybe muted the feeding response. I haven't quite puzzled out the limits of this, yet."

I finish my water, and gesture toward the window with my empty glass. "I don't suppose any of your other test subjects survived?"

He face goes blank, his expression flat. "You were the only person I found that wasn't dead or turned."

I laugh, the sound harsh and bitter. "So you murdered an entire town as an experiment."

His expression is stricken. "My vaccine works, though."

"On me!" I yell, leaning forward and nearly falling off the settee again. "Who else, Gideon? Who else?"

He bites his lip and shakes his head. "I had tried to tweak the formula to potentially lessen the aftereffects of a bite. The ones you're experiencing now. But the process is delicate, and when I had to make a new batch in haste . . . Something must have gone wrong. As I said, it was a mistake."

"You turned the folks from Summerland! The Duchess! And poor, poor Thomas!" My voice cracks as I remember his small frame, shuffling down the street, growling like an animal. "How is any of this worth whatever it is you're after?"

"It will be," he says, eyes wide. "Trust me on this. It will."

I want to believe him, to fall into whatever madness sweeps him along, but I can't. I'm tired of watching folks die.

"Maybe the damn thing just doesn't work, have you considered that? Perhaps you and me are a goddamn fluke, immune on our own, and it has nothing to do with your serum." Yelling feels good despite my pounding head and all over malaise, so I keep at it. "You didn't listen to me or anyone else, you risked the lives of every person in this town and everyone who managed to survive Summerland on a hunch! Because you were so certain that you were right even though you didn't have a lick of solid evidence to prove your point. I ain't a scientist, but even I know that one success does not prove a hypothesis true!"

My outburst leaves me retching once again, and Gideon gets the bucket, just fast enough at sliding it under me that I don't vomit all over my boots. He steadies me while I empty my stomach, holding my braids back out of the way until I'm finished. It might be a tender moment if I weren't so furious.

I fall backward, and tears leak out of my eyes. Gideon puts the bucket away and brings me another cup of water, one which I nurse while he begins to pace, his long legs taking him back and forth across the small room. Three steps left, and then back, and then left again. Watching him gives me something to focus on besides my roiling emotions and traitorous flesh. I'm so mad, so broken inside that I can't even speak anymore. It's like someone took out all the things that made me Jane—all the good parts, and the bad—leaving nothing but rusty razor blades in their place. And everyone I've ever cared about is either dead or in the wind. If they even made it out of Nicodemus alive. And if they did, what then? I remember how that horde harried us all the way from Summerland, and we'd had a wagon to make the going faster. There's little chance that they could outrun that horde on the open plain, and that thought makes me wish I had truly died. Maybe this is what despair feels like, a slow descent into an infinite abyss.

I've failed everyone.

"You're right," Gideon says, and my head snaps up, terrified that he can now add mind reading to his list of talents. But he wasn't responding to my dark thoughts. He hasn't stopped pacing, and his hands gesture wildly as he speaks. "I did jeopardize this town based on faulty science. I should've been more precise. I have to control for strength, maybe elapsed exposure time."

"Good on you," I say, voice clogged with tears. "You learned a damned lesson. I'm sure the fine, dead folks of Nicodemus would be thrilled to know that their town was not destroyed for nothing. Maybe we can have a party, invite the dead folks from Summerland as well. It'll be a potluck. Come one, come all, to the first annual celebration in honor of Gideon Carr's experiment yielding a useful result! It'll be marvelous."

The more I talk the angrier I get, and my hands itch for a revolver, or even a sharp rock to bash his head in. I grip the cup in my hand. It's tin and will no doubt crumple on such a hard head, but I'm willing to give it a try.

Gideon spins on his heel and comes toward me in a single explosive movement and I draw back, an instinct that brings back memories of my violent father, Major McKeene. For a second, I'm afraid I've pushed Gideon too far, and he's going to take his feelings out on me with his fists.

But then he falls to his knees in front of me. "You're right. I have done the unforgivable. I have to find a way to right this, to atone, to ensure the sacrifices of the people of Summerland and Nicodemus were not made in vain."

"There's only one sort of justice for what you've done here. And as soon as I can hold a blade again, I'm going to give it to you. I swear to everything holy, I will."

His eyes swim with tears, and he reaches for my good hand, clasping his fingers around both it and the cup of water. It's too familiar for the time we've known each other, but I don't pull away. I'm so empty inside, all hollowed out rage and despair, that this single bit of human contact feels like a balm to my soul.

I hate him, but I also don't want to be alone.

"I'm sorry, Jane. I'm sorry I put you through this. I'm going to be a friend to you, I promise. Please say you forgive me?"

I don't get to answer him, because a single shot rings out, shattering the window glass and kicking up feathers as it rips through the chair Gideon just vacated.

Gideon drops my hand and crawls backward out of the room like a crab scuttling for a hidey-hole. As he does, another shot destroys what is left of the window, the bullet lodging in the wooden flooring and kicking up splinters near my boots. There are no more shots, but the dead outside begin to stir, and I can just barely make out the sound of Gideon banging out of the back door, footsteps thundering away from the house as he flees.

This day just keeps on careening off the cliff, over and over again.

The front door opens, and a girl walks in carrying a rifle. The sunlight paints her outline, a pleasing one at that, and when the door closes I am only mildly surprised to see Callie.

"Helluva shot," I say. "Unless you were aiming for me."

cent

She gives me a tight grin. "Thanks, but no, I was aiming for that yellow-bellied bastard that just ran out of here."

"Well, I've got some unfortunate news for you," I say.

Callie shrugs. "Maybe next time."

There's a dark feeling welling up in me, one I've been fighting for a long time. It's part hopelessness, but it's mostly rage. I'm angry that I live in a world where people can listen to a man like Gideon Carr and whatever fantasies he wants to spread but continually ignore girls like me. If the fine folks of Nicodemus and the refugees of Summerland had evacuated when Katherine and I had told them to, they'd be alive right now. But they're not.

I tire of watching this tragedy play out.

Callie's eyes are shadowed and red, and I wonder how long she's been perched somewhere, waiting for the perfect moment to take her shot. She seems unconcerned about the dead outside, and that convinces me that I ain't the first girl Gideon Carr has experimented on.

"So he got you as well?" I say, gesturing weakly to my gangrenous arm.

"When he first came to town, before he went to the leaders of Nicodemus to try to do it all official-like." She gives me a sad smile. "I thought I loved him, you know."

"Did you help him dismantle the rear gate?" I ask, remembering the smaller-size boot prints.

She nods. "I thought they would just leave, that we could

close the breach up after. But they didn't, and it was every-thing we could do to get them into that barn before they overran the town." Her expression goes hard, but it's tinged with grief. I'm not the only one who has lost loved ones these past few days. "It didn't matter, anyway. I should've known it wasn't true. Gideon always lied to me. It's what he does."

"I'm starting to see that now." What else is there to say? We both got duped by his kindness.

Callie nods and swipes her hand over her nose. "My fam-ily is all gone. They're out there, walking monsters now. Or in pieces. I'm the only one left."

"Yeah, that's rough," I'm starting to feel unsteady once more, and I sigh. "If it makes you feel any better, I'm truly sorry you missed. And if I get the chance, I won't."

"You got murder on the mind then, Jane McKeene?" She smirks.

"If I don't die first," I say. I want to hold on to my anger and grief, but it's hard when I don't feel like doing anything but dying.

Callie walks over and takes the chair Gideon vacated. She wrinkles her nose in an expression that can only be described as utterly adorable, and something in my middle shifts. It's poor timing, but who am I to deny myself a little glimmer of humanity when I feel like an absolute monster?

She gestures at my bandage. "You're going to have to lose that arm."

And over her shoulder, the ghost of Jackson grins at me. I blink, trying to dispel the apparition, but he stays put.

"An amputation!" he says. "This is excellent." He settles himself near the window, leaning against the wall. He wears a different outfit now than he did the day he died, a sapphire-blue waistcoat decorated with peacocks, and dread is a heavy stone in my belly. His damned green eyes are crinkled with amusement.

"I think Gideon had some ether, down in his lab," Callie says, climbing to her feet. "It should make the process a little more bearable. And I want to make sure that sonuvabitch is gone, anyway."

"If he isn't, kill him," I say. I lean back against the settee and close my eyes again. Maybe this is all a nightmare, and when I open them I'll be back in the Nicodemus jail, Sheriff Redfern watching me with that inscrutable look of his.

Callie moves away, the back door slamming as she departs, and I turn my full attention to Jackson. He removes the hat he wears and sets it on a nearby table. He smiles, and I'm sure there's nothing good that can come of that look.

"Now this," he says, rubbing his hands together in delight, "is about to be a spectacle."

PART TWO

The Road to Perdition

— *One year and five months later* —

Washington is not a place to live in. The rents are high, the food is bad, the dead are everywhere, and the morals are deplorable. Go west, young man, go west and help save this country from the Undead Plague.

—Horace Greeley, 1865

— KATHERINE —

Chapter 24
Notes on a Card Game

Carolina Jones thinks he has a hand.

I know it, the same as I know to pull the trigger when the dead are in my sights. Carolina's dark face twists in concentration as he worries the unlit cigar in the corner of his mouth. Then he leans forward, a crease slowly furrowing his brow, looks intently at the four cards in the middle of the table: a six, a jack, a ten, and the ace of spades. He looks at the two cards in his hand, and sighs. It is a nice show. But the silly man is his own worst enemy. The merry beat of his leg bouncing under the table gives away the truth beneath the lie.

I have been traveling with Jones for months now, from New Orleans through Nicaragua and now on my final leg to San Francisco aboard the steamship *Capitán*. Carolina is one of the few people left in this miserable world who I trust. Not that I have ever been one to thoughtlessly place my faith in people. A misstep when I was thirteen taught me the brutal lesson that everyone will turn on you; it is just a matter of when and where.

A memory of Jane flits past as I consider Carolina, and I immediately dismiss it. It has been nearly a year and a half since we lost her in Nicodemus, and only recently have I been able to consider her passing without feeling a gut punch of regret and pain. For some reason, Jane's death affected me more deeply than just about anyone else I knew. I still have not puzzled out why.

So, then, Carolina. He is a fabulous traveling companion, the kind of man a single young lady fair of face could trust. One reason for this is that he prefers the company of gentlemen in his bedchamber. But another is that his kindness of heart is of the sort one is hard-pressed to find in this world. He was the one who spoke to the ship's captain on my behalf when I threw a deckhand overboard for getting too fresh. He's also the one who found Sue and me positions on this boat, working security for the lady passengers. He gave us a chance to earn a living and provide for Lily. We have fought shamblers together while walking through Nicaragua, and have spent a fair number of evenings drinking to our heart's content. . . . Well, Carolina had gotten drunk while I sipped politely at whatever rotgut was being served and Sue had murmured about the evils of drink. It would have been rude to refuse outright, but I know better than to overindulge. I am a lady, after all.

All of this to say, I know Carolina's tics and mannerisms as well as my own. Now, as I sit in the *Capitán*'s galley and play poker—gambling is a vice, but one must keep oneself busy on these long trips by sea—I cannot help but put all of his tells together: Carolina Jones thinks he has a winning hand. The man is a terrible actor, and I simply adore him for it.

"Are you in or out, Mr. Jones?" Dr. Cornelius Nelson sits to my left, his generous chin whiskers vibrating in agitation. Dr. Nelson is a Negro surgeon—"the best in New York," he will assure you, likely within the first few moments of introduction. Of course, I find that hard to believe, since he is apparently lacking in the good sense God gave every man. He has proposed marriage twice, and each time I have politely declined, even when he insisted upon composing an ode to my blond hair and blue eyes and dusky skin. It was all quite improper, and the height of embarrassment. On the third occasion I had been forced to draw one of my Mollies and threaten to feed his liver to the fish if he did not leave off.

It was completely out of character for me, and I wholly blame my time with Jane McKeene for the lapse in decorum. Jane loved pointing bladed weapons at people. It was part of her charm.

But I am not going to think about that.

Dr. Nelson has mostly left me alone since that day, but every now and again I can feel his glance directed at me. If I were interested in a husband, or in any of the requirements of marriage, he would not be a terrible prospect. Even after nearly a month of hard travel, he is still pressed and tidy, due in no small part to the efforts of his valet, Hector. Hector stands just a bit behind Nelson, his dark face impassive. Dr. Nelson is light-skinned, and with a shave and some careful avoidance of the sun he could pass as white, if he wanted. He apparently does not, since he is on the decks designated for colored folks. That is a thing I respect about him.

Jones rubs his chin as if deliberating, still deep in his chicanery, then shrugs and throws a few dollars into the center of the table. "I call."

I toss my money in as well. Dr. Nelson, who made the original bet, smiles, his eyes more on me than the pot. What a ridiculous man.

Two other crew members, Baldy Pennington and Lazy-Eye Earl, watch quietly from their chairs, their dark faces impassive. They folded after the first few cards were played, protecting their rapidly dwindling piles of coins against any further loss.

Lazy, who is dealer this time, flips over the last card—a jack. The good doctor only hesitates a moment before pushing what is left of his stack into the middle. After a few tortuously obvious moments of deliberation, Carolina calls once more. I do as well.

Dr. Nelson reveals his hand: a pair of tens, giving him a full house. But before he can make another move, Carolina Jones whoops in triumph. He tosses his cards on the table: a jack and a six, giving him a better house. Nelson's face falls; it's not often that the good doctor is so roundly beaten.

As Jones goes to scrape up the pot, however, I tap his hand, gently, like a school marm correcting a student. "I do believe that belongs to me." I lay my cards on the table near the middle for all to see.

A pair of aces.

The table goes silent for a long moment before Baldy begins whooping with laughter. "Oh, looks like the pretty little miss beat you again!"

Dr. Nelson mutters a curse and heaves his bulk out of the chair. He barely pauses to tip his hat before he strides out of the room, his man Hector rushing to keep up. I am certain his pride smarts even more now.

Once he is gone, I reel my winnings in from the center and grin at the remaining men.

"Another round?" I ask, widening my eyes innocently.

Lazy guffaws and climbs to his feet. "You can flutter those lashes all you want, little miss, but I know the score. You're as deadly with those cards as you are with your swords."

Baldy says nothing, just nods, tipping the remnants of the whiskey bottle on the table down his throat before standing and heading for the door.

I watch the men take their leave until it is just Carolina and I. He sits there, chewing on the end of his unlit cigar. "Pretty incredible hand you had there."

"Is there something amiss, Carolina?" I ask.

He leans forward, striking a match and finally lighting the cigar. "How much you pay him?"

I blink. "Pay who?"

"Doc Nelson's man. How much you pay him to tip you to everybody's cards?"

My heart thumps painfully in my chest, and for a few heartbeats I am fearful, truly afraid. I know what betrayal feels like, and I have let that pain drive me to become the woman I am today. I sincerely do not want to have to kill the one friend I have remaining in the world.

But I will do what is required of me, even if it means cutting down Carolina where he sits.

I shove the dark emotions aside and force a slow smile. "Ten dollars. How much did you pay him?"

Carolina laughs, the sound sharp and bitter. He leans back and draws deeply on his cigar. "Five."

"Oh, Carolina. You simply must stop being so cheap! If you continue to overestimate the generosity of people, you are only going to end up disappointed."

Carolina shakes his head and I relax. I slide a cut of the money across the table. We have been running something of a game on the swanky upper-decks passengers since New Orleans—not playing with each other, but not exactly playing against each other, either—and I see no reason to stop now. In a world that is morally gray, I somehow still believe in right and wrong.

And I refuse to change that until I must.

I tuck my winnings into the pocket sewn inside of my skirt, a trick I learned from Jane, and I think about San Francisco and the life waiting for me there. I have my heart set on opening a millinery. Something small at first, see where I can take it. Sue thinks it is a silly idea, but she has agreed to help me with the shop until she finds herself a husband. We have discussed it at length, and we both think it will be best for Lily, the stability of a life in a single place, settled and constant.

I might have to hire out as an Attendant when I first get to the city, or possibly work with one of the protection crews the Chinese run, although I am not certain they accept women. But either position would only be temporary. My heart is set on being a businesswoman.

It is that single, small dream that has kept me going over the past few months. I dare not lose it now.

Carolina draws deeply on his cigar, the sweet smoke filling the room. "How'd you get so smart?"

"A girl has to survive. It is a cruel world," I say.

Carolina nods, and once more we sit in companionable silence for a long moment, before Carolina says quietly, "We friends, Katherine?"

I laugh, because that is what you do when a man says something ridiculous. But I am not thinking about him. For a moment my breath flees, and my chest tightens. I am overwhelmed by memory, screams of terror and the moans of the dead. I think of Jane, of the last words she said to me.

Thank you for being my friend.

And then I let her die.

I clear my throat, bringing my mind back to the conversation at hand. "Well, since you have neither proposed nor propositioned me, I am willing to consider that we may indeed be friends."

He contemplates the end of his lit cigar, avoiding my steady gaze. "If we're pals, then that means I can give you some advice."

My amusement evaporates. I have had quite enough of men and their advice in my eighteen years. "You can try."

Carolina runs his finger along the bottom of his mustache. It is a familiar motion, one I have seen often when he is thinking on a complicated situation. "We're going to be in San Francisco in three days."

"That is what we have all been told," I say, my words clipped.

Jane wanted to go to California to find her mother. Perhaps that is why I have found myself on a ship bound for the Golden State. An ache blossoms in my chest, and I pick up my untouched glass of whiskey and drain it. The liquid tastes as smoky as my memories and burns all the way down. It feels like penance. That is the real reason I do not drink too often: I am afraid that if I find my way to the bottle I will be lost forever.

I shake my head to clear it; I know exactly what Carolina is going to say. "Your offer is generous, but I must refuse. I have business in California."

Carolina sets his cigar in a nearby ashtray before leaning forward over the table. "So now you're a mind reader?"

"You want to know if I will stay on with you. Keep working security for the *Capitán*."

He says nothing for a few heartbeats. From outside the galley comes feminine laughter and a man's answering rumble, followed by echoing footsteps. It is late, and people are settling in. No one lacks for company on the *Capitán*, if they are looking for it.

"It's a chilly night," he says. "How do you know I won't ask you to come and keep me warm? When was the last time you went for a tumble, Kate?"

I snort, manners forgotten for the moment. "Do not call

me that. And stop trying to provoke me. We both know that there is nothing I can offer that you want. If you are lonely, you should go find Dr. Nelson's valet. He was very complimentary of your facial hair."

Carolina laughs. "It is a very fine mustache," he says, smoothing the waxed ends, which curl up like catfish whiskers. Humor is always bubbling beneath the surface in him, whether relaxing after a game of poker or knee-deep in lake water fighting the dead. It is insufferable. And yet, it's one of the reasons I am overly fond of him. He reminds me of Jane.

"Stop being coy and ask your damn question so I can retire," I say. I am tired and out of sorts, the memories that I have tried so hard to bury are too near and too real. Even the money we have won tonight is not enough to loosen the hard knot of rage that has been festering in my middle since leaving Nicodemus. I have replayed my time there again and again in my mind, trying to find ways things could have turned out differently.

I have been unsuccessful.

"I know you intend to go to California, set up a business, maybe find your friend's momma," Carolina starts, choosing his words carefully. "And I think that's admirable. But what makes you think you'll be happy there?"

I pick up my whiskey glass and put it to my lips, only to remember that it is empty. I settle for sliding it across the table from hand to hand. "What makes you think I will be unhappy?"

Carolina leans back in his chair. "I think you're running, Katherine. There's a haunted expression you wear when you think no one is watching. And I want to help you, because you've been a great partner to me these past few months. Hell, I've come to look on you and Sue as sisters. Working regular on a ship like the *Capitán* offers protections against many of the dangers faced by those back on land. Ones you witnessed firsthand. You could be safe on this ship. Here. With me."

I smile tightly, but say nothing. He is trying to protect me, in the simple way men are always trying to protect women: by stealing away their freedom.

I know he thinks a lady with a face like mine would be putting herself at risk, trying to make it in a city like San Francisco on her own. Men and women have coveted my beauty ever since I was a girl. But because of Jane and Fort Riley I now know how to wield it like a sharp blade. And it is a weapon I am willing to use, if I must.

Before traveling west, I took Jane's advice and went back home. That is, once I managed to extricate myself from Fort Riley. The ruse I had used to get us safely to the compound had served us well enough, but when we arrived, Ida and her folks had lit out for the Lost States, back to their homes. It had been a loss, but then Ida was Jane's friend, and with Jane gone, well, there was really nothing keeping us together.

It was nearly a week before Sue, Lily, and I were able to make our way out of Fort Riley. The soldiers there were quite taken with us, colored and white alike, but we left with our virtue intact. That probably had more to do with our bladed weapons, an overabundance of caution, and extraordinarily good luck than any sort of chivalry on the soldiers' part.

Once we cleared the gates, we headed straight for the Mississippi and were lucky enough to meet only a few shamblers along the way. We found an abandoned boat not far from where we met the river, and within a week, we had reached the bayous around New Orleans. When I was thirteen, I ran away from the city, or at least tried to, landing myself in those bayous, which were outside the safety of the walls.

And it was there in those bayous, both familiar and strange, that I grieved for Jane. I trained with the Laveau girls once more and considered our next steps, and what would be best for the three of us. Sue found a book about California and how to travel there, and after I had read a bit of it out loud to all of us, she convinced us that that ought to be our destination. Everything seemed to indicate that the Golden State had been nearly free of the restless dead for years, most especially San Francisco. The high walls, designed by the modern genius Thomas Edison, were the stuff of legend, an impenetrable defense against the dead. And after decades of fierce policing and constant Army intervention in the countryside, all of California was a paradise free of ravenous hordes. The land was beautiful and serene, and the combined obstacles of the Rocky Mountains and the Sierra Nevadas kept the undead from traveling overland into the Golden State, for the most part. Jane had asked me to look out for Lily, and everything we read about California seemed to indicate it was a brand-new kind of place. The restless dead were a minor nuisance and not a plague, which meant that San Francisco had to be a better place.

Someplace I could carve out a space for myself and finally breathe.

And now that I have nearly reached my goal I have no intention of surrendering it to fear of the unknown. Maybe I would have, once. But not any longer.

I stand and stretch. "Carolina, I know you mean well. And I appreciate your concern, and your offer. But I assure you, I know what I am doing."

I turn to leave, and Carolina's parting words follow me out the hatch.

"I know you do, Katherine," he says. "I just hope that you aren't disappointed if it turns out you're wrong."

I pause only long enough to look over my shoulder. "Darling, disappointment is the only sure thing in this world."

There is no shortage of hard men in the west, the kind of men who have escaped falling cities and bloody battlefields only to find themselves on the other side of the Deathless Divide. These men kill and rob their way across the unsettled territories, stopped by only two equally powerful forces: the marshal and the bounty hunter.
—Western Tales, *Volume 23*

— J A N E —

Chapter 25
In Which a Dark Omen Appears

Near the docks in Monterey—just a few paces down from the receiving office where immigrants arriving in California are inspected like cattle—is a saloon. There ain't any sort of sign to mark the doorway, nothing to set this building apart from the rest of the street, and the men who stumble in and out couldn't tell you the name even as they were pouring themselves another dram of rotgut.

Places like this? They don't need names.

The inside is dark, dreary. The wooden floorboards are warped, the air hangs heavy with the stink of unwashed bodies, and the few lanterns that burn inside do more to heighten the gloom than to dispel it. There's a small hearth, but the fire there ain't enough to chase away the chill that clings to the room like a shambler that's latched on for a bite.

But folks mostly pretend not to notice any of that. This is the kind of place men go to forget who they once were. Gambling, drink, maybe the occasional murder for hire— this place has seen it all. One might think that in the end times there'd be no more use for such a den of iniquity, but the men within these four walls know better. They know that survival comes with a hefty price, and sometimes the only way is in the forgetting.

There ain't no good-time girls in this place. Maybe once, long ago, when miners and gold-struck boys would come through, set on making their fortune in the Golden State. Drinking a nip, sharing a dream before cutting a bloody path east through the forest and the people, no price too high for the chance at a future. People in the West will tell you it's the Indian you need to fear, but no Indian has ever been half so vicious as the white man. And the dead? Well, they took their cues from the best.

America had once been the land of opportunity, its possibilities endless for the chosen people who arrived on its shores. Now, it was a land rife with death, threats lying in wait around every corner, in each shadow, and in the eyes of the living left behind.

The saloon had adjusted its expectations accordingly.

I stride into the cantina with no expectation of service, or even a lukewarm greeting, and I ain't disappointed. This ain't any kind of place for a lady. But then again, I ain't no lady. Even less so now than I might once have been. I stomp into the room, Salty on my heels. The terrier growls and snaps at anyone we pass near, but I don't move to restrain him. The dog is a penance, not a gift, and there is only one reason why I'm here.

In the back corner of the room, furthest away from the door, sits my quarry: William Jefferson Perry, raconteur and ne'er-do-well. Callie and I have been chasing him for nigh on a week, and it had been sheer luck he'd decided to dash into California instead of skulking about Nevada. I'd had quite enough of Carson City, and getting word that he'd headed south was like hearing Gabriel blow his heavenly horn.

Perry's bowler is tilted low, long legs sprawled under the table. His pale skin ain't remarkable in this part of town, but the pistols he wears are. They're too fine, too well-made. Perry was a dandy before he was a murderer and a thief, and once a man has a taste for a certain style of living, it ain't easy to break. This is a hardscrabble sort of town, the kind in which a badly scarred Negro girl might be able to blend in. A well-to-do white man, though—less so. It's true, a number of people had frowned and shaken their heads when I described him: a white man with blond hair and blue eyes Ella May Barnhart had said were "like a mountain lake on a summer's day" in her journal. No one could tell me definitively whether they'd seen Ella May's secret lover. But the guns? Everyone had taken note of those six-shooters.

Now that I'm finally laying eyes on them myself, they look to me more decorative than lethal. There is something delicate about both the man and his weaponry—something Ella May, and many other women besides, mistook for softness. But there ain't nothing soft about Perry. The deputy in Carson City had started crying while the sheriff described the crime scene: the body of poor Ella May was so badly mutilated that the only way they'd been able to identify her was by a length of her hair, the fiery red unlike any other. It had matched the man's modus operandi: find a rich woman, earn her trust, carve her up, steal her money.

And now, after weeks of pursuit, here he sits, giving me a smile that is one part charm and six parts slime.

"Well, if it isn't Jane McKeene," the man says, his voice low and sultry. "Fierceness ne'er looked so beautiful, nor beauty so fierce."

If Perry thinks he can charm *me*, he's got another think coming. I'm not exactly partial to men and their wiles these days. I draw my pistol and calmly level it at his head. Most of the people in the room get up and make their way out, self-defense or plausible deniability, who knows. A moment later, the only ones left in the saloon besides the two of us are a few sots scattered amongst the tables, their heads down, too far gone to notice what's happening.

"William Jefferson Perry, you're coming with me."

He sighs, resetting the bowler back on top of his head. "What took you so long, I wonder?"

"No one crosses the Donner Pass in the winter. I had to go south through Death Valley."

He takes a drink from his glass, slow and deliberate, like I ain't got a gun pointed at him. "I've heard the desert comes by its name honestly enough," he says finally. "And yet, you survived."

"I'm resourceful."

He laughs, like we're just two people making conversation, and I want to put a bullet in his brain. "They told me that no matter where I ran you'd find me. There isn't any escape from the Devil's Bi—" He spits on the floor and gives me another look, this one less smoldering. "Well, I'm sure you heard the nickname. I won't be so crass as to swear in front of you, respecting the lady you once were. So, they say you've never lost a bounty."

"Who's this 'they' you're talking about? You got a mouse in your pocket?"

"You'd be surprised, the people that got their eye on you, Jane McKeene."

I snort. "You keep saying my name like you're trying to

summon a haint. Now come on and get up. The sheriff here is expecting us."

"He ain't the only one."

The men who were sitting in the opposite corner stand up, pistols drawn. William Jefferson Perry gives me a grin like the cat that got the canary.

I sigh. "Now why'd you have to go and make this difficult?"

"On the contrary, my dear," he says, "I think your choices just simplified."

The thing is people have always had a tendency to underestimate me. Which is fine. In fact, I even used to enjoy turning those expectations around on folks. But that was back when people were seeing the color of my skin and my girlish countenance and assuming I wasn't worth more than the dress I was wearing. Now, though, their judgment is based on my missing an arm, and I can't say I truly understand why. Just because I'm down a limb doesn't mean I don't have two perfectly good feet to plant in their rear end.

While Perry gloats I swing around fast as a jackrabbit and plug both of the men in the middle of their chests. The gun is loud in the small space, but this ain't the first time I've pulled a trigger, and I am without regrets. Their six-shooters clatter to the ground, followed by their bodies.

"Salty, get," I say, and the terrier takes off into the gloom to fetch the dropped guns.

The sound of a chair being shoved out comes from my

left, but before I can turn my attention to it, another shot rings out, followed by the sound of a body falling. A figure stands up in the shadows to my right and moves toward me and Perry.

"Took you long enough to join in," I say.

Callie shrugs. "I figured you had it handled."

"I was wondering if you were going to leave me high and dry like you did in Denver."

The corners of Callie's mouth turn downward. "Not now, Jane."

She's right that it's not the time, but that doesn't mean I ain't going to bring it up again. If there's anything I'm good at, it's holding a grudge. Callie is a solid shot, and I've been grateful for her company this past year and change, but she can try my temper sometimes with her casual manner.

"You want to check out those bodies and see if they're holding anything?" I say. "Or did you want to finish your beer first?"

Callie picks up an oil lamp from one of the tables and carries it to examine the carnage. When she gets to one of the first men I shot, she raises her pistol and shoots him between his eyes—he must have had a little life left in him and needed to be put out of his misery, or at least out of ours. It's much easier to transport a dead body than a living one.

Salty comes running back and drops a gun at my feet, before running off to get another. Guns aren't so plentiful out west as they once were, since there are so few gunsmiths left who fashion them. I'd heard tell of expeditions into the cities for valuables, but most of those stories end the way you'd expect. Taking guns off dead men in these outlying towns is a far easier way to earn a buck.

"Wait, please!" Perry finally breaks his silence; he's lost his smug smile and is beginning to realize that he ain't going to be able to charm or shoot his way out of this one. "I'm sure we can come to some sort of arrangement."

I smile. This is a script I know well. Every crook, murderer, and cheat thinks he can get the better of a bad situation by bargaining, and it is one of my few remaining joys in life to watch their faces the moment they realize that no one can buy Jane McKeene. There's only one thing I want, one thing that's brought me here all the way from Nicodemus, and it sure ain't money.

I pull a rope from my belt and wrap it once and then twice around Perry's hands, tying a decent half hitch. It's harder with only one hand than it would be with two, but I make do. Even so, Callie walks back over and gently nudges me to the side to take over the job. A flash of frustration zings through me, but time is short and she's faster at securing the knots than I am.

"Looks like these other fellas are the Andrews gang," she says. "We can take them up and claim their bounty, too. It ain't much, but it'll keep us in hot meals for a spell."

"Please," Perry burbles.

Callie looks up at me and raises an eyebrow. "What's he about?"

"Trying to get out of the noose that's waiting for him in Carson City, I reckon," I say.

"No, truly, I can help you. Gideon Carr. You're looking for a scientist named Gideon Carr!"

Callie and I freeze.

"You won't find him on your own," Perry continues, talking fast now. "He's in hiding. Got himself a benefactor, and a new lab."

I move my eyes over to Callie. She is still dumbstruck. Perry looks between us, nervously. I've known men to invent all manner of things when they realize they're beat, but I have no way of telling with Perry.

"He ain't lying."

Standing next to the bar, looking fine in a lavender waist-coat and a velvety bowler, stands Jackson, once more reading my mind. As usual, a feeling halfway between happy and sick rises up in me. I'm always glad to see his ghost, real or imagined; but I've gone back and forth over what his pres-ence means, and I keep coming back to the obvious: nothing good.

Callie's eyes narrow as she watches me, my gaze focused on what to her must appear to be naught but empty space. "He back?" she asks, voice low.

"Is who back?" Perry says, eyes wild as they dart around the bar.

"Yep," I say, ignoring him. "He says this fella here is telling the truth."

Perry nods, his Adam's apple working as he swallows. "I am! I just met the man, not more than a week ago. Brilliant, determined, said he had a plan to end the undead plague."

"That's Gideon all right," Callie says, and if there's a wistful tone to her voice I'm thinking it's just because we've finally gotten a hint as to where the tinkerer could be after all these months. Least, that's what I'm going to believe for now. I ain't going to let jealousy distract me.

"Callie still loves him," Jackson says, laughing deeply. "The same way you still care for me. The two of you really are peas in a pod."

"And just how did you know we were looking for Carr?" I ask Perry, turning away from Jackson.

"Them boys over there, the ones you just plugged. When I told them it was you who were after me, they said that you've been dogging Carr for months, taking bounties out west while you followed his trail." Perry laughs nervously. "Two killer Negro girls, one without an arm, tend to attract attention."

"So where exactly is this lab?" I ask, trying my damnedest to ignore the ghost of Jackson as he strolls over and examines Perry's wardrobe.

"Oh, that is the secret, isn't it?" Perry grins, even as there's fear in his eyes. The gloom of the cantina can't hide that he knows he's got something we want. "You let me go, and I'll send you a telegram once I get to Mexico with everything I know about Gideon Carr and his whereabouts."

"No way," I say.

But at the same time Callie says, "All right."

I grab her arm, move her away out of earshot. "You want to let him go? Even if Perry ain't lying about having met Gideon, how do we know he's going to be truthful about where he is?"

"Why would he lie?" Callie holsters her gun, rubs the back of her neck.

"Hmm, I don't know, the fact that he's facing the hangman in Carson City?"

She sighs. "The only reason we're out here is for Gideon, ain't it? We've been tracking him for damn near a year, I'm ready to be done with this."

The anger that she is so good at tamping down rises up now. It's telling, her willingness to bargain with this monster. When we'd left Nicodemus, me half dead and Callie emotionally broken, we'd sworn we'd do everything we could to hunt down Gideon and deliver justice. Along the way, we realized that the best way to track his whereabouts and eke out a living would be to take up bounties on the sorts of men who lived in the same shadows Gideon would be sticking to.

And, just maybe, it would help to cleanse our souls a bit in the process. But letting one go just to find Gideon?

I don't know what exactly is behind Callie's sudden change of heart. But I just purse my lips and nod.

"Okay, we'll bite," Callie says, walking slowly back to Perry. "But none of this telegram business. You tell us where he is now."

"Fair enough," Perry says. Callie unties him and he digs a vellum card out of his coat pocket. "This is the man who is funding Gideon and giving him shelter."

Callie takes the card and laughs, the sound hollow. "Thurman Leakes? We might have only gotten to California a few days ago, but we ain't stupid."

I put my hand on my hip. We'd heard a whole earful about Leakes as we'd walked north. The newspapers are obsessed with him, a relative unknown who quickly became the most powerful man in the state. Didn't matter that everyone knew he'd made it there by climbing over the bodies of others, greasing palms along the way. "You want us to believe that Gideon Carr is hiding out with the King of California?"

"Thurman Leakes is a dear friend of mine, and it was only because of these complications in Carson City that I am here and not relaxing at his estate." Perry straightens his waistcoat and stands. "Trust me when I say that is where you will find Gideon Carr. Thurman enjoys the company of . . . interesting people."

I can't help but wonder just how a bastard like Perry befriended Leakes. I have some ideas, though. "So that's it? A calling card for some robber baron? You think we're going to let you go for that?"

"Yes, I do," Perry says. "A deal is, after all, a deal."

"Well, a deal is only a deal so long as everyone is sticking to their end of the bargain. You didn't tell us where Gideon Carr's laboratory is."

Perry blinks at me owlishly. "That, my dear, is not something I am privy to. I gave you what I know."

"No, you didn't," I say, drawing my revolver and pointing it at Perry. "Sit."

"Jane . . . ," Callie begins as Perry sinks back into his chair.

"Tie him up," I grind out.

Behind me, the ghost of Jackson chuckles. "Now, there's my Jane," he says. "None of this making deals with criminals. Callie's losing her edge, you've known it ever since Denver. Shoot the bastard. The first chance he gets, he's going to carve up some woman the same way he did Ella May."

"Did you kill Ella May before you carved her up?" I ask, once Perry is secured again. "Or did you start in on her while she was alive?"

Callie's eyes widen, and she takes a step toward me. "Jane."

"Sweetheart, why don't you fetch the sheriff so he can verify these bounties," I say. My gaze flicks to Callie just long enough to see the tremor that has set into her. For a moment

I'm afraid that she will fight me on this, that she won't leave.

But then I see the resignation set in, and she does as I ask, just like she always does.

"Oh, Jane, I see what you're about," Jackson says. He disappears and reappears beside me, and his whisper in my ear sends a chill down my spine. "You never were one for half measures."

I shrug and holster my revolver. Perry relaxes just a bit, but only until I pull my knife from the sheath on my belt. He swallows hard, his Adam's apple bobbing up and down.

"Now, I believe you were going to tell me the location of Gideon Carr's lab?"

He shakes his head so hard that his hat comes unsettled. I knock it the rest of the way off with the flat of my knife, his hair mussing from the violence of the movement.

"I don't know, I swear," Perry says, talking fast. "Look, I already told you everything I know. If you're going to kill me, please, just make it quick."

I give him a grim smile and tilt my head, placing my blade next to his right ear so that the flat presses against his skull. "Now, where is the fun in that?"

To Perry's credit, he doesn't start screaming until I start in on the left ear.

The bounty of California is most evident in the sprawling grandeur of San Francisco, a city for the modern age. The wall surrounding the city was designed by the brilliant inventor Thomas Edison and has attracted settlers from all around the world with its promise of safety.
—Russell Carpenter, Westward into the Sunset, *1871*

— K A T H E R I N E —

Chapter 26
Notes on an Arrival

San Francisco is nothing like I had expected.

Fog covers the bay, heavy and wet, and we disembark at Angel Island. Although there are docks closer to the city, all passenger ships delivering visitors must send their passengers through the central processing station on the island to ensure that we are free from bites. There is another facility in the southern part of the city as well, but Carolina assures us that Angel Island is faster and better staffed. I am not looking forward to an afternoon of poking and prodding, but it is a necessary precaution, if an irksome one.

The center is small but heavily armed. Artillery guns point out toward the sea, defense against a military opponent, not the undead. I expect to see dead washing up on the shore as they do in just about every single other place where I have been, but the rocks are free from debris as we paddle past in the boat that tenders us from the *Capitán* to the shore. Perhaps the stories we have heard about California, a sun-soaked land of opportunity freed from the undead plague, might actually be true.

Once the tiny rowboat bumps up against the dock, Sue, Lily, and I climb out. Our baggage, which contains only a single knapsack and a good collection of weapons, sits in the bottom of the boat. We grab our gear while Carolina and another man hold the craft steady.

"I've got to go back and get a few more folks. Are you going to be okay?" he asks, ever concerned about our safety. Ironic, considering our job these past few months has been to protect passengers against the threat of the dead.

I nod. "We have your directions; it should not be an issue to find the boarding house. Thank you so much. For everything."

Sue nods in agreement and then Carolina and the deckhand turn the boat back toward the *Capitán*. And we turn our attention to the facility before us.

It is so early that the sky still has not shaded beyond the gray of the dawn, and yet there is already a long line winding up the steps to the building. Armed soldiers patrol up and down the line, rifles at the ready and a backup weapon of a machete tucked into their belts. The building beyond is white and squat and looks less like a government building and more like an Army barrack.

"This place looks like Fort Riley," Sue says.

"It does," I murmur.

"It gives me the creeps," she says, spitting for luck.

The processing station segregates by gender and race, and as Sue, Lily, and I make our way to the line for women, a woman in a uniform waves me over. Sue and Lily follow as I approach the official. The woman is Chinese, and my shock is very quickly replaced by delight.

This is something new after all.

"Do you speak English?" she asks, her tone brusque and dismissive.

"Yes," I say. "I am sorry, is there some sort of issue?"

"No, of course not, Miss . . . ?"

"Deveraux."

"Miss Deveraux, there's no need for Americans to wait in line with the immigrants. You and your girls can follow me."

I open my mouth to tell the official that neither Sue nor Lily are my girls, but Sue gives me a half headshake. The line is very long, and it seems as though I am once more enjoying the boon of my fair skin.

The official leads us into a small room and closes the door. The room contains a single chair and a desk, but that is all. There's a small fire burning in the hearth, chasing away the chill of the morning, and it is strange to be taken aside into such a place. She pulls forth a ledger and opens it before me.

"What is your business in San Francisco?"

"Oh, well, I am planning on establishing myself as a businesswoman—"

I break off when she stops scribbling and pushes the ledger across the desk at me, handing me a dripping pen.

"I wrote down marriage. Please print your names in the empty space and follow me."

I do as she asks, the scrawl barely legible in my haste, and after a quick perusal she nods and puts the ledger away. I exchange a glance with Sue, but she shrugs and we follow along behind the woman without another word.

We are led out a different door than we entered and down a path that leads to yet another set of docks. There is a gate with a guard between us and the waiting area on the docks, but the gate opens at a wave from our administrator.

"The ferry arrives at the top of each hour, and it will cost you each two bits to get to San Francisco," she says.

"That is it?" I ask, clutching at my satchel.

"Was I unclear?" The woman turns toward Sue. "You understand that slavery is illegal in the Republic of California, so if you are not being compensated you are free to leave at any time."

Sue's lips twist as she fights to hide a grin and she nods.

"Excellent, welcome to California," she says before striding back down the path from which we came. I walk through the gate to the waiting area. The young soldier guarding the gate tips his hat at us.

"Ferry should be along in a few moments," he says, his gaze lingering on me a bit too long to be appropriate.

We make our way toward the boarding area, and I shake my head. "Sue, what just happened?"

"Same thing that always happens, she thought you were white," Lily says.

"Good to see things here in California work the same as everywhere else," Sue says, chuckling mirthlessly.

Indeed, that is what I fear.

I have visited a number of varied cities, from the mishmash of Spanish and French architecture in New Orleans to the staid stone structures of Baltimore. And I had expected something similar when I arrived in San Francisco: imposing stone buildings, wooden clapboard houses, and sprawling grounds with manicured lawns.

But there is no clapboard or stone in San Francisco, at least as far as I can see. The Spanish influence is clear in the stucco and rounded arches of the Presidio that greets us when the ferry docks. The orange of clay tiles seems odd to me, even though I saw its like as we traveled overland through Central

America. But it is the landscape beyond that captures my attention. The steep hills rise up and down, and multihued buildings with intricate scrollwork and sweeping roofs that curve up into points at the four corners cling precariously to those inclines, like barnacles to a hull. San Francisco's architecture is part Spanish and part Chinese, and it is beautiful. I have never seen anything like it.

"Is that a dragon?" Lily asks from next to me, squinting at a carved arch that welcomes us to San Francisco in a half-dozen languages, only two of which I can read.

"Most definitely. The Chinese got a thing about dragons, well, about all animals in fact. They have a calendar that assigns a different animal to each lunar year."

I turn, and leaning against a piling is Carolina, looking fresh as a daisy.

"I thought you were returning to the *Capitán*?" I say.

He shrugs. "I figured I should see you girls to your lodgings first."

"How'd you make it through clearance so quickly?" Sue asks. "They think you were white as well?"

Carolina barks out a sharp laugh, because he is equally as dark as Sue. "No, I know a few fellows in the center." He wiggles his eyebrows suggestively, and Sue looks away, a tad bit scandalized. "But good to know that Katherine can still pass."

I shrug. "I suppose there are times when my pale skin

comes in handy." This is my least favorite topic of discussion.

"Are there a lot of Chinese in the city?" Lily asks. She has no patience for our conversations, and her eyes still hungrily drink in the beautiful arch and the words and symbols carved into it. From where we stand there is no sign of San Francisco's fabled Great Golden Wall, a relic from the Years of Discord when officials thought that the hordes in the East would make their way to the western coast of the continent. Perhaps we will see signs of it as we move farther into the urban landscape.

Carolina gestures toward the arch. "There surely are. The Chinese pert near run this city, and those peaked roofs are their contribution to the landscape. Vexes the white folks that ran up in here during the rush mightily. Of course, they ain't doing us any favors, either. The Negro sector is farther south. Unless you plan on heading to the white sector?"

I take a deep breath and let it out. It is not a sigh, but it is close. This is an old argument between Carolina and me. He has been urging me to pass since I boarded the *Capitán*. He simply will not accept that I can no longer surrender the Negro part of myself, any easier than I could give up an arm.

Sue strolls up beside me, her sword strapped to her back and a small carpetbag in her hand. In New Orleans she had traded her scythe for a broadsword. Same deadly reach, but a bit more versatile in a fight. She squints at the city before us and makes a sound somewhere between a snort and a sigh, mulling over Carolina's words. The fact that she is still by my side says much more about her than it does about me. She is loyal to a fault.

"I hope you ain't planning on playing Polly Plantation Owner again because I'm about done stepping and fetching," Sue says, her voice low. "You heard that lady back at the island. Slavery is illegal."

Mirth dances in Sue's eyes, but I am not laughing. I know the toll these small indignities can take over time. "Negro sector," I say to Carolina. And we begin to walk.

My nerves jangle as we enter the city. Lily carries a small sword and a pistol on her hip, and I have my Mollies, a rifle, and a pistol. But no amount of weaponry ever feels like enough.

"You weren't lying about the Chinese folks," Sue says, taking in an old woman tending a crowded market stall full of fresh fruit and fish. Her tone is not one of dismay or disgust, but wonder. My sentiment matches hers. I have never been to a place with so many different kinds of people living side by side.

"Yep," says Carolina. "The Chinese came here in the forties for the gold rush, just like everyone else, and when the dead overran Asia even more of them came. The West Coast is dotted with small settlements of Chinese folks, as well as people from Japan, India, and the Dutch East Indies. But San Francisco is the oldest and the largest Chinese community in the West. At first, the white folks who had settled the city welcomed them, since the Chinese worked cheaper than the Negroes or the Irish. They dug ditches, built levees, killed the dead, the hard work of establishing civilization. But then most Negroes moved on to Sacramento, a lot of the Irish headed north to the Willamette . . . and the Chinese got organized."

"Organized how?" I ask.

Carolina digs a cheroot out of his waistcoat and lights it as we walk. "They set prices for work and told the rich white folks who hired them that they could either pay those prices or go without. And every time new Chinese immigrants came into the city there were people who were already here to welcome them and give them the lay of the land. The white folks in charge got mad and tried to keep the Chinese out, even passed some laws up there in the state capital. But without the Navy or any kind of army to enforce them, it didn't matter."

"That is brilliant," I say. "To organize in such a way."

Carolina shrugs. "Unless you're a Negro. Our people have somehow ended up with the worst end of this market war. Whites refuse to pay us as much as they would pay the Chinese, and the Chinese refuse to hire us. To say nothing of how it's impacted the Californios, who were here before either the whites or the Chinese and have had to mostly leave the city. Don't let San Francisco fool you. It might seem pretty, but it's been built on the same volatile mixture of greed and exclusion as the rest of this country. Now, it's a powder keg just waiting for a spark."

We navigate our way down a side street, staying clear of the gutters, which are thick with muck. There are no cobblestones here, just red bricks that are curiously uneven, as if something had pushed them up from below. A breeze blows in from the water, taking away some of the stink of the city and leaving the scent of the ocean in its place. I shiver. I had not expected San Francisco to be so chilly, especially since the rest of our stops along the California coast had been so temperate. It is nothing compared to the winters I spent in Maryland, but there is a bite to the air that makes me wish I had a shawl.

We turn another corner and Carolina gestures toward a three-story building that dominates the block. It is painted red and the roof is emerald green, with inlaid writing on the front in what looks to be actual gold. A couple of very large men stand in front of the doorway, holding halberds and giving everyone who passes by a once-over. "That's the Sze Yup Society. It's run by the oldest established Chinese families in the city. They coordinate the labor pricing and negotiate contracts. There are smaller ones in places like Sacramento and down south in Los Angeles and San Diego, but this one is the biggest and most powerful in all the state. Nothing happens in the city without their okay." His lips twist, and his gaze goes far away for a moment. "And that includes in the Negro sector."

"This city is starting to sound like every other place I've been," Sue says, staring at the men as we pass. They wear their dark hair in a long braid in the back, but the front part is shaved. I try not to stare, but I am only partially successful. They are striking and imposing.

People from all over the world lived in New Orleans, their ships lying in the mouth of the Mississippi before they took their wares upstream. But very few stayed, and I am starting to realize how little time I have spent with anyone who is not white or colored. Now I wonder if it was because there were reasons I never considered, and I think of the way folks tend to group up with folks like them. Even on the *Capitán* I was careful to keep to myself, very rarely spending time with the Spanish-speaking men that worked in the engine room or on the decks. Some of them were from places in South America, others were from various towns in Mexico or California, but everyone had always stayed with those with whom they shared a cultural connection. It was just easier that way.

But now I wonder what kinds of things I might have missed by not reaching out to speak to them, to learn the things that they might know. And perhaps it is because the strangeness of San Francisco is a bit overwhelming and I am feeling a bit maudlin in being in such a gray city, but I miss Jane. She could talk to just about anyone, whether they understood her or not. She might have been a terrible listener, but I can imagine her waving at all the people in the streets here and, before we knew it, we would have made a friend or two (and likely a couple enemies as well). It is almost enough to make me smile through the usual pang of loss.

But more important, it makes me wonder: How can we make the world a better place if we are always at odds with one another for every single kind of reason under the sun?

Carolina takes us on a meandering path through the city, up and down hills, amid beautiful homes and shops, until finally we clear the last of the Chinese architecture, and the ornate buildings give way to squats. The faces that peek out between flaps are pale, and the hair dark, and it is so terribly wrong that even in a city with strong walls and its back against the ocean, where people from halfway around the world can live in luxury, there are still people struggling. The stories I had heard of California painted it as some vast promised land, and it is easy to see that there is coin aplenty here. But there is also poverty, and it strikes me once again that it is not simply the undead that make survival a constant battle.

The squats open up into grassy hills, and there is the slightest break before we come upon a collection of tents and haphazard structures. But these are different. The hollow-eyed faces we meet here have deep brown skin and crinkly, curly hair. The scent of offal is overwhelming, and there are fetid puddles everywhere I look. As we navigate between the threadbare squats my heart constricts. Now I understand the haunted look in Carolina's eyes.

"I thought California was supposed to be the land of milk and honey?" Lily asks, her expression of dismay saying everything.

"Maybe you have to head out into the mountains to find all the honey," Sue says. A bit of the old anxiousness flutters in my chest, and for the first time I wonder if we made the right decision coming to California. I had expected to find a Negro settlement that was robust and thriving, the kind of place where my keen eye for fashion and knowledge of color would be welcomed and have a civilizing impact on the place. But this part of the city is little more than an encampment, and it is only the sight of the wall in the distance that lets me know we have not left the city limits.

Carolina puffs on his cigar and sighs. "I'm afraid that the past few years have taken quite the toll on the colored population here. Most folks came here to flee slavery, but the work they found wasn't much better. When the dead rose there was an opportunity to work the patrols, but that was before the Chinese took over most of those jobs. Now the Chinese do all the menial work, leaving no real way for the Negro to thrive. It ain't like white folks are hiring us to do anything more than clean their houses."

"But how many of the Chinese who come here are trained? I thought China was a poor farming country," I say, as I realize that the only thing I know about China is opium and rice. "Didn't the dead nearly overrun the country in only a few weeks?"

Carolina shrugged. "That's most places. And rich white people don't care about training, they just want to feel safe. White people have the money, Chinese people have the numbers and are well organized, and everyone else is left out in the cold. Plus, space is getting scarce inside the wall. Now that the East Coast is gone people have started thinking about being behind walls in a way they haven't since the Chaos Years. This area is hotly contested, and someone has tried burning out the colored folks no fewer than three times. Most of these people lost everything in the last fire, including their loved ones. There ain't a lot to keep the Negro in San Francisco. Folks are hard-pressed to stay when there are better places to go. Ahh, here we are, Miss Mellie May's boardinghouse."

The building we stop in front of is barely standing. It lists ever so slightly and there are burn marks along the facade. It is a small sign of the fires Carolina mentioned, but there is more evidence all around us; as I inspect the land, I see the remnants of so many more buildings, all burned to the ground. No wonder this entire sector of the city is tents and hastily erected clapboard structures. No sense in building something permanent in this place, and anyone with a clue and the ability to leave has most likely gotten out.

We make our way up the stairs of Miss Mellie May's

house, and my heart is heavy. All my hopes and dreams have turned to ashes, and for the briefest moment I consider grabbing Carolina's arm and having him take us over to the white sector. Sue could pretend to be hired help, and Lily could be my younger sister. Things would be awful at first, but eventually I could perhaps learn to forget who I am, to ignore the snide comments about Negroes and don a mantle of gross indifference. And Lily is young and has spent the past few years passing.

But then I look at Sue, and I do not know how I could even consider dragging her to a place where her skin makes her a target every single waking moment. I think about the months I spent back in Summerland, laughing to hide my discomfort, pretending that I shared the same ideas about the world as those fine white families, and the way I felt as though a very important part of me was slowly dying, a brilliant rose robbed of light and sustenance.

This world may hate the Negro, but that is who I am. I do not care about the story my skin tells. I am a colored woman, and I will not let them make me hate myself.

Carolina raps on the door three times, and it is yanked open by an immaculately dressed Negro woman. She is nearly as dark as Sue and her complexion sets off the peacock-blue traveling suit she wears in a way that steals my breath. This woman, who I am taking to be the eponymous Miss Mellie May, is tiny, but exudes all of the ferocity of an alley cat.

A pencil-thin eyebrow cocks upward when she takes in our merry band. "Seamus, you bring me a bunch of riffraff to care for again?"

"Seamus?" Lily barks out. "Your given name is Seamus?" Sue and I exchange a glance, and she stifles a grin. The way Lily says the name, SHAAAAAYYYYYmus, makes it as clear as day why Carolina put that proper name behind him.

He clears his throat and, ignoring Lily, says, "I brought you boarders, Mellie. Paying customers. These girls here have come all the way from Nawlins on the *Capitán*, and they aim to make a name for themselves out here in the West. Did I mention they're paying customers?"

Miss May huffs out a little breath and puts her hands on her hips. "Well, that's nice, but seeing as how I'm heading to Sacramento for the foreseeable future, it's a little bit too late. Plus, don't think I've forgotten about the money *you* owe me."

I look from Carolina to the boardinghouse proprietress, and frown. "Do you two know each other?"

Miss May gives Carolina a bit of side-eye. "This fool is my brother, unfortunately."

"Her older and wiser brother," Carolina says with a rakish grin.

"If you're wiser, how'd you end up getting robbed by that saloon owner last time you were here? Too dumb not to remember to stay out of the gambling halls."

Carolina clears his throat and puffs on his cigar, his

embarrassment etched on his face. "Why are you going to Sacramento? You finally getting hitched?" he asks, deftly changing the subject.

Miss May rolls her eyes. "Juliet has an outfit up there escorting folks up into the mountains and back down again. It's a bit of a treacherous trip to her outpost, but a bunch of us left here are going to make our way there. There's nothing left for me in San Francisco." She lowers her eyes and blinks. "And before you start lecturing me about how important this place was to Momma, let me tell you that Mei's family came for her, again, and this time she went. She was the last good thing about this place and without her I am disinclined to stay."

Carolina's chagrined expression melts into one of sorrow. "Mellie, I'm sorry."

"Don't be. I should've known the moment I saw her that she was going to break my heart."

The pain written on the woman's face is naked and raw, and my sympathy goes out to her. Carolina is looking six kinds of uncomfortable, so I push around him to talk to the proprietress myself.

"Miss May, I am so sorry for your heartbreak. I'm Katherine Deveraux; this is my colleague Sue—just Sue—and our protégé, Lily Keats. You say there is a group of people here going to Sacramento, and I must say that I am intrigued by this prospect! Being newly arrived in San Francisco, I will admit I am a bit dismayed at the opportunities for Negroes here. I had heard that California was a land of opportunity for all. . . . Pray tell, how do the fortunes of colored girls like us look in Sacramento?"

Miss May's expression shifts into one of curiosity. "Well, I would say that the fortunes of enterprising young ladies are vastly superior in Sacramento to what they are here. The Chinese presence is smaller, and most of the white folks have fled north to Oregon. Not only that, but there is a strong contingent of Buffalo Soldiers up that way, many of them keeping the cavalry tradition strong and the area safe from the occasional dead. But, you say this little one is your protégé. What, exactly, are you girls about?"

I laugh, the sound high, tinkling, and amiable. "Oh, Miss May, we are experts in the defensive arts. As you can see from Sue's broadsword, she specializes in horde clearing; I myself focus on personal defense. Lily here is learning both disciplines, and though she is nigh passable at this point, I daresay that in a few years she will be a marvel to rival Hattie McCrea."

Miss May frowns. "I don't know who that is, but you girls do look well-fed. And capable."

Carolina knows an opening when he sees it. "Oh, the girls are more than capable, Mellie. I was trying to get them to stay on the *Capitán*, but I'm afraid I couldn't convince them."

"Well, of course not, that smelly old ship doesn't have anything to offer a cadre of audacious young ladies. I daresay it's hardly any better than San Francisco here. But Sacramento"—Miss May pauses and grins winningly—"there you could find your fortune."

I give her a polite smile, because her willingness to oversell Sacramento gives me pause, but I am a woman with limited options. If there is a chance for more and an opportunity to get there, I believe it to be worth investigating.

I raise an eyebrow at Sue, asking an unspoken question, and she gives me a quick nod, indicating her agreement. Sue and I are close enough after traveling together for the past year that I did not think she would object to this change of plans, but it is good to know that she is wholly on board.

"Well, then, I do believe we shall investigate the matter of the state capital a little more closely. May we come in?" I ask Miss May, and she stands back, allowing us to enter.

I pray we are doing the right thing.

Some say that the marshal is the most important personage in the West, seeing to order and keeping good citizens safe. But it is truly the bounty hunters who work to bring the lawless to heel, even if their methods are as brutal as the criminals they hunt.

—Western Tales, *Volume 23*

— J A N E —

Chapter 27
In Which I Consider Domestic Bliss

I follow Callie out of the sheriff's office and down the street to the hotel where we've secured lodgings. She was down in the mouth all through delivering Perry's body to the sheriff, which was less a delivery and more telling the sheriff a tall tale to justify why Perry was missing both his ears and his nose. The man had finally given up the location of Gideon Carr, a small house in Sacramento, but by then I was covered in blood.

Thankfully we had the Andrews gang as an easy scapegoat, and the sheriff too easily believed that the whole bloody scene had been a robbery gone wrong, with Perry double-crossing the Andrews and paying the price. Callie had deftly avoided my gaze during the entire conversation, her eyes always sliding away every time the sheriff looked at Perry and swore.

"Seem like you got a knack for finding people after they been through a trial," the man said, his words a not so subtle reference to what happened in Denver.

I shrugged. "Bad things happen to bad people."

Now, as we stride toward the hotel, Callie gives me the silent treatment, her anger a palpable thing between us. I know what's on her mind, but it ain't anything I'm of a mood to discuss. I'm still annoyed that she sided with Perry. I don't know that I like where this attitude of Callie Washington's is going.

I can stomach a lot of things, but pacifism ain't one of them.

We make our way through the fine double doors of the hotel, and the owner meets us in the foyer.

"You can't bring that dog in here," he says, gazing askance at Salty. He's been patiently dogging my heels, waiting for his supper. Even while Perry was screaming up a storm he sat nearby, adding his own chorus to Perry's yells. I kept expecting someone to come by the cantina to see what was happening, but no one did.

Humanity continues to disappoint.

Callie slumps. "Is there a problem, sir?" Her tone is like

THE ROAD TO PERDITION

an out of tune fiddle, strident and annoying. It pulls me from the memory of Perry and back to the now.

The hotel owner stands in our path. Color rides high in his pale cheeks—fear or rage, I can't tell. He straightens a little. "That animal is mangy. This is a luxury establishment, a place for good folks."

"The dog was in here this morning when we booked our lodgings. You walking our accommodations back?" I ask, voice low. I don't have to yell; the dead man's blood on my clothing is probably speaking loudly enough. I wear trousers, just as I have ever since we left Nicodemus, and the brown material bears stains from past run-ins with both the dead and the living.

Something in the clerk's expression changes, and I figure he must have heard the stories about my adventures. People out west are entirely too bored without a real threat from the dead, and they've got nothing to do but wag their tongues. There are even weekly rags dedicated to such stories. It's one of the things I've come to love about the frontier. Everyone is too damn busy surviving to gossip.

But here, in the city? It's another matter entirely.

"You got something to say?" I prod, tapping the butt of my talking iron, once, twice, to help him make up his mind. His eyes are drawn to both the motion and the blood that still cakes my fingernails. We paid the rate he quoted us—most likely higher than what any white person would pay to stay in this nowhere town—and just because he's looking to get rid of us now doesn't mean our money ain't green.

"You can stay," he says finally, his face pale. "One night. But you and your sister leave first thing in the morning." I smirk at the notion that Callie and I are related, and there is a small bit of joy in the man's fear as well. I'd rather have the same respect that he gives any other guest in his hotel, but if I can't have that, I'll settle for fear.

"Much obliged," Callie says, as though he's doing us a favor.

"Send up someone to draw a bath as well," I say. "And make sure the water is hot." I ain't playing this game any longer, kowtowing when folks are just giving me my due. I might not have been able to force the sheriff to give me my proper pay—he shorted us on the bounty because of the condition of Perry's body—but I can take on a hotel clerk. I tip my hat at him and head up the stairs, Callie and Salty right behind me.

As soon as we enter the room, Salty sniffs each corner before settling near the fireplace. I drop my lone saddlebag next to the door and unstrap my sword holster and pistol belt, the job made awkward due to my amputated left arm. I'm better at dressing and undressing than I was, but there are days when I would kill to have my left hand and forearm back.

Callie drops her saddlebags next to her side of the bed and goes over to the fire grate and stokes the coals back to life, Salty licking her face as she works until she finally pushes him away and he curls up on the hearth rug. I land myself in the room's lone chair, not wanting to settle on the bed while I'm covered in road dust and blood.

"You want to talk about what's vexing you?" I say to Callie's back.

"Nothing is bothering me, Jane."

"Not a single thing?"

"Well, I probably don't need to tell you that what you did to Perry is downright horrifying and completely unnecessary, but there ain't no way to unslaughter that lamb," she says, continuing to poke at the fire. "In fact, if there'd been an actual lamb, you probably would've killed that as well and tried to convince me that I wanted lamb chops for dinner."

"Lamb chops are delicious," I say, hoping I can at least provoke a ghost of a smile.

Nothing.

I sigh, because she's being petulant and all I want to do is take a bath and sleep for a month. But if I let her go to bed cross it'll last a whole week instead of just until morning. Hell, it's been two months since things fell apart back in Denver, and we still ain't talked about it beyond a few sniping comments here and there.

"Callie, leave that fire alone before you burn off your eyebrows and come here," I say. She glances at me over her shoulder before dropping the poker in its holder and slinking toward me. She still won't meet my eyes, and I use my good arm to tug her forward and into my lap. She's no cleaner than I am, and this ain't the first time either of us have been covered in blood. She huffs and I plant a kiss on her nose. She's still stiff, but she doesn't pull away when I rest my good arm in her lap.

"You're mad because you wanted to make a deal with Perry and I didn't," I say.

"No," she says slowly, like I'm stupid, "I'm mad because you tortured and killed a man after I gave him my word he would live. Again."

"Ah, so this is about Denver."

"Not everything is about Denver, Jane."

"But this is," I say, holding her on my lap when she makes to flounce away. "And here's the thing about Denver: I told you that I was planning on killing the O'Reillys right after we talked to the sheriff. And you know I ain't one to break a promise."

I'm about to tell her, for the thousandth time, how the O'Reillys deserved to die. I'm about to tell her, for the thousandth time, that *all* the people we've been chasing deserve to die. And worse besides. But the look she gives me shuts me right up.

The thing is, I know I'm right. But I'm not willing to lose the one person I got left over it.

After Gideon fled Nicodemus, Callie nursed me back to health. She sawed off my arm, kept the wound from getting infected, and made sure I had enough to eat and drink. All I did the entire time was imagine the twenty different ways I was going to kill Gideon Carr. I thought about small Thomas and the Duchess, Sallie and Nessie. I thought about Cyrus Washington with his careful manner and soft voice, the confident way he discussed the risk of the vaccine and his passion for his town. I even thought about Jackson and how those dead that had ambushed him on the prairie came from Summerland. Knowing what I did of Gideon's penchant for experimentation, I was soon convinced he'd had even more to do with the end of that thrice-cursed town than I'd suspected at the time. In my mind, Gideon had killed Jackson just as surely as he'd killed poor Thomas. Him, and his reckless pursuit of a cure.

Winter set in, and Callie kept us both alive, foraging for food in nearby towns until I was strong enough to go out hunting with her. Life became very different when the dead were no longer a threat, and she taught me how to take stock of the prairie for dangers that weren't shamblers.

It's hard to say just when I got sweet on Callie. It wasn't an all-at-once sort of thing. I reckon there's something about being stuck with a person for a moment that makes you start to see them differently. She told me stories about her family, about Gideon when she first met him; I told her stories of Miss Preston's and Rose Hill. I even told her about my heartbreak over Jackson, and my visions of him nearly disappeared. Things were good, and by the time we ended up in Denver we were sharing more than just stories. Unlike so much else in our lives, it felt . . . easy.

I guess falling for someone always is. It's the staying in love that's hard.

The Colorado Territory was the first time we fought, and I reckon that was because it was the first time we'd encountered other people in almost a year. The horde had wiped out most of the towns still standing in Kansas; whatever Indian nations were still about were good at keeping themselves scarce as Callie and I traveled west so that most days as we walked we were the only living souls about. But all that changed once we got nearer to Fort Laramie, a heavily fortified, bustling crossroads trading post in the Wyoming Territory. For some reason the horde hadn't roamed this far west, and the shamblers we did see were quickly put down.

Fort Laramie was the first time we encountered news of Gideon Carr.

It was a small thing, a newspaper article from the Denver paper. There, in the smallest font possible, was a headline that upended the foundations of my new life:

BRILLIANT SCIENTIST LOOKING FOR VOLUNTEERS TO TEST NEW VACCINE

It was like seeing a ghost, and it was all I could think about for days. How long until he turned folks after making a mistake? How many people had he killed already, the kind of people no one really cared about? Thoughts of Gideon and the people he'd killed went round and round in my head until I finally realized that no one was going to stop Gideon Carr.

Which is why I had to end him and his reign of terror.

It was about this time that Callie and I began to realize that we would be remiss not to find a way to earn some money. Since no one would hire a one-armed girl to be their Attendant and Callie had none of the necessary training, we started taking bounties. It was lucrative work, and the thing about bounties is that the sheriffs posting them are already past the point of desperation. Which means they ain't too picky about who delivers on them. And that was the case with the O'Reillys.

The bounty on those boys' heads had only been for livestock rustling and petty thievery, but they'd killed a family of Negroes. The O'Reillys had come onto their property pretending to be beggars, and the Turner family had welcomed them in and fed them, even gave them a place to sleep. And in return, once the Turners had gone to bed, the O'Reillys murdered all of them in their beds. It was the kind of crime that should have seen them hanged. But killing Negroes wasn't against the law in Colorado Territory, just like it wasn't illegal to kill an Indian in most places, and so the sheriff had only been worried about the crimes of theirs that had been perpetrated against white folks—cattle rustling, stealing a few chickens. If there had ever been any doubt in my mind that the lives of colored folks were cheap, the Turners' tragic end had put them to bed.

There was no court in Colorado that would hold those boys accountable for their true crimes. But more than that, while looking for the O'Reillys we discovered that they'd done some work for a man of science with a laboratory outside of Denver.

And so, when we caught up with the O'Reilly boys, I took the liberty of appointing myself judge and jury. But not until after I'd discovered everything they knew about Gideon Carr.

Everyone gives up what they know at some point. It's just a matter of how much cutting you have to do before they do.

We were too late in getting to Denver, Gideon was long gone by the time we'd arrived, but now we knew that Gideon Carr was hale and hearty and using lowlifes like the O'Reillys to do his dirty work.

Killing the O'Reillys had been easy, and after that, well, I realized that it was much simpler to collect a bounty on a dead ruffian than a live one. I've spent so much of my life fighting and killing the dead that the living seem like a cakewalk in comparison. Sure, they might fight back, but if you're quick and you're ruthless, there's not much to worry about. Either way, I was willing to do whatever I could to make sure Gideon Carr paid for his crimes.

And if Callie had any objections, well, eating fine food and staying in nice hotels shut them down.

Until now.

Callie doesn't say anything for a long time, and for a moment I'm afraid that I've gone and done it this time, that she's going to leave me in the night and I'll be on my own. I don't relish the idea of it being just me and Salty. But we're so close to finding Gideon now that I can practically smell him, and the thought of finally catching up with him after all this time is a sweet one. Maybe finer than Callie's kisses, truth be told.

That's when Callie looks me dead in the eyes, and her expression ain't angry in the least. It's indescribably sad.

"I ain't mad that the O'Reillys are dead. They were bad people, and the Turners deserved justice. I ain't even all that mad about Perry, because Lord knows he was a sonuvabitch. It's just . . . all this awfulness, it takes a toll, Jane. This doesn't feel like justice, it feels like revenge. And just what do you think is going to be left of your soul if you keep letting vengeance take tiny bites out of it?"

I snort.

"It's a good question," Jackson says, laid out on the bed, ankles crossed. He wears a fine suit of all black.

"No one asked you," I snap at him. Callie rears back, looks over at the bed, and climbs to her feet.

"This is what I'm talking about," Callie sighs, tugging on one of her braids. "You're talking to spirits, you're torturing people, you're killing because you can, and all the mirth has left you. This ain't you, Jane. This hunting for bounties and for Gideon, it's made you hard. You've locked up the best parts of yourself, and all that's left is a woman that I don't like, one who shoots first and asks questions later and talks to thin air in between."

"The ghost thing might be a bit much, and that's something I have to think on myself," I admit grudgingly. Since we've gotten to California, Jackson has been making more frequent appearances. Nothing good can come of that. "As for the killing, well, executing someone who deserves it feels like a fine bit of work, like planting a garden or washing your face. You know it needs done, and while the work itself can be tiresome, the result is invariably worth it."

"But who made you executioner?" Callie says, her voice low. "Do you really win anything if you end up just like the people you hate?"

"If it ends up with Gideon Carr in a pine box? Yes."

The bleak mood I've been fighting for months finally descends upon me, just as there's a knock on the door. Callie opens it and two Negro men bring in a copper tub as well as steaming buckets of hot water. They fill the tub halfway, and then leave two more buckets of water near the fire to keep warm. Callie hands them each a silver dollar and they leave with a tip of their hats.

As the two men leave, Jackson's ghost looks at me and shakes his head. "The girl loves you, Jane, as impossible as that might be. Listen to her." And then like always, the bastard is gone.

Callie and I stare at each other for a moment, not speaking, and I think this is my chance to tell her all the things I feel. This is where I should tell her that I'm sorry and I'll do better, that I'm not the person she thinks I'm becoming: heartless, ruthless, killing without an ounce of remorse.

But I respect her too much to lie to her. Because no matter what else I do, I plan on hunting down Gideon Carr. I plan on doing whatever is necessary to the people I meet along the way who have aided him in his foul agenda. And when I find him, I plan on making sure he feels every ounce of misery that he has inflicted on the world.

And I am going to take my time doing it.

"You go first this time," Callie finally says. "You're covered in blood."

I begin to undress, awkwardly, and she comes over to help. The moment for declarations has passed, and we are back to our usual rhythms. Her hands go to unbraid my hair, and I accept the help without complaint. She helps me climb into the tub, and I sigh as the warm water washes over my skin. For a moment I'm nervous, the same way I always am when I step into a tub. A bad experience with water as a child has always made me a little bit skittish, but as Callie starts to help me wash my hair my anxiousness melts away.

I get out of the bath. We use an empty bucket to drain most of the water, tossing it out the window that overlooks the rear of the hotel and pouring in most of the remaining hot water for Callie.

And we do it all without uttering a word.

I wash her back, planting a kiss on her shoulder when I'm finished. She reaches back and rests her hand on my neck, holding me close for a few heartbeats, steam wafting up around us. I'm half tempted to climb into the tub with her.

How is it possible to care for someone so much and still want more?

"Let's just forget about Gideon," she says. She releases me, and I take a few steps away from the tub. "We can head north, get ourselves a little homestead." Her head is bowed and her voice is low. "We've got funds enough to set ourselves up right. Or maybe go back east? We could do our own private tour of the great deserted cities and the dead will leave us be. It would be like back in Nicodemus, after the fall."

She ain't pleading, but there's a quaver to her voice. I sit on the bed, wrapped in a blanket, and say nothing. Because I don't like to break a promise, and what I'm thinking she won't want to hear.

None of this happiness is for me. Gideon Carr's death is my only future.

After Callie rinses with one of the buckets, she drops our clothes into the tub, washing them and stretching them out next to the fire, stoking it so that it's summer hot in our little room.

"Come lie next to me," I say, and she obliges without a word. I wrap my good arm around her, and sigh as she presses against me. The heat and the relief of having finally caught Perry after weeks of tracking him descend upon me.

I fall asleep without ever answering her.

Or maybe, that is all the response she needs.

When I dream, it's of walking hand in hand through the fields of Rose Hill with Callie. It's a sweet taste of what I can never have.

If there is any doubt as to the necessity of westward expansion, the rising of the dead has thoroughly ended the debate. For America to survive she must find new lands to claim, conquer, and rebuild.
—Senator Jerimiah Springfield, 1867

— KATHERINE —

Chapter 28
Notes on a Curious Wagon Train

We spend the night at Miss May's boardinghouse. She charges us only half the usual rate—a deal on account of three of us sharing a single room. The house creaks the whole night through, and I find myself missing the gentle rocking of the *Capitán*; but once I get to sleep, my rest is undisturbed, and I wake the next morning to sun filtering in through the window.

As I wake I take a moment to mentally revisit the events

from the night before. Miss May had related the real reason she was heading up to Sacramento: San Francisco was not safe for Negroes. A few years ago everyone had been content to leave the Negro sector alone. But now there was a scramble for space behind the Great Golden Wall, which is what folks call the wall around the city that keeps the dead out, few and far between as they were. There were quite a few men of science that predicted that now that the East was lost the hordes would try once more to cross the Rockies, and that some might succeed. Of course, the constant attention of the Army in California had thus far kept the number of dead to a minimum, but there was a panic in the city as everyone scrambled for land.

And the Negro sector was the one place where no one cared if a few buildings burned.

"The good people in this city have fled, because good people have no stomach to watch their neighbors be burned out and then have their plots bought from under them," Miss May said over dinner the night before. "And after this most recent fire, I have to say that I'm of a mind to finally head east into the mountains. I've heard there's a Negro settlement out past Sacramento, place up in the foothills called Haven. Let the whites and Chinese fight over San Francisco, I'm going to find someplace where I can have a little farm and not have to worry about waking up in flames."

That wasn't the only reason Miss May wanted to leave the city, though. There was also a matter, mentioned briefly, of

THE ROAD TO PERDITION

a close friendship gone south, but I was polite enough not to pry into the specifics. Miss May's tears while packing up a studio portrait of her and a Chinese woman provided more than enough insight.

My musings are interrupted by the door opening just a bit, the soft pad of feet on the wood floor drawing my attention. Before I can wonder what the noise is about a giant orange tabby launches itself onto the bed, gazing at me with luminous eyes for a heartbeat before walking onto my chest.

"Mrow," the cat says, as though we had already been introduced.

"Ah-choo," I say in response, because it must be said that although I enjoy the presence of felines, especially if they happen to be adept mousers, their existence does not agree with mine.

I sit up and scoop up the cat in one move. I no longer wear a corset; the loss of Jane set me off on a spiraling path of doubt and uncertainty, and in my endless revisiting of that day, I could not help but wonder if I might have been able to save her if I had been less restricted in my movements. I do wear a binder across my breasts during the day, but in my rest I wear only a sleep shirt (and a few throwing knives strapped to a holster on my thigh). Sometimes I think that Jane must be looking down at me from on high with that smug expression of hers, and it brings me a moment of gladness.

I set the cat down while I dress, and it sits and watches me with wide green eyes. I had not seen any sign of a cat yesterday afternoon while we'd helped Miss May box up her few belongings. But the cat looks well cared for, and there is something about it that reminds me of Jane, perhaps the way it looks at me as though I were the silliest creature on the planet.

Carolina told me a story about a man he had met from the Punjab who said that all things that die are brought back for another chance at life. The best people reach enlightenment, but the rest of us might have to come back as a lesser creature. Carolina had told me the story as a way of explaining that the undead plague had to be some sort of cosmic punishment for humans being so terrible to one another. But I had been quite taken with the idea of people dying and coming back as something like a grasshopper or a rat, and the way that cat looks at me makes my heart ache. Maybe Jane is not up in heaven being insufferable, after all.

"You will be glad to notice I am no longer wearing a corset," I say to the cat, because if it is Jane I would rather forestall a lot of meowing about my attire.

"Who're you talking to?" Sue asks from behind me, and I startle.

"Lordy, Sue! Creeping around like a thief is like to give me a heart attack."

She laughs. "I ain't the one fixin' to sleep the day away. I was just coming to fetch you." She holds a plate for me; there is cornpone and a nice slice of fried ham, and my stomach grumbles. "I saved you some breakfast, because Lily was eye-ing it."

"That girl is growing like a weed and has the restless dead's appetite to match," I say. "Thank you." I take the plate and begin to eat, the cat cleaning up any crumbs that fall. I eat standing up, and Sue watches me appraisingly.

"What?" I say around a mouth full of food.

"You disappointed that San Francisco is a bust?" Sue asks.

I chew as I think, turning my thoughts over and in on themselves. "I suppose I was looking forward to seeing the cosmopolitan city we had been dreaming about. But I should have known that it would suffer from the same ills as every other place."

Sue nods. Her expression is pensive, and the corners of her mouth turn down. "You ever remember Nicodemus and think maybe there's no point to all this fussing? Maybe we aren't supposed to be in control of our own lives. Maybe we just get to messing things up."

I frown. "Are you saying that you think that it's colored folks' fault that they're being run out of San Francisco?"

Sue shrugs. "I don't rightly know. I see everything that's happened here, what Miss May's seen, and I just feel like, when it comes to Negroes, it seems like our mistakes pile up faster and harder than anyone else's."

"I think that's because there are a lot of folks who are just waiting for us to fail so they can seize the opportunity to put us back into a cage of their making. If it had not been for Gideon Carr, Nicodemus might still be standing. He destroyed that town from the inside, because he thought he knew better than anyone else. It had nothing to do with any kind of inferiority of the Negro."

Sue nods and sighs. "It just feels like nothing is ever fair for us."

"I believe that feeling is the truth, hidden under so many things that feel coincidental but are in fact purposeful. Remember Ida talking about the Lost States? How the laws ostensibly made to ensure people are equal are enforced to keep people in servitude? Back in Nawlins, it just was not proper for a Creole man to marry a Negro woman, but he could keep her on the side if he wanted, no different from a wife. What do you think would have happened if all those well-to-do men started marrying Negro women legally, making them legitimate ladies of means?"

"Things would start to change," Sue says.

I finish my food and brush the crumbs off my skirt, the orange cat sitting back and grooming itself. "The world naturally trends toward injustice, and it is colored folks who bear the brunt of that. The moment it looks like a Negro will break out of those chains, both real and metaphorical, the faster folks are going to arrive with their torches. First, they will try to offer helpful advice; next, they will try to burn you out for your own good. I reckon if it had not been for the Years of Discord and the enterprising nature of the

Chinese folks in San Francisco, the white people here would have found a way to force the Chinese out. But they are too powerful, so white folks are directing their ire at the Negro sector instead. It is no different from what the writings of Mr. Frederick Douglass predicted."

Sue gives me a bit of side-eye. "I don't know who that is."

"I read some of his essays to you on the boat over here. Remember? 'Power concedes nothing'? Either way, Miss May is right. If the Negro wants to flourish, then they will have to find a place to put down roots and push them down so deep that nothing, not even the dead, will be able to pry them loose."

Sue grins and rocks back on her heels. "I never took you for a radical, Miss Priss."

I ignore her teasing tone. "Well, I suppose hearing Miss May's tales of woe last night have put me in a different sort of mind."

The truth is, I had been thinking about all sorts of things since losing Jane. I cannot help but remember the way she had never hesitated to call out some random bit of unfairness or chicanery. (As long as it was not her own, of course.) There is something admirable about being willing to stand up against injustice and name the devil true. And now that I am in a position to reinvent myself, to be a fine Negro woman here in the great state of California, I want to have the courage to stand against unfairness, no matter how difficult and ugly it might be.

Of course, everyone knows that it is much easier for a leopard to talk about changing its spots than to actually start to wear stripes.

"Either way," I say to Sue, bringing myself back to the moment at hand, "I am interested in finding the place past Sacramento that Miss May mentioned, Haven. Jane had a letter from her mother that told Jane to find her there." I swallow past the sudden lump that forms in my throat, taking a deep breath and letting it out before continuing. "Jane was convinced that it was another Survivalist stronghold, in the manner of Summerland; I find it curious that Miss May says it is in fact some kind of Negro town."

"Maybe things changed," Sue says. "We should head out and meet the wagon master before we leave. Despite what Miss May says, I don't know many men who are too comfortable with the idea of a woman working security. Might be a good idea to show him we ain't a couple of withering roses."

Sue is right. I wash my face, secure my weapons, and don a tasteful hat that contains only a handful of swallow feathers before following her down the stairs and out into the morning.

Sue had gotten directions to the staging area this morning, so she leads the way through the gray, misty landscape. The sun had finally deigned to grace us with its presence late yesterday afternoon, but it has hidden its face once more; the weather is cold and dreary, altogether damp, and while that may be typical for March in these parts, I am more acclimated to the heady temperatures of the southern climes after spending months making my way across Central America. I shiver and hug myself, wishing I had brought some sort of overcoat with me, and I make a note to see if there happens to be a dressmaker with some ready-made offerings in the vicinity. I can only imagine our trek into the mountains will be even cooler, and I have no intention of freezing my way across California.

The Negro sector of the city is mostly mud and sorrow. Miss May told us people had been leaving steadily since the most recent fire, especially since the fire brigade had not even bothered responding until long after the buildings that had been set ablaze were little more than smoldering ruins. "It doesn't take a knock upside the head to let me know when I ain't welcome," she'd said. This exodus of which we are now a part has been weeks in the making, and I have no doubt that it was the Good Lord's intention for us to escort them, defenseless as they are. It is true that there are fewer shamblers out west, but even one can wreak havoc on an underprepared group.

Not to mention the more human threat of bandits.

Upon arriving at the staging area, I am even more confident that Sue and I are doing the Lord's work. Families pile belongings into a handful of rickety wagons. Children and the elderly stand by, and there are only a handful of capable-looking adults, all of them with the lean and hungry look of a people used to going without. There are a few fashionably dressed men, mostly closer to our age, but they have a soft look to them. Dandies.

No one I see moves like a fighter, like someone trained in the rhythms and patterns of survival. And the weaponry? There is no way this wagon train is going to make it two minutes fighting the undead with the hodgepodge I spy as we approach. A few rusty rifles, one or two knives, and a thin sword with a tassel at the end that I recognize from our weaponry courses at Miss Preston's as being Japanese in origin. But it would not matter if they had freshly forged artillery; the people gathered here do not appear to have the slightest sense of how to wield these blades and firearms.

All of them, that is, with the exception of a Negro woman with a pair of overlong knives strapped to her waist. They are not Mollies, they are too short for that title, but there is something in the way that she moves that strikes me as familiar. I suspect that she is the lone person here that can handle themselves in a scuffle.

"That's the wagon master with the red vest," Sue says, pointing to a white woman with blond hair and a tight expression.

I cannot help but frown. "The wagon master is a woman?"

"I don't see anyone else wearing a red vest, do you?"

This turn of events has me flummoxed to the point that I have to rearrange my talking points in my mind. I like to rehearse conversations in my head before they happen, because otherwise I get a feeling like being in an unmoored dinghy on a storm-tossed sea. And that usually results in me giving a polite smile and agreeing to all sorts of nonsense I have no intention of following through with.

I take a deep breath and stride over to the wagon master, who has her head down, inspecting some sort of list. As I approach, she begins to speak without looking up. "Juliet, I simply cannot make heads or tails of this chicken scratch. Either way, we are simply going to have to reorganize. This just will not do." That is when she raises her head and frowns at me. "You are not Juliet. Who, may I ask, are you?"

Sue chuckles behind me. "You about to deal with some finery," she murmurs, which is what the girls at Miss Preston's used to call the rich white women who came through to engage an Attendant. And she is right. The woman's bearing makes it clear that she is used to being in charge.

"No, I apologize, I am not Juliet. My name is Katherine Deveraux, and this is my associate, Sue—no last name. We are mistresses of the defensive arts, and we are joining your wagon train at the invitation of one Miss Mellie May, proprietress of Miss Mellie May's boardinghouse. She has engaged us as additional security—"

"Thank you, Jesus," the woman says, interrupting my speech, and I start. "Pardon my rudeness," she continues with a warm smile. "I am Louisa Aiken and that woman over there with the blades and the braids is my business partner, Juliet. Also no last name, though Lord knows I have tried to convince her to adopt something for etiquette's sake."

Sue and I exchange a glance but say nothing. The woman's accent is from somewhere in the Lost States, but my ear is not good enough to place it accurately. She waves to the aforementioned Negro woman, who strides over. Once again I get that sense of familiarity in the woman's movements, but I am rather certain that I do not know her.

"Juliet, this is Katherine and Sue. Oh, you do not mind me calling you Katherine, do you?" At my headshake, she smiles. "Excellent. We tend to do away with formalities on the wagon train. Life out here on the frontier has done terrible things for my manners, and it is only getting worse. So why pretend otherwise? Juliet, these girls will be additional security for our trip."

Juliet squints at us. "You Attendants?"

I straighten and give her my best smile. "Yes! Well, I am afraid we have not encountered any situations where an Attendant would be of use in ages . . . but we completed our training at Miss Preston's School of Combat in Baltimore, the finest academy in all the nation, whatever might remain of it."

Juliet gives us a slow smile, like dawn breaking over the land. "You don't say. I'm a Miss Preston's girl, too. Was that miserable Miss Anderson still there when you left, or did she have the good sense to be eaten by a shambler?"

"Oh, she was there—as sour as a bushel of lemons," Sue breaks in, and Juliet laughs. Sue shifts to stand next to her, and the two trade stories of Miss Preston's while I turn back to Louisa.

"If I may be so bold," I say, "I take it from your previous declaration you may be interested in securing our services for the protection of the entire wagon train? Miss May had originally hinted that we might find employment as her personal protection."

The woman nods. "My original count was twenty people heading to Sacramento, and now we're up to well over a hundred and fifty. That's likely twelve or fifteen wagons—more than Juliet can ably watch out for if we run into a group of stray shamblers. If you girls are going our way, I'd be much obliged if you might be willing to work the whole train. I pay four dollars a day plus vittles."

"Make that five-fifty a day, each, and rations for our apprentice as well, and you have yourself a deal."

Louisa smiles. "Done. I think we're going to be fast friends. You've got a good head on your shoulders. I like that."

I nod in gratitude. The hope that had died a brutal death the day before begins to burble anew. I can do this. I can make a life for myself here. If this woman has managed to be savvy and successful, well, so can I. "We will secure our belongings and return forthwith. It was brilliant to make your acquaintance."

"Likewise," Louisa says, already going back to her list. "And welcome to California."

It might be thought that in a world of cutthroats and hard men a woman would fear for her life and her safety, perhaps even seek to engage her own protection. But just as men have found their fortune in these merciless lands, so have a number of the fairer sex.
—Western Tales, *Volume 23*

— J A N E —

Chapter 29
In Which I Am Once Again Fortune's Fool

I wake slowly the next morning, feeling better than I have in a spell. My body still aches a bit from so many days on the road, but my hair is clean and freshly braided and my heart is light. For the first time in a very long while I have a goal in mind, a destination that will lead me to the end of my search for Gideon Carr. I'll head north to Sacramento, track down this Thurman Leakes character, and find Gideon, and then after that—

After that I will seek out this town called Haven, and finally find my momma and Aunt Aggie.

But not until I put down Gideon. Because, as reluctant as I am to admit it, Callie is right: there's a sickness in my soul, a bleak sort of hopelessness that I've tried to fight for a long time. It was fed and nurtured during my convalescence, but each morning since seeing that newspaper article in Fort Laramie it has gotten stronger. Every day that I wake up and consider Gideon Carr out there in the world—setting up shop in a town somewhere, continuing to experiment on folks—I grow angrier. The only way to close this chapter of my life, to move on from the barren landscape of murder and human destitution, is to kill the man who put me on this path in the first place. Once he's dead, I can go back to fighting for something worthwhile.

Even if I'm not all that sure what that might be just yet.

Salty rolls over on the bed and whines at me, pushing his head under my hand the way he does when he wants attention. It's my first clue that something's amiss. Callie ain't too partial to Salty. He belonged to some drifter who tried to come at us in Utah, and I'd kept the mutt as a reminder that I could never let my guard down. But he turned out to be a good little dog. He'd mostly been trained to sniff out the dead, but he was also good at fetching and flushing small game. Callie had just thought he was dirty, which, he was. Because he was a dog. But Salty is in the bed, which means

Callie ain't, and that sets off all my alarm bells.

I sit up, and it's immediately clear that she's gone. Her weapons aren't where she left them last night. I scurry out of bed, my sudden movements dragging an excited bark from Salty, but I ignore him and take a quick inventory. My boots are still here, untouched, as well as my falchion, the sword I switched to when it became clear that dual-wielded sickles were no longer an option for me. My tool belt, which holds my pistol, a few throwing knives, and extra rounds of ammo, is still hanging off the foot of the bed. There's also a single blue dress, ugly and threadbare, across the room from my clothes from yesterday.

But my saddle bags, which held my extra clothes, share of cash, and my letters from my momma, are gone.

I sink to the floor and bury my head in my hand. Callie's left me high and dry.

After a moment, I scramble across the floor, the motion made even more awkward by my left arm being shorter than my right. If I wanted to get a strap-on arm, I could, everything from my elbow to my shoulder is intact and strong besides, thanks to months spent running drills back in Kansas, but I haven't considered it so far because they're made of wood and most of them are too blasted heavy. Plus, I always had Callie around to help when I needed it. Now, though, I'm thinking I might need to find a surgeon and see what he can do for me.

I grab my right boot and feel around inside for my

emergency stash. But instead of a wad of cash, my hand finds a single piece of paper. I pull it out and read the sentence scrawled across in charcoal.

I love you, but I am going home.

That's it.

I am abandoned and penniless, and a feeling somewhere between grief and rage chokes a sob out of me.

"You can't say the girl didn't warn you," Jackson says. He wears homespun, the same way he did the day he died, and I wonder if his attire has had some hidden meaning all this time. I've been too preoccupied with seeing a ghost to get to noticing intricate details and parsing out their meaning.

"She didn't tell me she was going to rob me on her way out," I say, dashing away a few tears that have managed to slip out and feeling sour about the whole thing.

"The heart works in mysterious ways, Janey-Jane. Besides, you can't fault the girl, can you? Think of how you would've felt if you were in her place. You pretty much told her to go pound sand when she asked you to run away and spend the rest of your life with her. She's angry and hurt. Ain't nothing for her out here in California, and you're too busy carving up men to even notice that she was offering you everything you've ever wanted."

"So you say." I stand and begin to dress, taking my time as I do. I don the dress rather than the shirt and trousers hanging by the fire; it's easier to get on and fasten the buttons one-handed.

For a moment I consider going after her. The sunlight that filters in through the room's window is still watery, which means she can't have more than a two-hour head start. If there's anything I've learned over the past couple of months it's how to track someone down. It won't be all that hard to find a Negro girl.

But doing that means I have to wait to head out for Sacramento. At some point the papers are going to pick up news of Perry's death, and I fully believe that Gideon knows I'm gunning for him. He may be mad, but he isn't a fool.

And so, I have a choice: love or vengeance.

But it's a decision I've already made, and one I keep making with each scoundrel I kill.

I sling my belt around my waist and wrap my rage and anger at Gideon Carr around me like a blanket. I bear Callie no ill will, my heart just ain't in it. I hope wherever she is, she finds someone who can love her the way she needs. The way that I won't.

Maybe I am the terror Jackson says I am.

And if that's the case, well, I aim to be as monstrous as necessary to get to the man who made me this way.

By the time I walk into the sheriff's office, I've stitched myself back together like oil cloth with twine, rushed and messy. The sheriff is a Californio, those tan-skinned men and women who can trace their lineage to the mixing of colonizing Spaniards and the native tribes of California, with a wide mustache that has been groomed into a pencil-thin line. He leans forward and reaches for his hip when I enter.

"Miss McKeene. What can I do for you?" His tone is a bit more polite than it had been yesterday, but, despite his manners, there's an edge to his words.

"I need money," I say.

The sheriff's eyes are everywhere but on mine; he's all alone and the room is dark, the lone cell empty. He's nervous. No doubt he's remembering the scene when he walked into the cantina yesterday. They don't call me the Devil's Bitch because I have a dog, after all.

"I showed you the telegram from Carson City yesterday," he says, voice shaking now. "Five hundred was the bounty if Perry was taken alive; since the gentleman was already dining with the devil, two hundred was the—"

I wave his words away impatiently with my left arm, which does nothing to calm his nervousness. To be honest, it is a bit fun to show off my amputated arm. Callie once pointed out to me two roughnecks speculating how I lost it; when I told them I'd traded it to a demon at a crossroads to make me a crack shot with the pistol I was twirling, their eyes had gone wide.

"Relax. I ain't here to dicker over Perry's payment. My partner ran off and I find myself in need of funds. I was just going to inquire as to whether you have any outstanding bounties."

The man takes his hand off his merrymaker and stands.

He's no taller than I am, but he makes a point to hitch up his pants all the same. "So that gal got the better of you."

"We did not see eye to eye on some things, as friends do every now and again. You got work for me or not?"

"As a matter of fact, I do. A bounty came up by courier from Los Angeles just this morning. Bank robber by the name of David Johnson. They think he might be headed for San Jose or Sacramento." He hands me the flyer, and a white man with a bushy mustache stares back at me. He's an utterly forgettable sight, the kind of man who could blend in anywhere. And the bounty is only a hundred dollars, barely even worth the work. He's probably shaved by now, and I'm going to have a hell of a time trying to track him down. It's not a job any working bounty hunter would take.

But I ain't got much choice in the matter.

I take the flyer and tip my hat to the sheriff. "Dead is okay, right?"

His tan skin goes pale and he nods. I shoot him a smile. "Ain't personal, you know how it is. The devil's always going to get his."

I tip my hat again and leave the tiny office, my vengeance once more on track.

The quickest, and safest way to begin your westward journey: wagon train! Call on Harper and Sons Outfitters for more information.
—*Advertisement in the* New York Times, *January 1876*

— KATHERINE —

Chapter 30
Notes on an Overland Journey

Falling into step with the wagon train as we head out of San Francisco and east toward Sacramento feels right. For nearly two years I have found myself on a journey—first from Baltimore to Summerland; then from that vile city to poor, doomed Nicodemus; and then east to Fort Riley; and then to the Mississippi. From there we boarded a ship, the *Miserly Widow*, followed by a trek across the wild jungle lands of South America, and finally to the *Capitán* until we arrived in San Francisco. During all that time, I felt a duty to protect those around me, as most of my companions have rarely been as adept at the defensive arts as I am.

It was not quite the work of an Attendant—no one expected me to dress them or consult on the best pairing of ribbons and such—but it at least felt familiar.

Still, there's a strangeness in walking along with these families that is new and fresh and a little terrifying. I had not expected there to be so many children—passels of kids running around and screaming and laughing and teasing one another as if we were on our way to the circus rather than fleeing the peril of the city. There are so many men and women, all Negroes, ranging from light like me to darker than Sue. And not a one of them has anything more refined than a kitchen knife to defend themselves. Sure, there are a few rifles here and there, but far too many of the people bear no arms, and the farther we get from the safety of the Great Golden Wall, the more I begin to fret.

The wall is quite a sight. Sue, Lily, and I had arrived on the seaward side, so we had not been able to see it at the time. But as we leave, the wagon train numbers near to 150 people and it would be far too expensive to load everyone onto a ferry so that an overland route is our only option, I begin to understand the way people speak about San Francisco, as though it were a wondrous place. It takes most of the morning for our entire train to leave the city as we wait for our turn. To enter one of the three guarded exits. The gate to enter and leave the city is massive, guarded on either end by a portcullis. Passing through the gate, which is a hole in the wall more than a true gate, is like walking through a railway tunnel. Electric lights chase away the gloom, and our wagon train murmurs in awe as the lights flicker. I have seen electric lights before, most recently in Summerland, but many of our party have not. And the tunnel is quite the experience.

Once we are through the tunnel the entire wagon train pauses on a slight rise outside the city to take in the wall. We are not the only ones, and there are a number of people just standing and looking back toward the city. The Great Golden Wall shimmers in the weak morning sunlight, the glimmer veining its way around the outside showing how the construct got its name.

"That gold is Thomas Edison's wiring," Juliet tells Sue and I as we gawk. "Theory is, should a horde try to enter the city they can fire up those circuits and give them what for."

Sue frowns. "You mean it ain't never been tested?"

"Not against any real kind of shambler attack," Juliet says, taking a deep drink of a canteen. "The Chinese built most of the wall during the Chaos Years based upon a design from their home country, but it was the white folks that made it gold. It took twenty years to finish, and every year they make it a little bit higher. By then, the plague had largely been wiped out around these parts. Who even knows if it'll do the job it was intended for? At least it's pretty."

We continue on our way, opting to be prudent and not waste the entire day marveling at the largest wall I have ever seen. Our security team consists of me, Sue, Carolina, who decided to join us on our travels rather than return to the *Capitán*, Juliet, and the white woman Louisa, who I am praying knows how to use that Japanese sword strapped to her back.

I admit I do not know how things will shake out should the dead attack. But I am praying the people of the wagon train are more capable than they appear.

Toward the end of the day I decide to bring up my concerns to Juliet. She is a Miss Preston's girl, and as such she will understand my concerns about ratios of defense and response time. Miss Preston's was no hack-and-slash like some of the other schools, our instruction was as much about service as strategy. I also decide to mention something because my worry has returned, a low-level buzz in my brain that refuses to abate no matter how much I focus on breathing and taking in the scenery. I have not had one of my fits in months, but here I am, perspiring and fairly shaking with my uneasiness over the lack of security on the wagon train.

I find Juliet walking toward the middle of the train, whistling a fine ditty like she is out for an evening stroll, not leading a group of people out of a city bent on their eventual destruction. I fall into step beside her, and she glances over with a grin. "You're about to tell me that we don't have enough security, ain't ya?"

I blink, and then return her smile. "What gave me away?"

"That pretty little frown line between your brows. Louisa

makes the same face when she's vexed about something. You're right, we don't have enough security. The lack of shamblers in most parts of the state gets people to feeling unreasonably safe, and my dear Louisa is no different. Especially since funds are short. I've told her a number of times what kind of havoc the dead can wreak on an unprepared caravan, but this is the best we can do, so we'll make do. Hopefully we can add some more able fighters to the train in Sacramento right before we start to head up into those hills."

"Louisa said it should take a week to get to Sacramento?" I ask, scanning the horizon for any signs of trouble. The road we walk is not far from the Sacramento River, and the barges and ships making their way inland are visible. Still, I dislike being out of the confines of a city. I suppose when one grows up behind a wall, it seems like safety, even when it is not.

"Well, we could make it even faster if we were to push ourselves, but the weather is still cool, and it'll just get colder as we head up into them mountains. There's no need to rush when we have neither the inclination nor the desire. Not a lot out here to harry us along."

"I find that curious," I say. "The apparent lack of the dead."

Juliet shrugs. "They say it's because the desert and the mountains wear the dead down long before they can reach the California Republic. A bunch of rich fellows even commissioned a study couple years back, and a few different churches have out and out proclaimed California the new Eden." Juliet laughs. "Either way, the only dead are the ones who are made here, and as long as folks are savvy about putting someone to rights when they pass, we're good."

I want to ask why San Francisco has a wall—especially one people are so enamored of—if the dead are not a threat, but a shout goes up from the front of the wagon train, so Juliet and I hotfoot it to see what might be amiss.

The oxen pulling the front wagon low out their displeasure and a group of men have all crowded around, scratching their heads. Carolina is there with them, and I grin when I see his face.

"Got your land legs back yet? Looking a mite bit unsteady there," I say.

My first few days at sea I had been abysmally ill, and Carolina had been kind enough to tease me over it at every possible opportunity.

He turns, and his frown melts into a bemused smile. "Very funny. Lucky I also carry a big sword to lean on." He waggles his eyebrows, and a few of the men around us chuckle while I smack his arm.

"Fresh!"

Carolina truly does carry around a large sword. He wields a two-handed broadsword that is very good at clearing an area, a weapon that happens to be strapped across his back. Just seeing him eases some of the worry in my breast.

What security we have is very good, so things could be worse.

"What seems to be amiss here?" I ask.

"Broken axle." Juliet lets out an exasperated sigh. "Barely half a day out of the city, and already a delay." She moves off, and Carolina steps in close to me.

"Can I have a word with you?" he asks, voice low.

"Of course."

We walk away from the wagon train, toward the edge of the road and up and around, walking a perimeter to make sure there are not any threats looming on the horizon. But all I see are wetlands and the tall, waving grass. Great white birds fish in the shallows, and every now and then the air is split by a particularly raucous cry that I trace to a black bird with a red upper wing. It is peaceful and beautiful, the sun hanging low in the sky as it makes its way home for the evening.

I wish Jane could have seen it.

"You talked to your young Miss Lily?" Carolina asks, pulling me from my reverie and sending me down another path of thought.

"Not since we left this morning. Why, did she get into a scrap with one of the other children?" Lily had been alternately sullen and aggressive since we left New Orleans. I am not worried about her, she has always been smart and self-reliant, but the way Carolina is looking at me right now has me nervous.

"Katherine . . . I think your girl Lily is haunted."

I am not quite able to swallow the bubble of laughter that burbles up, and it explodes out of me before I can quite call it back. A few of the families turn to look over where we are, and I give them a jaunty wave while I regain my composure.

"I'm serious, Katherine," Carolina says, his face impassive.

"My dear, while I appreciate that Lily might sometimes find herself in a right mood, and I truly do believe in spirits—I am from Nawlins; it is practically a crime there if you do not—I sincerely doubt that Lily is haunted by anything but the specters of what she has been through of late." I sober and stop walking, so that Carolina is forced to stop as well. "In the past two years the girl has been taken from her home and spirited west; watched a town be overrun, twice; lost her brother; lived amongst soldiers; fought the dead; and lost any kind of mooring to anything concrete in this world. That lack of stability would make anyone feel haunted."

The crease between Carolina's eyebrows deepens, and he studies me a little too closely. "Is this why you were so set on starting a new life in San Francisco?"

"Partly, yes. Lily needs a place where she can thrive, where she can find herself. She is young, and she needs a place to play and learn to read and do all the things girls her age are supposed to be doing." As I speak, I cannot help but think back to my own childhood. There were happy moments, but mostly I remember the fear of my body changing and growing, because I knew at some point I would have to take a husband, or a patron, like my mother and her friends did. That was just the way of things back in New Orleans. Some women took in laundry and some women worked as maids in the houses of the fine Creole ladies, but the smartest and prettiest ones lived off their charms. The thought of a man's hands on my body left me cold, and it still does. Nor is the idea of a female companion, like Miss Mellie May's lost love, something I desire. But until I ran away, there was never any kind of a hope for any other kind of a life.

And that is the last thing I want for Lily. No one should have to live like me, or Sue, or any of the girls at Miss Preston's. She deserves a life without the constant specter of death and loss—something more than the bite and the turning.

I pat Carolina on the shoulder and give him a smile, though there is not a bit of joy in my heart. "Carolina, thank you for bringing this to my attention. I am certain that Lily will be fine once we get to somewhere we can settle down for a while. All this traveling . . ."

Carolina nods and moves off, and I continue to patrol around the perimeter of the wagon train as we make camp for the night. The restless feeling inside my chest—part panic, part worry—returns, and I sigh.

I have to find a solution that provides Lily with a measure of stability and does not make me feel trapped.

I am just not quite sure what that looks like, yet.

One such legendary hunter is a one-armed colored woman that goes by the name of the Devil's Bride. Her true name is unknown. Few have seen her face and lived to tell about it. This humble recorder of history has heard it rumored that any who see her face are taken aback by her beauty, and the smile she wears as she gleefully chases down her quarry, whether they are guilty or innocent. But the truth is rarely so easily known.

—Western Tales, *Volume 23*

— J A N E —

Chapter 31
In Which I Am Flummoxed

The dank saloon in which I found Perry has shuttered its doors for the time being, with good reason, so Salty and I make our way out of town, merrily kicking up dust as we go. If I want to find David Johnson, I'm going to have to rustle him out of hiding. Knowing I'm on his tail is liable to do that—and there's no better place for gossip than a crossroads tavern.

Half a day's walk from Monterey is the small town of

Kearneyville. The place ain't much of anything, but it boasts two boardinghouses and a large hacienda, a fine oasis for travelers making the trek north from Los Angeles to San Francisco. Callie and I had spent a week in Kearneyville while tracking Perry, and I'd rather liked the small place. It was the kind of dusty little town where Californios, Indians, Negroes, and whites all seemed to get along because they all knew how to mind their own damn business. As long as you had funds to spend, you were welcome in Kearneyville.

The lone tavern, which takes up the front of the hacienda, is named Reckless Rosie's, and the establishment's namesake pours drinks behind the bar. Her boisterous laugh and generous bosoms are rather memorable. Callie and I had stopped in to ask about Perry on our way into Monterey and had quickly learned that there ain't one shady enterprise going down in these parts that she doesn't know about. She is a Californio married to a white man she calls "hon" who is both large enough to dissuade most folks with a lick of sense from fighting, and friendly enough to not scare away more respectable folks. The joint featured a lively bar area as well as a quieter dining room, and it was one of the few places I'd been since leaving Nicodemus that didn't make me tense as a bowstring.

Without a nickel to my name, I know it's pointless to step through her front door. Instead, I slip through a small orange grove and head for the back of the building, Salty panting and wagging his tail in excitement. Singing comes from the kitchen area, and despite the joyful colors of the red-clay bricks and brightly painted glazed tiles, I feel a pang of homesickness.

Rosie's mother, a tiny Indian woman called Maria, does the cooking. As I approach the outdoor area I find the door propped open and Maria outside working the firepit, pointing and yelling at a few younger boys as they wrestle a pig onto a spit. A handful of other women cut peppers and onions and oranges around a low trestle table. Even though it's more than half a continent away from Kentucky, it could be Rose Hill.

Like Rosie, Maria is happy to dish, but her price tended to be more in the line of a story than gold or silver. Just last week when I was here I'd seen her trying to draw water up through an ancient hand pump and had made the happy mistake of trying to help her. That had earned me an afternoon of helping out in the kitchen and a passel of tamales as payment. Rosie had laughingly explained to me that her mother had taken me for one of the girls the nearby landowners sometimes sent around to help as a sign of respect for the elderly woman.

"Your skin is the same as some of the Southern peoples," Rosie said, shrugging. "Your hair is just a little curlier, but who can tell about these things? Mama just thought you were sorda, since you just shrugged and smiled when she spoke to you." She shook her head and pointed to her ears to clarify her point.

"I don't speak Spanish," I said, not at all put out. The tamales had been delicious, and the expectation of help had never made me feel lesser than Maria or any of her other women who worked the kitchen. Honestly, it had been nice to spend an afternoon helping those ladies cook up some food rather than tracking down a man to kill.

I'm pretty good with a knife either way.

Today when I walk into the kitchen area, Maria waves to me and yells something in Spanish.

I smile sheepishly. "Hola," I call. "¿Cómo estás, Señora Maria?" That just about exhausts my knowledge of Spanish.

"Jane McKeene," Maria says, giving me a toothless grin and saying my name very slowly. There is a shrewd look in her eyes, and I have the feeling that she knows more about me now than she did before last week's mishap. "Sit. Eat." She hustles over to a trestle table and makes a show of brushing off a spot. I sit while Salty snuffles at the ground near the boys. They laugh and chase him, half trying to pet him and half grabbing for his tail. He runs under the table and growls. No one appreciates the difficulty of poor Salty's life.

A plate of food appears in front of me and I hold out my hands in the universal sign for being poor, but she waves me off.

"No dinero," I say, insisting.

"Eat, eat," she insists. "You must be hungry." And then she mimics cutting with a knife to the other women in the kitchen, coupled with a spate of rapid-fire Spanish. The women gasp and a few cross themselves in the manner of Catholics. I now have no doubt that Maria knows exactly who I am. News travels fast.

"Diabla," one whispers at me.

I raise an eyebrow. "What's a diabla?" I ask no one in particular.

"She-devil," a small boy says from under the table. I lean down to peer at him where he's snuggled up to Salty. The boy has the lean look of someone used to being hungry.

"You know Spanish?" I ask him.

"Yes. My momma used to talk to me in Spanish, but she's dead now." His tone is matter-of-fact, and his gaze slides away from mine. "She-devil. It's not a nice thing to say about someone."

I shrug. "I'm not a nice person." I dig into the plate of food, still half watching the boy. The meal consists of some kind of meat, beans, a couple of corn tortillas, and an orange. It's a feast, and the boy scoots a bit closer as though the scent pulls him to me. I roll up a tortilla and hold it out to him. When he reaches for it I pull it back. "I'll share this with you if you stay here and tell me what everyone is saying."

He nods and then clambers up onto the bench to my left. He notices my arm only after he's already sat next to me, and his eyes widen when he sees my sleeve, tucked up messily. "You don't have an arm."

I shake my head. "Nope. Lost it."

"How?"

"Bit by a shambler," I say, telling the truth for once.

"But shouldn't you be dead, then?"

I nod and grin. "But I'm a she-devil, and we dance with the dead for fun."

I share the plate of food with the boy, letting him eat his fill while I pick. He tells me his name is Tomás, and it brings me back to the last time I saw the Spencer boy, so long ago now; hearing that name again feels like an omen. From what I glean he's a true orphan. His father is in the wind; his mother used to help Maria out in the kitchen here in exchange for room and board, but when she died a few months ago, he stuck around and Maria kept feeding him. Not enough, though. He's skin and bones. But he's not half bad at translating; he repeats for me everything said in a murmur, and if anyone but Maria notices, they are aces at pretending not to care.

Or, maybe, they actually don't care. I've read the fraught history of this place, what I could find, and there is nothing easy about life here, even if the dead are fewer in number than in the East; I cannot be the only hard woman to stumble into this kitchen yard. The West is full of girls like me, victims of circumstance, or poor choices, or good old-fashioned bad luck. We harden into diamonds under the pressure, keeping our chins up and soldiering on. It's one of the things I love about this wild land. In the East, the dead could get you just as surely as pneumonia or yellow fever—quick, quiet, hard deaths. But in California it would be bears or bobcats or maybe a claim jumper, all noisy, violent ways to go. California was a wild land full of strong, ferocious people, and I liked that.

Once the women have finished their work they begin to wander off, and Maria comes over, one of the older boys who spit the pig helping her to sit. The smaller boy next to me shrinks into my side, and I see the bigger boys eyeing him in a way I don't like.

"They pick on you?" I ask.

"They said I'm not worth anything because I don't have a mama," he says. "I have no name, and my papa was a gringo. There ain't no home for me."

"You stay here next to me until they leave," I say, because I am not above backhanding some sense into a kid if I have to.

I might be a monster, but even I'm not about to let some kid be terrorized.

Maria settles and offers me coffee, which I happily accept. Once it's poured she gives me a toothless grin. "Callie came through this morning, told me you would probably be by to look for her. You two have a fight?"

Maria sees far too much. I shake my head, pushing aside

my discomfort. "Actually, I'm looking for a man. Any of your ladies seen him?" I pull the bounty sheet for David Johnson from my dress pocket, unfolding it and handing it to Maria. She frowns and sucks her teeth, and then nods.

"I heard a rumor that Luz complained about a white man bothering her girls, getting a little rough. This could be him. Lots of money, not enough sense. Though, that's every man." Maria laughs, and I chuckle along with her.

"Luz's is on the way to Stockton?"

"Yes. You want me to send word that you're looking for him?"

I shake my head. This was a lost cause. I knew it before I even set out, but I suppose I'd hoped I could get a lucky break. Stupid, Jane. Just goddamn ridiculous.

Going after David Johnson would waste time I didn't have. I had to get to Sacramento before Gideon Carr could disappear once more.

"Thank you for lunch, Señora Maria." I take a chunk of leftover fat and drop it on the ground for Salty. The boy immediately sets in on the remaining beans on my plate, and I realize that he was trying to be polite and not eat everything before he knew I'd had my fill. For some reason, that makes me like the kid even more.

Maria hands me another orange from the bowl on the table and gives me one last toothless grin. "After I heard what you did to Perry, lunch is the least I can do. That man." She says something in Spanish, and I look to my translator.

His cheeks go ruddy. "I shouldn't say that out loud. I'll get in trouble."

"Good idea," I say, tipping my hat to Maria as I stand to leave. She holds up a hand, stopping me before I go.

"I give you information and lunch, so you do me a favor." It ain't a question.

"What's his name?" I ask.

"Richard Smith. He has a ranch toward the edge of town, heading north. He took liberties with Anna's daughter," she says. Her expression is mild, but the meaning is clear by the hardness in her voice. "His house has a blue door. He looks a lot like this man," she says, tapping the wanted poster so I'll get her point.

I nod, because I know the place. "Dead or alive?"

Maria gives me a gap-toothed grin and shrugs. "Use your knife."

I stand and tip my hat at her, the same hat I've worn ever since I left Summerland, before scooping up the wanted poster and tucking it into a pocket. Maria is doing me a favor, because I need the money. And I ain't above trading one bastard for another.

One less monster in the world will always be a good thing.

Tomás stands as well, and it ain't until I'm walking back through the orange grove that I realize the boy intends to follow me.

"You can't come with me," I say.

"Why not?" he asks.

"Because it ain't safe."

He lifts his shirt and along his side is a jagged scar, old but violent enough to stoke my rage.

"Those boys do that to you?" I ask, half ready to go back and teach them just what cruelty reaps.

"No, my papa, before my mama left him. He came back and killed her, and he said he was going to kill me, too. He slashed me, but I ran, and by morning he was gone." He lowers his shirt. "You don't know Spanish, and all of California speaks it. You keep me safe and I can translate for you."

His logic is sound. The Californios, descendants of the Spanish invaders and the native Indian population, have managed to keep their traditions strong. Perhaps without the dead upending the world the ways of the Eastern states would have taken a stronger foothold out here, but as it is the places I've traveled have thus far felt more like Spain than Baltimore. Haciendas and ranches rather than farms and Georgian architecture. Most everyone I've met speaks at least a little English, but Spanish seems to be much more common; having an interpreter would be very useful.

But how am I supposed to care for a kid while tracking Gideon Carr?

Jackson appears behind the boy and gives him the once-over. He's dressed in a flamboyant red waistcoat and dark suit, and he jerks a thumb in the child's direction. "This kid is smart, and almost the same age as Lily. I think she'd like him. Plus, you know his father will eventually find him and kill him. Men like that, they can be slowed but they can't be stopped. You gonna let that happen?"

I sigh and rub my hand over my face. "Okay, fine, you can come with me." I point at his bare feet. "As soon as we get some money, we're finding you a pair of boots. Now, you know where this Richard lives?"

He nods slowly.

"Good, you point the way."

The boy blinks, and for a moment fear is writ large on his features. His eyes widen and his lips part as he realizes that he's made a deal with la diabla, and for a moment I think he will change his mind and stay.

But then the boy sets his jaw. "You will want to go the back way, through the fields, otherwise he will shoot you before you even get close. Follow me."

As we take our leave Jackson tips his hat at me and says, "This, Jane, is how you find your way back."

I pull out my knife with a low chuckle.

I sincerely doubt that.

As the wagon train crested the Sierra Nevadas and the entirety of the Golden State was laid bare before our eyes, I knew that I had never beheld true beauty until then.

—*William Meyers,* A German Immigrant in the West, *1872*

— K A T H E R I N E —

Chapter 32
Notes on the Impossible

Traveling to Sacramento while protecting 150 souls is exhausting.

At night we sleep in shifts, everyone taking a watch, and it feels like I have barely rolled out my blanket and shut my eyes before I am being shaken awake.

"Your watch," Sue says with a wide yawn.

"Thanks," I mumble before climbing out of my bedroll and stumbling toward the low burning fire.

Every able-bodied adult in the wagon train has taken a shift, and as I walk toward the fire and the pot of coffee burbling enticingly, a few of the younger men try to catch my eye. I ignore them, focusing on pouring coffee in my cup, and Carolina sidles up next to me with a low chuckle.

"Even rumpled and half asleep, you still manage to turn heads," he says, holding his tin mug out so I can fill it for him. I pour him a healthy measure, and when one of the dandies comes over with his cup held out and a flirtatious half smile on his face, I look him dead in the eye and return the pot to the fire.

Carolina, of course, is beside himself. He dogs my heels as I walk toward the perimeter of the Conestoga wagons, stretching my muscles and yawning widely as I finish waking. "You're a heartbreaker, Katherine Deveraux."

"That has nothing to do with me and everything to do with them," I say, blowing on my coffee before sipping it. There is chicory in the brew, and I drink it appreciatively while we walk. "I have already had to tell more than one of them that I am not interested in courtship, thinking about courtship, hearing about courtship, or talking about the possibility of courtship. What is it with men thinking every woman they meet must be half in love with them?"

"You can't blame them, Katherine. You're the prettiest face in three states, and it's only natural for a man to want something beautiful in this life."

I sniff. "Well, then maybe they should consider taking up painting instead of trying to wife me up."

Carolina laughs, drawing looks from a few of the other folks nearby. I realize now that it is no accident most of the dandies have signed on to my shift. Drat. This is Doc Cornelius and his puppy eyes all over again.

Taking in the garb of the men on patrol with me, I am a bit surprised once more to see that not everyone in San Francisco was in as dire straits as Miss Mellie May. Quite a few of the men sport gold teeth and tastefully embroidered waistcoats, clothing better suited to a drawing room than the rough-and-tumble wilds of the trail. Still, the fact that they are here on the road with us is a testament to the fact that stacking up a bit of coin does not erase the hardship of being colored. When I was a child, the richest woman in the French Quarter was a dusky-hued Negro woman who was the daughter of a French viscount. That did not keep her from having to pay twice as much as white women at the market. It just meant the pinch did not bother her nearly as much. All the money in the world cannot make a colored person worthy to some folks.

I wonder yet again what we will find in Sacramento, and beyond, in this town of Haven. Yesterday, I stopped and chatted with a few of the folks I was watching out for, asking them what they had heard of this town. No one knew much, but one woman, a schoolteacher, had handed me a flyer.

"This was in the *Voice of the Negro* last month," she said. I had heard of it; it was the only Negro-run newspaper in the West. "They're looking for men and women to help with construction jobs in the town."

The advertisement was a crude drawing of a town, complete with a water tower and a nearby lake. "Negro-Friendly!" was emblazoned across the top, and a list of needed trades as well as "Haven is happy to welcome all colored folks!" It looked like yet another town of Negroes trying to make a go at life in this new frontier. But they seemed overly eager for new citizens . . . and for some reason I cannot help but think of Summerland.

Carolina said the Survivalist ideology never much caught on in California, mostly because the robber barons and their survivor capitalism was too strongly entrenched; and the Negro population was too small, the Indian tribes too dispersed after the Spanish were finished terrorizing and exploiting them. The Survivalists never had much of a chance. But that did not mean California was without its ills. Those captains of industry were no better than the evils we had left behind. Just a different kind of paint on the same woes.

Now, as Carolina and I make our way around the perimeter of the camp, him telling me some story about a boy he once met in New York City before the Years of Discord, I am thinking on plots and threats and working my way through another small panic. Our wagon train is comparatively small;

most families are sharing space because they'd had few enough possessions. I cannot help but think of how much these folks have already been through. Many people came west after they found their freedom—walking, working on steamers, whatever they needed to do to survive. They have already paid a steep enough price for a better life, and it is time they had it.

I refuse to let anyone fall into anything like Summerland, no way, no how. Why, what kind of Miss Preston's girl would I be to let these good, hardworking people flee San Francisco only to land in a hell of another sort? If Haven is just a Survivalist trap in disguise, a way for those dastardly sorts to lure hapless Negroes to their cause, then I will find a way to crush that town and undo those men.

How? I have no idea. But that does not mean I should not try.

It is what Jane would have wanted.

A shout goes up from the rear of the encampment, and Carolina gestures for me to check it out while he holds his position. I run over to find a couple of boys holding farm tools and poking at a man lying on the ground. A small shaggy dog stands a few feet away, barking excitedly.

"What happened to him?" I ask, as other folks begin to walk over.

"He just ran up and collapsed," one of the boys says. "I think he's dead."

"Stop with the poking," I say. "Is that your dog?"

The other boy shakes his head. "No, ma'am. He was chasing the man."

People are starting to gather, too many. I gesture to one of the dandies who had been making eyes at me earlier. "Get everyone back to their places on the perimeter. It could be bandits, some sort of a trap," I say. When they do not hop to I put my hands on my hips. "Sorry, was that last direction unclear?"

The man tips his hat at me, muttering as he goes, and instructs the other folks running up to do the same. A large man comes over—Doc Nelson, from the *Capitán*. As though I did not have enough vexation in my life.

"Miss Deveraux," he says, slowing his gait. "I was wondering when we might have opportunity to converse again."

"Dr. Nelson," I say with a nod, trying to keep the annoyance out of my voice. "I did not realize you were part of this wagon train."

"I did not join until a few towns back. It turns out that my prospects in San Francisco were not as bright as I had hoped."

"That seems to be a common theme. Would you mind taking a look at the man on the ground?"

Someone has brought a lantern over, and now it is easy to see that the man, who appears to be white, was on the losing end of a very bad fight. One of his eyes is swollen shut, and his breath comes in rabbit-quick huffs. Blood soaks through his clothing, and there are slices all over his face and his body, as though someone went after him with a knife. But they are a curious sort of injury.

Who would slice at a person rather than stabbing them outright?

"I'll know more once he wakes, but it looks as though he has been badly beaten. There are also several lacerations here that look like knife swipes."

The sound of a gun cocking echoes across the otherwise still night, and I look up. There, just outside the circle of the lantern, is what appears to be a woman. It is the long single braid hanging over her shoulder that gives her away. The tiny, shaggy dog goes over to stand next to her, still barking at the man on the ground next to Dr. Nelson.

"Salty, hush," she says.

It takes me a long moment to realize the woman only has one arm, her left sleeve is pinned up like I sometimes see with old war veterans who have had a grievous injury. The woman is terrifying, and there is something about her presence that seems familiar.

"Good evening," she finally says after a long moment. "Sorry to inconvenience you folks, but could you possibly step away from that man? I aim to kill him, and I ain't as sharp a shot as I once was."

Her voice is raspy, as though she is not used to speaking aloud. But it is a voice I know, a voice that has echoed in my mind a hundred thousand times since that fateful day in Nicodemus, my constant companion in nights spent lying awake thinking of the only girl I have ever called a friend.

My heart pounds, loud enough to echo in my ears, and the world seems to tilt just a bit, even though I still stand. Time slows to a crawl, and a million thoughts race through my brain. I blink, and the apparition is still there, the figure resolving itself into an image from memory.

"Jane?"

The woman tilts her head to the side, and adrenaline shoots through me. She calls across the distance, "Katherine? What the hell are you doing in California?"

And that is when the man lurches up from the ground, gasping, eyes wide with fear.

There is only a single shot, the sharp report bouncing off the wagons and echoing in on itself. The man's face explodes outward, and blood and brain splatters Doc Nelson. My mouth falls open at the sight of the man's ruined face, and nausea roils in my stomach. I am no squeamish miss, but this is a bit much even for me.

The folks still standing around exclaim in horror, and more than a few run to the edge of the wagons, whether out of fear of Jane or because they are also ill at the sight of the corpse. I blink and try to avoid looking at it directly, as though avoiding the horror on the ground will cause it to disappear.

"Jesus, Joseph, and Mary," Doc Nelson says, pulling out

a handkerchief and wiping the blood and gray matter from his face. He turns to me with wide-eyed horror. "You are acquainted with this woman?" It is clear from his tone that he is considering that perhaps I would not have made such a great wife after all.

Jane, for her part, is nonplussed. She does not even seem to notice the chaos she has wrought. She holsters her pistol and whistles back into the darkness. A skinny, brown-skinned boy with floppy hair and dark eyes dressed in the loose-fitting farm garb of the Californios runs forward.

"Tomás, grab Salty, would you? And run back and get that blanket we nicked. We're going to need it to wrap the body."

The little boy snatches up the dog and runs off, his eyes carefully avoiding the dead man on the ground. Jane moves over to the body and begins rifling through his pockets. My chest tightens with panic, and I take half a stumbling step back. Doc Nelson holds out a hand to steady me, and I shove him away harder than I intend.

"Jane, what on earth happened to you?" I demand.

Jane shrugs. "Nothing much. The Jane McKeene you knew died in Nicodemus, and good riddance." Her voice is flat, emotionless, and I take a step toward her before she looks up at me with coldness in her eyes.

"If you know what's best, you'll take yourself and your friends back inside the safety of those wagons and leave me to my business." She looks back down at the body. It is a dismissal, and a cruel one at that. I want to hug her, to tell her how much I missed her, how much she has occupied my thoughts since Nicodemus. But fear and confusion keep me rooted to the spot. Every line of Jane's body is tense, and it is impossible to miss the dark spot on the blade of the knife that hangs from her belt.

She brutalized this man before his death.

My heart aches, and tears spring forth. I dash them away before anyone else can see. After a year of mourning my friend she has returned from the dead.

And I have no idea what to do with that.

But, dear readers, the stories of the Devil's Bride are untrue. For I have discovered the truth about the woman, a girl really, who has been given such moniker. And the truth is she is an angel of justice, avenging those who have been wronged in equal measure to their trespass.
—Western Tales, *Volume 23*

— J A N E —

Chapter 33
In Which I Find that Reunions Ain't Always So Happy

I kneel next to Smith's body and begin to check his pockets to give myself time to gather my wits. Katherine still stands over me, beautiful and horrified, like a fine lady from a novel. I could almost see her stalking across the moors, fleeing an unloving husband. The breeze blows her skirts back as though to emphasize the point, and I shake my head to chase away the vision.

When Smith ran I wasn't quite sure where he was headed, since there are a dozen sloughs and marshes in this area. I'd already worked him over pretty well, so I didn't think he'd get very far. But when he'd turned toward the wagons and firelight in the distance I knew I was in for a scene. Most folks are squeamish about killing, and there was no way I was going to let Richard Smith live.

I needed a body to turn in for David Johnson's bounty, after all.

"Miss, I don't know who you are, but you should step away from that body." A Negro man with the fanciest set of mustaches looks down at me, a fancy snub-nosed revolver pointed right at me. He stands beside Katherine, as though he's of a mind to keep her safe. I laugh.

"This another of your admirers?" I ask Katherine, and she just shakes her head mutely.

The man's eyes widen as he looks from me to her. "You know this woman?"

"This woman is Jane McKeene, and Katherine and I went to school together. And I'd thank you to quit pointing that smoke wagon at me."

"I'll do no such thing. I need you to step away from the dead man."

"Not a chance. Might I get the pleasure of your name, sir, if you're going to start shouting out commands?"

"My name is Carolina Jones," he says.

"Carolina? Is that a given name or an homage to your home state?"

"It's neither, miss. Now please step away from the body."

I keep rummaging through Smith's pockets, of which there seem to be an awful lot. The man is fairly made of pockets. "I think not, Mr. Jackson. I'm a bounty hunter. This body is worth a hundred dollars, and anything that is on his person is now my property."

"I don't believe that's true," he says. "And it's Jones, not Jackson."

"Begging your pardon," I say. "And just how many bounties have you collected, Mr. Jones, that you seem fit to have an opinion on such a matter?"

"None, Miss McKeene."

"Then I should say that I am the expert amongst us." Arguing with this man is a welcome diversion, which is the only reason I indulge him in the least. He's distracting me from the tortured expression on Katherine's face. There is nothing I can do to erase that look, so the sooner I can wrap up the body and take it with me the sooner I can be quit of this place.

The past is the past, and until I finish killing Gideon Carr I need it to stay just the province of memory.

"Bounty works like this, Mr. Jones," I say, as though he's asked even though he ain't. "Once someone puts a price on a fella's head, he should know better than to run around with valuables in his pockets. And it seems like enterprising folks who go to the trouble of chasing down murderers and thieves should get a bit of gratuity for their effort. I mean, ain't that just capitalism? Well, lookee here." I pull out a folded wad of

2

cash from Smith's waistband, at least a hundred dollars from the look of it; I grin before tucking it into the pocket of my dress. "Not too shabby."

I go to pull off Smith's boots when Carolina Jones's tiny pistol cocks back with a click. "Miss McKeene, as one of the stewards of this wagon train I'm going to ask you once more to leave off—"

The man's tone grates, so I draw my merrymaker and point it at him. "Mr. Jackson—excuse me, Jones—I do not care if you are the mayor of Sacramento. This is my bounty—what's on the body, and the body itself—and I will dispose of it how I see fit. Now clear on out before I have to make a bolder statement than that. I'd hate to have to ruin those lovely mustaches."

"Well, you're about as reckless as ever," comes a low voice.

I turn to find none other than Sue, standing a little off to the side.

"Sue," I say, my voice low.

I am certain I want nothing to do with this happy reunion. Katherine was enough on her own, but now Sue . . . I am not quite in control of myself, and my breath comes quicker than I'd like. I drop my arm back to my side, burying the tip of my pistol in the dirt. A wave of longing and sadness buries me, months of suppressed emotions, and I damn near burst into tears. I spent so long thinking everyone was dead, that I was the last Miss Preston's girl left in this whole miserable hellscape. It was easier that way. Because then I didn't have to lie awake at night wondering if they were safe, or if they'd turned shambler. "Why must you vex me as well? I already have Katherine over here looking at me like I murdered her puppy."

"Seems to me like you would if there were money in it," Jones says, disgust lacing his voice.

I give him a hard look. "You have no idea who I am, sir."

"You running bounties, now?" Sue says in her same easy manner, as though there ain't a year and change and most of a continent standing between the last time we saw each other.

I gather myself, stand and holster my pistol, ignoring Mr. Jones, who stares at me like a wild cat has managed to talk. "It's a great way to survive as long as you don't mind killing."

Sue tilts her head at me.

"Jane, this man has been tortured," Katherine says, finally speaking.

I shrug, feigning nonchalance. "Things happen."

Tomás comes running back, Salty on his heels. Katherine takes a step forward, looks at the boy and the dog, and steps back to where she was, moving a little bit behind Sue. I ain't sure why, but that bit of indecision breaks my heart just a little. I ain't so changed from who I once was. I just have a purpose beyond survival, now.

I should probably thank Gideon Carr before I plug him. He gave my life meaning I didn't know I needed.

I take the blanket from Tomás and begin to wrap up Smith's body. "I don't suppose any of you have a horse and wagon I could borrow to get this body to the closest town?" I'm not of a mind to head back toward San Jose, but I will if necessary. Now that I have the kid tagging along with me I can't exactly sleep in the back room of a brothel or any ditch that seems safe enough. It's boardinghouses and legitimate hotels from here on out. And those cost money.

For a moment, I miss Callie desperately. She could explain to Sue and Katherine how I ended up here, the weeks of sickness, learning to adapt without my left arm, teaching myself to re-center my weight in a fight and wield a falchion. I'd spent months honing myself into a weapon in order to make the trip overland, and the journey itself had only sharpened my edge. At Miss Preston's I'd been a pistol. Now I was an artillery cannon.

But Callie ain't here.

Someone clears their throat. It's the man who'd been examining Smith when he came to. I'd forgotten the man was even there. "Miss McKeene, we haven't been properly introduced, but I am Dr. Cornelius Nelson. If I might be so bold: if we were to help you transport this body to the nearest sheriff, would you perhaps consider riding with us to Sacramento? I believe I have some oil cloth that might help preserve the body from pests. And with murderers like this man about, and the occasional shambler a constant threat, we could use a woman of your skills on these treacherous roads."

"Ain't no one said the man was a murderer," Jones says.

"And who else in this wild country have bounties upon their head?" the doctor asks. "He was most likely a ne'er-do-well in any case."

"If this man even had a bounty on his head," Jones says, giving me a hard look.

Either way, I do need to get this body to a sheriff, and I was heading to Sacramento in any case.

If this ain't Providence pointing me right at Gideon Carr, then I don't know what else it could be.

"Deal," I say with a pointed look to Carolina Jones. It would take time and money to transport Smith's body on my own, and both come at a premium these days. And traveling with a wagon train will be much safer than walking overland by myself, especially as I have Tomás to consider. He might be tough, but no child is prepared for what this life can bring.

"We'd best talk to Juliet and Louisa before making any additions to the security detail," Jones says, and I know he and I ain't about to be friends anytime soon. He's put his pea-shooter away, but even in the low light of the single lantern we've been jawing by I can tell he's got a mighty big dislike for me.

Good. I ain't fond of pushy men, either.

"I do not think there will be a problem," Katherine says,

her voice low. "We are shorthanded as it is, and things will only get more dangerous as we get closer to Sacramento and head up into the mountains."

"Mountains?" I say. I want to know what Katherine is thinking, but her horror has finally melted away and her expression is worthy of a seasoned gambler. "I thought you were headed to Sacramento?"

"We are," Sue says. "But after that we're going to a town for Negroes, place called Haven."

The town name freezes me, and I have to take a deep breath to steady myself. Haven, the town where my momma and Auntie Aggie are supposed to be. For a moment I consider what *that* reunion might look like, and the happy thought dies a violent, fiery death. If reuniting with Sue and Katherine is any indication, seeing my mother again would be a heartbreak.

"Well, then, when the sun comes up I'll talk with your Louisa and Juliet about joining up with y'all. Doc, you'll see to this?" I ask, gesturing at Smith, who seems to be finished leaking out into the dirt.

He nods. "Most assuredly."

"Don't go dissecting the man like I know you butchers are wont to do. I won't risk getting shorted on my bounty because you want to take an up-close look at his spleen. He's already lost enough of his brains, after all." It's a terrible joke, but the horrified expressions are worth it.

I tip my hat at the rest of the gathered assemblage. "Sorry to have disturbed your rest. I hope to more properly make acquaintances in the morning. Katherine, Sue, good to see you looking well. Tomás," I say, turning and jerking my head back toward the dark.

"Jane, wait," I hear Katherine call, but I ignore her. I have had more than enough feelings for a single day. I stride away decisively, out of the light of the wagon train and back into the comfort of the shadows, Tomás and Salty at my side.

While there are a number of rough locales in the West, civilization
is also firmly entrenched thanks to the early efforts of the Spanish.
Truly, California is a wonder of contradictions, but the near lack of the
undead makes every hardship worthwhile.
—*Russell Carpenter,* Westward into the Sunset, *1871*

— K A T H E R I N E —

Chapter 34
Notes on a Bounty Hunter

By the time the sun peeks over the horizon, I am more than
ready to be on the way to Sacramento.

After Jane retired to wherever she was planning on spending the night, Sue went back to sleep, and I spent the rest of
my patrol walking around in a haze. If there had been any
real danger, I would have been in quite a pickle. No matter
how I tried to pull my attention to keeping watch my brain
eventually skittered back to the question at hand:

How was Jane McKeene still alive?

I watched Jane get bit, saw her arm bleed and the chunk of flesh the undead woman took in her attack. I bandaged Jane's arm myself, tying the rag tightly so she would not lose too much blood. There is no mystery as to why Jane lost an arm, but how could she have survived being bitten?

Unless, of course, Gideon Carr's vaccine worked.

That is the thing that niggles as I walk yet another circuit around the Conestogas, watching as the wagon train begins to start its day, people waking and stoking their fires to make breakfast. Watching all those dark faces go about their business reminds me of the promise of Nicodemus, of the possibility of the success of a Negro settlement. Sorrow washes over me.

If Jane could survive the bite, if Gideon Carr's vaccine truly did work, perhaps Nicodemus might have been saved.

Perhaps we should have stayed and fought instead of running.

I shake my head. No, the town would have still fallen. But the possibility that there could be a working vaccine, though, that given time we could all have a better chance of surviving the restless dead, that is a heady thought, nearly as exciting as knowing that my friend lives once more.

But the Jane I saw last night is different. The woman who shot that man looks like Jane, and she sounds like Jane. But while Jane was always reckless—goodness knows that most of our fights at Miss Preston's were over her penchant to run into things without thought—this version of Jane is something else entirely. She had not flinched when she pulled her gun on Carolina, and seemed ready to kill him all because he was being rather irksome.

Something happened to her in the last year and a half, and it has nothing to do with the bite of the undead.

Still, Jane has always gone cold when she is hurting, and so rather than consider her to be this person indefinitely I resolve to discover the root cause of her hardness. And then I shall decide what to do next.

Another walk around the perimeter and I find Juliet and Louisa next to the fire, a fresh pot of coffee brewing. Louisa takes one look at me and grabs a tin cup, fills it, and hands it to me.

"Heard the gunshot last night. Carolina said there's a bounty hunter you know that might be pitching herself to us." She sips her own coffee and looks at me over the brim of the cup. "You trust this woman?"

"Well, about that . . ." I am unsure how to approach the matter. I want Jane to come with us. I need to know what happened to her—how she survived, what brought her to California if not her mother. But I am also afraid. I do not know much about the life of a bounty hunter, but everyone knows that they make a living dealing death. Having her in our midst might jeopardize the wagon train's safety. And I am not sure that is a risk I want to take, with dozens of families just trying to find their way to a better life.

That said, we do need more security on the wagon train,

especially as we draw closer to Sacramento and then move into the mountains. The climb will put us in a precarious position, with few options should we be set upon by the undead or highwaymen. So I am left with asking Jane to stay on.

Even though she might be just as dangerous as any other threat.

Juliet glances from me to Louisa and back to me as she waits for me to continue. When I do not, she says, "This girl, you know who she is, right?"

I nod, the direct question loosening my tongue. "We went to Miss Preston's together. We, um, lost touch, so it was quite a surprise to see her last night, let me tell you." I force a laugh. I am not about to tell them the last time I saw Jane, she had been bleeding out from a bite.

Louisa and Juliet share a look, and Juliet shakes her head. "That ain't what I meant." She reaches behind her and pulls out a paper. It is a few weeks old, from the same Negro press as the flyer for Haven, the *Voice of the Negro*. She flips through until she comes to what looks to be an installment in a serial. "True Stories of the Wilding West," it's called; this episode is entitled "The Devil's Bride."

I take the paper from Juliet and sink into a crouch as I read.

As I was traveling through Denver in the Colorado Territory I came across the terrible tale of the Turners. Like so many True Stories of the Wilding West, theirs is one that started with hope and the promise of a better life, and ended in tragedy.

Beatrice and Harold Turner had fled the hellish Lost State of Mis-
sissippi in the midst of the Years of Discord, fighting their way west,
past hostile natives and a plague of restless dead. But when they settled in
Colorado and began raising sheep and children, they figured their fighting
days were over.

They were wrong.

I look up from the article and shake my head at Juliet. "What does any of this have to do with Jane?"

"Keep reading," she says.

Impatient, I skim through the article, picking out the details: the Turners were kind and gentle people with a passel of kids; when they invited travelers to stay with them in the spirit of hospitality, they came to be murdered by a family of vicious brothers called the O'Reillys.

I skip over the sordid details and innuendo characteristic of this sort of pulp news serial, and finally come to a passage near the end of the piece.

Thus, a hardworking Negro family is murdered without any jus-
tice, the world indifferent to their fate. After all, we Children of Ham
know the curse that has been laid upon us—not the curse of bondage, but
rather the curse of neglect. This country does not see, nor seek to remedy,
the suffering of the Negro, and we are taxed to bear the wrath of white
inadequacy.

Yea, in most cases, our story would end with the deaths of the Turners.
But, Dear Reader, you will be heartened to know it does not.

For out of the ashes of America rides an avenging angel, a Negro woman with but a single arm who serves justice by way of pistol and blade. The criminals and thieves of the Western states murmur her name in awestruck fear:

The Devil's Bride.

For she is the one woman who can ensure the devil gets his due. And she was certain to make sure the O'Reillys paid in full.

I read every word of the rest of the article, marveling at the description of Jane riding the O'Reillys down on a white horse and lopping off each of their heads with a single chop, and then throwing those same heads at the feet of the neglectful sheriff outside Denver.

"I did not know Jane could ride a horse," I murmur as I come to the end of the article.

"I can't," Jane says, startling all of us out of our stockings. She grins mischievously, and it is almost like having the old Jane back. Almost—the smile does not quite meet her eyes. "You should know better than to believe everything you read. Now, I suppose you must be Juliet and Louisa, the wagon train masters?"

Juliet nods; Louisa studies Jane with a shrewd look. "So you didn't chop off those people's heads?" she asks.

Jane's grin fades, and the look she gives Louisa is flat and cold, like a rattlesnake turning its regard on a mouse. "Oh, I did. I suppose folks will say it's because I was aiming to make a point, but the reality is it was just more expedient. There were a few of those O'Reilly brothers, and it takes a long time for me to reload." Jane waves her shorter left arm to make the point. "I did shoot the last one, but only after he answered a few questions I had for him. I also gave them a bit of payback for the misery they visited upon the Turners."

I think back to the knife wounds on the man from the night before and my blood goes cold.

I do not know this woman.

Jane gestures at the coffeepot near the fire, like she has not just confessed to torturing and murdering a group of men. "Might I grab a bit?"

Neither Louisa nor Juliet move or speak, they are that terrified of the bounty hunter before them. I hand Juliet back her paper and grab the pot of coffee. "The thing you will learn about Jane is that she is ever so expedient when it comes to ending a conflict."

Jane glares at me as I pour the coffee. "Don't do that."

"Do what?"

"Bright side." She takes the coffee and takes a drink before continuing. "You try to make things seem like they're better than they are."

My mouth falls open in surprise at the casual cruelty, but Jane is no longer paying attention to me. Instead, she has crouched down between Juliet and Louisa.

"Now, to business. The good doctor who is amongst your charges has been kind enough to offer conveyance for the bounty I ran down in the night; in return, I'll keep this wagon train and everyone in it safe from any man or creature that would see to cause them harm. I know you don't know me from Adam. But I can tell you this: I was trained in combat at Miss Preston's and my skills have only been sharpened in my long trek from Kansas to California. I've worked wagon train security before, and I am damn good at it."

"That's madness," Louisa says. "No one can make that trip overland and live to tell about it."

Jane smirks and takes a sip of her coffee. "Ah, that's one of my primary qualifications. I'm very difficult to kill."

"If that's so, how'd you come to lose your arm?" Juliet asks.

"Shambler bit it," Jane says.

The air whooshes out of my lungs. I have no idea what game she is playing; I do not know the rules, and I am not even certain I understand the goal. Dread begins to wash over me. I have felt many things around Jane McKeene, but fear has never been one of them. It is not a sensation I like.

"Which is the other skill I bring to this outfit: I'm immune. It's not only that I won't turn if bitten; shamblers won't even attack me. I'm guessing you can see how that would be useful."

Louisa gives Juliet a look and turns back to Jane. "You cannot be serious."

"As a heart attack, I'm afraid."

"I've heard that Negroes have been known to be resistant to a shambler's bite, but I had no idea—"

"I'll stop you there," Jane says, and her temper flares, just for a moment, though it just as quickly settles. "That old overseer's tale about Negroes being immune is a bunch of hogwash. My immunity comes courtesy of a science experiment gone wrong. In fact, that is the reason I need to get to Sacramento. I have business there in connection with said scientist. So I will be heading that way regardless of your employment. This is your opportunity."

Louisa looks to Juliet once more and shrugs. "Miss Preston's," she says. "I can't say you don't come with premium credentials."

"Carolina told me you were able to draw down on your bounty in the dark and in less than a heartbeat," Juliet says. "We could always use a decent shot."

"Six rounds, pistol only," Jane says, standing. "I'm no good with a rifle, and I like to look people in the eyes as I kill them, just so they get the courtesy of knowing who it was that did them in. I charge four dollars a day plus vittles for me and my boy, and I'm only going to stick with you until Sacramento. Like I said, I have my own business to attend to once we get to the city."

"And what is that?" I ask, my temper at her indifference getting the better of me. "What is this business you have in Sacramento?"

She finally looks at me, and I would swear that I feel an icy wind blow through the camp. "I'm fixing to kill Gideon Carr," she says, and I half believe she actually might have gone and gotten hitched to Satan himself. "Good seeing you again, Katherine."

As she walks away, Juliet and Louisa shake their heads.

"Damn," Juliet says, voice low.

"I know," Louisa answers, fanning her flushed face. "I've half a mind to court her."

The two women share a laugh, but I'm too busy watching Jane walk away and thinking how she has not called me Kate once since we have reunited.

I cannot help but wonder if there is anything of my old friend left.

How many men has the Devil's Bride killed? One sheriff I spoke to in Carson City said he knew of at least ten men. "She's quick and she's efficient, even if she's only got the one arm. Anyone fool enough to find themselves on a wanted poster should pray they meet the devil instead of his erstwhile bride."
—Western Tales, *Volume 23*

— J A N E —

Chapter 35
In Which I Respond to an Inquiry

Tomás is less than thrilled to discover that we'll be traveling with the wagon train to Sacramento. "Miss Jane, everyone speaks English here! There's nothing for me to translate."

"That's all right," I say.

"But, how am I supposed to earn my keep if I don't have a job?" he whispers, and the look of naked fear on his face makes my heart twist. I stomp the emotion flat.

"I still need a helper, and you can be my assistant, got it?"

"Do I get a gun?"

I swallow my laugh and shake my head. "No, but you get Salty. You know this pup was trained to sniff out the dead, right? So you and Salty are going to work like an early-warning alarm. It's a dangerous job. Think you're up to it?"

He nods, his heartbroken expression melting away into one of excitement. "We'll be the best casimuertos lookouts, ever." He yells something to Salty in Spanish and takes off for the front of the wagon train, the dog running after with happy barks.

Fortunately, with the dead so few and far between out here, I ain't got to worry about the poor boy getting in over his head with some shamblers. Besides, we ain't going to have much more time together one way or another. Sacramento is going to be the end of the line for me and Tomás. It ain't like I can take the boy with me to kill Gideon Carr. I'm sure they got orphanages in a city like that.

I recheck my weapons before doing a quick head count as the train gets ready to move. Nigh about 150 people, and only twelve wagons carrying them. The group Callie and I traveled with from Carson City to Los Angeles wasn't much larger than this, but it had four times as many hired guns as Louisa and Juliet have assembled here. I know people believe California is safer because the dead ain't as much of a threat, but the truth is it's easy enough to die from an ambush by living folk, not just the restless dead, and there ain't enough people carrying guns to protect this group if we're set upon. Though, now that I think about it, that doesn't surprise me. Even here in the grand and glorious west it's surprisingly hard for a Negro to come by a talking iron. Most places have laws against Negroes bearing arms, and it's hard to find a gunsmith willing to sell to colored folks in places that don't. The Californios might be a little less picky about where their money comes from, but most of them ain't going out of their way to help a Negro. California is just as mean a place as the rest of this thrice-cursed land.

Louisa, who I now know to be the wagon train master, calls the march and we head out. She told me that it would be four more days' walk to Sacramento—a slow pace, on account of the fact that we've got a whole bunch of children and older folk with us, most of whom have to walk. In other wagon trains the young and old could ride in the wagons with the household goods; in this one space was at a premium.

We've gone less than a mile when Katherine sidles up to me. I ignore her at first, though truth be told I'm glad she's sought me out. Her presence means she ain't completely given up on me. It's a nice sentiment.

Too bad I've nothing for her.

Katherine looks the same as she did the last time I saw her. She's dressed smartly in a traveling suit in a shade of deep blue, the skirt just long enough to keep within the realm of modesty. Her boots have been polished to within an inch of their life, and her tool belt holds a number of throwing

THE ROAD TO PERDITION

knives as well as her Mollies, silver and sharp. Her rifle is slung across her back, and even that looks shiny and new. If there were an advertisement for Miss Preston's, Katherine would be the poster girl. Her hair is swept up under a bonnet, and she's as pretty as she is deadly. There's something reassuring about seeing her looking so hale and hearty, and for the first time since I've known her I don't feel the pang of jealousy that I usually do. Instead, I'm just glad that some good things in this world manage to survive and endure.

The last thing I want to do is sully that with my sins of the past year. Maybe joining up with the wagon train wasn't my best idea, after all. I don't want Katherine to ever look at me again the way she did last night, as though I'd just burned her favorite dress. Callie's abandonment is still too fresh, and I don't think I can stomach disappointing anyone else I care about right now. This is why I was better off on my own. More people just means more complications.

"Jane, might we talk?" she asks, her voice gentle. As though I'm a skittish cat and not the woman who plugged a man right in front of her.

A man who wasn't even my bounty.

"I'd rather not," I say.

"And I would rather we did," she says, crossing her arms and stomping along beside me. The other folks from the wagon train have given us a wide berth. "I have questions, and you cannot just ignore me. You know me better than that."

I shake my head, because it's true enough. The more you try to ignore Katherine, the more vexatious she becomes. But I don't like the tremor in her voice, somewhere between sadness and fear.

"There's nothing I'm gonna say that you'll like."

"Jane, there is nothing you could say that would surprise me. Not after what we went through. Besides, you already admitted to surviving the bite of the dead. It is not as though things could get more unbelievable than that."

"Fine, I reckon it'll be an awkward few days if we don't talk. And I get the feeling that saying no would just give you even more reason to harass me."

"I am not harassing you! Last I saw you, I thought it was the end, Jane McKeene. I spent over a year reliving your death and feeling like it was somehow my fault. You saved me in Summerland, and I let you die in Nicodemus. At least, that is what I thought. You . . ." She stomps her foot. "You . . . cannot even die properly!"

I try to stifle a laugh and fail, because it's such a Katherine expression, and it makes my heart feel light after the year I've had. But then I remember what awaits me in Sacramento, and the look on Callie's face when she'd asked me to run away with her and I'd quietly refused, and my mirth fades away. "I suppose some catching up is in order," I murmur.

"I supposed so as well," says Sue, coming up on my left. She falls into step with Katherine and me, and there's something right about Miss Preston's best girls fighting together once more. It's a strange thing to consider that even though Miss Preston was a monster, training girls only to send them to their death, she gave us all this. Camaraderie, something worth fighting for . . . I ain't about to say that my time spent at that school was worth it, but after all I've seen I understand only too well that finding someone to watch your back is a hard thing indeed. It was good fortune that brought the three of us together in Baltimore and again in Kansas.

The least I can do is tell them a story to honor that memory.

"All right," I say. "What do you want to know?"

"We want to know how you survived being bitten," Sue says. "Stop being coy."

"Did it have anything to do with Gideon's vaccine?" Katherine asks.

I press my lips together until the pain centers me. My lips are chapped, and the bottom one splits, the blood coppery on my tongue. "I don't rightly know. He would say yes, but others in town had been vaccinated as well and that didn't save them. I think it's more complicated than that."

"It usually is," Sue says. "Go on."

And so I tell them everything.

I share how I woke up in Gideon's house surrounded by shamblers, and I re-create for them his confession that he'd made Nicodemus his own pet science experiment. As I talk, I become angry all over again, and by the time I share how

Callie missed nearly ending the man and was there to take my arm, I am shaking with rage.

"Jane," Katherine says, laying a hand on my arm. "Jane, look at me."

But I can't. I can't bear to see the pity in her face.

I jerk free and put a bit more space between us, to remind myself that this is a temporary respite. I don't get to have these friends. I don't get to enjoy their camaraderie or the balm of their sympathy. All I get are pain and death and suffering until Gideon Carr has breathed his last.

So I keep my gaze on the horizon, step it out so that I'm a few paces ahead of her and Sue, and stick to the telling of it.

"I spent the next few months in recovery. Callie was immune as well, so we stayed in Nicodemus with naught but the dead to keep us company. There were provisions enough for the winter since it was just the two of us, and no one was coming anywhere near a town overrun by shamblers. I would sometimes watch them walk by the window, count how many folks I knew. A few Miss Preston's girls, some folks I recognized from Summerland . . . but most were strangers. It must have been harder for Callie, because she'd lived a good bit of her life in Nicodemus, knew most of the people who were eaten or turned that fateful night.

"But one day, I was looking out the window, and there she was. Miss Duncan."

My throat closes with the telling, and I have to cough to force the words out. Katherine and Sue watch me, and their gazes weigh heavily on the back of my neck. Even though the sun is shining, and I'm surrounded by people I know, I feel as alone as I did that day back in Nicodemus. "It was snowing, and she was just walking the street, like the dead tend to do. It's like currents, if you can believe it, watching them move around. I suspect there's a pattern to it, though I could never tell what it was.

"I suppose I was still a bit weak and feverish from the infection, because I forgot for a moment where I was, and all that had happened. I ran outside after her, barefoot in the snow. I was just . . . so happy to see someone I knew. I stopped her and tried to talk to her, but her mouth just kept moving, making that shambler moan. And I became so . . . mad, just furious. I pushed her down, but she got up and just kept walking. And I did it again, and she got up again, back to walking, like a windup toy. That's when Callie found me, pushing and crying and yelling. And once she brought me back to myself I swore I would take all my rage and pain out on him." I take a deep breath and finally turn around. "So that's what I aim to do. I've slashed and shot my way across this great land just for one last chance to murder that bastard. No matter what."

Tears track down Katherine's cheeks, and she dashes them away. "Jane, I cannot imagine what you have been through. But coming all this way, tracking down Gideon for revenge, it is—"

I shake my head, and it silences her. "Callie, she . . ." I

consider telling them about the feelings between me and Callie, how close we'd grown over the past year, but I decide not to. Some things just ain't for the telling, and even though Callie is gone, I want to keep the memory of our time together for myself. "She eventually tried to talk me out of it, said getting my revenge wouldn't bring anyone back. And I know she has the right of it, but I can't stop. I'm like poor Miss Duncan now, I have to just keep moving in that direction. Because if I don't, I will just lie down and die from the despair of it all."

"But what about your mother, Jane?" Katherine says. "The wagon train is going to Haven. That is the town in your momma's letter! You managed to rendezvous with us against nigh on impossible odds. If that is not the workings of the good Lord, I do not know what is. It is obvious He would rather have you find your mother than Gideon Carr. There are always going to be bad men in this world, men who trample everyone in their path for whatever their foolish heart desires. But you cannot kill them all, Jane. Leave Gideon Carr to God, Jane, and see to the ones you love."

I laugh, the sound hollow. I consider for a moment seeing my momma, filling her in on my adventures for the past few years. I'd embellish the tale, make myself a hero instead of the fallen woman I've become. It would be exploits of glory and derring-do, and I'd make it sound like a lark instead of a trial. She'd clap her hands with delight and be so proud of her daughter, a girl so audacious and refined that no one else could compare.

Just the thought of it is exhausting.

"I think that the good Lord might have his hands a bit full at the moment, and I am willing to step in and take up the burden. It's the only thing I want now, to see Gideon finished, to see him *realize* that he is beaten. Besides, that girl is gone, Katherine. She died in Nicodemus. I'm a revenant now, and the only thing I want is to kill the man that murdered me before he can hurt any more people. Now, I think that's enough talk of revenge for one day. Tell me how you all came to be in California."

Katherine and Sue exchange a look before Katherine tells me of leaving Nicodemus and how her friend Carolina Jones had helped her, Sue, and Lily escape Fort Riley on the eve of her wedding.

"You ran across the prairie in a wedding dress?" I ask, because if anyone could do it, Katherine could.

"Well, we rode horses. Of course, the poor things were lost to the first pod of undead we ran across, but we escaped unscathed. Carolina said we should make our way west by boat—he had a lead on a sea captain looking to cater to a Negro clientele, and so we headed to New Orleans and stayed with some friends of mine."

"So, is this Carolina sweet on you?" I say, asking the obvious question. It's worth it for the horrified expression on Katherine's face.

"What? No, absolutely not. Carolina does not prefer my type of company, if you know what I mean."

"What, bossy?" I say, even though I know exactly what she means. She shoves me playfully, but just as quickly as it arrived, the moment is gone.

"So what happened to Callie?" Sue asks.

"She left me back in Monterey. She seems to have found some charity in her heart for murderers. Just not for me." I'm surprised by the amount of hurt that comes through in my voice, and Katherine sighs.

"Oh, Jane," she says, and I realize I've given away more than I wanted to.

"I ain't seen Lily," I say, deftly changing the course of the conversation.

"She's around," Katherine says, and now it's her turn to sound guarded.

"She good?" I ask.

"As much as can be expected," Sue says, and I get the feeling that there's something they don't want me to know.

Thankfully, people start screaming, distracting Katherine and Sue away from any more story time and halting any further potential for exploration of my feelings. But the shout that goes up ain't any kind of good news.

"¡Casimuertos!" Tomás says, running toward us full tilt. "Miss Jane! ¡Casimuertos! They're coming for us!"

The bounty and safety of the West has made clear that every good Christian should abandon the East, foresworn as it has become, and build a new Eden upon the prairie and the mountain, sharing the gospel with those who need it most.
—Pastor Jonathan Smith, 1870

— K A T H E R I N E —

Chapter 36
Notes on a Troubling Sign

Jane's small helper and scruffy dog run toward us, the dog barking excitedly and the little boy yelling in a mixture of English and Spanish.

"Hurry, hurry, Miss Jane! They're in the river and coming right for us. There's more than I've ever seen before!"

The poor child is wide-eyed and shaking with fear, but Jane is as calm as a sea captain navigating familiar waters. She directs the boy back toward the middle of the wagon train, giving him instructions in a low voice, as Sue and I draw our weapons and turn toward whence the boy came.

Our group had decided to take a route that paralleled the Sacramento River rather than the more direct roads. There were two reasons for that. First, because it was easier to make any long trip with a reliable source of drinking water nearby, and although steamships and barges navigated the Sacramento River, it was still potable. If our group had any kind of funds we could have made the entire trip via steamship, but walking was infinitely more affordable than negotiating passage with a boat captain. The second reason was that this route was much less traveled. Bandits and thieves worked the roads with higher traffic, and, generally speaking, when it came to traveling as a colored person, the less attention paid to your movements, the better.

Of course, none of that prudent planning is going to save us from a surprise encounter with the restless dead.

Jane keeps pace with Sue and me as we head toward the river, but our progress is stopped by Carolina and Juliet heading away from the direction the Californio boy indicated.

"There's too many of them," Carolina says. "I don't know that the three of you will be able to put them down in a melee."

"How many are we talking?" Jane asks, drawing her falchion. It's a fine blade, and even Sue gives it an admiring glance as she readies her broadsword.

"At least fifty," Juliet says, visibly rattled. "It's the most I've ever seen in the entire time I've been here. The train will have to make a run for it."

"Are they all in the river?" Sue asks.

Carolina nods. "I'm wondering if a ship was somehow infected and overrun upstream. Either way, once they make the bank they'll be a real threat."

"Keep the wagon train moving," Jane says, and points northeast. "It looks like there's a bend here. If you can get everyone past this spot, it should be clear upstream."

She is right. The river travels quickly here, the water wide and deep, but its course makes a sharp turn, which the dead have bumped into in their trip downstream. I watch as a few wash up and scrabble out of the water, lurching through the reeds and bushes that grow thick along the bank.

"Go, we can take care of this," I say to Carolina and Juliet. I am not nearly as sure as I sound, but they nod and hurry away.

Jane is already striding decisively toward the water's edge. "Stay behind me and let me work. As long as I move slowly they should be no problem. Just take care of the ones that get past. Don't tax yourselves."

"Well, ain't she bossy," Sue says. But it becomes clear why Jane barked out such an order as the first few restless dead draw even with her.

It takes the undead a good bit of maneuvering to navigate through the weeds and onto firmer land. A couple slip and fall in river mud, the same as any heedless person might, but Jane does not run up to them to end their forward progress. Instead, she waits, and whistles a merry tune as they regain their footing and stalk toward her. They are not lurching and grasping for her the way they might a regular person. Instead, they walk right past her, one going so far as to bump into her before Jane swings her sword around and takes off his head.

Shock washes over me as I see Jane was not exaggerating about the side effects of Gideon's vaccine. She is completely invisible to the dead. It is like she does not even exist to them.

She throws a roguish grin over her shoulder at me and even has the gall to give me a saucy wink.

But then there is no time for anything but work.

More restless dead are gaining the bank, and Jane takes down better than half of them, her movements slow and deliberate. Sue and her big sword very nicely work cleanup on the ones that scramble through the grasses too quickly for Jane to decapitate. I quickly see that I am extraneous, and I instead track the progress of the wagon train as it makes its way past us and up the road. As I watch, it turns toward a bridge, crossing and heading away from the river.

Within a few minutes, the fifty dead have dwindled to only a few, and the bank is thick with blood and bodies. Jane wipes her sword off on a woman's fine velvet dress and sheathes it before rejoining Sue and me. We all head back to the wagon train.

"I thought the plan was to follow the river," Jane says, pointing to the train beginning to cross the nearby bridge, the column stretched out like a cat sunning its belly.

"It was," Sue says.

Without oxen and heavy loads we can move faster than the wagon train, and we catch up to our group quickly. Lily runs to greet us, and she freezes.

"I thought you were dead," she says, giving Jane a terrified look.

"I am," Jane says, voice flat.

Lily does not quite know what to do with that, and the parade of emotions that flit across her face echo the way I am feeling by the minute: angry, then sad, then cautious, and finally, concerned.

"Lily, is there something amiss?" I ask.

She grabs on to the lifeline I throw her with both hands, turning her attention back to me. "Upriver, the water is filthy with shamblers!" she says. "Juliet says we need to head away from the water."

Jane's face goes stony, and she strides ahead to where the middle of the wagon train is crossing a long bridge now crowded with Chinese and Californios pointing to the water. They hold pickaxes and shovels, and I realize that we must have stumbled upon one of the work crews building levees along the river. It was the talk of San Francisco, where the people of the city were eager to have more predictable travel to Sacramento and to lure more people to the state. The project was intended to make more of the area alongside the river conducive to farming by alleviating the massive flooding. A lack of workers and soaring costs had delayed the project; it was now slated to be completed in 1890.

"Tomás!" Jane yells, and the small boy comes running over. We approach the nearest Californio, who looks to be in charge of the day laborers, and, with Tomás interpreting, we inquire what happened. He relays the story of the dead appearing in the water—ten yesterday, a few more this morning, and now more than a hundred of them.

Sure enough, the water churns with the dead. The current is a bit too swift for more than a handful to gain the bank, and without the curve of the river that benefitted the dead behind us they cannot maintain their footing. Either way it is clear that they are coming from somewhere upstream.

Jane thanks the man for his time and we catch up with the wagon train, which is now cutting a path away from the river to the north. A few dead try to lurch after the train, and we easily dispatch them. We walk in silence for a few moments, Tomás and Lily eyeing each other suspiciously, the little dog hopping sideways and barking whenever one of the restless dead get too close. We are almost rejoined with the wagon train when Jane utters the question on all of our minds.

"What the hell is going on upriver?"

No one responds, of course. We do not know anything more than she does. But I hope the answer is one that does not spell our doom.

When the Devil's Bride ran up against Alfred and Lucy Brampton,
a couple of no-good swindlers who had left a trail of dead and broken
hearts in their path, she did not hesitate. Reports are that she walked
into a saloon that the couple frequented, asked their names, and shot
them down before either could respond.

And good thing, to be sure, for the Bramptons had a wagon full of
colored children, stolen from their parents, that they had planned on
selling into slavery.

Had she known this about these fiends? Or had her heroism been a
happy coincidence?
—Western Tales, *Volume 47*

— J A N E —

Chapter 37
In Which Our Plans Change

Predictably, the topic of conversation on the wagon train runs
to the dead. How could it not? Most of these folks came west
to escape shamblers, to find new lives away from the killing
and dying. Of course, it ain't like they haven't seen the restless dead in California before. Just not like this, fresh and
fast and ravenous. The dead in the ocean were old and raggedy, easily dispatched by beach patrols. The old shambler
that wandered the landscape here was usually an oddity, a

prospector or trapper that died in the wild and came back without any kin to plant a nail in their forehead.

But this was something completely different, the beginnings of a horde, flowing down the river, out to sea. Assuming the river did not bend fortuitously and provide a landing spot for them and their endless hunger.

Yes, the people of California had fled the dead, yet here it all was, pursuing them like Pharaoh harrying Moses and the Israelites across Egypt. Only in this case the Red Sea seems to be in on the chase. I wish I was surprised, but I ain't. Seems to me whenever anyone finds but a little bit of peace, the dead inevitably show up to wreak their special kind of havoc.

It's nice a body can rely on something these days.

We veer away from the river, a panicked hustle that can only be maintained for an hour before Juliet has to call a halt as older folks and kids begin to drift too far back. We're heading due north instead of the more northeasterly route that would have taken us to Sacramento, and that vexes me. Something is causing the dead in the river, and even though I pray that it's just an overrun boat like Carolina Jones suggested, I fear that Gideon has laid waste to yet another town in the course of his despicable experimentations.

I take a deep breath. We've stopped next to a placid stream that burbles and sings, and the landscape is beautiful, but the direct opposite of how I feel.

Katherine, Sue, and I do a quick survey of the perimeter before posting guards. Our shifts will start earlier tonight, and with good reason. Folks are skittish at seeing the dead, but I hear more than a few conversations that already try to minimize the danger. "It's probably just a boat," someone says. "Maybe a family turned and their town went as well, there are dozens of little hollers up this way." They're trying to tell themselves a story that makes California the land of safety and sunshine, and in lying to themselves they're putting us all at risk.

Well, not me. I ain't got a thing to worry about.

Tomás has stuck to me like tar since we sighted the dead, and I lay a heavy hand on the boy's shoulders as he bumps into me once more. "You feeling okay?"

"No," he says, a quaver in his voice.

"How long has it been since you saw casamortos?" I ask.

He frowns at me. "It's *ca-SI-mwhere-TOES*," he says, emphasizing each syllable. "Casimuertos. And I've never seen them, only heard stories. They . . ." He falls silent for a moment and I watch as the families in the train pull down chairs for their aged and get to the making of their evening meals. Tomás sniffs. "They said that I would be taken away by the casimuertos because I didn't have a mama anymore."

"That's not true," comes a voice from behind us, and I turn to find Lily watching us with a scowl that looks hauntingly familiar. For a moment my heart squeezes as I remember

Jackson puzzling things out with a similar scowl, and it's almost like thinking about the man summons the ghost.

"Lily always was the kind of girl who'd adopt any wounded creature she came across," Jackson says. "Soft heart." He lights up a cheroot and puffs on it merrily, the smoke wafting into the late-afternoon air. Today he wears a waistcoat of dove-gray silk, his suit crisp and shoes shiny. It's an outfit the real Jackson never would've worn on the trail. He was too practical for such nonsense.

"Lily, could you take Tomás and show him how to gather firewood?" I ask. "Something tells me we're going to want more than usual tonight."

She gives me a baleful glance; there is much she wants to say to me and ask of me, but she hesitates. I've always capitalized on the doubt of others, now more than ever. The girl causes my heart to clench, and I aim to avoid our long overdue conversation as much as possible. I've chosen this path and nothing will derail it, especially not the sadness of one girl.

Lily reaches out to Tomás and pulls him along. The boy is almost a head shorter than her. They go off into the thicker trees along the creek, still well within the perimeter, and Salty bounces along after them.

"Don't go too far, the dead are behind us but they might head this way," I call.

I walk away from the wagons and back in the direction

from which we came. The mystery of the dead appearing so suddenly and in such large numbers digs at me. Gideon Carr was rumored to be in Sacramento, and now there's a river full of hungry corpses. Isolated outbreaks are not unheard of, but—

"She is growing like a weed," Jackson says, with a hint of wistful sadness. It's the first time I've ever heard the ghost express any kind of emotion other than amusement at my dire circumstances.

"I thought you were gone."

"I'm never gone long, Janey-Jane. But I will say that this is your chance. Give up on your revenge and make sure everyone here gets to Haven. This, I think, is your shot at redemption." He stubs out his cheroot on the bottom of his shoe and tucks the rest in a vest pocket.

"Redeem myself for what?" I snicker, turning to watch Tomás and Lily navigating a large piece of deadfall, their arms full of tiny kindling sticks. "My list of sins is far beyond absolution at this point."

"The sin that matters most, of course: killing me."

I whip around to look at Jackson, but he's gone to ether once more. Katherine walks up, and she frowns at me turning this way and that.

"Seeing ghosts?" she asks.

"Always. What's going on?"

"Juliet is going to gather everyone to talk over what to

do now," Katherine says primly. "She feels that continuing toward Sacramento, which is at the source of the river that is now teeming with dead, is not the smartest option."

"I need to get to Sacramento," I say, turning back toward where the city lies. It's only a day's hard walk away at this point. I am so close to ending this, to finding Gideon Carr and snuffing him out. So close . . .

"Well, I suppose walking upstream against the dead would be no problem for you," Katherine says, "but I don't think the rest of the wagon train is so cavalier about encountering a horde."

"The horde is the least of it. You think there's no connection between an army of the dead appearing and Gideon Carr being in California?"

"How do you know that Gideon is even here, Jane?"

I snort. "Someone said he was, and they had every reason to tell the truth."

Katherine's expression flits from confusion to horror, and she blinks. "What happened to you? Nicodemus was a tragedy, and we all suffered a loss there, but this cannot all be about Gideon—"

"Gideon Carr murdered an entire town in his pursuit of glory and in his attempt to fix the world according to his ideology," I say, my voice getting louder as I talk. "The man killed hundreds of people and learned nothing. Did you know he was running experiments in Denver, paying people to let him inject them and then convincing them to let themselves be bitten by the dead?"

Katherine's eyes widen. "Jane—"

"With the information I got from the youngest O'Reilly boy, Callie and I found what was left of his lab up in the mountains. Seems that when Gideon couldn't find willing volunteers he was only too happy to pay for less willing ones. All in the name of *science*. That ain't a man that can be left alone, to hope he'll learn a lesson. He has to be stopped."

I take a deep breath and let it out, fighting for a measure of control. People have started to gather, and quite a few of them watch me with hooded expressions. The last thing I need is a melee with a bunch of well-meaning folks.

"I got my priorities. If the wagon train ain't going to Sacramento, then I guess I ain't gonna be accompanying this wagon train."

"But we are going to need you for security, now more than ever." Tears fill Katherine's eyes. "Jane. You gave your word."

"My word don't amount to a hill of beans," I say. "Gideon Carr's head on a pike is the only thing I care about."

The clang of a bell halts our conversation. It's a giant cowbell that Juliet uses to rally everyone around the cook fire. Once a good crowd has gathered, Juliet puts the bell down and gazes out at each individual face, as though she's memorizing them. Of the 150 or so people in the train, roughly thirty have gathered to hear what Juliet has to say, mostly men. Sue joins Katherine and me nearer to the fire, and she elbows me to get my attention.

"Lily's doting on that boy of yours," Sue says.

"He ain't my boy, just a stray that decided to tag along," I murmur. "His life's been nothing but tragedy, though. He could use a little warmth."

Sue grunts in acknowledgment. "That dog is something else. I ain't never seen an animal like that."

I glance over and there's a slight grin on Sue's face that makes me smile as well. "Sue, I never took you for an animal lover."

"Well, perhaps that's because you never asked, Jane Mc-Keene." Her tone is mild, but the words are sharp. How much of me and Katherine's argument did she hear?

Juliet is speaking now, and we turn our attention to her. I should grab my gear and set out, because no one is going to press for keeping on to Sacramento, not with the dead in the way, but I also am curious to hear what they decide.

"As you all know, we abandoned the river route because it has been beset by shamblers. Carolina and I tried to scout a bit upriver before we changed routes, but it was too risky. Traveling along the river to Sacramento is more dangerous than a lot of you were counting on, and we ain't sure what's causing the surfeit of dead, either."

A commotion goes up as everyone starts talking at once; Juliet lets the chaos go on for a moment but then she raises her hand and motions for everyone to settle down. "Katherine

Deveraux, one of our experts in the defensive arts, spoke to some folks working on the levees."

"Yes," Katherine says, drawing herself up. "We consulted the lead man on a work crew and he said the number of dead first appeared yesterday and have been growing in number since. From that bit of information, we can ascertain that it is likely that a town upstream fell to the dead. A large town, from the looks of it. I have seen this sort of thing before, and I concur with Juliet: we should not continue our route to Sacramento. Rather, it might be safer to turn directly toward the mountains, skirt the city altogether. That way we can avoid the thickest part of the horde, should there be one."

People begin to descend into a commotion once more, and a finely dressed Negro with velvety dark skin and a closely cropped beard raises his hands in an attempt to quiet them. At first it seems they might ignore the fellow—he doesn't look much older than me—but he carries himself with an air like he's used to being deferred to, and soon folks quiet. Once he holds the attention of most of the assemblage he grins winningly.

"Hello, all—Thaddeus Stevens, I believe most of you know me." He tips his hat, and a few of the women closer to the fire titter appreciatively. "I beg pardon, Miss Juliet and Miss Deveraux, but this new plan is simply not acceptable. Surely this swath of dead is an unfortunate accident but hardly indicative of an epidemic. I know you both come from meaner lands, but this is California. Why, we have more bears than shamblers here." He laughs, drawing agreement from the rest of the group.

"I reckon anything more than zero is shamblers enough to fell a town." All eyes turn toward me, and the mirth dies away real quick. "The arithmetic ain't hard where the dead are concerned. One bites one, which bites two or maybe three, and inside of a day everyone's turned. Nowhere is safe from the undead plague."

Mr. Stevens gives me a long assessing look, and I tip my hat at him. His gaze finds my arm, and his self-satisfied smirk turns to wide-eyed wonder. I can tell at that moment he realizes who I am.

Celebrity is a burden.

"My point," Stevens says, dragging his eyes away from me to take in the rest of the assemblage, "is merely to say that we should ascertain this threat before we abandon course. Especially since quite a few of us had planned on remaining in Sacramento if we found it amenable."

"Mr. Stevens is right," Carolina says, chewing on the end of a cigar. "And I'm still of a mind that we should get some more respectable hired guns before we attempt to navigate the dangers of the mountains anyway, what with bandits and all. I think Sacramento is still an option, and we should try for it."

It doesn't escape me how Carolina looks in my direction as he mentions "respectable hired guns" and I try not to let it bother me. But next to me, Katherine is less composed.

"Carolina, we cannot put these people in harm's way on a hunch," she says, crossing her arms and glaring at the man.

"Which is why we should send an expeditionary team," Stevens chimes in, the smug expression back in place.

I get the feeling that Stevens is often taken with his own cleverness.

"An expeditionary team?" someone from the crowd asks.

"Yes! Our own Lewis and Clark, as it were. We can send a smaller number of well-armed individuals who can quickly assess the situation up toward the city, see if this anomaly is the result of the fall of Sacramento or if it was in fact some sort of accident that has already been dealt with."

A dozen conversations begin at once. People talk excitedly and fearfully, so I don't point out to Stevens that, even if Sacramento has not been overrun, heading toward the largest settlement around is exactly what the dead would do. Assuming all of them ain't being carried downstream by the river, some would begin their determined march toward any place that could provide a good meal.

It seems to me that these folks have a lot of opinions on things they know nothing about.

Juliet and Louisa confer in low tones, and Katherine sets a hand on my arm, leaning in close to address Sue and me. "What do you think? Is there any prudence in acquiescing to the train's consensus? Heading upriver to see the situation better?"

"I think done is done," Sue said. "When have you ever

seen that many dead? Where there's smoke . . ."

A shrill whistle cuts through the discussion, and Juliet addresses the group, hands on her slim hips. "Enough. Now, Mr. Stevens, that is a fine idea, but it's a lot to ask of anyone to put themselves at risk in that manner."

"I'll go," I say. My words land heavily, and the stares of everyone land on me, heavier still. Katherine's heaviest of all.

"Alone?" says an older matron seated on the other side of the fire next to Stevens. "Into a town that might well be fallen to shamblers?"

"That's right, ma'am. I'm immune to the shambler's bite."

The matron laughs, and she's not the only one. "And how, young lady, did you manage that?"

"I sold my soul to the devil, of course."

Her smile withers on the vine, and silence falls over the crowd.

"Right," I say, more than a little amused at their reaction. Being the Devil's Bride ain't all a curse. "If there ain't any other questions, I'll be on my way. I can be up and back before you folks know it." Of course, I ain't coming back until I kill Gideon Carr, and maybe not even then.

A murmuring goes up once more, but this time it's cut short by Stevens, who must fancy himself a leader of some sort. "This is a fine idea. However, you shan't be going alone. I volunteer to escort the esteemed Miss McKeene on her journey." He flashes me an indulgent grin, and I return a blank stare. I never gave him the pleasure of my name, and it bothers me that he obviously knows who I am when I don't know a lick about him.

"I didn't realize you were a shambler expert, Mr. Stevens."

"Hardly," he says, bowing his head in respect. "But I know an opportunity to learn from the best when I see it."

"Dear God," Sue says next to me, disgust lacing her words. She's right. This man is entirely too much.

"I am going as well," Katherine says. I turn to face her.

"No," I begin, but she holds up a hand like a schoolmarm calling for quiet.

"I abandoned you once, Jane, and I will not do it again." She gives me a sad smile, and panic wells up for the first time in a very long time.

I can't keep Katherine safe from the dead, but trying to stop her once she's made up her mind is a fool's errand. I open my mouth to argue, and she sets her jaw so I snap it closed.

Hell's bells. Katherine Deveraux is going to be the actual death of me.

Sue sighs heavily. "I guess that means it falls to me to stay here and protect the train while you two have all the fun."

"Someone has to tend to the flock," Katherine says sweetly.

As soon as Katherine volunteers, two more men raise their hands to join us, but Carolina quickly shuts them down when he points out they have no weapons. That's when a younger man steps forward.

"I'm decent enough with a blade, and I got kin up in Sacramento. I'd like to see firsthand whether there's a chance we can make a go at the city."

There's a woman next to him with a deadly look on her face. She holds a baby and the child lets out a long wail as the woman pulls the fellow in close and talks to him in clipped whispers. But before long, she stomps off while he remains. I wonder what could make a man desperate enough to volunteer for such an endeavor against the wishes of the one he loves.

"Well, damn it all," Carolina mutters. "I'll go as well. I know the route to Sacramento and can guide us upriver. But we're burning daylight. We need to suss out the situation as soon as possible, because if Sacramento truly has fallen, this wagon train is in danger of being devoured."

Katherine nods, her spine straight. "Then let us depart."

When I first arrived in California my nose beheld a scent so sweet, so fresh, it was like I had never truly breathed good air until then. How had I lived so long without the crisp scent of pine, the salty air of the seas, and the medicinal musk of those strange transplants from Australia, the eucalyptus?
—*William Meyers,* A German Immigrant in the West, *1872*

— KATHERINE —

Chapter 38
Notes on an Expedition

Carolina, Mr. Stevens, and the young father who introduces himself as "Jebediah, but you can call me Jeb," return to their wagons to load up their packs, as Jane and I check our weaponry. We each carry a rig outfitted with a few throwing knives, as well as long knives that will come in handy in close-quarters fighting. Jane carries a pistol on her belt, as does Carolina, but Jeb, Mr. Stevens, and I all opt for a rifle as our firearm of choice. Jane has her falchion, Carolina his claymore, and my Mollies are strapped across my back while a half-dozen throwing knives weigh down the belt at my waist. Their weight is a comforting presence as we set out.

Neither Jeb nor Mr. Stevens carry any sort of sword or knife, and it does not take long for Jane to make her opinion known on the matter. We have barely gotten out of sight of the wagon train before she starts needling them in a sharp tone about their lack of versatile weaponry. She sounds like Miss Anderson when she used to get in one of her moods, although I am not foolhardy enough to make the comparison out loud to Jane.

Jeb says nothing, but Mr. Stevens clears his throat, his aspect more than a little chagrined. "I'm afraid I've never considered the need for bladed weapons, to be honest. My parents came to California in the Years of Discord, and I have lived my entire life here. A rifle has always been suffi-cient for the occasional shambler encounter."

Jane's harrumph makes Carolina smile, although he is quick to hide it. The two of them have gotten off on the wrong foot, so to speak, but I am confident that if they were to spend a few moments conversing they would realize they are cut from the same cloth. Well, at least the old Jane was. I make a note to myself to ensure that at some point they exchange more than just guns pointed at each other.

Jane has not finished poking about the men's lack of swords. "What about you? You like this dandy here, ain't never considered it, either?"

"Rifle was all I could afford. Swords and long knives are

expensive," Jeb says, his words deliberate and careful. His cadence bears faint traces of the South, most likely one of the Lost States; perhaps he was raised there. "I've needed more protection from the living than the dead since my family and I arrived in California, and live folks tend to respect a gun more than a sword."

Jane's face flashes despair before she once again shutters her emotions. There is much left unsaid in his proclamation, and I think once more about the burn marks on Miss Mellie May's boardinghouse. Not all threats can be dealt with like the dead. I must admit, upon reflection, that there is a simplicity of fighting for one's life against obvious monsters.

Jane purses her lips and gives him a short nod. "Well said. Have you got some skill with a blade?"

"Some," Jeb says.

Jane reaches to her right pant leg and unbuttons a section next to her thigh. She detaches a short sword in a scabbard. All together it is the length of her thigh, and Mr. Stevens is agog—from the brown length of leg Jane reveals or from the fierceness of the weapon, I cannot say. But the look he gives her is one I am quite familiar with, and I cannot think Jane will be pleased to know she has an admirer.

"Here," she says, handing Jeb the blade. "In case things get a bit more intimate." To Mr. Stevens, she says, "you just try to stay out of the way of the work."

"Miss McKeene," he says, straightening his coat, "I assure you my rifle skill is second to none."

"Uh-huh," Jane replies, and we fall into silence as we walk.

Our plan is simple: retrace our steps back to the river and then cut up along the bank, keeping a good distance from the water, hopefully far enough to evade notice. This serves a dual purpose. First, it gives us a point of reference for our assessment. If the rash of shamblers was caused by an isolated incident, like a boat being overrun, then we should see a sharp decrease in their presence as they are washed down river. Though the restless dead are very good at bobbing along for what seems like forever, they cannot swim. Second, retracing our steps gives us a chance to put down any enterprising undead that somehow ambled onto the bank and had seen fit to follow after us, keeping everyone back at the wagon train safe.

This is, of course, only theory. If there is a horde approaching overland as well, all of our efforts will be for naught. But despair means certain death, so we are optimistic.

We make our way apace—Jane scowling, Jeb distant, Mr. Stevens following close behind Jane like a puppy, Carolina vaguely amused by the whole endeavor—until we get within sight of the river.

The edge of the closest bank is still almost a mile away, but we don't need to get any closer to see that the outlook is not good. I half wonder if it's a trick of the light making the water look as though it boils.

Mr. Stevens reaches into his pack and withdraws a bronze

spyglass, holding it up to his eye. He stills like a rabbit sighted in the short grass, and slowly he lowers the glass from his eye. His skin goes gray, and the man looks as though he has had the fright of his life.

"My God," he breathes. "What are they doing?"

Jane takes the spyglass from Mr. Stevens without asking and looks herself. Her expression is grim as she hands it off to me.

As I take my turn with the spyglass, my heart falls. The dead are thick in the water, flailing and bobbing. A few gain the bank at the S curve where we fought them earlier, dragging themselves onto land and then heading in the direction the wagon train came from, back toward San Francisco. The dead are too numerous for this to have been a random ship or even a small town that was overrun. And all of them look to be freshly turned, with none of the decay one would see in a larger horde that had been building over time.

"They're heading west," Jane says. "Yep. That's a proper horde."

I pass the spyglass off to Carolina and turn to her. "You are thinking Gideon Carr did this," I say, intuiting her thoughts from the murderous look on her face.

"Perry, the bounty that told me Gideon was in Sacramento, said he had a new lab. Doesn't matter what happened in Denver or to Nicodemus, or with Ghering's failed experiments back in Baltimore . . . These men and their prejudices dressed up as science." Jane stalks off a little ways into the woods, swearing up a blue storm as she goes, and I turn back to the rest of our group.

"Jane thinks this horde came from Sacramento," I explain. "The work of a man we knew back in Kansas."

"Gideon Carr, the inventor you told me about?" Carolina says, passing the spyglass to Jeb. The man looks for only a moment before handing it back to Mr. Stevens. Like the other man, he also looks like he has had the shock of his life.

"A scoundrel and a blackheart, he is," Jane says returning. She stares at the water for a heartbeat, a muscle in her jaw working. "How far is it from here to Sacramento?"

"Twelve, maybe fifteen miles," Carolina says. "I think we've got our answer as to the source of this endless stream of shamblers. Can I assume you've reconsidered your plan to press east?"

"On the contrary," Jane says, the mad glimmer returned to her eyes, "I'm now even more determined to find Gideon Carr."

I want her answer to surprise me, but it does not. Not now, not after all I've seen from her since our reunion, and not from the things she admitted came before. She is never going to give up. Not even if it kills her. And for all her skill and strength, I do not see any other end to this quest for revenge. There is a very slim chance Gideon Carr is working by himself, Jane seems to forget how good the man was at building alliances and using others to further his agenda. Had he not done exactly that to Jane and I in Summerland? I have very little doubt that Jane will find Gideon Carr, and when she does she will rush in and meet her tragic end.

"Of course you want to find the man," I say. "And I am going with you."

Jane freezes for a moment. "Are you mad?"

"No," I say, my voice casual and even. I must choose my words carefully. If Jane thinks I am doing this out of pity, or sentiment, she will only find a way to abandon me at the first opportunity. "I am simply repaying my debts. You saved my life back in Summerland, and I owe you. If you want to go on some wild-goose chase to kill a man who has cheated death at every turn, that is your decision. But this is mine. I pay my debts."

Jane sighs heavily. As I suspected, she will not argue. Emotions make her uncomfortable and tetchy, but obligation? That is a tune Jane McKeene will dance to.

I do not relish journeying upstream toward Sacramento, but I meant what I said. I will not abandon Jane again. I am not nearly as afraid of dying as I am of grieving for her once more.

"Miss McKeene, take my spyglass. It should aid you in this quest of yours." Mr. Stevens holds it out, and Jane takes it with a nod. I am certain the man fairly swoons from her momentary regard.

"We'll be cutting up past Abbottsville," Carolina says. "And then Oroville. That will allow us to stay clear of Sacramento. We'll then follow the Feather River up into the mountains. A piece of advice if you . . . Well, once you're finished with your business, and heading up toward Haven: take note of the Klamath and the Paiute tribes once you get up into the mountains. They'll mostly keep to themselves as long as they don't see you as a threat."

Jane nods, and as Mr. Stevens begins to tell her a bit more about the journey to Sacramento, Carolina pulls me aside, frowning. "Are you sure this is something you want to do?"

"She was—" I catch myself as I watch Jane bid farewell to the other men. "She *is* my friend, Carolina."

"Well," he says, giving her one last look. "I hope she's worth it."

If the Devil's Bride is any kind of monster, as some say she is, then
I fear for our land. Because the West is a bloody, brutal place, and it
seems fitting our heroines should be cut from the same cloth.
—Western Tales, *Volume 43*

— J A N E —

Chapter 39
In Which I Have Regrets and Count My Blessings

Katherine and I have only gone a few miles further upriver when we decide to settle in for the night. We see a small town, but we don't consider knocking on doors and asking for hospitality; there's no way to know whether the folks here are friendly to Negroes or not. But as we draw close to the town, we soon conclude it doesn't matter.

Everything is dark and quiet. Windows are shuttered, and there ain't a soul to be seen. The town laundry, the sign written in both English and Chinese, is still and unattended.

There is no light visible in any of the houses, and the lone general store boasts broken windows and empty shelves. We decide to take a shortcut through the main street, and there's an ominous feeling to the place that keeps us moving quickly.

"Where do you think they have gone?" Katherine asks. "We have not seen a soul since we left the wagon train."

"Maybe word reached the town here faster than the shamblers," I say, glancing toward the river. "If whatever precipitated this horde happened a few days ago, people could've cleared out ahead of the danger. Crossed the river and gone north, or made west, right for the ocean."

Katherine says nothing, but her countenance makes it clear just how terrible an idea she believes this whole endeavor to be.

We put another mile or so between us and the river, ground we'll have to retrace in the morning to get to Sacramento, before we make camp. By the time we do I'm exhausted. Between chasing down Richard Smith and working the wagon train, I haven't had a decent night's sleep in a week. The night Callie left me. I sit and lean against a tree, head tucked into the collar of my coat. It's cold enough where a fire would be appreciated, but we have no idea where dead might be in these parts, and we decide not to risk it. Plus, the dead are not the only danger out here. The less chance of discovery by anyone, living or dead, the better.

Katherine digs a canteen and some pemmican out of her pack, handing me a decent chunk, and I chew on the dried meat while she fills my cup. The sun sets quickly, as though it, too, is eager to get away from the dead, and soon the dark presses in. There ain't much of a moon to speak of, and the night is quiet except for the occasional rustle in the underbrush, the hoot of an owl.

"Jane," Katherine says, voice low.

"Hmm?"

"Did you think about me?" she asks. "And not just me," she hurriedly continues, "but Sue, Lily, or any of the other Miss Preston's girls? I remember you used to dote on Ruthie . . ."

It's the kind of question a body can only ask in the dark, when there's no light to show the hurt and loneliness behind the question.

"No," I say, voice flat.

Moments pass by, only the night sounds marking the time.

"Actually, that ain't true," I say after a long while. I want to leave this gulf between us, to keep her and Sue at a distance. But Katherine is so damn persistent, and I'm so tired of being cold and angry. It's like my rage at Gideon Carr continues to burn up anything good inside of me, and I just want a moment's peace, just a few hours to feel like a person and not an instrument of destruction. "I did think of you. I thought about each and every one of you. I wondered if you all had made it to the river or even out of Kansas. I thought about whether you'd gone back to that flooded city where you grew up, if Sue had finally found herself a husband and become a mother like she'd dreamed back in Miss Preston's. I used to imagine getting better and heading east to find you.

"But that was only the first few days after we separated. After I saw Miss Duncan stalking around the streets of Nicodemus with no trace of her humanity left . . . Every time I thought of any of you, all I could see was you all turned shambler."

Used to be that thinking about the long winter trapped in Nicodemus, surrounded by nothing but the frozen dead, made me feel panicky. It hasn't been that way in a while, though, and I owe Katherine honesty. She's pledged herself to my cause, even knowing what I intend to do and how I intend to do it.

That's more than even Callie did. And the thought of it threatens to overwhelm me in a way that nothing has in a long while. I've let the drawbridge down just a bit, and now emotions storm the gates of my heart.

And I'm just so damn tired that I let it happen.

"Katherine," I continue, "if it had been you I'd seen that day instead of Miss Duncan—dress torn, neck open, eyes dead—I wouldn't be here right now. I never would've left Nicodemus. I would've just laid down in the middle of that snowstorm and waited to die. So, no, I didn't think about you. Because that's how I survived."

"That's good, Jane," Katherine says, her voice heavy with emotion. "But it was not me, and I am here. No matter what else has come before, I am alive and I am here. With you."

I figure she's going to say more, but after that there's nothing but the sound of our breathing and the stillness of the night, and soon we fall into the abyss of our own ruminations.

I wake with a jolt, drawing my gun instinctually. Katherine crouches next to me. I can just barely make her out as my eyes adjust to the predawn light.

"Jane," she says, the sound little more than a breath. "I think we are in a bit of trouble."

I strain my ears for the sound of the dead, those characteristic moans and the stink of rot. I exhale in relief as I realize there's nothing.

"You got a match?" I whisper. At first I think maybe she didn't hear me, but then I see slow movement, and the silence is broken by the hiss and pop of a match strike.

The flare of light illuminates the small clearing in which we've laid down. Katherine's eyes are wide, the blue nearly black in the low light.

Surrounding our little copse of trees, swaying from side to side like a congregation caught by the spirit, are the dead.

It's just like that night back in Summerland. Then, I hadn't understood why the dead had hesitated, warily, before attacking us. Now, I know it to be some side effect of Gideon's vaccine—he and I had been at the front of the small army we had led against the incursion, and until we had attacked, they had similarly declined to make the first move.

Callie had explained it as we'd traveled west. "It ain't something that happens before you get the bite when it's just the vaccine in your blood. But a shambler bite and the vaccine makes the dead weird, like they're waiting for orders. You ever hear of a snake charmer? Well, I heard once there were these men in India that could sing to these snakes that are more poisonous than a rattler. They could make them sway and keep them under control so that they didn't strike. We're like that now with the dead. As long as we move slow and steady, they won't attack anyone at all."

I hadn't fully believed it, but yesterday down by the river had proven Callie's hypothesis correct. I still ain't entirely sure how the whole thing works, it ain't like I've had a chance to ask Gideon, but I know what I've seen with my own eyes and I have a plan.

"Okay," I say, checking my gear, the sword sheathed on my back. "Sit here next to me. We're going to wait a little, until the sun comes up. Then we'll deal with this in the light."

"Jane—" Katherine begins, but I lay a hand on her knee.

"If they haven't come for you already, I don't think they will. They're confused—I think it's a side effect of the vaccine. I believe they won't think either of us to be a target unless we attack them. So, we bide our time."

I slowly draw a knife and place it on my outstretched legs as Katherine settles herself next to me. She's shaking, and I try to comfort her the best I can, which ain't much at all.

The sun rises slowly, casting the world in shades of gray. I stand, Katherine remaining crouched down on the ground as I slowly approach each of the dead. They don't move, their milky gaze fixed on some distant point, even as I press the knife into the base of their skulls. One by one I slide the blade in to sever each of their brain stems, and gently lower their bodies to the ground, not disturbing any of the others as I do.

After a few are put down, however, the rest turn toward me, like I'm north on a compass, and my hands take on a tremor.

This ain't something I ever want to do again.

It's hard work, stabbing and catching their weight, and Katherine draws her swords as I work, but she trusts me and doesn't jump to her feet, doesn't make a single sudden move.

She trusts me, even though I ain't given her a single reason to since we've been reunited.

I complete the task quickly, and when I lower the final shambler to the ground, leaving the largest man for last, Katherine jumps to her feet, swords drawn, her earlier fear replaced by a fine kind of rage.

"This is why the dead behaved so strangely in Nicode-mus," she says. "Just waiting outside of the town for so long."

I nod. "Possibly. Gideon told us the dead were evolving. I

can't tell what was a lie and what was the truth with him. But what I do know is this"—I gesture vaguely to the corpses that surround us—"has happened more than once when Callie and I were traveling overland. This weird sort of waiting."

"And after we'd escaped Summerland and we were on that farm—" she begins as if to herself. Her eyes move from the dead to me, seeing if I heard her before she silenced herself.

But I did hear. My knife falls out of my hand and sticks upright in the grass, the blade buried in the dirt.

Jackson. He said that the dead were waiting for him, the morning he got bit. He said they were down in the tall grass and then they sprung up when he walked by. As if they'd been waiting.

Because of me.

"Janey-Jane, you knew it in your heart," Jackson says, his voice near my ear. "Why do you think I've been following you here there and everywhere? You just didn't want to face it, the fact that what Gideon Carr did to you had consequences beyond your control."

I turn my head to the side. There is no ghost. Perhaps there never was. Only the subconscious knowledge that I truly do bear some responsibility for Jackson's death, and the cold reality that he is never coming back, that my heartbreak will always be total and complete.

I shake my head. But I wasn't bit then. I wasn't immune.

"Jane?" Katherine calls to me, but her voice is far away.

Bite plus vaccine, Callie said. Unless Callie was wrong. Maybe everyone was wrong. What if the behavior of the dead is the key to identifying an effective vaccination, just seeing how the dead reacted to a living body? If the dead are disinterested, then it means the vaccine has taken. But the whole process takes time, both Callie and I had been vaccinated for months before being bitten.

By that estimation I wasn't immune when Gideon and I walked past the shambler wheel in Summerland, but perhaps by the night of the undead attack I was. It could be too many unvaccinated folks make the dead react like usual, so then, maybe some of the Summerland patrols actually are immune and that's why the dead acted so strangely back then. A real scientist could work out ratios and ranges and all that, but I ain't a woman of science, I'm a woman of action.

Either way, the vaccine does work. Just not the way Gideon Carr thinks it does.

Stupid, stupid man. He had the answer in front of him all along, one everyone could have lived with. All he needed was to parade a body in front of the dead and gauge the reaction to check the efficacy of his vaccine. None of his exposing folks to the bite was necessary. Gideon's focus was just too narrow to see it.

And Jackson is dead because of it.

My anguish quickly explodes into rage. I lean down and pick up my knife, cleaning it off on the dress of a white woman. I want to push everything back, to close the door on the cage of my emotions, letting only my anger run free. But it's too late for that. Katherine's presence has compromised my defenses and laid my heart bare, and now there's nothing to do but deal with it best I can.

I can see what she's doing, trying to save me from myself. But she doesn't need someone like me in her life. I am unrepentant and feel no shame for the lives I've taken. It's inevitable that I will disappoint her, just as I have everyone else. And the sooner she figures that out, the better.

"These dead are newly turned," I say, cold and calm, once I've gained control of myself enough to speak. "We should get moving. I reckon the horde must be growing, which means they're only going to get more numerous."

Katherine's hand is over her mouth. "Jane, I did not—"

"All is well, Katherine," I say. My voice is as flat as the Great Plains themselves. "It's just one more reason to plant a bullet between the eyes of Gideon Carr."

By far the greatest indication of the grandeur of California is the ability of the common man to eke out a successful living, whether by farming, trapping, or trying his luck in the mountains where gold is plentiful and the dead are not.

—The Great California Republic, *1868*

— KATHERINE —

Chapter 40
Notes on a Disaster

Jane and I quickly break camp and head out. She is quiet in the wake of the revelation about Jackson, and I regret the part I played in it. Sometimes I think it is better when the causes of our miseries are mysteries to us; when the reasoning is clear, it almost becomes too much to bear. And as we make our way upriver Jane tries to come to terms with the idea that she might have played some inadvertent role in Jackson being bitten. Jane has no face for poker, even as she thinks she does;

her every thought or feeling is telegraphed across her face. I see the familiar mix of anger and sadness in her expression as she bares her teeth and quickens her pace, but there is a newer darkness there as well, and it causes me to feel breathless as my familiar anxiousness begins to overwhelm me.

I want to tell Jane that none of this is her fault. She was vaccinated by Gideon Carr against her will before she even knew what effect it would have. She certainly had not summoned Jackson to our side as we fled that awful place. But if she continues down the path of killing Gideon regardless of the cost, well, that *will* be her choice. And whatever heartache she reaps will be exactly what she has sown.

But I am not sure she cares about anything beyond her revenge.

We find a well-used road and, silently, agree to follow it rather than cutting our own path through the woods. The road twists toward the river, then, about a quarter mile from the water, turns to run parallel to it. At first I am wary of the dead doing their damnable jack-in-the-box act as they once did to Jackson, but hours pass, and we do not see anyone else, living or dead. The sun is warm and bright, and the coat I wear is more than I need for such temperate weather. California truly is a marvel. No wonder so many sing its praises. The wheat and alfalfa that grow on either side of the road are green and lush, and the birds sing songs of joy and renewal. That the dead have managed to find their way into a place of such promise is an American tragedy. Nothing remains untouched in this world for long, and it is hard not to fall into despair at the futility of our condition.

"Jane," I call, a thought occurring to me.

"What?"

"What are your plans for Tomás?"

She scowls and shrugs. "I ain't got any plans for the boy. I figured that there would be an orphanage in Sacramento where I could drop him."

I blink. "You figured you would drop the boy at an orphanage."

"Yes, I can't be out here caring for a youngster. I only brought him along because I thought I'd need him to translate for me."

"But, he is a *child*."

"Yep, and one that can speak Spanish, while I do not. But our time together nears its end, so I suppose he'll have to figure out the future on his own."

"Jane, you cannot just abandon the boy! He has no one."

"I know that," she snaps. "But he ain't my problem."

I bite my tongue, stopping myself from any further conversation on the matter. I had thought to bring it up to distract Jane from the problem of the vaccine and Gideon and Jackson's end, but only because I had made the mistake of thinking perhaps there was some affection between Jane and the boy.

It was a miscalculation, to be sure.

"What is your favorite bit of Scripture?" I ask.

Jane snorts. "I find the Bible tedious. I prefer Shakespeare. Or that new writer, Twain. I find their writings somewhat more relevant to my experience."

"You cannot find the Bible tedious! It is a beautiful book with some absolutely wondrous passages. I have always found Galatians to be particularly uplifting, since you did not ask. 'And let us not be weary in well doing: for in due season we shall reap, if we faint not.'"

For some unfathomable reason, Jane smiles. I cross my arms. "I do not see why that passage is amusing."

"'Conscience doth make cowards of us all.' That's from *Hamlet*. Do you know what that's about?"

It is not as though I am ignorant of Shakespeare; *Romeo and Juliet* and *A Midsummer's Night Dream* were frequent favorites for the showcases in a few of the entertaining houses back in New Orleans. I never had cause to watch any of them as a child—mostly because they were performed in the nude—but I can tell Jane has something to say, and so I just look at her until she does.

"*Hamlet* is about a prince trying to kill the man who killed his daddy, which happens to be his uncle."

"His uncle is his father?" I cannot keep the horror from my voice. Classic or not, this play sounds depraved.

"No, the murderer is Hamlet's uncle. After he kills Hamlet's father, he marries the queen, Hamlet's mother. His daddy's ghost is the one who clues him in on the whole plot, but Hamlet's not sure if he can trust the ghost, so he goes through this elaborate plan to get the new king, his uncle, to confess. In between, he spends most of the play talking about how awful everything is, and how unfair his life is. Finally, Hamlet ends up stabbing his uncle, but not before Hamlet himself is poisoned." Jane goes quiet for a moment, and I wait. "Anyway, if I can get my hands on a copy, I'll read it to you. It's very good. A lot of people die, but they deliver these great soliloquies before they go. Well, at least the men do."

"I would like that," I say, and I mean it.

Our travels have brought us to a crossroad and, just beyond it, a bridge. We're close to Sacramento now, and the dirt wall levees here are finished and intact. They're also built higher than they were downriver. A levee is a wall of a sort built between a river and the land on either side, dirt and rocks piled up wide and high. The Sacramento River's levees are covered with tall grass, and from where we stand the water is not quite visible. But there are no dead, and that is a good sign. I am still a bit rattled after this morning, and more reluctant to face the dead than I have been in years.

I am not fond of surprises.

We climb the road to the bridge. Here, the river is muddy and narrow. It's not half so majestic as the Mississippi, but it is still a power in its own right. The water looks slow, but as the odd corpse or tree branch bobs by the speed of the current is revealed.

"Looks like the bulk of the horde has passed through," Jane says.

"What's that?" I ask, pointing to the city in the distance, where there is a line of smoke rising, as if from a factory. Perhaps Sacramento is still safe after all.

Jane fishes the spyglass out of her pack, lifts it to her eye, and lets loose with a string of curses that would cause even the most experienced working girl to blush.

"Look," she says, thrusting the bronze tube at me.

When I hold the spyglass to my eye, the city is painted in smoke and flame. Figures make their way through the chaos, but the jerky motions are not that of the living. Sacramento may have once been a jewel on a river, but now it is a fiery hellscape.

"My God," I breathe. If Sacramento is overrun, that means the dead we saw downriver were just the beginning. Soon, tens of thousands of shamblers will be making their way, unabated, toward San Francisco.

The promise of California is no more. Even if the dead could not find their way en masse across the Rocky Mountains, the West will still succumb.

The dead always find a way.

"Well, what now?" I ask.

Jane's jaw clenches. "We continue on to Sacramento."

"You . . . even if Gideon had been here, you cannot truly think he would have remained in the city, do you?"

"No," Jane finally admits, reluctantly.

It is the first real sign of reason I have heard from her since our reunion.

"Halllooooo," comes a call.

Down in the river, heading right for us, is a grizzled old white man in a small rowboat. He appears to be a prospector; he wears a dusty, battered hat, canvas pants, and an unkempt beard that has mostly gone to gray.

"Hello!" I call back, because it would be rude not to. Jane just glares at the man.

"You wouldn't happen to have a bit of rope or an oar, would you?" he asks.

"No, sir," I say, cupping my hands around my mouth so that my voice carries. "You would not happen to know what is happening upriver, would you?"

"Didn't your homestead get a rider? They sent out a hundred men on horses the first night. The city has fallen! They say some rich folks were having a soiree, as they do, and one of them must have been infected. All turned! No one knows how one of them could have gotten bit. But that's how it started."

The little boat picks up speed as it approaches, and goes under the bridge we are standing on. Jane and I switch sides to keep talking to the old man.

"It was a rich person who first turned?" Jane yells.

"So I heard. But who knows? Some folks was claiming the infection came from some food they'd had sent up from the Chinese in 'Frisco; others say it was a Californio day laborer who turned first. There's more than enough blame to go around once folks get to speculating."

The man is drifting downriver now, and Jane leans over the railing of the bridge so he can better hear her. "Why is the city on fire?" she calls.

"Who knows?" The old man shoots back with a cackle. "Most likely some fool thinking he could end the threat of a horde before it could get out of the city. But I was at Gettysburg, I know the truth. The dead always get theirs."

"Thank you for the news," I say. "And good luck!"

"As long as I'm still breathing my luck is fine! You and your girl be careful."

Whatever else he says is swallowed up by the distance.

"Well," I say, looking at Jane. The muscle in her jaw is working again, and I can only imagine what is going through that mind of hers as she sorts through our options.

"This is Gideon's doing," she begins. "I know it. He's behind what happened here. You want me to give up on my revenge, but Katherine . . ." She closes her eyes, and a tear escapes down her cheek. It is the first time I have seen her cry since Jackson. She swipes it away angrily and no others follow. "I ain't . . . I *can't* let Gideon Carr get away with what he did to me and everyone else."

I hold my breath. If Jane is still bent on finding Gideon, the only place we are going to find a clue as to his whereabouts is in that city of death on the horizon. Even if Jane is beyond fear of anything but failure, I am not. I close my eyes and say a silent prayer.

She gives the smoke in the distance one last look and

sighs. "The only lead I had was in that city, and I ain't about to quit now. I'm going to see this through, and neither fire nor flood is going to stop me."

I swallow around the lump in my throat. My anxiousness is nearly overwhelming, and I want to give in to the feeling. But I cannot.

I can only keep moving.

The silence weighs heavily between us. I could try to navigate my way back to the wagon train, but traveling by oneself is dangerous. If I follow Jane to Sacramento I will be walking right into the middle of a horde. And while Jane has nothing to fear from the dead, I am very much not vaccinated and vulnerable.

But I meant what I said to Jane back when we left the others. Jane might not see anything in herself worth saving, but I do. And until she sees it, I am not about to leave her alone.

"Well then, let us keep moving. If we wait any longer there is like to be naught but ashes left."

And then I stride down the road toward the city, my shoulders square and revealing not a single hint of the terror that thrums through my veins.

A prudent bounty hunter knows when to let a quarry go for a better offer. After all, not all men are worth hunting to the ends of the earth. Considering the cost is what smart bounty hunters do. Plunging head-long into any bounty that comes a body's way is what dead hunters do.
—Life on the Range, *1868*

— J A N E —

Chapter 41
In Which I Contemplate My Future

Katherine Deveraux is a fool.

She walks beside me as we make our way to the city, the smoke growing in volume as the fire in the city spreads, and I want to send her away, tell her to go back to the wagon train. I'd thought my determination to continue on to the city would make her turn tail. What rabbit runs into a fox's den? But that is exactly what Katherine is doing, walking with me to a city of the dead without any care for her own fool neck.

And she's doing it for me.

The further we walk, the angrier I get, so that when we pass through a small shantytown on the outskirts of the city proper, I grab her arm.

"Why are you doing this?" I demand. This close to the burning city the air smells of wood and cooking meat, and the smoke makes my eyes water. We can only see a little ways before us; the smoke billows around the tent city we walk through. The ground is muddy, even though I don't know the last time it rained, and I figure it must be water pushing up from the river in some way. The stink of squalor is barely noticeable, only when the smoke clears enough for me to get a whiff. Breathing is hard, and my lungs labor, the smoky air making me cough.

There is not a soul to be found, and even if Gideon Carr had remained in the city after the dead rose, there is no way to ride out a fire like this. We haven't even walked into the city proper and it's already unbearable. I know he ain't there, just as Katherine does.

But at my snarled question she raises a blond brow at me. "What do you mean? I should think it was obvious. You want to kill Gideon Carr, and you think we will somehow find him in this city. And so, here I am. I do have to admit that I think we should probably wait until the fire has died down," she says, coughing delicately. "This smoke is abysmal."

I'm not paying attention to our surroundings, I'm too

focused on my frustration with Katherine, so it takes me a fraction of a second too long to realize that there are shapes lurching toward us through the smoke.

"Katherine," I say, drawing my sword. "Turn back."

"No," she says, not yet seeing the dead around us. "You want to march into the mouth of hell to find Gideon Carr, then I will accompany you all the way to Satan's throne."

"No." I push her behind me, using my elbow to steer her around. The way we came is clear, but in front of us the dead are beginning to congregate. I take a step backward, forcing her to do the same.

If they swarm us, Katherine is dead.

Despite the hazy smoke that swirls around us I can finally see clearly. I have a choice: Gideon or Katherine. Stupid, stubborn Katherine, contrary and ridiculously loyal to boot.

Gideon Carr has not yet taken everything from me. But if Katherine dies, he will have won.

I take another step back. Katherine is still behind me, and I use my body to block her and draw my sword slowly. She tenses, finally seeing the threat before us, and I keep going, walking backward a single slow step at a time. Katherine is bright enough to understand what I'm doing, and we continue to move back the way we came. The dead haven't charged, and I have to hope that keeping myself between her and them will keep the situation calm.

"Jane," Katherine says, her voice hoarse. I hazard a glance

over my shoulder, and I see the problem. A handful of the dead, not many, have started to appear from between the rows of the tent city.

"Just keep moving," I say. The dead seem confused, like they were this morning. They jerk this way and that, sensing Katherine but unable to ascertain her direction. A lifetime passes between every step we take, but eventually we have put enough space between us and the tent city. When we reach the road leading us back to the river, I push Katherine.

"Run," I say.

And she does.

A few of the closest shamblers break after her, but I put them down easily, tripping a couple. The rest of the horde stays within the hazy smoke of the tent city, and once I'm certain we won't be followed I take off after Katherine.

We run for a while, and eventually I put my sword away in the sheath that crisscrosses my body. Katherine waits near the bridge we crossed this morning, and I sigh heavily, enjoying the crisp, clean air. We didn't make it very far.

"Well, that way is no good," Katherine says, coughing a bit. "Maybe we should see if we can get north of the city and come in from another direction. Or what about the railways? Following the train tracks might be a better plan."

"No, Kate, it's over." I shake my head. "Gideon Carr is in the wind again. It ain't worth wasting any more time on this. We'll head back to the wagon train, and I'll figure out what to do on the way. He's here somewhere, and it's only a matter of time before he pops back up again." I ain't giving up on finding Gideon Carr altogether, but I have to be smart about this. Losing Katherine to this search ain't going to help anything. It's just going to be another death on my conscience. One I simply could not live with, if I'm being honest with myself.

She gives me a wide grin and nods. I scowl. "You ain't got to be so happy about it," I grumble.

"That is not why I am smiling. I just never thought I would be so glad to hear you call me that detestable nickname."

I shake my head and sigh. I wasn't exactly looking forward to charging into a burning city, dead or no. But now I'm right back where I started. I have no idea how to find Gideon.

"Come on, let's go back to that wagon train."

We reach the wagons before nightfall. Turns out even our little adventure hadn't put all that much distance between us and them. The reactions to our arrival are mixed—quite a few folks are stricken to hear that Sacramento is no more, but mostly everyone seems to be relieved that they are gone from San Francisco, where the horde is inevitably headed, and that we've returned to bolster their protection detail, especially now that there are shamblers about.

"I suppose we'll see how Edison's Great Golden Wall fares against real resistance, now," says a skinny colored woman who bears a striking resemblance to Carolina Jones. I cannot help but agree. San Francisco is in for a fight.

After supper, Thaddeus Stevens, blowhard extraordinaire, brings out a leather-bound Bible and reads a bit of Scripture for those comforted by such things. Quite a few of the single ladies on the train, and no small number of the married ones as well, jockey for position as he reads by the firelight. I am unsurprised to see Sue seated to his right, eyes closed as he reads. She was always taken by ridiculous folks. It's why we were friends at Miss Preston's. Even Carolina stands on the edge of the circle giving Stevens cow eyes.

Katherine and I seem to be the only ones not smitten by the man.

"Don't you want to join the Bible study?" I say to her, nodding toward the group.

"Jane, please. Even the good Lord has limits on the trials He expects us to endure," she mutters, too low for any ears but mine. I swallow my laugh.

"Neither of you are of a mind to take in the Scripture?" Juliet asks, walking up behind me and Katherine on cat feet.

I snort. "What kind of muttonhead reads Revelations at a time like this?"

"Honestly," Katherine huffs, and it is so very much *her* that this time I do laugh, the sound carrying. The moment of pure happiness takes me by surprise, and a number of heads at the fire turn to look at me, their expressions suspicious and wary, and just as quickly as it appeared the joy evaporates.

No one wants to see a killer happy. And for good reason. I fight my residual mirth back into the shadows of my heart.

Juliet gestures for us to follow her, and I put aside my ruminations and walk. Focusing on just doing the next thing has gotten me through the darkest of times, and I have to stick with what works. We follow to where Louisa, Carolina, Jeb, and the skinny woman who spoke earlier sit. She introduces herself as Miss Mellie May, Carolina's sister, and her regard for me is a bit more than I am comfortable with. I make a mental note to ask Katherine about the woman later.

There's an air of tension to the assembled group, and it's no wonder why. The Bible study continues behind us, which means this is the kind of meeting where having everyone chime in ain't the best idea. That never means anything good.

"Sorry to round you all up like this, but we're in a bit of a pickle," Louisa says.

"We've taken stock and realized that changing our route means we don't quite have enough rations to make it through the mountains," Juliet says. At Louisa's sharp glance she shrugs. "No point in mincing words."

"How many days do we have?" asks Carolina.

"About four, if we make it count," Louisa says. "I'm guessing a few of the families might have something squirreled away, but most folks gave everything they had to get out of San Francisco."

"Is there any chance of hunting?" I ask. "I've seen game aplenty in my travels."

"This time of year, it'll be difficult," Carolina says. "Especially with so many homesteads around. That's a lot of rabbits to feed a hundred and fifty people."

Juliet points a stick in the dirt, and in the glow of the lantern begins to draw. "This is the river and the path we were going to take into the mountains. I propose we take a new path, along the Siskiyou Trail. We'll head north, and there should be a good number of towns where we can stop, and where they'll hopefully have supplies we can purchase."

"Assuming the dead haven't beat us there," Miss May says.

"If the dead flank us, we shall have much more than low rations to worry about," Katherine points out.

"Well, we are just going to have to make sure that doesn't happen," Carolina says. "My concern is more about the towns we're passing through. Do you think anyone will sell us supplies?"

"And at a fair price," Jeb says.

"I can probably assist with that," Louisa says.

"Yes, and me as well," Katherine says, a sad smile on her face. "No one ever assumes me to be a Negro, and that is something we can use to our advantage in this situation."

"We can ask Doc Nelson as well," Carolina says. "He dislikes passing, but I believe he would make an allowance in this case."

"We'll still be strapped for funds," Juliet says. "In addition to a shorter route and a cheaper opportunity for us to resupply, we'd planned on picking up more folks in Sacramento."

"You can take my bounty," I say. "I need to get boots for Tomás, and proper clothing as well, but the bounty on Johnson was a hundred dollars. That's a fair amount."

Everyone looks like they want to argue, to refuse, and I wish I could rescind the offer. I'm likely going to need the funds in the future when I head off to find Gideon. But it ain't like I can't take another bounty. Besides, the body ain't even Johnson's, anyway.

"That will likely get us through." Juliet nods.

"What kinds of risks are we taking, going this new way?" Jeb asks, staring at the drawing in the dirt. "Will bandits be a threat?"

"The Army has been very good at patrolling the trail and keeping it pretty safe in the past," Juliet says. "But I'm guessing they'll have their hands full trying to put down this horde. We'll have to be careful, but no more than we were before. The dead are now by far the greatest concern."

"And that means speed will be our challenge," Louisa says, her expression grim. "That horde might be headed west, but that won't last forever. We're going to want to be somewhere fortified before their numbers swell in San Francisco and they move east again, away from the water."

"Some folks have talked about abandoning the journey

THE ROAD TO PERDITION

into the mountain, instead making for Abbottsville or one of the other towns in the foothills," Jeb says. "It won't offer any protection if the dead come, but it might be preferable to an ill-fortified trek into the mountains. Telling folks the plan might help make up some minds."

There are nods of agreement, and I glance back down at the map, trying to put it into the context of what I know about the Golden State. "How far is it, exactly, to Haven?" I ask. Just saying the name of the town out loud makes my heart beat a little faster. Hope or fear, I'm not quite sure. I consider the possibility of getting to Haven and finding my mother and Auntie Aggie, introducing them to Sue and Katherine . . .

I can't picture it.

There won't be a single lick of joy for me until I kill Gideon Carr. That's the promise I made.

And I keep my promises.

"About a hundred miles north to Corning," Juliet says, pointing to a spot on her hastily drawn map. "Another forty miles hard climb up the mountainside to Haven itself. So about two weeks hard walk, maybe three."

"What makes you think the mountains will be safe?" Jeb asks. "How long will it be until that horde turns toward the rest of the state?"

Everyone falls silent considering it, because he has the right of it. Eventually the dead will come knocking.

And what then?

"Colder weather will help when it comes," Juliet finally says. "The snow is brutal and deep up in the Sierra Nevadas. So we really only have to worry about the next few months. Here's hoping the horde sticks to the lowlands for now. As long as this Haven has strong walls and proactive measures it should be safer than just about anywhere else."

"Besides," I say, "nowhere stays safe forever."

I can feel Katherine's regard. I don't look at her, but her gaze fairly burns a hole in my back. She's most likely thinking the same thing I am.

In less than a month I'll either find my mother or I will discover that she never made it west at all. And if she and Auntie Aggie are gone, then there will be nothing to keep me from spiraling completely into the darkness.

Not even Katherine.

If one should find themselves hiking through the lush Central Valley of California, be sure to stop by one of the many homesteads and taste the fabulous offerings of California agriculture: oranges, almonds, and a multitude of other fruits native to warmer climes. The Golden State's harvest is bountiful and plentiful. You will find hospitality aplenty as well.

—General Augustus Redmond, 1875

— K A T H E R I N E —

Chapter 42
Notes on the California Trail

We walk.

It seems to be all we do for a very long time. Juliet warned us, gathering everyone up after our meeting, laying out the challenges, the cost of this endeavor. Many had their concern about the toll such a pace would take on the elderly and young, while others had seemed unsurprised that there was yet another burden to be borne. I do not think there was anyone who, in their hearts, ever believed that the trip to Haven would be easy, but that did not mean it was not upsetting to hear how brutal the journey would truly be in the aftermath of the fall of Sacramento.

And yet, the reality of it pales in comparison to anything we were told.

Each day, we wake as the sun is barely cresting the horizon, over homesteads and fields, mostly fallow this early in the year—that is, if we are lucky enough to even get to sleep the previous night. We break our fast with a meager meal of cold beans and head out, walking as fast as the oxen can be coaxed to go. The trees change from leafy beeches and cottonwoods to towering pines, but the muddy, rut-marked road remains the same.

We are far from the only travelers on the trail. Every day we meet more people, some fleeing the ruin of Sacramento, others from towns that had the misfortune to be in the path of the dead's march to the sea. Pale-skinned Chinese, brown-skinned Californios, and white people convinced that something better waits for them just around the next bend.

It is the white folks who seem to be taking the new surge of undead the hardest.

"They just came out of nowhere; we were lucky to make it out with our lives," I overhear a woman say in Abbottsville as we are purchasing what we hope will be enough supplies for our trip into the mountains. Jane dropped her bounty in the first town we had stopped in, some little nothing of a place that didn't even have a real name, her grisly payday filling the coffers of the wagon train—but that town's general store's wares were not sufficient for our needs. Abbottsville's stores are better stocked, but that, we find, brings its own challenges. The place is filthy with people who believed that they had been safe from the undead plague out here in the west. The cost of the supplies are three times what they should be, but the upcharge is not due to the fact that we are Negroes—it is the demand.

Everyone is heading north, although not for the same reason.

"I heard the Chinese were behind the infection in Sacramento, so they could charge more for their protection teams," says a white man with a mean look to him and a sidearm I would bet money he has no idea how to use. As I wait to pay for my purchases, the man has the temerity to say to me, "Me and mine are heading up to Oregon. No Chinamen, no darkies. Did you know the Oregon Territory has made Negroes illegal?"

"Pray tell me, sir, how does one make another person illegal? That does not sound very Christian."

He has no answer for me besides a dark look as he walks off to harass some other poor woman. If I slip an extra prayer into my nightly communion with the Lord that the man should get some comeuppance, well, that is no worse than such a man being allowed to bring children into this world.

But other than a few hostile travelers competing with us for scarce resources, our hardships are caused more by the journey itself than anything else.

Jane purchases new clothes for her and Tomás, warmer clothing that will be necessary for the colder temperatures of the mountains. I watch her spending time with the boy every evening, helping him sound out words in a book of poetry she picked up. The boy works hard to please Jane, and I even catch her smiling at him a time or two as he figures out a passage on his own.

Though I could never have foreseen the eventual benefit it does seem that accompanying Jane on her foolhardy adventure to Sacramento served its purpose. With Gideon in the wind and so many reminders of Jane's old life around her now, and the possibility of her family being in Haven, she has regained a measure of her old self. I have seen momentary flashes of the friend I knew, warm and kind and jovial, and I know that it is but a matter of time before she quits her quest for vengeance altogether and becomes the girl she once was. Well, if not the Jane McKeene of old, at least a close approximation.

My heart nearly bursts when I think upon it too long, whether from despair or joy, I am not quite sure. But I hope to never again see the cold stare of the woman who shot a man and seconds later began to casually rifle through his pockets, as though his death were as remarkable as a sneeze.

I pray Jane is finally on the road to once more being her fierce, loyal, frustrating self.

One of the ladies in the wagon train knits Jane a scarf and Tomás socks to wear under his boots, which are a tad too big. When Jane offers to pay her, the woman blushes prettily and waves her off. I think maybe she is a bit sweet on Jane, who does cut a dashing figure in trousers and broadcloth, the falchion strapped across her back and a pistol hanging low on her hip.

Jane has no shortage of admirers on the wagon train.

When we stop in the evenings, exhausted from the days' labors, Mr. Stevens finds his way to Jane's side more often than not. She is surprisingly tolerant of his attentions, to the point that I finally inquire, after a week of hard travel, "Jane, you do know the man is courting you, right?"

Jane pauses, mouth agape, a spoonful of beans halfway to her mouth. Whatever manners she might have learned at Miss Preston's have evaporated; she eats more like a farmhand than an Attendant. She never was much one for etiquette, and the wildness of these lands has only encouraged her to be more herself.

She slowly sets her spoon back on her plate, using the remnant of her left arm to keep the dish from toppling.

"What are you talking about?"

"Mr. Stevens. The man is courting you."

"Don't be a ninny, Kate. The man is doing no such thing."

We sit in a grove a short ways from the well-worn Sis-kiyou Trail. It is a spot that looks to have served as a refuge for a number of travelers, complete with a firepit and a small surplus of firewood left by the previous visitors. Because of the trials and tribulations during our trip our wagon train now counts only a hundred souls, as people opted to stay in towns along the way. An entire group of our wagon train broke off and decided to head to Eureka, turning west at a fork in the road despite Louisa and Juliet's counsel. With our hundred we count a meager four wagons. Most of the oxen teams have been doubled up as people sold the beasts off for extra cash. We would make better time with more oxen, but fewer mouths to feed is always a good thing.

"Stevens ain't looking for a wife at all," Jane continues, nearly upsetting her plate with the force of her spoon smacking the bottom. "That man loves the sound of his own voice too much. He doesn't want a wife—he craves an audience."

"Believe what you want, Jane, but I know what I see."

And as if to prove my point, Mr. Stevens sidles over at that moment, giving me only the most perfunctory of greetings before sitting down and engaging Jane.

I scoop my beans slowly, with a self-satisfied smirk, as the realization of the truth of my proclamation dawns on Jane's face. I know this is a sin, but there are few things I enjoy more than being right. I have been praying to the Lord to be a bit more humble. He just has not seen fit to show me the way as of yet. And as Stevens offers Jane his corn bread, and she just stares at him half in shock and half in revulsion, the range of expressions marching across Jane's face is so delightful that I have to excuse myself lest I give away the joke.

But the most delightful thing by far is that Mr. Stevens does not seem to realize Jane would sooner murder him than shower him with kisses. But the fact that she has not pulled her revolver on the man seems to be yet another indication that Jane is finding her way back from the darkness.

All in all, the last couple of weeks have been an encouraging sign that I can one day have something close to the friend I lost in Nicodemus.

I take my empty dish to the wash bucket and scrub it before putting it in the drying rack nearby. I wave at Sue as I pass, but she either does not see me or does not want to be bothered. She is deep in conversation with Roy, a large, nicely built Negro blacksmith who joined our train in Abbottsville, a rare gain when we had been losing members of our wagon train steadily. Roy had been an apprentice to another man and was ready to strike out on his own. Sue seems quite taken with him and he with her, and it is then time for my own painful revelation as I consider that by the time we get to Haven I might indeed be left to my own devices, just Lily and me. Well, as much as Lily needs me. She has been mostly self-sufficient during the trek.

There is a commotion at the edge of the wagon ring. The

sun has been staying up later as we move closer to summer, and the slanting golden rays of sunset still illuminate the land. I hustle over to where there seems to be a scuffle of some sort. Bartholomew, one of the boys from the wagon train, swings and misses at a man in a plaid red shirt and dungarees. The man's face is indistinguishable beneath the low brim of his hat, but he moves out of the way of the punch with an easy grace that I cannot help but admire.

"I said I'm not here to cause trouble or to steal from you. I'm looking for Jane McKeene. Bounty hunter known as the Devil's Bride."

I recognize the voice, and it quickens my pace.

"Mr. Redfern!" I say. "How in God's name are you here?"

Bartholomew turns toward me. That is the moment Daniel Redfern chooses to swing, catching the boy by surprise and felling him like a termite-infested tree.

"Dammit, I'm sorry," Mr. Redfern says, bending down to help the boy up, who is more than a little dazed.

One of the other boys on watch comes running over, and I pass Bartholomew off to him. "Alexander, would you be a dear and take Bart back to his people. Throw his arm over your shoulder, yes, just like that. I will deal with our guest."

The boys walk off, Alexander giving Mr. Redfern one last uncertain look before doing as I asked.

"Well, this is more than a shock, I should say, Mr. Redfern. I had taken you for dead back in Nicodemus."

"Miss Deveraux. It is . . . good to see you." His speech is labored, and the reason is clear. Mr. Redfern must have been on the losing end of a previous bout, if his blackened eye and swollen lips are anything to go by. He looks like a rough character, indeed.

My heart pounds. I do not believe in coincidence, and Mr. Redfern being here cannot mean anything good. Not for me, and most certainly not for Jane. But I will not let this man see my worry. "How did you come to be in California?"

"Same way as just about everyone else, I suppose," he says. His voice is gravelly, deeper than I remember, as though the world has pushed him down and his voice bears the scars.

"Well, that is hardly helpful," I say, my frustration grounding me for a moment. Annoyance is an easier emotion to contend with.

"Look, I need to talk to Jane," he says, not even bothering to continue the charade of polite discourse.

"Then talk." Jane walks up with more than a little swagger. Her fingers rest on her side arm, and I tense. This could get very bloody.

He tips his hat. "Jane McKeene."

"Daniel Redfern," she says, but does not move a muscle otherwise. "You got business with me?"

"I hope so," he says, his gaze unwavering. "I want you to help me track down and kill Gideon Carr."

The bounty hunter gazed into the eyes of the homesteader's wife, his expression steely. There was no use telling her that her husband was dead, and a ruffian besides. She was a delicate flower, and he would do everything he could to spare her from any more pain. He might be a man accustomed to a rough sort of life, but he could still appreciate beauty.

—Western Tales, *Volume 40*

— J A N E —

Chapter 43
In Which I Realize Life Is Ludicrous

Seeing Daniel Redfern—beaten and bloody, but alive and mostly well—is a shock I haven't had since the first time Callie kissed me. She and I had been holed up in Nicodemus, huddled together for warmth, and she'd leaned over and pressed her lips to mine, transforming our awkward friendship into something even more fragile and exciting. In that moment, I'd been happy, aching as I was for the warmth and passion of that kiss, but as soon as it was over, the thrill melted into

THE ROAD TO PERDITION

sadness. I knew, even then, that whatever the feelings were that were blooming between us, they—we—were doomed. Hadn't Jackson taught me that, over and over again?

Now, the same mix of feelings washes over me at seeing Daniel Redfern, because there is no way our time together will end well. He's been a harbinger of despair in my life, and seeing him once more makes me wary of what is to come next.

But there's also nothing I want more than Gideon Carr's head on a pike. And if that's his goal as well, then perhaps our destinies are intertwined for the better, after all.

I lift my chin up and look him dead in his eye. "I'm listening, Redfern."

"Daniel," he says, and quirks his lip. "I thought we were on a first-name basis."

"Have you eaten yet, Mr. Red—er, Daniel?" says Katherine, ever mindful of whatever etiquette the situation requires.

"No, and I'd be grateful for some chow."

We lead him through the wagons and toward the cook fires. Redfern holds his side as he moves, and I twist my lips. There are fresh lines in his face, and he looks older. I suppose we all do. It has been a humdinger of a year.

"Who got the better of you?" I ask.

"Gideon's hired men. He's gotten a bit more cautious— one might say paranoid—after I almost did him in down in Los Angeles."

"I thought he was in Sacramento?"

"This was before. He did the hardest part of winter in the southern climes, even crossed over into Mexico for a bit."

"How long have you been tracking him?" I ask.

A muscle clenches in Redfern's jaw and his gaze goes far away. "Since Nicodemus."

We walk past Sue, and when she spies our unexpected companion, she gets up from chatting with her beau to follow us to the cook fire. As we get Redfern settled in with some beans and a tin cup of water, Sue elbows me in the side. "Ain't that the sheriff from Nicodemus?"

"One and the same," I say.

"How'd he end up here?" she says, not even bothering to whisper.

"I came looking for Jane," he says. "I'd been hearing tales of the path she's been cutting through the Western states for months now; after the fall of Sacramento, I made my way to Abbottsville, evidently only a day or so after you'd been through. I followed the trail hoping I could catch up to you." He reaches inside of his vest and pulls out a newspaper, the *Abbottsville Eagle*. On the cover is a badly executed sketch of yours truly. I'm wearing a set of bandoliers and carry an oversized pistol, my lips overly large and my teeth pointed. Nearby is a group of terrified women and children. THE DEVIL'S BRIDE SIGHTED IN ABBOTTSVILLE, the headline reads. CITIZENS, BE WARY! At least they got my amputated arm correct, the end of the shirt pinned up neatly in the picture.

"Oh, for Pete's sake," Katherine says, yanking the paper and tossing it into the fire. "The imaginations of these men . . ."

"I don't know," Sue says slyly. "They got those messy braids right."

"I was gonna ask you to redo them, but your hands seem otherwise occupied since you've been busy with that blacksmith," I say sweetly.

Sue coughs, and I'm glad to see I've scored a direct hit.

"Daniel, perhaps you could start at the beginning," Katherine says, settling onto a vacant stool. She tugs her skirt over her knees primly, as the knife strapped to her thigh causes the material to ride up. Her hands move too much, she readjusts her bonnet and smooths her hair, telegraphing her nervousness to anyone who knows her. She ain't happy about Redfern showing up.

Sue and I take seats, and once we're settled Katherine turns to Redfern like she's hosting a soiree. "The last time we saw you was before Nicodemus fell."

"That's right." Redfern nods. "While I came to know who Gideon Carr really was in that doomed town, Kansas was not our first meeting. I worked for the Carr family right after I left the Lancaster Combat School. Like Attendants, we were placed with families of means. I was assigned to Mayor Carr's security team, one of those whose job it was to provide personal protection for him and his family. I had a knack for combat, and for surviving; within a few months, I'd become one of the mayor's most trusted men, and that's when he assigned me to his son's personal protection detail. At that time, Gideon was attending the School of Thanatology in Baltimore, where we first met. I'm sure you ladies remember the very public failure of Professor Ghering's experiments?"

I nod. "Indeed. Thank you for saving my neck," I say, quite belatedly.

He shrugs. "I wasn't trying to save you, exactly. Just ending the threat."

Sue lets out a laugh. I immediately regret showing him my appreciation.

"Weeks earlier," he continues, "I was waiting for Gideon outside the lab where he had been collaborating with Professor Ghering. I was supposed to escort him home. That's when I heard a cry from inside the lab. I found him on the floor, next to a cage in which he had a shambler imprisoned. He'd been bitten. I immediately dispatched the shambler, and I was turning my pistol to Gideon when he got to his feet and begged me to let him live."

"It seems like that might've been a mistake," Sue says drily.

"In hindsight, yes. But at the time I figured there was no harm in waiting to see if the boy changed. I would have had a hell of a time explaining things to his father if his son died by my hand, shambler bite or no."

"And you've always been one to put yourself first," I say.

He shrugs. "I'm still here, aren't I?"

"But Gideon Carr did not turn," Katherine interrupts, ignoring our back and forth.

"No. He didn't." Redfern gazes down at his plate, a hard

look carving its way into his features. "He believed he'd found a cure. A way to stop the plague. But while the formula had worked on Gideon, other test subjects hadn't fared so well with the same injection. Professor Ghering continued to work on Gideon's formula, and Gideon grew increasingly frustrated with the man. He convinced his father to let him build a lab in the basement of their family estate so he could work in private, and he began testing his vaccine on members of the household staff. Those who objected were let go; those who agreed, well . . . I believe you can imagine what happened to them.

"Gideon had yet to duplicate the success of the test he'd done on himself, but the results of his failed experiments steadily piled up, and so Mayor Carr sent him to Summerland, where he'd have more freedom to test his vaccine, as well as put into practice his mechanical defense systems. By this time, the Survivalists had brought in Negroes from the Lost States into the town to fill out the patrols. Gideon had all the test subjects he could ever desire. Sheriff Snyder's only rule was that he couldn't test his vaccine on any white residents."

A sharp pain shoots down my jaw, and I realize I'm gnashing my teeth. I could thrash Redfern for standing by and watching all this happen. Katherine is similarly vexed; the color that rides high in her cheeks is visible in the waning sunlight.

"You knew that this was going on and you did nothing to stop it?" Katherine says.

"I didn't do nothing," Redfern says grimly. "Although it is true that I waited too long to intervene. I wasn't sent to Kansas until I was put on the train that carried you out there, and almost immediately I sought out the leadership in Nicodemus, in an effort to figure out how to save everyone in Summerland. But . . . well, you know how that ended."

"How did Gideon end up in Nicodemus?" I ask, trying to push aside my emotions and not end up all in my feelings. If I fall into that dark well I might not ever get out, not even after Gideon Carr is dead. The sheer injustice of it all has already set my blood to boiling. Anyone else would have been stopped long ago, but Gideon Carr keeps getting opportunities to hurt people over and over.

That has to end.

Redfern clears his throat, and I pull myself back to the moment. "Gideon's only religion is science, and I don't think the Snyders ever really trusted him. He grew frustrated with their rules, with the lack of resources they provided him, with their patronizing regard for his experiments. It wasn't long before he was seeking out a place that was a bit more willing to see the potential of what he promised."

"So Gideon Carr found his way to Nicodemus," Sue says, lips twisting.

"Callie told me he said she was special," I say, my heart cracking. "But she was just the one test case where his vaccine worked."

"Not the only one," Daniel says, lips pressed together in a thin line.

I laugh, the sound hollow and dry. "He got you, too?"

"In Baltimore. I was the only member of the household staff that didn't turn, but mostly because he never got the chance to jam me in a cage with the restless dead. It wasn't until after Nicodemus that I was . . . that I discovered I was immune." Redfern's gaze goes distant, and I wonder if he's remembering those few days after the bite, the nausea and sickness and deep abiding despair. "Sometimes I wish the vaccine hadn't worked on me, either."

I know exactly what he means.

Gideon did have successes, here and there. It's seeming more and more like my survival hadn't been an accident, but actual proof of an effective serum, the perfect combination of science and time. If Gideon Carr had been a mite less impatient Nicodemus might still be standing, a town full of healthy, unafraid people able to survive the dead . . .

But none of that mattered. He'd rushed things, failed to let his setbacks humble him, and refused to listen to anything but his own inclinations. The end result was tragedy. There's a lesson to be learned from that, and I don't aim to repeat Gideon's mistakes.

"So what's the story here?" I ask, mulling over the possibilities as they unfold before me. "You could have killed Gideon in Nicodemus. Or Summerland. But you've traipsed halfway across the country through endless dead to hunt him down. Why?"

"Because—" Redfern begins, and anguish clogs his throat. His eyes fill with tears, and he swipes his hand across his face to chase them away. "He killed Amelia." And then Daniel Redfern is sobbing outright as the wall of his emotions break.

"I knew it," Sue mutters, before digging a handkerchief out of her sleeve and handing it to Redfern, who accepts it gratefully. I can't decide if I'm more sympathetic or horrified to see the man lose control of his emotions, even over Miss Duncan, but Katherine is less insensitive, and she scoots her stool closer and takes Daniel Redfern's hand, patting him reassuringly until he manages to compose himself. He gives her a grateful smile and takes a deep breath before continuing.

"I knew as soon as the gates were down that Nicodemus was lost. And Gideon Carr's handiwork was obvious to anyone who has seen how quickly his experiments can go awry. I was ready to leave Nicodemus then and there, but Amelia was determined to stay and help people. Because it was the right thing to do."

"She was bit," I say, and he nods. "She was there, during my convalescence. Seeing Miss Duncan like that . . ." I trail off, because there ain't much more that needs to be said than that.

"I wandered south in a daze," Redfern says. "There aren't a lot of places that are safe for Indians, let alone one traveling by himself. And it wasn't like I had any place to go." He shrugs. "I had no plan. For the first time in my life there was no one to tell me what to do and where to go, and I had no idea what to do with that. I was lost, no meaning, no purpose. The dead were no threat to me any longer. And yet, I couldn't die. The only thing left for me: to hunt down Gideon.

"I eventually made my way to Denver. There was an article in the paper, talking about Gideon lecturing about the possibility of a vaccine. I almost had him there. He escaped before I could confront him. But I've been tracking him ever since."

He turns to look at me and shakes his head. "I'm sorry to ask such a thing of you. But I figure if anyone wanted Gideon Carr dead as much as I did, it was you."

"Plus, I've always been happy enough to run off and kill someone who deserved it," I say.

He gives me a terse nod. "If what they say about you in the papers is even half true . . . well, I need help, and you seem more than capable of killing Gideon."

I don't say anything. It annoys me that Redfern is asking for my help, especially since the last time I saw him he gave me that lecture about minding my own business, but he's right. I want the tinkerer dead.

And I want to be the one to do it.

I think about the old man in the boat. "Did Gideon cause the fall of Sacramento?" I ask. I know what I think the answer to be, but I need the confirmation.

"The West is almost devoid of shamblers," Redfern says.

"And yet, Sacramento suddenly falls to a horde, right after Gideon reportedly sets up shop there? Does that sound like a coincidence to you?"

"The precedent has been set," I drawl. A body in motion tends to stay in motion, like old Sir Isaac Newton said. Unless acted upon by an outside force.

"Jane." Katherine's hand is on my arm and her eyes are full of barely restrained emotion. I can already hear the lecture she wants to give me. She wants to remind me that this doesn't have to be my fight. I could stay with her and the wagon train, make our way to Haven and maybe a future away from so much killing. She wants me to let go of my anger and try to move past my rage, to be the Jane McKeene I once was.

But I can't.

Redfern's got a lead on Gideon, and I've already lost track of the man before. And every time I do, disaster follows. The man is a menace to society, what remains of it, and he must be stopped. Even if Katherine is right—that there is a place for me and a life that could be good and safe—it's not going to matter. Not as long as Gideon Carr remains at large.

The only problem is convincing Katherine that me running off to kill Gideon Carr doesn't mean I don't care about her. Because if I leave, I am certain it will break her heart.

And I ain't sure how many chances I got left.

If California be the only hope of this fine land, a state settled by zeal-
otry and greed, then I fear for the rest of these great United States.
Indeed, we must ask ourselves if the dead are not so much a happen-
stance of the world, but a plague visited upon us for our many sins.
And if that be the case, then running shall not change a thing.
—Senator William P. Henry, 1870

— K A T H E R I N E —

Chapter 44
Notes on a Terrible Idea

As I listened to Daniel Redfern's tale my worry grew with
every word. His timing is terrible, and the tale he spins is
even worse. The more he talked, the harder Jane's expression
became. Now I am afraid that the hints of lightness I have
seen over these past couple of weeks were but my imagination. I have worked so hard to bring Jane back to her better
self, and here is Daniel Redfern to send her once more into
that darkness.

I refuse to let that happen.

I stand and gesture to Sue and Jane. "I am sorry, Daniel, but could you excuse us? We need to have a word."

"Of course," he says, standing as etiquette dictates. He watches us walk away from the cook fire with a mixture of interest and sadness. How much of it is an act and how much is truth? I have always been a very good judge of people, especially men. Spending time among women who make their living off a man's passions very quickly shows a body the best and worst of the sex, and Daniel Redfern makes me feel vaguely on edge. More so than ever before.

But mostly, I fear that Jane going with this man on a mission of violence will result in her end. She saved me once. Now, I have to save her from herself.

Once we are out of earshot I round on Jane. "I do not trust that man."

"Me either," says Sue, crossing her arms. "That man is too handsome by half, even looking like the loser in a boxing match. It's positively distracting."

"Sue!" I exclaim. "Be serious."

"I am," Sue says with a slow smile. She turns to Jane. "But Katherine is right. He's leaving something out in this yarn he's spinning. You've been hunting Gideon Carr for months, how is it that your paths are just now crossing? The man never struck me as being ineffective. He should've sought you out long before now."

"Exactly," I say, nodding along as Sue speaks. "Maybe the legend of the Devil's Bride has spread far and wide, but that does not explain his sudden appearance. He is hiding something."

"I'm going with him," Jane says. "I'm sorry."

"Jane, be sensible," I say. I can feel the work I have done over the past few weeks, helping Jane piece herself together as we traveled, begin to come undone as she considers turning back toward the bloody path of revenge. "We are only a few days from Haven, Daniel Redfern can wait until then. Perhaps we can resupply and find allies willing to go with us to confront Gideon."

I had hoped that upon getting to Haven we would find at the very least a functional town and, perhaps, Jane's mother and Aunt Aggie. I know Jane can be saved from the darkness in her soul, but I am afraid that I am not enough to get her to reconsider her path. Not again.

"I don't think this can wait," Jane says, her voice low. Something flickers in her gaze. "Katherine, I have to see this through. I've given up so much already, and someone has to stop him. I cannot bear to let this opportunity slip past."

I stamp my foot, because Jane is irksome under the best of circumstances and this is far from that. "If you think that I am about to let you march off with a man who has put his interests before ours, to our detriment, by the by, on more than one occasion, you have another think coming, Jane

McKeene. You know how I feel about this muttonheaded quest of yours, but running off with Daniel Redfern is a whole other level of lunacy. You are going to get yourself killed because you are too impulsive by half—"

Sue's deep laugh halts my tantrum.

"I swear, the pair of you are a match set, stubborn and overly dramatic to boot. You are both so determined to be contrary that it's a wonder you managed to escape that terrible town that had you all jammed up."

Jane raises an eyebrow. "And I suppose you've got a plan?"

"Of course. Just because the two of you never ask my thoughts on a matter doesn't mean I'm beef-witted. Jane, you're going to run off with Sheriff Redfern and get killed doing something reckless because you cannot help yourself. And then, Katherine, you're going to spend another year feeling sorry for yourself and doubting every decision you make." Jane and I fall silent, chastened, and Sue gives us a smug look. "Now here's what I think: Jane, you're my friend and all, but I learned long ago never to get in between you and something you got your heart set on. You want to kill that fool from Nicodemus, have at."

I swallow hard. "Sue, this is the opposite of helpful."

She shrugs. "Maybe. But someone has to be levelheaded here. Personally, I think spending all this time chasing down a single man is a lot for a body to handle. Way I see it, Jesus gets everyone sorted out when they get to the afterlife, so one way or another that man will get his."

Jane nods slowly. "I've always counted you as a friend, Sue. So thank you."

"I ain't finished," Sue says, exasperation lacing her voice. "It's obvious Katherine is going to have to go with you, both to save you from your impulses and so she doesn't go mad with worry over your carcass."

"Not a chance," Jane says. "I can't have Katherine's death on my soul."

"As if I am so easy to kill," I huff. "Sue is right. Your purpose may be Gideon Carr, but you are mine. I go with you, or you do not go at all."

"Is that a threat?" Jane asks, eyebrow arching.

"Yes, it is."

Jane hesitates before sighing dramatically. "Fine. But if you're angling to keep me from killing Gideon you may as well stay here."

"I am not, Jane. But you shall not go down this path alone. Because you have people who love you. You always have."

Something like sadness passes over Jane's features, but it is gone quicker than lightning. She gives me a dismissive wave. "If you say so."

And just like that, we are agreed on a course of action.

Jane nods toward Sue. "I don't have to worry about you coming along as well, do I?"

Sue snorts. "Heck no. Besides, someone has to keep an

eye on Lily and Tomás and talk Carolina out of the snit he's bound to fall into when he discovers you've gotten Katherine tangled up in one of your terrible schemes."

We leave early the next morning, just as the sun sends tendrils of pink across the deep blue sky. Mr. Redfern has not a single weapon and we are able to convince Juliet to part with both a shotgun and a Bowie knife for the man. Our plan is simple: hike straight into the mountains to Smith's Forge. It is an abandoned mining camp, and the place where Mr. Redfern says Gideon is holed up. Upon finding Gideon Carr, we will end his life.

"How do you know that Gideon Carr is still in this mining camp?" I ask as we walk, because I think Mr. Redfern is withholding vital information.

"Miss Deveraux, I believe I told you this already. Two days ago. That was when I ran afoul of Gideon's hired guns. There are three of them. Not sure where they're from, but all white, all of the rough sort that prowl these violent lands. We shouldn't have to worry about them until we get closer to the encampment."

"And just why exactly do you think Mr. Carr will still be in this place?" I ask.

"Because from what I could tell he's set himself up a nice lab out of the way from just about everything. And the kind of equipment he would have brought with him is expensive and hard to find. Not to mention that Gideon Carr is not a man to abandon what he sees as his life's work."

I do not ask any further questions, because Jane is giving me a sidelong glance and I do not want to provoke her. She is taken with this nonsense, and while all my concern is for her and what is left of her soul, it is a fact that when pushed in one direction she runs in the opposite. So while I doubt the veracity of Mr. Redfern's claims, I cannot show Jane my hand just yet.

We walk for two days straight, into the Sierra Nevadas, our trek consisting of little-used footpaths marked mostly by deer tracks. The nights are freezing, and the days are not much better. The sun shines warm and bright, but the last of winter's chill clings to the shadows as true spring has not yet made its way up the mountain. Our first night is spent huddled next to a fire, the temperature freezing cold. It seemed improper to take supplies from the wagon train for this tomfoolery, so we only grabbed a bit of pemmican and a hard biscuit. It is only the discovery of a fine trout stream on the second day that keeps us from feeling the pinch of hunger. While it is too early for berries or any other forest greens, Jane is able to dig up a few cattail roots in the mud along the creek to round out our evening meal.

"It's only about another day and a half walk from here," Redfern says as we enjoy our repast. I search his face for any signs of guile and find none. We finish the rest of the meal in silence. Jane, for her part, seems calmer than she has been in a spell. I have no idea what is on her mind because she says very little, and that worries me more than anything else. I have never known Jane McKeene to keep her thoughts to herself, and I wonder as we walk if perhaps I have underestimated the hate she carries in her heart. Perhaps I was too late. It could be that she was already too far along her path for vengeance by the time we became reacquainted. The possibility sends me on a spiral of despair, and I fall into a morose silence as we bed down for the night, my thoughts a heavy burden.

Redfern volunteers to take first watch, and I am so tired and dejected that I do not even think to keep a watch on him, falling asleep as soon as I close my eyes.

It is a mistake.

It is still dark when I wake to the sound of a gun cocking next to my temple. I open my eyes to the foul breath of a man grinning down at me.

"Well, 'allo there, lovely," he says, his voice thickly accented. Without thinking I grab his hand, wrenching his thumb around while I move my knees and bring my leg up to kick him in his middle. He falls over with an *oof*, and I climb to my feet with a pistol in hand.

"It's no use, Kate. We've been had," Jane says. Someone stokes the dying embers of the fire, and as the flames cast a bit of light her plight is illuminated. Another man holds a gun pointed at her back, and every weapon from her rig lies in a pile on the ground.

"Miss Deveraux, please disarm. I promise no harm will come to you," Redfern says. He gives the man who threatened me a meaningful look.

"I think she broke my thumb," he growls.

"Irish Tom, please," comes another voice, one that is all too familiar. "We are on a tight schedule."

The pistol is taken from my hands and Gideon Carr steps into the light of the dying fire, looking just as hale and hearty as he did the last time I saw him in Nicodemus. His eyes are shadowed, but otherwise he is just as I remember him.

"Katherine." He nods in greeting.

"Miss Deveraux, please," I say, crossing my arms and lifting my chin. I may be beat, but I still have my pride.

A smile ghosts across Mr. Carr's lips, and he inclines his head once more in acknowledgment of my rebuke. "Miss Deveraux. It is delightful to see you again, although I am sorry at the circumstances. Please disarm. I would hate to have Irish Tom do it for you."

"And just what is this schedule we are on?" I demand. I do not quite keep the tremor of fear from my voice and Mr. Carr looks exhausted and resigned.

"I have an experiment in progress," he says, his voice heavy, "and I have to get back to see the results. So let us be off."

There is only one rule of the frontier: shoot first and aim well. Well, I suppose that is two, but if you can't hit the broadside of a barn the first one don't matter much, does it?
—Bounty Hunter Shorty Allred, 1868

— J A N E —

Chapter 45
In Which I Fail

By the time Gideon and his men secure our weapons and belongings and are ready to move, the day is dawning. I cannot decide what I hate more, the fact that Gideon Carr has once more bested me or that Katherine has been looped into my misery.

I knew bringing her along was a stupid idea. Her well-being had halted my trek in Sacramento amongst the smoke and the dead, but now . . . Now I am so close, a heartbeat away from ending Gideon Carr, and I am left to consider that I might have to choose between killing Gideon and saving Katherine.

Even worse is the fact that should Katherine's life end up on the altar of my vengeance, I ain't quite sure what my decision might be.

As we leave our campsite Redfern catches my eye, his gaze sliding to Gideon and then back to me. "I'm sorry," he mutters. "It was the only way."

I have no response for him. My emotions are a maelstrom and it's taking everything I have just to walk the path to what I assume is Gideon's lab.

The moment I heard Gideon's voice my body went cold. Fingers, toes, even my nose felt like they were encased in ice. And still do. It's like all my anger and anguish have stolen the warmth from my body, leaving me with an empty shell filled with snow. I struggle to put one foot in front of the other, my rage so all-encompassing that I have half a mind to lurch for Gideon and give killing him my best shot, even though I know my life would be forfeit.

I wondered how it would feel to see Gideon Carr again, but I never could've envisioned this frigid fury. To be fair, most of my imaginings had been me strolling into a saloon and finding the man laughingly playing a round of cards. I imagined I would call him out in front of the whole room, so that when I did finally shoot him I would have the law on my side. Not that the law has ever done much for Negroes, but still. It would be a clean kill, a quick one, and then I would get on with living the rest of my life.

I did not imagine myself a weaponless statue made of ice, trying to bide my time until I could finally kill the man properly.

"At least now we know why you volunteered for first watch," Katherine says to Redfern. Two spots of color ride high in her cheeks, and her blue eyes flash like lightning. I would only be half surprised to see her rip out Redfern's heart like some kind of ancient warrior. Her gaze meets mine, and she lifts her chin and gives me a small smile.

A bit of the ice melts away.

Well, ain't this a fine kettle of fish.

"I want my money, Gideon," Redfern says.

The tinkerer waves a dismissive hand in Daniel's direction. "Yes, yes, of course. I'll give it to you when we get back to camp."

"You sold us out," I say, voice flat.

"I told you, I'm a man who knows how to survive," Redfern says, expression hard.

And there ain't much to say to that.

The woods we pass through are beautiful. The creek we slept near burbles along beside the path merrily, and birds call to each other high in the trees. A handful of trees are flowering, and even the ferns that grow in the shadows are an impossible shade of green. It's gorgeous country.

It's hard to appreciate when there's a six-shooter pointed at your spine.

We quickly gain the camp proper, and Redfern's betrayal is revealed in its totality. He had been the one to suggest that we break early in our trek and forage for our supper. If we'd continued, we would've stumbled upon Gideon's hidey-hole in minutes. It ain't much of anything—an ugly mud patch carved out of the majesty of the woods. Gideon must have full run of the place, because there ain't another soul to be seen. A couple of rough canvas tents, two buildings, one that lists dangerously to the right, and a water wheel that turns in the creek, the squeak of it enough to drive a sane man mad.

We are prodded toward the one solid-looking building. The man Gideon referred to as Irish Tom pushes me forward.

"Irish Tom. Is that your given name?" I ask. The man gives me a dark look but says nothing.

"He's named Irish Tom because he killed ten Irishmen up in Oregon, claim jumping," Gideon says. "The accent you hear is English. Please do not provoke the man, Jane."

"That's a terrible basis for a nickname," I say, but at Katherine's sharp look I press my lips together, keeping my ruminations to myself.

The door opens, and a younger-looking white man wearing a leather apron is behind it. Relief breaks across his features at the sight of Gideon.

"Very good, sir, glad to see you are back. Ah, with additional test subjects?"

"No, Plimpton. I'm hoping Mr. Shiner is our final subject. Jane McKeene here is a success story, so she will be helpful in the distillation of new serums. Please escort them to the two-person berth. How is Mr. Shiner doing?"

"Still stable, sir. No signs of transference."

Gideon nods, moving aside so that Irish Tom and his boys can herd Katherine and me toward a cage. "That's forty-eight hours. Let's go ahead and move him into phase two."

Plimpton nods in response and moves off as my eyes adjust to the darkness of the inside of the building. It's clearly a lab, despite it's humble exterior, and no expense has been spared. It's even more spacious and better outfitted than the lab at Summerland had been. Back then, before I knew the true depths of Gideon's malice, the lab had seemed magical. Now, every beaker and glass tube gleams ominously.

Katherine and I are pushed into a shambler cage, the iron door slammed behind us. She rounds on me as soon as the hired guns move away, her jaw set.

"I know, I know," I say. The chill is finally melting from my bones, leaving me to consider my options. "You were right about Redfern."

"Of course I was," she snaps, but fear is etched onto her features.

"This definitely is not my preferred outcome, but at least

I've finally found Gideon," I say, forcing a tight-lipped smile.

"Really, Jane?" she says, her usual timbre pushed higher by her emotions.

Redfern walks past, pausing by our cage and eyeing me once more before he follows Plimpton and Gideon Carr into a room in the back. When the door opens I get the glimpse of a man, eyes wide with fright.

"Please," the man begins, but whatever else he has to say is cut off by the slamming of the door.

"Oy, let's get out of here. I've got no desire to listen to this again," says Irish Tom, and he and his friends leave out the front.

"Jane—" Katherine begins, but whatever she's about to say is cut off by the sound of a shambler moaning loudly, and a man screaming in terror. It's too much like the lecture Katherine and I witnessed back in Baltimore, and she covers her face in horror.

"I think I know what phase two is," I say. My stomach turns. It's been a long while since I've heard anything like the sounds of the man pleading and begging followed by the sounds of the dead feeding. The screams of terror prickle the skin on my arms and start a fire of panic in my belly.

I don't think—I just start slamming my shoulder against the door of the cage, probing it for a weakness. Katherine, however, is just staring at the floor.

"Help me!" I say to her. "We need to get out of here, and

we're not going to get a better chance than now."

"You are right," she says, putting a calming hand on my shoulder just as I'm about to slam the door once more. She points at the ground by the cage wall. I follow it to see a glint of gold.

It's a key.

"Redfern must have dropped it," she says as she slips it into her skirt.

"So he is on our side?" I ask, voice low.

"I do not know if that man is on any 'side' but his own," she says. "But it appears that he has some sort of plan. The only question is whether we can trust it."

"Come on," I say, gesturing toward the locked door of the shambler cage. "We can figure it out once we're free."

"Jane, wait," Katherine says, and I turn to follow her gaze. The door opens, and Gideon and his assistant file out.

"In the report please note that the subject transitioned one minute after being bitten by the dead," Gideon says, wiping his hands on a rag. New lines etch his face, and he looks miserable. "Also of note, the lack of yellowing of the eyes. I suspect that indicates the infection did not fully develop. Perhaps we should do a weeklong incubation period to see if that impacts resistance."

"One minute," Katherine says, and I share her horror. That's faster than I've ever heard of anyone going shambler. What was Gideon trying to do? Did he even know anymore?

"You're doing it all wrong, you know," I say after Gideon's assistant has left. Redfern is nowhere to be found. My mind spins out a plan as I talk.

Gideon walks over to an open journal on the nearby counter and begins making notes. "Jane, please. I don't have the energy to spar with you," he says. "I'm tired and no closer to a workable serum than I was when I left Nicodemus. There is nothing you can say to me that I have not told myself, many times over. I have worked so hard to find the answer, and no matter what I do I find myself with yet another life on my conscience." He scrubs his hand across his face. He looks half ready to cry, and his anguish makes me mighty uncomfortable, which is saying something. "I'm not a monster, you know, never mind what you may think of me."

"This looks mighty monstrous to me," Katherine says, voice low.

Gideon nods. "I am fully aware of how this looks, Miss Deveraux. Trust me. No one hates me more than I hate myself." His gaze goes distant. "But it will all be worth it once I find an answer." Gideon turns away and takes out a pen and ink and begins to make notes. I'd expected to find a madman, a slavering lunatic jabbing needles into sobbing victims strapped to tables like in the weekly serial "A Dutiful Wife" where a woman marries a man only to realize he has conducted experiments on all his previous brides, changing them into monstrous creatures. The man we've found is someone else. Still, I can't reconcile this man with the boy I felt soft toward in Summerland. It's like he's traded his soul for a scientific breakthrough and no one has told him that his Faustian deal was a poor one.

"Well, the good news is your vaccine works," I say.

Gideon startles from his work. "Do not mock me, Jane. I'm afraid I've lost my mirth in the past year."

"I ain't. It works. Well, at least the serum you had in Summerland did."

He pauses and turns toward me, giving me his full attention. "What do you mean?"

"It works, given time. The problem is you're too damn impatient. Seven days incubation time? I'd had the vaccine months before I got bit. And Callie had been poked an entire season before she ran afoul of her shambler. How long was it between when you injected yourself in Baltimore and when the dead man bit you?"

He stands and walks over so that he is an arm's length away from the cage. A little closer and I can reach through the bars and throttle him with one hand, pulling his cravat tight enough to choke him.

He doesn't sense the danger. "A month. Maybe two," he says, voice quiet.

I nod. "You don't need to keep sacrificing people to the dead like some kind of mad scientist from a serial, all you got to do is wait, see how the dead react to a body that's been vaccinated, and mark when they no longer see a person as food."

"My god," he says, some of the weariness fading from his face as he strides away, reaching for a notebook. "I suppose your hypothesis is based on observation?"

"My suppositions are *always* based on observation. There's a muting of the hunting instinct when a person is successfully vaccinated. You've seen it yourself." I fairly swear to myself as he moves back out of reach.

"But that doesn't account for the eventual bites," he says, warming to my point.

"That's because the hunting instinct is muted but not completely removed. Sudden movements, loud noises? Those still kick shamblers into a frenzy and prompt an attack."

"And after the bite, because the original strain has been introduced, the subject's blood appears the same as one of the dead." Joy breaks over his face, and he takes a half a step toward the cage. "How did I miss that? An effective serum will nullify the hunting instinct once deployed." Gideon turns to his notebook and begins muttering as he scribbles.

"What was that, Jane?" Katherine asks me, voice low.

"A distraction," I say.

"Was any of that true?"

I shrug. "No clue. I mean, everything I told him was true, but I ain't a scientist. I don't know if time or something else is why Gideon's serum doesn't work. I was just hoping to get a hand on him so I could throttle him."

"We need a new plan," she whispers. I nod.

"Also," Gideon calls from where he stands, drawing my attention once more, "I never got to tell you this because Callie tried to kill me, but I discovered why Maeve and her girls turned along with all the other folks in Nicodemus. A problem with the potency." He takes off his spectacles and rubs his face, and it takes me a long moment to realize he's talking about the Duchess. "I truly am sorry about that one."

The memory catches me like a right hook and leaves me reeling. For a moment I'm back in Nicodemus, harvesting the Duchess and her girls, and then tiny Thomas. I'm whole and horrified, but my terror of that moment is nothing compared to the things I've seen in the meantime. I've been across the depth and breadth of horrors on this continent and seen just about every misery folks can inflict on one another firsthand. And perpetrated a few horrors myself.

Maybe that's why Gideon's sorrow feels genuine. While he has the screaming victims in spades, he is just as rational and unfailingly polite as he was when we first met him. He truly believes that he is fighting the good fight, that all of this is for a very good reason. And that is somehow more disturbing than any alternative.

Gideon Carr ain't insane. The man is exactly what Katherine is afraid I've become, driven and blinded by a singular goal, and for the first time I understand her fears.

"I don't get you, Gideon Carr. You helped us in Summerland, and you tried to help me in Nicodemus even if you were a bit wrongheaded about it. Was any of that real? How does a body get so twisted up that you abandon your humanity?"

Gideon gives me a wistful smile and my heart flip-flops a bit. He really is a beautiful boy. But he is so utterly and completely without a single shred of empathy that he's more a shell of a human being than a real person.

"I don't know, Jane. You tell me."

I open my mouth to respond, but nothing comes out. I am speechless.

Katherine squeezes my left shoulder, and I glance up to see her give me a small smile, even though her eyes are wide with barely suppressed terror. Something of my existential crisis must show on my face, because she tells me in a low voice, "You are nothing like him."

"I think we eventually become the thing we fear the most," Gideon says, standing, a syringe in his hand. "And I'm sorry for what I'm about to do, but I truly want to test your hypothesis."

I'm on my feet before he finishes the sentence. My rage is a comfort, and I'm grateful for its return. I wasn't sure what to do with the feeling of indecision and despair that had begun to creep in, but I know exactly what to do with my anger.

"You even try it and I'll—" My threat dies on my lips as pain shoots through my body. Every inch of me tingles and sizzles, and I crash to the bottom of the cage. Next to me Katherine has done the same thing, completely felled by whatever just happened. She groans, and as we writhe on the floor Gideon opens the cage door.

Carefully, he kneels down next to Katherine, lifts her arm, and pushes up her sleeve. He pulls a syringe from somewhere within his coat and jabs it into her skin, pushing the plunger and emptying the needle of the dark liquid within. He then rises and closes the door before we're able to gather our wits.

"I truly am sorry. I will have someone bring you some food and water. Just focus on your breathing, and the pain from the electric shock will fade." He pauses before saying, "And thank you, Jane. You may have just provided the crucial bit of information I needed. I knew I was right about you."

I stare up at the top of the cage, tears of rage leaking from the corners of my eyes.

No more.

When I get out of this cage, I am going to skin Gideon Carr alive, and nothing is going to stop me.

I am afraid the dream of California is ended. The dead have taken Sacramento and move en masse to San Francisco. They converge on the wall, their moans echoing day and night. I am the last one left here in the compound; everyone else has fled, taking to the sea. The poor scrabble at our doors demanding assistance that we cannot give. Will my wall hold? I have no idea. But I will not be here to witness the outcome.

—Henry Forsyth, Assistant to Mr. Thomas Edison, 1882

— K A T H E R I N E —

Chapter 46
Notes on Scientific Discovery

I am on fire.

Every inch of my body is aflame, and there is a particular ache in my neck. I want to sit up, but that would require moving, and I am perfectly content to just stare at the top of the cage for a moment and listen to the growls and moans of the undead in the next room while the flames under my skin abate.

After a long while, when I feel a bit more myself, I sit up.

Gideon Carr is gone, and Jane lies on her back crying angry tears. Her fist is clenched and there is murder in her eyes. I clear my throat.

"Well, I daresay I am not dead, so it could be worse."

Jane does not respond, so I continue talking.

"I suppose he means to keep me here for a month and then throw me to the dead. A bit biblical, is it not? Lions seem more humane than the dead. I never thought I could sacrifice myself like those saints, gouging out my eyes for love of my beliefs. But now, I think perhaps they did not really have much of a choice."

Jane sits up. "I'm sorry."

I blink. "What?"

"I'm sorry. I took you for granted. Now, then, always. I threw away Callie in my quest to find Gideon and then I turned around and did that same thing to you. Even after that moment in Sacramento, I still was willing to drag you along on this madness."

I smile sadly. "That is not who you are, Jane."

"I know. And I'm sorry I have never been a very good friend." She takes a deep breath and scrubs her sleeve across her face. "Thank you for never giving up on me."

A lump wells up in my throat, and I nod. "Never. I will never give up on you. "

She does not say anything, just looks out at the lab. A parade of emotions marches across her features, and I do not press her. The important thing is that she is letting herself feel something once again.

Especially since I feel something unnatural within myself.

Whatever Gideon injected me with has left me feeling sore and hollowed out, and I doubt that was the desired effect. My vision goes blurry, and I find myself blinking to keep myself in the moment. I want to lie down and just *be*, but Jane is plotting, and I must be ready.

"I'm certain some of those concoctions have to be explosive," she says, changing the subject. "Of course, I can't tell one thing from another. Maybe there's something in the man's notebook that will help."

"Jane, listen to me."

"You didn't happen to keep back a knife, did you? I suppose a broken beaker could do just as well as a knife," she mutters.

"I think I am dying."

Jane pauses and turns to me, slowly. "Kate."

"I am being serious," I say, collapsing against the bars of the cage.

She kneels beside me. "How do you feel?"

"Awful," I say, and it is the truth. I am dying. I can feel it. This is no usual sickness. A fever already burns through my body, and my fingertips are going numb. I came with Jane to try to save her, and maybe I did.

But I have sacrificed myself in the process.

The door to the lab opens, and Mr. Redfern enters. "Why

are you still in there? Come on, before Gideon comes back." He has our weapons in his arms, and I am sorely relieved to know the man stayed true to our cause. I take the key from my pocket to open the lock, but my fingers are clumsy and Jane has to take the key from me. She has no sooner gotten the door open, slipping out of the cage, when we hear the conversation of approaching men.

"I think taking a blood sample now will let us track the resistance to the introduction of a more active form of the sickness. If Miss McKeene is correct about the incubation time, we can see how the blood is changed."

Jane grabs a beaker, smashing it against a table just in time to stab the jagged edge into the neck of the man who enters first. It is Plimpton, and he burbles a scream as blood fountains out in an arc. He is on the floor before the man behind him is through the doorway.

"What in the—"

But before Gideon can finish his thought, Jane has shoved him up against the wall, pressing the bloody edge of the broken beaker to his neck. Redfern quickly shuts the door and steps back by the table with the lab equipment.

"Go ahead," Gideon says, struggling to get the words around the pressure on his throat. "Goodness knows I've thought about doing the deed myself. But if you kill me now, who will help Katherine if something goes wrong with the injection I've given her?"

"Don't try to weasel your way out of this," Jane growls.

"All of the lives lost because of my experiments," Gideon continues, thickly, "they are but a small fraction of the number of people who will die if I don't finish my work."

"It's a fantasy, Gideon," Jane shouts. She pins him in place with the edge of the glass. Gideon's eyes go wide. "Everything I said to you, about time taken after vaccination? It was all just a damned guess. You don't know for certain what you're doing any more than I do. The people you've killed died for nothing."

"You don't know that," he squeezes out, and swallows. A thin line of blood drips from where the glass meets his skin. "If anyone is going to figure this out, it's me. How long do you think you can stay on the run, keeping the people you care about safe from the undead? We need a cure, or the human race is finished. Everyone you know will die eventually. Everyone but you. Do you want that on your conscience?"

"If you're our only hope for the future, the human race was finished a long time ago," Jane says. Her tone is rife with malice. "And as for my conscience, well, if we're all done for, what's one more killing on my soul?"

"Jane!" I shout through the bars of the cell, over the pounding in my head. "You do not have to do this. We can take him with us. We can make him face justice. You and Mr. Redfern and I, we all know what he has done."

"It's too much of a risk, Kate, and it's more than he

deserves," Jane says, turning slightly back toward me.

In the moment she takes her eyes off Gideon he picks up a glass container from where it sits upon the table and swings for her head. Jane deflects his attempted blow, and the container sails toward another that sits over an open flame. The glass smashes, the liquid inside splashes, and flame licks across the counter, shattering more glass as it goes. Jane was right. Some of the things on the counter were flammable.

All of them, to be exact.

Gideon shoves Jane toward the burning counter and runs back the way he came, out the door and toward the woods. Mr. Redfern jumps over the dead man on the ground to follow.

Jane waits only long enough to skim her pistol from its holster before she makes to give chase.

"Wait!" I shout, and she whips around to face me.

"Kate," she says, as if just remembering I am here.

"Gideon is cornered, and Mr. Redfern is giving chase. Let him go, Jane. Let God deal with him and his sins. All of this violence has gotten you nowhere, just the same dead end over and over again. Please, let it go." Already the smoke grows thick, and I cough as I pull myself out of the cage, barely able to move, and crawl on hands and knees across the floor toward the door. The stink of blood has set off a flurry of activity in the back room as the dead, heard but not seen, begin to react to the disaster.

A burning beam crashes to the ground a little ways off,

sending out a hail of sparks. She glances at it and then at me, and my heart shrivels at the hard expression on her face.

"I can't let him get away," she says, before dashing out of the door. It is just that easy for her. She had a choice and she has made it.

Jane has left me behind to die.

Even the deadliest, savviest bounty hunter will eventually make a mistake. And that will be the last one he ever makes.
—*Bounty Hunter Rufus Green, 1875*

— J A N E —

Chapter 47
In Which My Fight Ends

Gideon Carr is yellow, just as I'd always suspected. He takes off running down the path to the woods, yelling all the way. Redfern is hot on his heels, and I am right behind him when a bullet nicks the brim of my hat.

I duck behind the nearest building, the one that lists to the side, and take stock of the situation. Tom and his boys run toward me full tilt, without the common sense God gave a flea. Just running out in the open, begging to be shot.

I lean around a rotting timber and oblige Tom and his

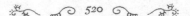

boys. Moving targets, but I'm a better shot than I used to be. I hit Tom in the chest, and each of his boys in the gut. They go down, screaming from the pain. Something about their anguish grabs at me, and I feel remorse like I ain't felt in a long while. Those poor men can't help that they were dumb enough to get wrapped up in Gideon Carr's machinations, and I pity that they met their end out of nothing more than stupidity.

But then I remember Irish Tom killed ten men to get his nickname, and I push the remorse aside, hard. I doubt his compatriots were any kind of saints, not as itchy as their trigger fingers were. And I have three bullets left, all of them bearing Gideon's name.

I run down the path toward where Redfern and Gideon dashed, but I don't see a damn thing. My heart is pounding, and despair fills my mouth with ashes. Angry tears prick my eyes and I scream out my frustration.

Gideon Carr is once more in the wind.

The chance I finally had after a year to end the man has dissipated like smoke in the breeze. I have given up everything and let myself travel down a road of violence and pain, and for what? I have nothing, *nothing* to show for it.

That's when it sinks in that I have left Katherine to her doom.

Greasy black smoke billows from the building that housed Gideon's lab. I look down the path where Daniel and Gideon disappeared, and I hesitate a second before sprinting back toward the lab as fast as I can. Gideon Carr deserves to die, but Katherine doesn't.

The door to the lab hangs off its hinges, and the smoke is thick. I try to run inside, and the flames are so high that I am pressed back by the heat. Only a madwoman would enter such a scene.

I holster my pistol, crouch down, and run inside anyway.

I cannot stand, because the air is thick with smoke, so I crawl along on hand and knees toward the cage. It's an awkward and slow business with only one hand, but I make do. My eyes water and I cough, the smoke a damnable curse, but I cannot leave without Katherine.

"Kate!" I call, but there's no answer.

I find the body of Gideon's assistant and right next to him is Katherine, her dress soaked with his blood. I sob in relief when I see her. Her breathing is shallow. I have to get her out of the building before the whole damn thing comes down around us.

I sit on my rump and use my right arm to hitch her up into my lap. And then I dig my heels into the floor and push both of us back toward the door. The air is too smoky to stand and this is the best I can do. It's hard work, and my middle burns from the awkward effort. The backs of my legs are not much better, but I just grit my teeth and keep going.

I ain't got any other choice.

"Jane?" comes a shout. Redfern? I cannot tell with the roar of the flames.

"In here!" I manage to yell back, despite my coughing.

"You're gonna die if you don't get it together," Jackson says, his ghost standing amongst the flames. He wears white head to toe, fairly gleaming against the smoky backdrop of the lab. I grunt and push-pull back another couple of feet.

"You ain't real," I say. Toward the back of the building timbers fall, and as they do the air leaves the room in a whoosh. I gasp. The fire is stealing all the breathable air, and I realize that I will be smothered long before the flames reach me.

"No, I ain't," Jackson says. "But if you don't move faster, you're gonna be just as dead as I am."

"I loved you and you broke my heart again and again," I say. "But I love Kate as well, and I ain't letting her die."

He grins at me and tips his hat. "Finally. Be happy, Jane McKeene. Whatever that looks like."

And maybe it's my imagination, maybe it's the way the fire is burning, but the smoke around me clears enough so that I can see the door just a few feet away.

I grab the back of Katherine's dress and stand as much as I can, pulling her toward the door. The air begins to cool and continues to clear, and then we are out in the lovely spring air.

I cough, my lungs aflame. Katherine is still unconscious, even though she breathes, her chest barely rising up and down. I keep pulling her until were are safely clear of the building, my eyes watering and coughing fitfully as I do. Once we are a good distance away, I collapse next to Katherine, spread eagle, and take deep, clean breaths.

"Jane."

I sit up, and Gideon Carr looks down at me, his pistol pointed right at me. Defeat crushes me, and I lift my chin as I peer up at him.

"I liked you, you know," I say, a coughing fit overtaking me for a moment before I can continue. "In Summerland. I thought for a moment I could let myself fall in love with you. That maybe, just maybe, you were different."

Gideon's grip relaxes. "I know."

"Can't you see that all you bring is pain and misery everywhere you go?"

He tilts his head. "Then I guess we are more alike than I ever supposed. I liked you, too, Jane."

I nod and give myself a moment to mourn what might have been. "I suppose you're going to kill me now."

He nods. "You know I have no choice. Neither of us ever did. Good-bye, Jane McKeene."

A shot rings out, loud and incredibly close, and I have a moment of weightlessness. But then Gideon's eyes widen and he drops his revolver as a crimson rose blossoms on his chest. His lips part, but no sound comes out as he falls to his knees and then collapses to the ground.

"Well, I for one always thought he was a bore," Katherine says, her voice little more than a whisper.

I turn. Katherine still lies on her back, but she holds my pistol, and her hand relaxes as she coughs, the gun falling to the ground while her body arches with the effort.

"You . . . killed him," I say, stupidly.

Katherine gives me a look that screams, *Well, that's obvious.*

"It was a good shot," I say.

"Best at Miss Preston's," she rasps out.

And then, for no good reason I can think of, I begin to cry.

Katherine is in no good kind of way. Her skin is clammy and there's a terrifying blue tint to her lips. I struggle to lift her to her feet, and she groans.

"We've got to find you a cot or something," I say, just as she begins to heave. I hold her as best I can while she vomits, and Redfern chooses that moment to come running back to camp. He skids to a stop, looks at Gideon Carr's body and then Katherine.

"He injected her," he says.

"Yes," I say. "Is there any place we can take her?" Behind me, Gideon's lab continues to burn.

Redfern nods, takes Katherine's other arm, and together we walk her toward the back of camp, away from the burning lab and toward the creek. There's a small cabin complete with a dusty cot, and we set her down gingerly. She immediately passes out.

"You stay here, I'm going to go and make sure those boys you killed don't return."

I nod and do what I can to make Katherine comfortable. I gently untie her boots and loosen her dress a bit. I hover over her like a mother hen until Redfern returns and tells me,

"Two days. If she hasn't died by then, she'll be fine. All you can do now is make her as comfortable as possible."

So that's what I do. While Redfern burns the dead I fetch water, an awkward task with only the one arm, but I make do. The lab collapses on itself, and the fire has burned so fast and so hot that it smolders, no longer a real threat, by the time I decide to try a bit of foraging. I find a henhouse out behind the decrepit building, and although the chickens are in a bit of a tizzy I find a few eggs for a nice broth. Killing one of the chickens would be better. But there will be time for that later.

On my way back I take a little detour, out into the woods, away from the camp proper. And there, where no one can see me, I fall to my knees and pray.

Now, let me be clear that I do not hold truck with a lot of that Bible nonsense, and I ain't sure why any kind of benevolent God would let mankind carry on the way it's wont to do. But Katherine believes, and so I pray for her because she cannot do it for herself.

And then I cry. I sob for Katherine and Gideon, and the lost chances in a world that doesn't give a whole bunch of opportunities to girls like me. And once I have carried on a bit, I scrub my sleeve over my face and go back to living.

There's a cook set in the cabin and a wood stove that's cold, and by the time Redfern returns, sooty and smelling of smoke and the stink of cooking meat, I've got a pot of water boiling, an egg and salt added to give it something worth-while. He takes one look at the stove, walks outside, and comes back with a handful of wild onions. I find my Bowie knife in my pile of weapons next to the door, not sure where they came from but I'm willing to bet Redfern bears some responsibility, and he slices the onions up with my knife and adds them to the pot while I check on Katherine. She's sleeping, her breathing a little wheezy but that is only to be expected. Redfern and I sit on the floor next to the cot and pass the eggy soup back and forth, eating straight from the hot pan since there ain't a dish to be found. It's disgusting but filling, and I ain't of a mind to complain.

No one would care if I did, anyway.

After the soup is gone, with the stove chasing the chill from the room, I turn to Redfern. "Why'd you give us over to Gideon like that?"

"Every time I got within a day of Gideon he'd spook and take off. So I figured it would be better to approach him as a friend than an adversary," Redfern says. "I offered to bring you to him for a price."

"Were you planning on killing me?"

"No," Redfern says. "Everything I told you at the campsite was true. I just left out that you were my ticket to winning his trust. It turned out okay in the end, but if you're upset, I understand."

I shrug. I ain't quite sure what I feel. I'm about to say *I would've done the same*, but that ain't true. Not anymore. I look over at Katherine and think about how close I came to being someone like that and feel a little ill.

Of course, that could be the soup.

"Daniel, I've always appreciated you saving my neck back in Baltimore," I say, "but I promise you, if Kate dies, I will put one of the two bullets I have left in your brain."

He doesn't move, doesn't react in any kind of way. And then, after a while he gives me a slow nod. "That's fair, Jane, that's fair. I suppose I should get to hoping that Katherine doesn't die."

I give him a toothy grin, but he doesn't return it.

And so our vigil begins.

California might be everything that folks say about it—hot, dusty, treacherous—but I quite find that I love it, from its murderous mountains to its desolate deserts. California is just one more place on the globe, and ain't naught but what folks make of it.
—Harold Payne, 1879

— K A T H E R I N E —

Chapter 48
Notes on a Happily Ever After

Despite feeling like the handmaiden to death I do not die.

I wake to Jane puttering at a stove, singing some bawdy tune under her breath, the scent of onions and meat filling the room. As I cough and sit up she spins around, and a sly smile blooms across her face.

"Daniel is going to be so relieved," she says, filling a glass of water and bringing it over to me.

"Why is that?" I scrape out, once I have managed to drink a bit. I feel like a hollowed-out shell of a person, weak and listless. I lie on a cot in a room I do not recognize, but after a few long moments I realize I am in a cabin. Gideon Carr's, who I shot over Jane's shoulder while lying on my back.

Still the best shot at Miss Preston's.

I am never going to forget that moment.

"Because I told him if you died I was going to kill him."

I blink, Jane's declaration dragging me away from the memory. "You cannot go around threatening murder whenever someone annoys you." I begin coughing again, and she refills the water, offering me a fresh glass.

"I don't see why not, it's been working for me thus far," she says, but there is mirth in her eyes. The shadowed look is not completely gone, but it has been beaten back enough that something of the old Jane shines through.

While I drink a delicious chicken broth, and marvel at the fact that Jane McKeene is a fabulous cook, she updates me on what has happened. It seems that I was indeed laid low by Gideon Carr's serum, and that I have lost nigh on three days' worth of time. We have been gone from the wagon train longer than planned, and if they have managed to complete their travel unmolested they should be in Haven by now.

"Where is Mr. Redfern?"

"He's been scavenging around the camp for whatever might be useful. So far we found a wagon, no oxen or horses, though, and eight chickens. Well, seven now," she says, looking meaningfully at the pot. "I found some of Gideon's notebooks, although most of them burned in the fire.

There's some useful stuff in there, things like diagrams for that water-heating contraption we saw back in Summerland." Her expression shutters for a moment, turning back to whatever horror she discovered in her digging. "He was busy," she says, finally, and I can only imagine the magnitude of the savagery he wrought.

"Well, then, I guess this chapter is finished. That means we should think about making our way to Haven." I start to stand, and Jane pushes me back onto the cot.

"We, me and Redfern, have been doing just that for the past three days. You need to spend another day getting back to good. It's at least three days' walk over rough terrain, and you've had a shock."

"I am fine," I say, but Jane is correct. Just trying to stand has left me feeling shaky and woozy.

Jane grabs the bowl and refills it. "You're lucky Redfern and I found bowls the other day, otherwise you'd have to eat out of the pot like a farmhand." At my look of horror Jane laughs and hands me more soup.

I drink the salty broth, it really is the most delicious thing I have ever had, and Jane sits on the floor next to the cot, sprawled in a way that makes her seem larger than she is. When I have almost finished the soup she clears her throat.

"Kate, I want to thank you," she says finally, and I raise an eyebrow in her direction.

"For nearly dying?"

"No," she says, laughing. "For trying to save me from

myself. I've never had a friend as loyal and as true-blue as you, and that means a lot to me."

I grin at her, but before I can say anything she continues.

"Of course, you're also vexing as hell, bossy, and a know-it-all to boot."

"Jane! Language," I say on impulse, and we look at each other and laugh until Mr. Redfern walks in, his expression full of questions.

"Miss Deveraux, I see you are awake. Welcome back to the world of the living."

"Yes, Mr. Redfern, thank you. I suppose you must be relieved."

He looks at Jane and smiles, and it seems to me a seedling of friendship must have been planted between them during my recovery.

"Yes, verily. Now, let's talk about our plans for getting away from this cursed place."

We stay in the encampment for two more days before we leave. Even after two whole days of lying abed and drinking a gallon of chicken soup, I am still weak when we begin our trek into the mountains.

Mr. Redfern found a map in and amongst a trunk of Gideon's effects, as well as a daguerreotype of Gideon and his parents that Jane immediately threw into the wood stove—the girl is ever so superstitious—and by locating the approximate area where we expected Haven to be we mapped out a route along trails.

Like our trip to the encampment, the way is mostly deer track, and we can only travel for a couple of hours before I have to rest. Jane carries four chickens in a cobbled-together cage, their clucking and peeping making clear their feelings on the matter, while Mr. Redfern leads the way, breaking trail in some areas so that we can negotiate the way. It is tough going, and the nights are much cooler than the days. I had thought our trek with the wagon train on the Siskiyou Trail had been difficult, but it pales in comparison to our mountain trek.

But our persistence pays off, and on the sixth day of our trip, just as Jane is beginning to make hints about eating another chicken, we hear the sounds of hammering. The deer track we are on deposits us onto a small road, and there, carved out of the trees and located upon a wide, swift moving creek, is Haven.

It is larger than I imagined, with at least ten solid houses as well as a church and what looks to be a saloon or general store. People go this way and that on their business, and it might seem completely normal excepting that there are a fair number of Negroes.

It looks as near to Heaven as I have ever imagined.

Mr. Redfern turns back to Jane and me. "Well, here we are."

"Indeed," I say, leaning against Jane. I am still a bit taxed from the after-effects of Gideon Carr's injection, and the relief that we have finally reached our destination fairly overwhelms me.

"Why don't we see if anyone has seen Sue or Juliet?" Jane says. But we do not have to go looking because Sue finds us.

"Jane! Katherine! Sheriff Redfern!" Sue yells from the frame of a house in the midst of being raised. The folks working together get the frame up and in place before she strides over to us. She beams as she gathers both Jane and I up into a massive hug. "You ain't dead!" she exclaims, releasing us and giving us a huge grin.

"We are not," I say.

"But we are tired and thirsty and need somewhere to put our poor chickens," Jane says. Sue's exuberance has made the chickens flap in the cage. Feathers fly up and around us.

"Those chickens are going to be bald by the time they get to a henhouse," I mutter, waving away a stray feather that tries to creep up my nose.

"They've had a taxing journey," Jane says. "It ain't their fault."

"Well, you two are just in time," Sue says. She points behind her to the house being raised. "That's for me and Roy. We're getting married!"

Jane whoops in delight, and I cannot help but clap my hands with happiness. I might be tired, but we all begin to jump up and down in excitement, which of course just causes the poor chickens no end of grief.

Our celebration is interrupted by a scream splitting the otherwise lovely day, and a woman with lightly burnished golden skin runs toward us, tears streaming down her cheeks. Her hat, a lovely powder-blue confection that matches her day dress perfectly, flies off, and a couple of men rush to retrieve it. She is beautiful, so much so that it is impossible to look anywhere but right at her.

"Jane, my baby, is that you?" the woman wails, now fully into her hysterics. We all freeze in our felicitations because the woman bears an uncanny resemblance to Jane.

Sue smiles and squeezes Jane's shoulder. "She been waiting for you," she says, voice hushed.

Jane for her part looks as though she has seen a ghost, her eyes wide and skin gone ashen.

"Momma?" she whispers.

The woman gathers Jane up in her arms even as Jane has frozen, shock making her limbs rigid. Sue and I take a few steps back to give Jane and her momma room. On the other side of Jane, Redfern melts into the gathering crowd. Apparently heartfelt reunions are not his thing.

"Jane, what happened to your arm?" the woman wails, and the question unmoors Jane. She takes a step back, putting space between herself and her mother.

"Is Auntie Aggie here?" Jane asks, hope brightening her

eyes. She looks past her mother to a woman that had been walking with her, a couple of small boys holding each of her hands.

"Oh, Jane, I am so sorry. Aggie didn't survive the trip out west. Her heart, you know. But this is Edith, do you remember her from Rose Hill? And look, these are your brothers, Jane. Are they not the most precious? Robert, that's my husband, well I'm not quite sure where he's gotten to. He's the mayor! I am once again a woman of consequence."

The woman continues on, telling Jane about her life in Haven, and her long trip from Kentucky to the sea, and then by boat to California. But Jane is not listening. Tears streak down her cheeks, her face twisted with an anguish her momma either cannot or will not acknowledge.

Without warning, Jane drops the cage holding the chickens, the fragile cross-hatching shattering. The chickens fly up a few feet, feathers flying in all directions. Jane's mother takes a few steps back, and Jane, without a word, turns on her heel and walks back the way we came.

— JANE —

Chapter 49
In Which the End Is Near

My first two weeks in Haven are spent shoring up the town's defenses and avoiding my momma.

The former is on purpose, the latter is a fortunate happenstance.

Haven needs a strong wall. The mountains provide some protection, but the dead are stalking California now, and it is only a matter of time before they come knocking on Haven's door. People are arriving every day, brought in by the same advertisement that Jeb and the others from San Francisco saw. It seems to me that making sure any town is safe should be a priority. Even if we can all agree that it ain't forever. But something is better than nothing, so strong defenses it is.

And so, I get to work with the help of Sue, Katherine, and a few others.

A better wall, a water wheel built off Gideon Carr's notes from his thrice-cursed but useful notebook, and a series of fortified fences to provide a necessary boundary against shamblers, whenever they arrive.

There's also a diagram for some sort of battery in the notebook, and while I have no idea what the schematic says—it seems to be written in math, that foulest of all languages—Mr. Stevens is quick to pitch in. We might even learn how to erect an electric fence soon.

As for Mr. Stevens, he's very helpful and always underfoot, and one night at dinner my mother has the audacity to say, "Jane, I do believe you are being courted."

"A body has to want to be courted to be courted," I say, and it puts an end to the conversation right quick.

Suffice it to say, my reunion with my mother is nothing like I'd imagined. Our conversations are full of stop-starts and long pauses. I ask about Auntie Aggie, about how her end came about, and Momma begs off because it's too painful. Edith ain't much help. She never knew Auntie Aggie very well, and all she can tell me is that she was buried somewhere alongside the trail on the way from Sacramento. Her heart, like momma said, gave out. And that is that. Sometimes the people we love fiercest leave the world like a whisper.

It's a blow that I ain't been expecting. Momma also doesn't want to hear anything about my trials and tribulations on the way to Haven. Whenever Robert, a fine man with velvety brown skin and a keen mind but perhaps questionable taste in women given how he dotes on my mother, asks about the combat school or my life up to now, Momma gives him a sharp look and declares, "Let's not talk of such things at supper." It's like there's no room for my life in her portrait of domesticity. The dead, and all the woes they bring, have no place in her world.

Day by day, my discomfort grows. While everyone else seems to adore Haven—Sue is jumping the broom, Lily attends school and helps Miss Mellie May with her boardinghouse, Tomás teaches all the other kids swears in Spanish, and even Katherine has found some aptitude as a teacher of the defensive arts—I am at a loss. Haven is a sheep's pen and I am a wolf, lean and hungry and deadly. I do not belong here.

But the hardest thing to accept is that my momma really did forget about me. She's been building a new life, one of love and warmth, while I've been struggling just to survive, to hold on to my humanity. Aside from our first meeting, during which she performed her grief and joy for the whole town, she has seemed more put out by my presence than happy. I find myself helping out where I can with the building of houses and the planting of gardens rather than spending an extra moment with her. The whole situation causes a curious sort of bitterness to rise up, and I tend it like a spring seedling, feeding it my grief.

Not that I don't love my momma. I do. But I don't think I like her much as a person.

The old Jane would've gone along to get along, but that girl died in Nicodemus, and thank God. It's been a spell since we've been in each other's presence, and the more time I spend with the woman that birthed me the more I realize that my memory ain't nothing like the reality. I start to remember all the small hurts inflicted by my mother, all the bad times that greatly outnumbered the good. It doesn't help a lick that she's got little ones to chase about. She dotes on Romeo and Tybalt in a way she never could me, and it's clear that they are well loved even if Edith tends to most of their needs. They will be beautiful boys when they get older. I try to remind myself that the babies are my younger brothers and I shouldn't envy them but I do.

I don't fit.

Spending time with my momma and her new husband makes me feel like a dark cloud raining down on her happiness. She loves being the mayor's wife, and she flits about her duties like a goddess of industry, overseeing the stores and preparations for next winter, immaculately dressed even though Haven is far from any sort of cosmopolitan society. It's not far from what she did at Rose Hill. Only I suppose without the stress of trying to pass as white.

Meanwhile, I feel as though Haven is smothering me. Or maybe it's just the staying in one place. When I was on the road my nightmares couldn't catch me. Here, they come to roost.

Most nights I wake in the middle of sleep, a scream half trapped in my throat as terror stalks me. Or, if I let myself go idle too long, I fall into imagining once more that terrible end that befell the Turners or wondering where Redfern's other Survivalist towns are, the ones he let slip that one time in conversation. When I asked him he said, "I'm sure they've met their end by now, Jane." But what if they haven't? What if there is a version of me out there struggling against the weight of hatred and injustice as I once did? What if my time could be better spent out in the world, righting all of the wrongs that I can?

The more time I spend in the idyllic setting of Haven, the more I wonder about such things, until my feet itch to leave.

But Sue is getting married, and while our friendship ain't what it once was, especially since I am fighting very hard to keep my dark feelings to myself so as not to ruin her impending vows, she is my oldest friend. And I cannot leave before she gets hitched.

May is a whirlwind of activity, and even as I'm helping to stitch Sue a trousseau, which I can still do surprisingly well, even one-handed, I'm thinking about leaving. So much so that one afternoon, a few days before the wedding, Katherine loses her patience with me and snaps her fingers an inch away from my nose.

"Jane, I was asking you if you plan on wearing those trousers of yours to Sue's wedding or if we should see about cutting down another one of your mother's dresses. Where are you these days?"

Katherine, Sue, and I are in the sitting room of the rooming house recently built by Miss Mellie May and her brother, Carolina Jones. Salty lies on the rug at our feet, Tomás by his side. Lily has been trying to embroider a hem with tiny daisies for nearly an hour, and every time she pokes herself she swears and Katherine murmurs, "Language, Lily." Miss May comes in and out with refreshments as we work, and I should be happy. This is everything I thought I wanted.

But I feel like all my insides are made of rusty blades, rubbing together in an awful way. Only, this time, I know why.

Both Sue and Katherine have resided in the boardinghouse since it was completed. I'd intended to move there as well, if for no other reason than to be near the people I cared about. Carolina and his sister had taken over looking after Tomás while I was chasing Gideon Carr, and it was a brilliant fit. They adore the boy more than the sun itself and I didn't have the heart to break up their happy family, but it was another reason to take a room. Plus, I wanted to live somewhere other than my mother's house. I had coins enough, and I was a fifth wheel within my family, even with Edith there, but when I'd mentioned it Momma had taken herself to her room and refused to come out until her husband, Robert, had begged me to reconsider.

"Gone. I'm gone," I say now, in answer to Katherine's question. When she arches a blond brow all the things that have been rattling around in my head the past few weeks come spilling out, how of all the places I've been, this is the first place that just doesn't seem to need me.

Haven is a great place for folks like Sue, those who want to settle down and get to raising a family. For me, this ain't where I belong.

I want something more.

I want the purpose I had when we went searching for the Spencers in Baltimore or struggled to escape Summerland. I want the freedom I had when Callie and I made our own way across the continent. I want the sense of justice I felt when I lived by my wits and hunted the men and women who plagued civilized society. Less killing would be nice, I don't miss that, but if killing is the price of freedom then I'm willing to pay it.

Katherine gives me a long look before putting down her sewing. "You are leaving."

"Yes," I say. I don't tell her anything beyond that. If anyone can understand how I feel, it's Katherine.

"Not before my wedding, I hope," Sue says, and for the first time in all the years I've known her, there is murder in her eye.

"No," I say with a smile. "After. I promise. And I will even wear a dress."

Katherine looks down at her lap, as though that was no longer the question she wanted answered.

"As far as I am concerned you can wear a flour sack as long as you're there. Katherine is the one pushing to make sure we all look like cream and cocoa," Sue says.

"This is the first wedding I have ever been to, will you please just let me make us all beautiful?" she wails.

Our answering laughter fills me with light and joy. But I still know, deep in my heart, that it is time to go.

And as everyone else laughs, Katherine is looking only at me.

It is a gorgeous wedding.

Sue and her beau hop the broom and we all cheer. Even Daniel Redfern has managed to make a rare appearance for the celebrations. There's no proper preacher in Haven (to the town's credit in my opinion) but Thaddeus Stevens is all too happy to officiate. His voice goes on and on about love and commitment and by the time Sue kisses her blacksmith I'm half asleep.

After the service, as we all make our way to the tables set up for the occasion, Thaddeus Stevens stops me. "Ah, Miss McKeene, might I have a word with you?"

Before I can answer he's taken my bouquet of wildflowers

and handed it off to Katherine while pulling me away from the flow of people. She gives me comically wide eyes, and my belly fills with acid.

Oh Lord.

Mr. Stevens leads me to his house and the workshop behind it where he's been going through Gideon's book, trying to puzzle some of the more complicated designs. Momma has already declared her intent to have one of the hot-water-making machines installed in her home once Mr. Stevens can fabricate them reliably. I wonder where they're going to get the required metals for such a thing, but very soon none of that will be my problem.

We enter his workshop, and I'm not quite sure what to expect but I have my pistol strapped to my thigh under my dress in case he gets the wrong idea. But he turns to me not with a ring, which is a relief, but with a metal contraption pieced together out of odds and ends.

"Oh, you made me an arm," I say, and all the tension melts away.

"Yes, Miss McKeene," he says, and then he's falling to one knee and it's like some kind of nightmare. Only if it were really a dream shamblers would be eating his face and honestly I'm kind of praying for the dead to appear as he begins to speak.

"Miss McKeene, I have admired you since the first day I beheld you, and you bravely shot an outlaw that had stumbled into our humble encampment."

I do not mention it wasn't really an outlaw, but a bad man all the same.

"Mr. Stevens—Thaddeus?" I say, and his expression brightens. "I'm going to stop you right there. Whatever you're about to say next, well, we should pretend it was just you saying how you were so moved by my sad situation that you made me an arm and not any kind of romantic proposal."

His expression falls but he remains on bended knee. "No?"

"No, sir. See, I'm clearing out tomorrow, back to murdering and the like, you know how it is, and I don't really have any use for a husband."

Recognition dawns on his face and he stands. "Ah. But you do have need of an arm."

"Well, seeing as how you went to the effort and all, it seems like it would be a shame to put it aside to wait for someone else to lose an appendage."

He smiles and helps me fit it on, showing me how it secures with the leather strap. There's a kind of hook that moves on a tension wire, and when I flex my upper arm the hook opens and closes. The mechanism is terrifying.

I love it.

"Would it be possible to put a blade on the end, there?" I wonder aloud. "Just, you know, considering the possibilities."

"You are an incredible woman, Jane McKeene," Thaddeus says, and I laugh.

"I know. Now, let's go dance."

The sun is barely cresting the trees when I set out to leave the morning after Sue's wedding. Robert is there with the babies to see me off, Edith in with my mother. I hadn't been planning to tell her I was leaving, but at some point in the evening, after Sue and her fellow snuck off to try out the bed Carolina built for them, the wedding had turned into a farewell party.

Thaddeus Stevens is by far the world's worst secret keeper.

Momma had been quite upset and left, but I just let her go. She's taken to her bed again, but this time she's going to have to find her way out all by herself. I won't do it for her anymore.

I kiss the babies, and they laugh and show me their teeth. Robert looks tired, but he offers me a wan smile. "She understands, you know, even if it seems like she doesn't. She asked me to give you this." He hands me a letter written on my mother's signature lavender-and-cream stationary. Somehow she managed to get this paper across the country but not Aunt Aggie.

I smile and tuck it into my front pocket. I won't read it. I'm going to burn it the first chance I get. I think it's probably better that way. For just once I'll keep the soft warmth of fantasy over the cold edge of reality.

I've only gone a few paces down the road when somebody calls my name. I've already said all my good-byes and the sun is bright in my eyes so I can't tell who it is. But as Daniel Redfern comes into view I smile.

"Well, howdy, stranger," I say.

"I overheard you last night and thought maybe you'd like some company," he says. "It's dangerous to go alone."

"I thought you didn't like to get involved in things," I say, reminding him of our conversation long ago when he was sheriff. He grimaces.

"Trying something new. People can change, you know."

"So I hear." I look back toward town one last time, hoping to see a different silhouette, but the road is empty. It's better this way, anyhow. I can't really ask Katherine to give up her life here to help me . . . what? Liberate any remaining Survivalist towns? Reclaim the Lost States? I don't really even have a plan, just an inkling that I'm needed anywhere else but Haven, California.

Daniel and I start walking, in companionable silence, when a voice yells after me, "Jane McKeene, you stubborn muttonhead, you better not leave without me!"

I turn to see Katherine running toward us. She carries her rifle with one hand and holds her hat on her head with the other, and little puffs of dirt rise up behind her. Her knapsack crisscrosses her body, and I have never been happier to see her. She pants when she reaches us and I frown.

"Are you wearing a corset?"

"Jane, I am not going to discuss my undergarments in the company of men," she says, looking at Daniel. She leans closer and says, "Yes, but it is very loose, please stop nagging me."

A feeling, warm and bright and happy wells up in me and I have to fight to keep from crying. But I push it down, because there is something I must say.

"Kate, you have to stay."

She pauses in fixing a loose piece of hair and stares at me. "What are you blathering on about, Jane?"

"I can't ask you to come with us. Daniel and I, well, we're immune to the dead. You ain't. It's too dangerous for you to go with us."

"First of all, you have no idea whether I am immune. You do not know that Gideon Carr did not finally perfect that serum of his any more than I do. We can test it out the first time we find a pack of the dead and adjust our expectations from there. Second, I am your friend, Jane, your *best* friend, and I would be no kind of person if I did not go where my friend needed me most." Katherine takes a deep breath and sniffs. "Besides, Haven is gloriously boring. And all the fashion is at least two seasons out of date. I have no desire to hide away from the world. In fact, I recommend we head to New Orleans first, by ship if possible. I miss the salt air."

Daniel Redfern nods. "That's not a bad idea if we're planning on going after any of those remaining Survivalist towns. There's one right near the mouth of the Mississippi River."

"Excellent," Katherine says, stowing her rifle in a back holster and clapping her hands. "Let us get to it, then."

"Kate," I say, as we turn our merry band toward the road.

"I'm glad you're here. But more than that, I'm glad you're my friend. You saved my life when I couldn't save myself."

"Oh, honestly, Jane, stop being so silly," Katherine says, adjusting her hat even though not a hair is out of place. She blinks a bit rapidly, but not a single tear falls. "Of course I am your friend. What a ridiculous statement. What else could I be? And let us not forget that you saved my life as well."

Redfern clears his throat. "No one seems to be glad I'm here."

Katherine gives him a sly look. "To be fair, we are still waiting to see whether you can be trusted. Your history leaves a little to be desired, sir."

Daniel Redfern laughs, the first real laugh I've ever heard from him, and I am put out. I am much funnier than Katherine.

He shakes his head and adjusts his hat. I check my pack and weapons one last time, my new metal arm clacking in a strange and easy sort of way, while Katherine grumbles about ungrateful ninnies that continue to underestimate her. I swallow a smile, and for the first time in a long while feel more full of light than dark.

"Hey, what ever became of my lucky penny?" I ask Katherine.

She frowns. "This one?" she says, pulling it out of a pocket. "Kate, it doesn't work if you don't wear it."

"Honestly, your luck charm never worked for me." She thrusts it toward me. "Here, take it."

"Help me put it on," I say, and Katherine dutifully hangs it around my neck, where it is a warm, heavy comfort. For a moment I imagine I am wrapped once more in Auntie Aggie's soft embrace, but the moment fades, and I am a little glad. I have had enough of being haunted.

"Are we ready?" Daniel asks, beginning to look like he has regrets.

I shoot him a too-wide grin. "Yep. All set."

And then we head out, off to find the truths of the world.

Author's Note

As I sat down to write this sequel, it was difficult to figure out where to go next. What new adventures made sense? What would readers be willing to sign up for after *Dread Nation*? How do I tell a story that is both honest and sensitive? I'm not sure I accomplished anything I set out to do, except for one: put Black people back into history.

The more I thought about it, the more I knew I had to visit the narrative of Black Americans in the Old West. I love Westerns, but they have long been the province of steely-eyed cowboys and plucky frontierswomen, always white. The mythos of the American Old West has nearly wholesale ignored the rich diversity that could also be found in the average frontier town. People from all walks made their way west immediately after the Civil War with hope for a new life and ran up against hardship and the Natives who were already there. But whenever I read any history book my primary question is always the same:

Where are the Black folks?

Black Americans were everywhere in the American West: herding cattle and plying their trade as ranch hands, establishing homesteads and trying their hand at farming, and, yes, fighting against Native Americans. Before that, they could be found enslaved by the Five Civilized Tribes, eking out an existence in Indian Territory or fighting and dying alongside staunch abolitionists in Kansas. Although Black people, both free and enslaved, lived throughout the West, they are rarely the heroes of any popular narratives.

Deathless Divide is no more a historical text than *Dread Nation*, but I hope there is something within these pages that provokes a hunger to know more about the actual daily lives of Black people during the late 1800s in America, something beyond slavery and suffering and an offhanded reference to the Underground Railroad.

And, of course, a reading list to help you get started:

The House on Diamond Hill by Tiya Miles

Black Indians: A Hidden Heritage by William Loren Katz

Black Cowboys in the American West: On the Range, on the Stage, behind the Badge, edited by Bruce A. Glasrud and Michael N. Searles

African American Women of the Old West by Tricia Martineau Wagner

And, as always, happy reading!

Justina Ireland